Tawseef Khan is a qualified immigration solicitor and holds a doctoral degree from the University of Liverpool, where he examined the fairness of the British asylum system. He is also a graduate of the creative writing programme at the University of East Anglia, where he received the Seth Donaldson Memorial Bursary. His fiction has appeared in Lighthouse and *Test Signal: a Northern anthology*; his non-fiction in the *New York Times*, *The Face* and *Hyphen*. His debut non-fiction book *Muslim, Actually* was published by Atlantic in 2021 and *Determination* is his debut novel. He lives in Manchester.

Praise for *Determination*:

'A compassionate, beautifully told portrait populated by lives that circle the UK's lamentable immigration story. This is a story of determination, also grief, hope, loss and desperation, as well as a reminder of the care, patience and kindness at the human end of a broken system'

– **Guy Gunaratne, author of *In Our Mad and Furious City***

'Tawseef Khan dramatises timely quests for migrant justice amid the grinding frustrations and punitive hypocrisy of the modern British state. Resisting stereotypes and easy moralising, this is absorbing, witty, eloquent fiction, as well as a trenchant political critique'

– **Tom Benn, author of *Oxblood***

'*Determination* is a hymn to empathy, alive with care and love . . . This is a novel not just to spend time with for the joy of the richly detailed world Khan has created but to be enlivened and challenged by. Embedded in his compelling and compassionate novel is an emphatic rebuttal to the racism and xenophobia rife in this country'

– **Rebecca Watson, author of *Little Scratch***

'A heart-breaking, honest, and deeply important story, providing a window into the world of a UK immigration lawyer and the lives touched by her work. This is a moving, immersive, and vital piece of fiction'

– **Jyoti Patel, author of *The Things That We Lost***

'This is a story of people trying their best to be human in a system that dehumanises those it is supposed to care for and those brave enough to work in it'

– **Damian Barr, author of *You Will Be Safe Here***

'A novel as believable as any memoir, offering a kaleidoscope of lives and characters, all of whom seem to extend beyond these pages. A truly astonishing and self-assured piece of work'

– **Adam Farrer author of *Broken Biscuits: and Other Male Failures* and *Cold Fish Soup***

'Funny, fast-paced, feminist and full of characters you're rooting for, *Determination* is a legal thriller with a difference. Laying bare that it's the so-called justice and immigration systems that are criminal, Tawseef Khan's page-turning novel shows how a protagonist as complex, charming and challenging as immigration lawyer Jamila changes the world, one bureaucratic challenge and one home-baked cake at a time'

– **So Mayer, author of *Truth & Dare***

DETERMINATION

DETERMINATION

TAWSEEF KHAN

FOOTNOTE

First published in hardback in 2024
This paperback edition published in 2025 by Footnote Press

An imprint of Bonnier Books UK
5th Floor, HYLO, 105 Bunhill Row,
London, EC1Y 8LZ

www.footnotepress.com

First printing
1 3 5 7 9 10 8 6 4 2

A CIP catalogue record for this book is available from the British Library.

ISBN (paperback): 978-1-804-44232-6
ISBN (ebook): 978-1-804-44091-9

Printed and bound in Great Britain
by Clays Ltd, Elcograf S.p.A.

The authorised representative in the EEA is
Bonnier Books UK (Ireland) Limited.
Registered office address: Floor 3, Block 3, Miesian Plaza,
Dublin 2, D02 Y754, Ireland
compliance@bonnierbooks.ie

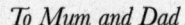
To Mum and Dad

Part I

One

Jamila sat up so fast her elbow caught the table lamp and sent it crashing. She grabbed the lamp and her phone from the floor. 7:30am. Crap, she had missed her alarm. Fallen asleep on the sofa with the television on standby. Muscles tense, she stumbled up the stairs.

Forty-five minutes later she left the house with wet hair, wearing yesterday's suit and an unwashed shirt, the inside collar smudged with dirt. She wanted to reach the office before the morning crush, but her journey stalled along Great Ancoats Street. Idling before the sad retail park, traffic at a standstill, she revved her engine and scowled.

Her phone rang through the speakers.

'Jamila, where are you?'

'As-salamu alaykum, Dad. I'm heading to work, what's up?'

'We missed you last night.'

'I couldn't make it, I texted,' she lied.

'I'll be late in today. I have an appointment.'

'Didn't I tell you before, it's fine? Enjoy your life, you're retired.'

'I just thought I should report to my boss.'

Jamila shook her head, imagining her father – her predecessor, mentor and occasional nemesis – grinning from the other side of her desk. She switched on the radio to distract herself. Itchy fingers flicked between stations. Thrashing guitars raised the hairs on her arms before the music cut out.

'Mrs Shah, it's Hassan. Can I come and see you?'

She thumped a button, cut the call. Hassan Khemiri was one of her most troublesome clients; there was always a problem of some sort with him. If he complained about being hung up on – of course he would complain – she would blame her poor signal.

The cars ahead started moving. She rolled forward, picked up speed. Construction workers dangled from scaffolding, hammering at high-rises, the shells dark and empty, like mouths full of rotting teeth. Tired old mills becoming pricey new flats. She drove over the Ashton Canal, a depressed vein in the city's rumpled topography, past the derelict mills and warehouses that gave the city its face of soot and stone. The sky was predictably murky. Ten minutes late, she parked up behind the office and scooted through the slippery alleyway, rain-sodden leaves buttered into the tarmac.

A line of clients began at her front door: ten, maybe twenty of them, in woollen fleeces and thick jumpers and jackets with knitted scarves and gloves. Hassan Khemiri waved from the middle. 'Good morning, Mrs Shah.'

'Hi,' she replied stiffly, smiling broadly at the others. 'Hello, Mrs Jackson, Namaskar, Auntie-ji, it's good to see you again. As-salamu alaykum, Mr Din.'

Commuters in their cars roared past the office towards the city centre. Beyond the dual carriageway, the 8:57am express train to Euston rumbled south. It blew its horn, as it did every morning, infuriating her. At the end of the block, the newsagent Mr Bankowsi brought out his pavement sign. She squinted to read the headline, but as with most things in her life, the prescription on her glasses was out of date.

Once at her desk, tea in hand, Jamila stared at her calendar. Friday 2 November 2012. The end of another hectic week. She dipped a bourbon biscuit into her mug, preparing herself for the day ahead. As she brought the biscuit to her mouth, half of it broke away and fell into her lap. She grabbed a tissue and dabbed carelessly. She wasn't here to be judged on appearances.

Still, as Jamila stood to clean up in the bathroom, Nazish Durrani knocked on her door and marched in. 'Where you going? You ask for medical report. I have it.'

Nazish was a thirty-seven-year-old asylum seeker from Pakistan, short and heavy, with long, curly hair. She never usually came in this early.

'Give me a minute, Nazish, I dropped something—'

'Leave it,' Nazish said breezily. 'I've seen you looking worse.'

Looking worse? Jamila blushed and sat down. Luckily, the desk hid the stain. She took the papers from Nazish: the top right-hand corner was printed with the trusty NHS logo, the last page signed by the Consultant Psychiatrist. 'Great, I'll add it to your file.'

'No. Read it. Tell me if it's okay.' Nazish leaned against the desk.

Jamila laughed. She allowed Nazish to speak to her like that, with a bluntness no other client would get away with. In fact, she enjoyed it. 'Why don't you take a seat?'

Nazish suffered from dysthymia, the letter said in stark medical prose: *a chronic form of depression aggravated by her precarious immigration status*. This had been clear to Jamila from the conversations they had shared while preparing Nazish's case. But every success began with evidence.

Nazish's eyes were awaiting Jamila's diagnosis.

'We're well on our way, Nazish. I think this letter will be good for us.'

Nazish was replaced by another client, then another, accompanied by a flurry of telephone calls. Jamila forgot about the stain on her trousers and managed each person as her staff gradually materialised: Rubel appearing out of breath at 9:20am, adjusting his hair and tie; Babar at 9:35, dawdling and texting as he strolled; Sadia at 10:15, looking frosty and taking it out on her handbag, which she lobbed towards the coat stand at the back of the room.

Her father wandered in after eleven. He had made a show of passing the office over to her at the beginning of the year and then continued coming into work. Initially, she assumed he was smoothing over the transition, but here he was, ten months later, watching, testing, intruding, unable to let go. But rather than confront him, she had found it far simpler to go along with the status quo.

The clients in reception stood for him and he saluted them, then headed inside. Before lunchtime, he came and sat on the cushioned bench at the back of her office.

Jamila was dealing with a new client from Angola, who wanted to develop a property business in Britain and apply for a visa as an entrepreneur.

'No,' she told the client, 'a property developer can't apply for a Tier 1 visa. But you could set up a real estate marketing agency. That could do it?'

Her father nodded in approval and, despite herself, Jamila felt her neck grow taller.

The client left to think it over; her father leaned forward. 'You never came round last night. Me and your mum were waiting,' he said.

'Sorry, I got busy.' She had finally started watching her recording of the summer Olympics, highlights of the women's gold in tennis.

'Come over tonight? We're taking the kids to see the fireworks in the park.'

'Tonight? Uh . . . '

The telephone rang and Jamila answered it immediately, grateful for the interruption. On the line was a young woman who had adopted a child in Nigeria and wanted advice on bringing her to Britain. As they talked, snapping, crunching sounds peppered the air: her father peeling and eating pistachios.

Jamila glared at him.

'Why don't you go and have your lunch?' she suggested once she had hung up.

6

'No, I can wait,' he said.

'The kitchen will get busier.'

'We can go together. We'll catch up.'

Just give me some space, she wanted to shout. She didn't want to catch up with anyone. She gestured to the door. 'I'll meet you there. Mera acha bacha neyn ain?'

'Main koi bacha van?' He quivered with laughter. 'Is that how it is? No time, no respect for your father?'

She leaned into the transgression, smiling, feeling a slight mania emanating from herself. All her life, her father had ushered her out of his office. 'Aren't you my good little girl?' he would say, stroking her hair. Ever since she was three years old, when he first started practising immigration law from home. Their house was tiny then, with just one living room. Whenever a client turned up – and they turned up at all hours – he would send her, Jahida and their mother huffing upstairs. Displaced in their own home, they had no choice but to stay busy until he signalled for their return.

Somebody fumbled with the door. A head poked through the gap.

'Mrs Shah, why don't you care about my case?'

She opened her arms. 'Mr Khemiri, my friend! How could I forget your case? You call me every day about it.'

Hassan, her bad penny, had perfect timing. They had spoken for an hour last night, after dinner, while she proofread letters on the sofa. He had demanded a re-do of his asylum interview from years ago – a pipe dream. But in that moment, she preferred him to her father.

'I'll be a minute, Dad. Start without me.'

As a child, her father tried to bribe her with promises of gifts and money in exchange for being left alone, but his tactics had always failed to work on her. Whenever he was busy with a client, she and Jahida slunk down and darted into the living room, switched on the television and turned it up to full volume before cackling as they ran back up the stairs. And now, as her father crossed his legs and leaned back, her tactics were failing to work on him.

'I think Mr Khemiri and I need to discuss something privately, isn't that right?'

Hassan stood with the door shut behind him. He was a wiry, grizzled-looking man from Algeria, with sun-baked, terracotta skin and a leather bomber jacket. She caught a woody, musky scent from him, with an underlying sweetness.

'Of course, Mrs Shah. Top secret,' he said. His sunken eyes glittered.

Her father spat out a piece of pistachio skin and got up. The two men crossed paths – her father stalling before he drifted from the room, his shoulders crumpled in defeat.

'So, enlighten me then,' Jamila said, looking up at Hassan, who hovered close by. 'What vital development was there between last night and this morning?'

'I tried telling you before. I want to change my caseworker. I don't like her, she's rude.'

Her head fell into her hands. 'Please, Hassan. Not this again.'

'Why do you always say that, huh? "Not this again." It's important.'

His winged ears twitched.

Jamila's stomach was growling by the time she left work. She had seen to at least fifty clients and attended almost a hundred calls: a standard work day. But though she wanted nothing more than to go home and eat and relax, her father had coaxed her into accepting his invitation.

Kingsway was jammed, commuters in snarling cars fleeing the city for the comfort of its suburbs and satellite towns. She joined the line and drove to her parents in Didsbury, where the trees were still heavy with leaves in pink and peach and rust, the streets were wider and the air sweeter, smelling of compost and the cold.

She parked by the grammar school, with its spiked gates and regal main building. The grounds were pitch black, the building tawny under spotlights. Silvery clouds moved beneath an impassive sky. Twice a week she was supposed to visit her parents. It was a deal she had made with her guilt – and them – before moving out fourteen months ago. And in the beginning, she had enjoyed those visits – for the most part. They watched political documentaries and gossiped about family, and her mother made sure to cook something special. On Sundays, Jahida came along too. But Jamila hadn't been in weeks.

She switched off the car and tried to get out.

She couldn't face her parents' enthusiasm for life when she felt decidedly apathetic. She didn't want to answer their questions about her absence when she had no desire to talk. Not out of duty, not for her niece and nephew – not even for her mother's food. She started the car again. Instead of watching political documentaries and making plans, all she wanted was to be alone.

Two

'Help me, Mrs Shah!'

That Sunday, Jamila lay in bed with her eyes half-closed, phone pressed to her ear, mind tangled in her dreams. Moments ago, she had been eating a sandwich of metal spoons, her teeth shattering into pieces like in a cartoon.

'Please help me. They take my husband and I don't know what to do,' said the woman on the end of the line. She began sobbing.

'I can't understand you. Take a minute. Compose yourself.' Jamila sat up and pushed her hair from her face. The world was blurry. Morning fought through the linen curtains.

The woman on the phone sniffled, then attempted to breathe in deeply.

'Now, tell me from the top, what happened? Who took your husband?' Jamila's voice was dull and thick with sleep. The wintry November air goosebumped her skin. She put on her glasses, slipped her arm back under the duvet and stared ahead at the clock.

For God's sake. It wasn't even 9am, and on her day off too.

'Immigration Enforcement. One hour ago, they force their way in. My children screaming, my husband telling them we have application, but they don't care. They grab and hurt him. They take him away.'

Jamila could hear their children wailing in the background. Children who had witnessed ten men enter their home and overpower their father, shouldering him through the house and into a van parked out on the street. Immigration raids at dawn; four times in the last three months. Desperate calls when the sun had barely risen. She closed her eyes.

'Did they say where they were taking him?'

'Huh?'

'Did they give you any papers?'

'They break our door . . . we still sleeping. They grab him so quick, shouting, *shouting* . . . '

So the woman couldn't help – she'd have to start from scratch.

'Please help, Mrs Shah. I'm going crazy.'

Jamila had stopped telling clients that she wasn't a Mrs; they could think what they wanted. Even when she had tried explaining, most persisted anyway, insisting that Mrs was a mark of respect, and with time she resigned herself to a title and authority that wasn't completely hers. She was twenty-nine and unmarried by choice. She had no time for sleep, let alone a needy partner.

'What's your husband's name again?'

'John. John Kulasingam.'

'Kulasingam, of course.' She remembered John. He was a quiet, thoughtful man, with a warm sense of humour. Gold filaments in his eyes and silver specks in his goatee. She was less fond of his wife, however. Jamila had been turned off the moment she had hightailed it into the office one afternoon and sat down while Jamila was shovelling in a quick lunch between consultations. Impossible to silence, she spoke more than she listened, and that was annoying too, being cut off while explaining the same thing again and again.

'When will you get him out? Today? Tomorrow?'

The eternal question. The one she had no clear answer to.

'If not tomorrow, then a day or two.'

'Mrs Shah, I need him here. He helps with the children.'

They had three children: two girls and a boy, who accompanied them to Jamila's office after school, sweet in their matching uniforms, the girls with braided hair and ribbons. The youngest had Williams syndrome, a rare developmental disorder. She remembered running into the family at Bruntwood Park over the summer. She had gone there with Jahida and her kids, and two cousins and their kids. While supervising the older children on the zip line, Jamila had spotted John sitting in the sandpit with his youngest, filling her bucket, turning it out to make a sandcastle. Even at the office, he sat with his daughter, feeding her bananas as his wife held court. The image made her ache, momentarily, surprisingly, for something – she didn't know what – before she cut it off.

'I'll go to the office and see what's happening.'

She wondered if there was still time to lay in silence beneath the covers. It would take a while before the detention officials would process John. But no, it was too late. Her mind had awoken. At least now it had something to focus on. She showered quickly and dressed, not bothering with makeup or her hair. Within half an hour, she was ready to leave.

The cold outside shocked her. She saw her breath in the air, white against the white sky, against the black branches and tree trunks. Briefly, she entertained notions of a different day: a lazy morning reading in bed, meeting her friend Samir in town for coffee, the evening spent with her parents, Jahida and the kids. She couldn't picture herself doing any of it. No, this was better.

Driving down Cheetham Hill Road, she shivered as she waited for the car to heat up, the cold of the steering wheel seeping through her leather gloves. She parked at the back of the office, where hooded youths gathered in the evenings, huddled around a glowing blunt. She quickly binned the discarded beer and vodka bottles. The shutters mewled and rolled open.

The first time she had seen this building, she had been, what, eight years old? It was the height of summer. She and Jahida were swinging from the trees in the garden; their parents promised ice lollies if they got into the car. They were driven to a block of shops in Burnage where they were greeted by a woman with a blonde bob, pink lipstick and an officious-looking smile. The property she led them through was a former hair salon. Huge windows drenched it in light. To Jamila it smelled of dust and old clothes and strangers' homes. Of coldness.

But her parents sensed an opportunity. At home, they revealed their intentions to put in an offer. They had discussed moving for months, ever since coming downstairs for breakfast one morning to find their kitchen windows broken and the filing cabinet empty, papers strewn across the living room. For weeks, Jamila could only sleep with her mother's hand soothing her chest. Their parents came to a decision. The work had taken over enough of their lives. Their home shouldn't be an office. There needed to be a separation.

'Maybe you two will run that office together some day,' her mother had said to them.

Jahida was ten years old and already acting like a teenager. She rolled her eyes, got up and left the room, leaving Jamila to stay behind.

Jamila was a quiet, guarded child, happiest when reading or playing in the garden. Firefighter to naan maker to bin collector, her career choices shifted daily. But this opportunity had never been presented to her before. Sucking on the dregs of another ice-pop, two threads of raspberry-coloured juice rising up the sides and the sharp plastic seams cutting into the corners of her stained mouth, she watched her mother and considered what those words meant.

Mrs Kulasingam called again the moment Jamila sat down. 'Where is he? My stomach hurts.'

Jamila took no time to reassure her.

'Look, you have to let me get on. If he calls, tell him to contact me.' She had to get him out, but knew from experience that she would never reach the officials today, not at the weekend. She called the local Home Office department anyway. All she got was a dry voicemail, instructing her to call back during office hours. As if they only detained migrants during office hours. She tried the detainee casework team in Liverpool. She called the various detention centres: Pennine House and Morton Hall and Campsfield House and Haslar, even Brook House and Harmondsworth near Gatwick and Heathrow Airports. Each of the numbers rang out or ended in curt voice messages with the same basic information, but no guidance on what to do in the event of emergency. She could only sit back and wait for John to call. Once he reached the centre, once the detention officers had taken away his smart phone and replaced it with a prehistoric handset without a camera or the internet (to 'maintain order' officials insisted), once he had been assigned to a room and a compulsory roommate, he would call.

In the meantime, she reacquainted herself with the facts needed to build a case for John's release. More than ten years ago, her father had helped John to claim asylum as a Tamil refugee fleeing the Sri Lankan civil war. That application had been hindered by the Home Office's tenuous grip of the situation in the country, and then by a backlog of over 450,000 cases. When Jamila had taken over his case a year ago, she had prepared an application for 'leave to remain' on his behalf. At that point, John's eldest daughter had spent almost seven years living in Britain – the benchmark for children. Seven years going to school and making friends and speaking the language and picking up the local accents, of eating mashed potatoes and beans and watching cartoons of pigs and trains on television. It wasn't right for them to start over elsewhere.

Jamila turned to the medical documents. She knew that John had been tortured by the Sri Lankan authorities before arriving in Britain – *knew* this, had seen the scars for herself – but she had to check the reports again. Every case sat in the lap of the gods, no matter how strong her evidence. The randomness of it all was gruelling. Every negative decision left her questioning herself.

Certain words and phrases in his medico-legal report stuck out to her: *detained by the government authorities ... beaten with blunt instruments ... kicked and burned and asphyxiated ... 28 scars, 24 of which were found by the clinician to be evidence of torture ... depression and Post Traumatic Stress Disorder directly related to his mistreatment ...*

She could divorce the precise medical terminology from their fullest meaning. Same, too, for the submissions she had once drafted as her father's protégé. John's testimony of police custody described him being beaten with gun butts and wooden poles, kicked in the chest, scalded with burning rods before being doused with petrol and threatened with being set alight; she read it impassively. But turning a page, she caught the outline of a human figure, a drawing that doubled up as a map of John's body, charting the scars dispersed across his back, stomach, arms and legs. Marks she had seen in photographs, misshapen, discoloured, in some cases waxen – forging an intimacy with John's body stronger than she'd had with any boyfriend. She looked away.

At 12:30pm, he rang.

'They bring me to the detention centre near Manchester Airport. Please, I can't leave. I have a pregnant wife and three children.'

He was close by, in Pennine House. 'What about paperwork?'

'They said I'm an illegal immigrant. I told them I have application.'

'Go to the library and fax me whatever they've given you.'

'Do something, Mrs Shah. They hurt me.' His voice cracked.

In spite of her years of practice, those three words made their way through her. What could she do about that? Who would listen if she tried calling attention to this? Her chest swelled. Nobody at the Home Office would be interested.

The fax machine sounded like it was in pain too, spluttering as it expelled hot air and, eventually, paper. As decisions to detain went, the papers were unremarkable. No specificity, no originality whatsoever. John had stayed in the UK beyond the dates of his initial visit visa. The authorities believed he was at risk of disappearing – though with three kids, how far could he run? Then Jamila realised something: John had been taken to Pennine House. Pennine House was for short stays. In other words, the Home Office wanted to remove him from the country.

She rifled through her drawer for her phonebook. She had fifteen numbers for the teams working at the airport, seven crossed out because they were no longer in service. She dialled the others, one by one, getting through on the fifth attempt.

'Hi, can I give you a reference number? It's K3104534.'

It took a few seconds for the detention officer to load the file.

'What do you need?' he asked, surly and gruff.

'Can I speak to the caseworker?'

'Nobody's here until Monday. You should call then.'

John's file balanced in her lap, the papers weighed a ton – a whole decade of his life in this country. She fortified her voice.

'But my client has an outstanding application. We submitted it a year ago. His youngest daughter has a learning disability, he's her primary carer.' She hoped this last part would carry an additional punch; perhaps it could shame them into granting John an automatic release.

'I can't see that on the system here,' said the officer.

'I have the acknowledgement letter in my hands. Don't your departments liaise with one another?'

She gave the officer a few seconds to respond, but he had no interest in engaging with her. Finding a human ear in this business was hard. She softened her voice.

'Tell you what, I'll fax over a copy right now.'

She teased the papers from their binding.

'Mr Kulasingam isn't even fit for detention. He's a victim of torture.'

The voice turned cold and mechanical. 'As you know, we regularly evaluate and review a person's fitness for detention.

16

I'm sure somebody will consider this information when it's next appropriate . . . '

She stood over the fax machine again. As sheets of paper entered one side and exited the other, Jamila thumbed her mobile.

She had received two messages, the first from Samir confirming their coffee at three. It was clear that she wouldn't finish in time and even if she did, she'd be in no mood to socialise.

She bashed out a message: *Stuck at work on a 999. How about next week? Sorry!* This, she followed with a shower of hearts and sad looking emojis, allowing more emotion than she could muster in reality.

Samir replied instantly: *Oh, Wonder Woman, is it? You don't even try to avoid it. Fine, don't forget your cape.*

Her heart panged. Samir was her closest friend. They had grown up together, living just streets apart. Even then, he had always sassed her. She idly flicked through their old messages, and those with their school friend Maryam. There were multiple attempts to arrange a meeting or even a call. She missed them. But, as with every never-ending battle, there was work left to be done.

The second message was from her mother: *What time are you coming? Jahida will be here from 6.*

Without replying, she returned the phone to her pocket, relieved. She would not have to feign interest in other people or herself. Unlike friends or family, her clients' emotions were predictable and her work followed a well-worn formula.

Once the fax went through, she confirmed the officer had received the papers – actually held them in his hands. In the Home Office, faxes were often misplaced or never picked up at all. It must have been the only government department that insisted on using them. She pictured their Croydon office: a sixties tower block with garish carpets, burning cigarettes and clacking typewriters. They were out of step at every turn.

'When can we expect a response?' she asked.

'Soon, I'm sure.'

She sighed. It was futile to push him. He was just a small cog in a half-put-together machine, and they were drilled in never deviating from the official script.

She updated Mrs Kulasingam.

'You said you were getting him out today.' Her voice shook with accusation.

Jamila bristled. 'I can't when the caseworkers aren't there.'

'Then when?'

'When I come tomorrow, I'll keep pushing.'

As soon as Jamila got off the phone she wrote to the Home Office again, restating the facts, only this time including the sticky business of emotion. John's wife was heavily pregnant, their youngest daughter dependent on his care. Too many lives were being ruptured.

Through the blinds the sun slipped over the horizon. Close to 7:30pm, she watched the shutters roll down the back door, bleached by the security light, the dark sky folded in around her. The air smelled of gunpowder; she heard the odd firework popping not far away. She had forgotten it was Bonfire Night tomorrow, and in the parks the Sunday displays would begin soon, crowded by grinning idiots and their squealing little children.

Jamila barely registered the route she found herself taking. She drove away from the mithai shops and fast-food restaurants – and the families – of Longsight and Levenshulme, heading for the concrete anonymity of east Manchester, past the football stadium and velodrome, up the Alan Turing Way. Her stomach grumbled. She had survived all day on tea and garibaldis, but had John eaten? They had submitted his application within the time limit, provided plenty of evidence, waited patiently for a decision, and still the Home Office had screwed them over. There were multiple lives in immigration cases, multiple opportunities to succeed. This was a comfort when a case was refused. But when those chances looked to be running out, she beat her brain to a single question: could she have done something differently?

She parked in her driveway and got out. The house was cold, unlit, uninviting – it received her as a stranger. For the last fourteen months, she had been living in Cheetham Hill in a semi-detached house that was doubly attractive: cheap enough to afford a mortgage on her modest salary and a good eight miles from her parents in Didsbury. Almost thirty now, she couldn't believe how long it had taken to move out of her parents' home. They expected her to stay with them until she got married, so she went ahead and bought the house without telling them. Upon receiving the news, they tried to arrange tenants for her. They sulked when she announced that she was moving out, then cried as they carried her things to the van. But here it was, her sanctuary.

She had painted the rooms white, but the walls were bare, waiting for her to customise them with ideas collected from magazines. She tried to visualise these scraps as her own, trying to imagine herself as the sort of person that chose a Mondrian for the pleasing order of its lines, and not because it fitted an aesthetic that made her appear cultured and cosmopolitan. For now, even her furniture reflected nothing of her tastes. Everything she owned, she had rescued from her parents' garage: a paisley-print sofa with broken springs, a coffee table with a crack in its glass inlay, three consoles with faded varnish, which she used as stands for thirsty, brown-tipped plants.

She put her bag down and checked on Bertha in the living room. Her pet snake was coiling around a branch in her vivarium, her smooth skin neon beneath the UV lights. Independent, rational and straightforward, Bertha was the perfect companion.

The kitchen was the real draw of the house, renovated on account of the cooking and entertaining she had imagined doing there. It was bright and airy, with navy cupboards, gold handles and white marble countertops. There were also dirty plates and cups scattered around the sink, plastic containers stacked there for days, tacky with oil, crusty with sediment and sauce. She walked in, took a ready meal from the freezer and placed it in the microwave. She played with her phone until it was bubbling, then took the cannelloni into the living room and sat on the sofa.

She switched on the television to a piece about the American elections. None of it filtered through. John, his wife, the children – everything circled back to work. Before she had even finished eating, she called him.

'They're going to deport me, aren't they?' he said.

'No—'

'You can be honest. They will kill me if—'

'No, John. We have options. It's not that easy to—'

'Yes? Like what?'

'We can ask the Home Office for temporary admission, apply to the tribunal for bail, appeal to the High Court for an intervention . . . '

'This place is like prison, Mrs Shah. The walls are so cold . . . so white.' His voice echoed, as if he was speaking to her from another realm.

Jamila recalled his police testimony – it must have seemed like he was being punished all over again. Her attempts to provide comfort always felt pointless, but she pushed herself. 'I know it's hard, but I'm fighting for you. I'm going to get you out.'

'I hope so, Mrs Shah.'

A series of fireworks erupted in the neighbour's garden. She flinched and stared at the food warming her lap. All she ate these days were ready meals. She had been through every supermarket option. They were bland and unhealthy, always too small and devoid of real nourishment, but instead of cooking, or eating her mother's food, she continued to subject herself to this plastic rubbish. It didn't matter: she ate not for taste or pleasure, but to get through the next day's work.

She pushed these thoughts away and replaced them with the names of the men and women who had been detained in the last weeks and months. Through the television screen, she saw their faces. Ali Ashour and Gul Bibi, Israel Anyaoku and Elisa Duni. Among the tedium of grandmothers wishing to visit their grandchildren and husbands wanting to join their wives, these were the people that stayed with her. Each one had swallowed her previous Sundays. Each one imploring her to evaluate the strengths and weaknesses of their cases, the strategies they could employ to slay their dragon. Each one grasping for certainty on how quickly she could get them out.

Three

Immigration Enforcement
Home Office
Dallas Court
South Langworthy Road
Salford
M50 2GF

Our Ref: K3104534
Your Ref: Shah/Kul/370
Date: 9 November 2012

Dear Mr Kulasingam,

| John Kulasingam | Sri Lanka | 25 May 1977 |

Your application has been refused for the reasons set out below.

Personal Circumstances

You were born and raised in the town of Nallur in northern Sri Lanka. You had two brothers and two sisters. For as long as you can remember, your father and brothers were members of the Liberation Tigers of Tamil Eelam ('LTTE', also known as the 'Tamil Tigers'). You also had dealings with the group, which was unavoidable since they controlled your town, but you were not an official member. You focused on providing for the family as a fisherman.

In January 1996, during the third Eelam War, your father and brothers left home to fight on behalf of the LTTE. As a result of the heavy fighting around the Kilinochchi area, you and your family became displaced in the violence. You were captured by the Sri Lankan armed forces and tortured as a suspected member of the LTTE. When you were released in October 1996, you had lost contact with your mother and sisters, and lived in a camp for internally displaced people in the Vavuniya region. This is where you met your wife, Mary. When the early peace efforts began in 2000, you and your wife fled the country.

Immigration History

On 17 May 2002, you entered the UK as a visitor with your wife and claimed asylum. On 5 January 2004, your asylum application was refused. Your subsequent appeals were also refused and you became appeal rights exhausted.

On 18 January 2005, your representatives made further submissions. You stated that the political situation in Sri Lanka is volatile, where real and perceived members of the Tamil separatist movement are violently suppressed. Due to a backlog of asylum cases, you did not receive a response from the Home Office. Consequently, your case was entered into the Legacy Case Resolution Programme. On 23 March 2011, we decided not to grant you any leave.

On 17 October 2011, your representatives lodged an application for discretionary leave to remain.

Consideration of your Case
Risk of Return to Sri Lanka

'On 19 May 2009 the Sri Lankan government announced its military victory over the Liberation Tigers of Tamil Eelam (LTTE) following a 26-year-long

internal conflict. Over this period at least 70,000 people are estimated to have been killed and some one million displaced.' [Foreign & Commonwealth Office (FCO) profile, Sri Lanka, 2011.]

'Following the conclusion of the civil war in Sri Lanka, the Sri Lankan authorities' interest in failed Tamil asylum seekers has not increased; if anything, the level of interest in them has decreased.' [Upper Tribunal Judge Covey, in his determination of your appeal, 2 August 2011.]

Thus, since the end of the civil war, the Sri Lankan authorities' focus is not on Tamils from the north and north-east of the country, but persons considered to be LTTE members, operators and fighters, or persons who have played a role in the international procurement network of financing and providing it with arms. We note that you were, in fact, not an LTTE member, so we do not consider you at risk if you were returned to Sri Lanka.

Circumstances in the UK

The submissions made in your most recent application have also been carefully considered under the provisions of the European Convention on Human Rights. Article 8 (1) states that: *Everyone has the right to respect for his private and family life, his home and his correspondence.*

You have been living in the UK with your wife since May 2002. On 30 January 2005, your eldest daughter, Jasmin Kulasingam was born, followed by your son, Henry Kulasingam on 12 December 2006 and your daughter, Jessica Kulasingam on 7 July 2008 Your wife is currently pregnant with your fourth child. According to the evidence provided, you have strong ties to the Tamil community in Manchester. You have also submitted letters of support from your friends and family in the UK as proof of the social bonds you have created here.

It is accepted that you have a family life with your wife and children. We are satisfied, however, that it is reasonable for your family unit to return together to Sri Lanka. Your children are young and will adapt to the culture and climate of the country. You and your wife are healthy adults, capable of working to maintain your children financially, and providing for their safety and welfare.

Your eldest daughter has accumulated 7 years continuous residence in the UK. According to the Immigration Rules, as amended on 09 July 2012, a child who has spent such time living here could be entitled to leave to remain. But the Rules also state that it must be unreasonable for the child to leave the UK. In this case, we do not believe it is so. If your daughter were to return to Sri Lanka, she would be returning with her parents and siblings, as part of a family unit. There is a strong school system for her to integrate into. Alternatively, if she were to remain in the UK, you would not need to stay with her. Your family life could be continued through modern means of communication, such as internet messaging and telephone calls.

According to a report from her Consultant Paediatrician, your youngest daughter was born with Williams syndrome. You state that this makes it impossible for you or your family to return to Sri Lanka, where the level of care towards people with disabilities is substandard and severe societal discrimination exists towards the differently abled.

But the threshold set by Article 3 ECHR is a high one. It is not simply a question of whether the treatment required is unavailable or inaccessible in the country of origin, it is whether the applicant's illness has reached such a critical stage that it would be inhuman treatment to deprive him of the care he is currently receiving and send him home to an early death. Here, this is not the case. Exercising discretion in your favour would be to treat you in a more favourable manner when compared to other persons who are in a similar position and have been refused leave.

Exceptional Circumstances

A Rule 35 assessment was carried out by one of our medical practitioners on 7 November 2012. As stated in our letter earlier today, the doctor assessed the marks on your body and stated that they may be consistent with torture but could also be self-inflicted.

This is consistent with the assessment of UT Judge Covey, who rejected your claims of torture and severe mental health problems:

'You submitted a report from the Medical Foundation in support of your treatment at the hands of the Sri Lankan authorities. Dr Kamlana reports that the scars and lesions found on your body are consistent with your account of detention and ill treatment. However, the mere existence of scars does not indicate that the injuries were sustained in the manner described. Even if the doctor's conclusions are taken at their highest it can only be accepted that the scars were caused deliberately. The doctor cannot be expected to state by whom, and in what circumstances, these scars were caused.'

Indeed, when assessed by our medical practitioner, you said that your mental health was 'bad', and that you had contemplated suicide in the past, but you were not currently feeling suicidal. The doctor found that you were eating normally and exercising regularly. Since he has not suggested that your detention is inappropriate and there has been no recommendation to release you, detention will be maintained.

Yours faithfully,

N. Gupta

Four

'It's so awful, baj. All the crap they spouted to engineer this refusal, it's pathetic.' Jamila's voice broke as she staggered out of her chair and turned on the answering machine, then wandered through the staff area, switching off the lights and computers, checking that the windows were closed. 'I was just hoping they would back down through the application, you know? Even if they rejected the torture again, they would have to acknowledge the rights of his kids.'

'Are you surprised?' Jahida replied. 'They're heartless monsters.'

Jamila tightened her grip on the mobile. 'Did I say I was surprised? I'm pissed off. How do I argue with their stupid logic?'

'I don't know, but you're not going to figure that out tonight, are you? Come round.'

'I'm not in the mood.'

'Then take the night off. Watch something, eat, play one of your nerdy video games. Tomorrow, talk to Dad. He'll steer you.'

'Mmmn.'

A pressure welled inside her, but she wouldn't reward the Home Office with tears.

All week, she had kept her foot on the pedal. She had called detained casework first thing on Monday morning, laying out the facts, believing for a minute this could be easy. A short interlude. The Home Office would recognise its mistake and grant him a reprieve.

'I haven't gotten to that file yet,' the caseworker said when she finally got through.

Jamila paused. 'When will you? It's kind of urgent.'

'I'm hoping to this afternoon.'

'I'll call you back then, shall I?'

'If you want, but I can't guarantee anything.'

The caseworker had laughed, like they were colleagues sharing banter. But Jamila kept on calling, through her father's unhelpful comments ('It doesn't matter what you say, they always follow their own timing'), through Mrs Kulasingam's growing anger ('Your father would have got him out. You keep saying you will too, but can you really?'), through her failing attempts to comfort John, whose voice sounded like it had been crushed into parts so small it was little more than vapour ('I can't sleep. They locked me in my room, but I can hear the planes taking off outside').

By Wednesday evening – the fourth day of John's detention – Babar, her bookkeeper-cum-protégé (owing to the fact that she had recently started giving him legal work to do), had learned no more than her. 'The caseworker is apparently looking at it,' he said, toeing the ground in frustration.

She decided to accelerate: 'Let's make a Rule 35 referral, put the onus on these idiots. Maybe if they see the scars on his body, they'll come to their senses.'

According to the law, vulnerable adults weren't allowed to be detained; John's previous experiences of torture and ongoing mental health issues meant that detention would harm him.

Babar shook his hands out of his pockets, looking as though he were about to enter a boxing ring. 'I'll type it up. You tell me what to write.'

'I'll do it,' Jamila said. She had nothing waiting for her at home.

She repeated a summary of his police testimony, the scars on his body, the diagnosis of post-traumatic stress disorder. She asked for his immediate release.

Now, two days later, this sickening response. And on her way home, in every light on every street, in the windscreen of every car, a scrolling digital sign: *But can you really, can you really, can you?*

She entered her house and sank into the sofa. Her boots anchored her feet to the ground, but her mind flew somewhere above her, buzzing with ideas. She had to act. She couldn't leave it like this.

But the Home Office had shut for the weekend, there was little she could do. For once, she listened to her sister. She went upstairs and changed into a hoodie and pyjama bottoms. In the bathroom, she tied up her hair and began washing the day from her face. She used to relish this routine, the stillness it invoked after the commotion of the office. The house, with its vast emptiness, with no noise apart from the television at night and the birds at dawn, was a quieting influence. Tonight, however, she felt nothing.

She dried her face on a towel and went downstairs. Another spinach cannelloni, another episode of that vampire show. She brought out the family sized crisps and chocolate peanuts, and binge-ate while playing video games. For a while, she was glad to be absorbed into that reality, but when her avatar was killed, she switched off the console and glanced around the room. What to do now?

The silence wrapped its fingers around her neck. This is how it was: over the course of an evening, an empty weekend, what was once a respite came to suffocate her. She moved to the edge of the sofa, craving the office ruckus. Sure, her mother was a phone call away, she could have accepted Jahida's invitation, she needed to reschedule that coffee with Samir, but she put it all off. She had nothing to offer them.

Bertha nosed aimlessly around her tank. Back and forth, back and forth. Jamila wondered how her friends treated her endless cancellations, always putting the office first, client catastrophes before birthdays and weddings. Did they take her seriously or perceive it as an affectation, somebody who chose to appear busier and therefore grander than she really was? They can't have been that bothered really; they continued to reach out to her.

Still, there was pleasure to be drawn from a life like this, she told herself. It was like going to the gym – back when she made time for the gym – pushing her body to its limits on the treadmill; the tight, elastic feel of her muscles absorbing the stresses of the weights' machines. At the end of a working week, she felt like she had run a marathon.

Scrolling through her phone, she went to his social media profile. He who used to be hers. What would this house have smelled like with him in it? How would it have sounded with him sitting next to her? Her finger hovered over the message button. Her breath and chest fell to nothing.

She couldn't do it. Couldn't reverse a decision that had already been made. Nor did she have the capacity for moping or mourning. No, rather than think about him, she preferred to swaddle herself with work, games and food. Her gaze went to the papers on her table then, their edges lifted as if they were ready to fly away. She grabbed them and started scribbling.

The next morning, she went in and called John. 'Honestly, I didn't expect this – I mean, I had an inkling, but I didn't think they would do it. The decision is stupid and offensive – it's just plain wrong.' Anger leaked through her professional tone. This was the fear that loomed over every client, that the Home Office would wake up one day and decide to remove them from the country, only bothering to justify it afterwards.

'Is this about money?' His words collided together. 'You're wanting more from us?'

'What? No.' She was shocked. If this was about money, she wouldn't have been in the job at all. She could make more money practising almost any other area of law – the very suggestion insulted her.

'I want to see my baby being born, Mrs Shah. I want to be a good father, good husband.'

She paused. 'And you will be. How are you holding up?'

'I try to keep busy, exercise. They have gym, but why no swimming pool, huh?'

His laughter had a hollow ring, but she joined in to be polite.

She called his wife.

'You said that you could get him out. You did. You promised me and then you did nothing . . . ' Jamila held the phone away from her ear. ' . . . We're going to find another solicitor.'

She knew it was her job to absorb their frustrations, but Mrs Kulasingam needed to know that she had nothing to gain from their loss, that their fates were entwined. 'If that's what you want, go ahead. You won't find a solicitor like me.'

But her empty office didn't seem to agree.

Jamila waited for the threat to transfer John's file to another solicitor to materialise. In the meantime, she had work to do. Suggesting that a seven-year-old stayed in the country while the rest of her family returned could not be in her 'best interests'. She sought out the latest country reports on the situation in Sri Lanka. Though the Home Office had dealt with this previously, now that things were moving into fourth gear it came into play again. And contrary to the line the Home Office parroted after its secret meetings with the Sri Lankan government, it wasn't safe for Tamil asylum seekers to return home. Many had fled back to Europe and disclosed everything: '*When I arrived in Sri Lanka, two men stopped me from leaving the airport. They led me through a series of rooms and then into a van. Why did I come back to Sri Lanka? They asked me. Why had I left in the first place? They tied my hands and legs together and kicked me, then hit me with burning rods.*'

The UN had issued the guidance that scars on a body could incriminate a person, suggest they were once of 'interest' to the government.

John had so many scars.

Jamila spent hours over the weekend composing her response, converting her semi-legible notes into paragraphs of legal argument. It was what she enjoyed: burrowing into the depths of a matter before surfacing to construct an argument from what she had found. Both stages were integral: there was no house without foundations, no bone without marrow. She wrote and rewrote her submissions, reflecting, even while attempting to sleep, that the final document had to be concise to convince an overburdened caseworker, and flow with logic and elegance.

On Monday morning, she stared at the typed pages in front of her. She was putting the Home Office on notice: if they didn't release John and grant him a visa, she was taking them to the High Court.

She rubbed the back of her neck. 'Is this the right step, Dad?'

Her father sat opposite her, picking at a plate of rusk biscuits. 'What step?'

'The pre-action protocol, Dad. For John.'

'What other option do you have?'

'Shouldn't you be telling me? You're the oracle here.'

In the last day or so, John had lost faith in her. He was willing to meet his fate in Sri Lanka; he just wanted to say goodbye to his children. His voice had sounded so calm, so at peace, it terrified her. If only she had trained as a psychologist, as she had wanted during her college years, she would have known how to respond. Instead, she had none of the training, but a similar expectation that she would diagnose and treat traumatised individuals. If the protocol or subsequent judicial review failed . . . she couldn't bear to imagine the consequences for John. It was a last hope. But there were consequences for her too, potentially. She had heard the stories: High Court judges humiliating immigration solicitors, threatening them with official investigations if they felt the grounds before them were baseless. 'Why do we do this to ourselves?'

Her father smiled, saint-like. 'You do this because of Allah. Because you're good.'

Goodness and God. Surely, he had more to offer than that.

Maybe she wasn't cut out for this. Every time a client was being pushed onto a plane, every time she stepped out before a judge with decades more experience, no matter her preparation, the queasy feeling in her stomach had her questioning whether this job was her vocation.

'You're so lucky to be in sitting in that chair, Jammu.'

'Yeah?'

'What would you rather be doing?'

Did he mean in the case or in life generally? She skimmed the protocol for mistakes.

'Just give the Home Office five days. If there's no response, we go to court,' he said.

She made him blow on the pages before faxing them, as her clients did when they made him pray over submissions before she lodged them with the Home Office. They still descended on him, complaining of ailments like loneliness and illness and broken hearts. For a moment, she also believed that his touch, his words could change her destiny.

'Insha'Allah, John will come out,' he said.

She reached over to her father's plate and broke off a piece of rusk.

It turned into crumbs between her fingers.

All she had to do was wait. As other clients and cases competed for her attention, Babar checked in with the caseworker every morning and afternoon.

By Friday morning there was still no news. The protocol was supposed to speed things up. She couldn't wait anymore. But as she contemplated calling the caseworker herself, her mother called. She was too busy to talk, but then Hassan Khemiri appeared at her door, tapping the Arabic newspaper in his hands, like a man who had won the lottery, and she gave in.

'Your Dad and I are still deciding when to go to Pakistan,' her mother said.

She strained to listen over Hassan's incoherent babbling. 'What? I thought you'd decided on Easter?'

'He's changed his mind.'

'Why?'

She knew why. Christmas was the least disruptive for the office. The Home Office ran a skeleton staff over the holiday period, so they had always travelled in December. He couldn't let this place go.

'Has he not mentioned it?'

'He's on his lunch, I think.'

'He wants you to come as well.'

'Oh, I can't. Not at Christmas or Easter.' The clients couldn't stand her absences. Even at a dentist's appointment, their frantic messages jammed her phone.

'Why not? Your dad managed it.'

'And how stressful were those holidays? Dad constantly calling the office, dealing with crisis after crisis while we shopped in Anarkali. Had me staying behind the last few years, didn't he?'

'Everyone deserves a holiday, Jam.'

She sounded so concerned, but had holidays ever crossed her mother's mind when she started badgering her to study law? 'Look at how your father has built this business for us,' she had said when Jamila was seventeen and contemplating university. 'Jahida refused to take it, but you could help your father's name to live on. Everybody in Manchester knows and respects him. What a shame to let that die.'

All her life, Jamila had followed her father. She had waited in the cold outside hardware stores, takeaways and supermarkets, while clients – appearing from nowhere – mined him for advice. The resentment of sharing him with others, his attention always divided, had been formative. But in private moments, she recalled the opening day at their office: the partitions her father had built to make a reception, staff room and consultation room out of the salon, the kebabs they ate in celebration when he came home and told them of the people who had visited, the way his chest had swelled in his cheap three-piece suit. Having seen the respect her father inspired, restauranteurs refusing to accept his money for meals, mechanics touching his feet for blessings, she wondered if she could emulate him.

She, too, had wanted to help people.

'I'll take a holiday when things aren't so hectic. Maybe I'll go to Pakistan without you.'

'Why, what's wrong with travelling with your parents?'

'I'm almost thirty, Mum.'

'What does that mean?'

'You know what it means.' They still saw her as an extension of themselves, in a way that had stopped applying to Jahida the moment she got married. Whenever they did something together, Jamila slipped into becoming a child again. She let it happen to herself, as if it was incontestable, the natural order of things. But she had to experience Pakistan without their mediation.

When the call finished, Hassan launched into rumours of a government amnesty for asylum seekers. She nodded, thinking instead of Pakistan. The country that she loved, that was hers, but not fully; where she was adored by her family, and as the second grandchild to be born abroad, was a glorious spectacle. They spoiled her relentlessly. But, over time, that reverence faded, and she became a spectacle which invited scrutiny. Why, as a teenager, did she hide her changing body in oversized band T-shirts and baggy jeans that made it difficult to tell if she was a boy or a girl? Why, in her twenties, was she still stubbornly unmarried when 'marriage was half the faith'? Her justifications, in crumbling Punjabi, emphasised the difference between her and them. They thought her insolent; their persistence fatigued her. Still, her aunts and uncles needed to shift their perceptions: she was responsible for their destinies. It was from his office that her father used to send them money. Now her office, she did the same every month, but the respect for it was still awarded to her father.

Hassan waved his hands in front of her. 'Why aren't you listening? Oh, you never listen.' His ears were beginning to redden.

'Sorry! Please tell me from the top.'

Jamila said a special prayer for herself at Jummah and, when she returned from the mosque, she went straight to her office and called the caseworker.

'Yes . . . Kulasingam . . . We lodged a pre-action protocol letter on Monday morning. I wanted to know if you'd looked at it.'

The caseworker was unavailable, but her colleague offered to check the system.

'It says here that a decision has been made to release your client. He should be out by tomorrow morning.'

'Oh, brilliant!' Jamila's tense shoulders dropped a little. 'Do you know why?'

'It doesn't say.'

'Will he be granted leave?'

'It seems so.'

'And does the client know?'

'You can give him the good news yourself.'

Jamila's heart was racing. More than anything, she felt relief. Only a week ago, the Home Office was promising to separate John from his family. They had booked him on a flight home. What had changed? All she had done differently was threaten them with a beating in the High Court. Sadly, it was a question that would never be answered. They had traumatised the family for nothing. She knew better than to expect a sound reasoning for their decisions, and perhaps the reason didn't matter. After all, John would be free.

She went out to the staff area to share her news. 'Guys, it's finally happened.' It sounded more ominous than she'd intended.

Sadia tailed her from the reception desk. 'What what what? Tell me now.'

She turned to her. 'John Kulasingam is going to be released.'

Sadia high-fived Jamila and squealed.

Rubel stood up, buttoned his suit jacket and walked over. 'No, really? When?'

'I just spoke to the Home Office. He'll be out tomorrow.'

'You worked so hard. I knew you'd do it.'

She looked around. 'Where's Dad?'

Babar stepped forward. 'He just left. Congratulations, Mrs Shah. I can't believe it.'

'Neither can I.' She touched his arm, thinking of all the calls he had made on her behalf. 'I'd better call his wife.' She was the bridge between the client and the Home Office, the bearer of bad news and good.

She found the number in her recent contacts. She couldn't wait to tell John's wife, to listen for the shift in her voice as it accommodated her victory. Jamila had proven her wrong. That was some achievement.

She held out her mobile. It rang on speakerphone.

'Mrs Kulasingam, hi,' she began brightly. 'It's Ms Shah from Shah and Co. Solicitors. I've got some great news for you. The Home Office is going to release John. He'll be with you and the kids by tomorrow. If not tomorrow, then Monday.'

There was an awkward pause.

'Mrs Shah, they release him already. He's with me now.'

Jamila straightened up. 'What?'

'They saw sense in the end, but thank you for trying.'

There was a ringing in Jamila's ears. *He's with me now.* The Home Office had said tomorrow. The words seared themselves onto her cheeks. She looked up at Rubel and Babar, found them staring at her with shock, then undisguised pity.

Five

Some three weeks later, one icy Tuesday in early December, Jamila escaped to the kitchen for a break. Situated in the bowels of the office, down a couple of stairs, it was a damp, dark little room.

From here, the circus that accompanied the office was also muted. She stood on the balls of her feet and stretched out her calves and tried to release the tension that had been trapped in her body lately. She placed her hands on the work surface and did the same with her arms. She worked her spine, straining backwards then bending forwards, grunting like an old man. Her torso lay almost prone on the work top, strung out like a cat, fingers slipping against the clammy wall tiles, when the door whipped open.

Sadia stared at her.

Jamila snapped upright. She adjusted herself, smoothing the wrinkles in her blouse. She couldn't find a moment's peace anywhere. Her cheeks scorched and prickling, she eyeballed Sadia, who stared back, uncowed by Jamila's glare.

'What were you doing?' Sadia asked.

'Nothing,' Jamila said awkwardly.

'John Kulasingam is here.'

Jamila pulled her lips into a firm, closed smile, eager to regain the authority she had just lost. 'Fine. I'll be there in a minute.'

Sadia headed back to her desk, failing to withhold her laughter as she left. Jamila flipped on the kettle and tried to forget her embarrassment. It didn't matter who had arrived, these precious minutes were hers. She scrolled mindlessly on her phone. When the kettle had boiled, she dunked a teabag in a mugful of hot water, added milk and sugar, then stared out of the tiny window at the pigeoned roofs, the opening so small that even a child couldn't crawl through.

She returned to her office with her tea. In the weeks since he was released from detention, John had stayed away – postal delivery of white chrysanthemums and a Thank You card aside. Instead, they shared phone calls that always failed to alleviate her continued concern for his wellbeing. With everyday cases, she abandoned thoughts of the clients as soon as they left her office. But with vulnerable clients that were forced into precarious positions, the pressure, disappointment and anger formed a lump against her chest. All she could do was give him space, so not until she had received his papers did she ask him to visit.

Now, he rapped on the door.

'Mr Kulasingam! It's so good to see you. Please, take a seat.'

John was wearing a polo shirt and jeans. For the first time, the scars on his forearms were exposed for all to see. But he massaged those scars, hiding them behind his hands. When had she last seen him? She had trouble recalling this interaction with her usual clarity. A month before his detention maybe, when he had come to her wanting permission to work, grinding his teeth at the cost of necessities for the new baby.

So much had happened since then.

'How are you? How's your wife?'

'Good,' he nodded. 'Baby coming next month.'

'Ah, so she's resting at home.' Jamila tried to sound invested. 'For the best, I think.'

He couldn't stop smiling. Through that smile, Jamila recalled his insistence that all was well after his release, though their telephone conversations were always fragmented, punctuated by these long, distracted silences that led nowhere. He had always sounded like she had disturbed him from a deep sleep. Again and again, she urged him to see a doctor, but he only promised to think about it.

'You know I did everything I could, right? I tried to get you out as quickly as possible.' It sounded petty, especially directed at someone who didn't care how his freedom had been won. But his wife had been so frugal with her praise, even after their victory. 'I tried to make their lives a living hell,' she said, borrowing a Punjabi phrase from her father. She knew a part of her was also speaking to herself.

'You did so much for us, Mrs Shah. The flowers were my wife's idea.'

Jamila hadn't known that. What was it his wife had said in an early meeting? 'Sometimes the fear grips me that they will take us away from our children and I feel like my lungs are on fire.' Her mouth had puckered and quivered, which she had tried to hide with a bit of her shirt sleeve. The threat of removal haunted every parent. Jamila stared at the chrysanthemums sitting droopy and browned in a chipped vase at the end of her desk, her soreness waning.

'I guess we should focus on more positive things then. Your visas are here.' She leant over the side of her chair and fished for John's file in the pool of successful cases she kept on the floor beside her. 'They've given you and your family five years' leave.' She slapped his file on her desk and prised out his residence permit. His fingers trembling, he held it with a reverent gaze.

'With this you can work, access public funds—'

'I don't want anything from them, only this.' He gestured to his permit, his jaw set.

'Well, you have the option if you ever need it. They've returned your original documents, so check if there's anything missing.'

John turned the second packet out onto her desk and sifted through the items: his expired Sri Lankan passport, his children's school reports, his daughter's medical reports, scans of the latest pregnancy. She watched him, trying to match the person who had been totally crushed by detention with the person sitting before her. The person who she had thought about while driving home from work, eating dinner and watching vampires on TV, his deadened voice colliding with the sounds and images on screen. Now, his clean, clipped nails and citrus-scented aftershave suggested he was doing better, but surely returning to the outside world hadn't been that easy?

From this side of their exchange, she would never know, could only grasp at the air.

He lifted his head. 'It's all here.' He smiled again, as if their working relationship was ending in the smoothest, most uneventful circumstances.

'There's one more thing . . . I think we should sue for unlawful detention.'

'Huh?'

'You shouldn't have been detained, John. There are rules against it happening in this country. The Home Office should be punished.'

John clutched the envelopes to his chest. 'But I don't want to punish anybody.'

'Maybe punishing isn't the right term. It's holding them to account. If we don't, then who will? They'll keep on doing it, to other people, other families.'

John had won, but she couldn't forget the Home Office's indifference to his case. She had done everything right: set out the legal facts, established his right to protection, presented these details in easy, digestible language, and they refused him as casually as refusing the offer of a drink. She wanted to protest the system's wicked unpredictability, how the long arm of the law could wrap itself around anybody's neck – anybody who lacked the necessary power and status. 'Think of it as giving back,' she said, fighting for the right words. 'You doing something for people in your position.' At the very least, the Home Office deserved it for humiliating her, telling her that he was being released tomorrow when he was already out.

'I just want a peaceful life, Mrs Shah . . . '

It was clear she couldn't change his mind. She fell back in her chair. 'Fine, but they broke the law. Somebody should hold them to account. You have a year to change your mind.'

John stood to leave. 'Maybe we could have a hug?'

Jamila didn't readily embrace her clients. It happened only when one of them rushed over and collapsed in her arms, leaving her no choice but to hold them.

This time, she got up and approached him.

He was incredibly still in their embrace. She pressed her hands against his back, feeling the weight of the last two months between them, a weight that clouded her throat and made it difficult to let go.

'Come back in five years and we'll apply for indefinite.'

Would she still be here, she wondered.

'Yes, Mrs Shah.'

His voice vibrated against her chest.

It was early, for once, when the staff gathered for lunch. She heard the boys' voices as she approached the dining room. Her father's was the loudest, lecturing them on the connection between true spirituality and dedication in their office work. She rolled her eyes. When she entered, Babar thrust his phone at her, the screen so bright it erased the text. She stepped back and squinted – on the screen there appeared to be a menu. 'God, are we not done with Christmas planning yet?'

Babar and Rubel had spent all morning trying to finalise where they would go for the staff Christmas party. She was already sick of it. She bent her body away from him and looked for some place to sit, albeit slow enough to catch how her comment had dimmed Babar's eager enthusiasm.

Babar rubbed his lips and stared at the table. 'Oh. No. Christmas is decided. This is—'

'A celebration of my daughter's success,' her father said. 'I'm treating everyone to lunch. Babar was simply showing you what we ordered. Afghani food.'

'Dad . . . ' She didn't deserve a celebration and wasn't in the mood for one.

'I had to. You won a big case.' Her father pulled out the chair beside him. 'Come, sit here.'

Babar and Rubel carried the food and cutlery in from the kitchen.

Sadia returned from an appointment and joined them too.

As they ate, they discussed the news. A typhoon in the Philippines. Palestine awarded observer status at the UN General Assembly.

'How many marriage proposals have you received lately, Mrs Shah?' Rubel asked suddenly, his lips wet in anticipation of her answer.

'Come on, Rubel. You can't ask that,' Sadia said, though clearly she was interested too.

Jamila bridled at the assumption she would discuss her private life with her employees. Her private life was nobody's business. And yet . . . when she took over the office, she hadn't expected to receive more marriage proposals in one month than most people got in a lifetime. 'Nothing since last week when Mr Khemiri insisted that I marry him to help his case,' she said eventually. It wasn't much of a personal revelation – they all knew Hassan well.

'Isn't he already married?' Rubel said.

'Not much of an offer, is it?'

Her father puffed out his chest. 'Why didn't you say? I would have put him in his place.'

She laughed at his sudden machismo. 'How many clients will you do that to?'

'Wait, there are others?' He searched her face in bafflement, then looked away, silent. She wondered whether he had recognised this as an occupational hazard when she first took over from him. What advice did he have on managing these proposals – and the men who saw her gender as an opportunity, like they could demand something more from her than representation? Would he shame them all?

'What did John say about suing them?' he asked after some time.

She shook her head. No advice at all then. The truth is, he had no concept of what it took for her to assume his seat – and all that his clients now expected of her.

Her father patted her back. 'It's good to accommodate. Even in Hudaybiyah, the Prophet turned back from war.'

'We won and that's what matters,' Rubel said.

She tried to absorb this. The Home Office might have released John from detention early, without informing her, but the fact that he had been freed at all was a result of her actions. Her sleepless nights. Her work. Victory couldn't be snatched from her, no matter how the Home Office had undermined her. She had won. And yet, weeks after the decision, Jamila continued to feel like she was submerged, stretching out to grasp the potent, dizzying sensation of success, like an oyster that was too far away.

Six

Nazish

Nazish had known exactly who she was waiting for at Shah & Co. Solicitors that sunny August afternoon: the woman who had saved her life. But since they had never met before, she had no idea what to expect.

The floorboards had creaked and Nazish looked up at a tall woman with fine features, generous hips and frizzy hair. She wore a boxy grey suit, her shirt badly creased, her thick mane tied back in a ponytail. But she wore no makeup (the women in this country caked it on) and there was warmth in her pale face and big honey-brown eyes, a corona of piercings in her ears.

'I was hoping you'd have your old file with you,' she said, reaching for the brown packet Nazish had brought and left on the desk. The lawyer moved with a jittery energy. She looked to be in her late twenties but had sounded older over the phone. Could such a young woman, one who couldn't even dress properly to boot, be trusted with her case?

'You're my solicitor?' asked Nazish, raising a brow.

'Sorry, yes, I'm Jamila Shah. I thought we could use the privacy of meeting upstairs.'

Nazish nodded, and Jamila sat down to read the documents in the packet. As she did, Nazish looked around. The premises were strange for a solicitor's firm. Scuffed skirting boards, cheap ceiling tiles and woodchip wallpaper slathered in lavender paint. The carpet hadn't been spared the shoddy paintjob either – in one corner paint pooled and cracked. Had she chosen the right solicitor? Well, it hadn't been a choice. No other solicitor would have her.

'What can you do for me?'

Her directness might have been considered rude by some, but Jamila seemed to find it amusing. Her lips parted, revealing a wide, gap-toothed smile. It reminded Nazish of her grandmother, who believed smiles like that brought good luck. 'The next steps are obvious. We pursue this appeal of yours. Luckily, your previous representative lodged the forms in time, so we just need to prepare for the hearing. It'll take a while. We must get this right.'

'How?'

'Start gathering documents to support your case. I'll make a list. We need a new statement. We need to tell your story in a way that's impossible to refuse again.'

Nazish held her stomach with her hands as she absorbed this information.

She hated stories. She didn't read novels and she didn't watch television. She couldn't stand it when friends lingered over their tales, stretching them out for attention and effect. Yet here she was, expected to tell hers again. For the second time now. Or was it the third? We don't like your story, tell us again. That was how the immigration system played with her and she despised it too.

'What do you think of my case?'

'The Home Office are proper arseholes. Absolutely shocking decision to refuse you.'

Nazish noted the rage that reddened the woman's face. It pleased her.

'Honestly, I think your case is winnable. We'll need to work for it, though. No judge is handing this to us on a plate.'

Nazish folded her arms. 'Main apni puri koshish karoungi.'

'And I'll work hard for you, too.'

'But, let me tell you,' Nazish pushed her shoulders back, relishing her words, 'I'm not easy. People think I'm trouble and I'm at peace with this.' Being trouble was the only way she could stop life from completely flattening her. It was the only way a woman like her survived. But when Jamila laughed, Nazish's cheeks flushed.

'You're not my first difficult client. I'm not so easy myself.'

Jamila began putting the documents in order. Nazish couldn't quite believe how, just a week ago, she had been trawling the internet for a solicitor willing to represent her. If sweet Pamela, her fellow Yarl's Wood detainee, hadn't shared the details of her own representative, she would have floundered. When the stupid Home Office refused her asylum claim, Nazish decided to resist. What she hadn't imagined was how quickly they would take her away, how quickly her solicitor would abandon her. The vulture, who had charged her £3,000 at the start, offered excuses about competence and authority, 'Not being able to deal with such cases'. She wondered if he meant lesbian cases, but sitting here, she decided that it was a blessing.

'Your first statement, the one prepared by your previous solicitor for the initial asylum claim, isn't bad.'

Jamila teased a staple loose from the pages, spreading them across her desk.

'We can use this as the basis of an updated statement. Add your recent activities, our rebuttals to the refusal, we'd be in a good place, I think—'

Nazish shook her head. 'Mujhe aisey nahin chahiye. I want you to start my statement new.'

'Why?'

'I want you to use the statement I wrote myself. I emailed.'

'But why though?'

'I just told you. This statement is not mine.' She felt Jamila studying her over her round glasses and pulled her shoulders back again. For this partnership to work, Jamila had to respect her need for authenticity in this process.

'Naz – can I call you Naz?'

Nazish pursed her lips. 'No.'

'Fine, Nazish then. I'm just trying to help, okay? If we prepare a statement that's different to the one you submitted before, we'll get crucified at the hearing.'

Cooperative, that's how they had described Mrs Shah in online reviews. Friendly and accommodating. So why wasn't she listening? 'First time, I did what they wanted – I tried to tell a perfect story – but what did that do? Kuch bi nahin. No, this is my life, my story, and there are so many gaps, so many things I don't remember. If I can't tell it as I want, I prefer to go home. Or to some other solicitor.'

She didn't mean this – she had knocked on enough doors only to have them shut in her face – but sometimes the other side needed testing. Nazish reminded herself to breathe. She inhaled deeply as Jamila eyed her, then switched on the computer. It didn't take long to print the email. For the next ten minutes, she compared the two statements.

'I think I can make it work,' Jamila said, eventually. 'For both of us.'

'What?'

'I can work out a compromise. Let's get on with our storytelling.'

Nazish forced Jamila to find a common point of entry. What they agreed upon was this: Nazish was born in Islamabad, one of three children, the middle child. Her mother was from Kashmir, her father from Khyber Pakhtunkhwa, and this, Nazish grew up believing, gave her a unique right over Northern Pakistan; the entire region was her home.

'My nana-ji was Kashmiri too,' Jamila said. 'I love it there.'

This was the place where ancient pathways converged, to which civilisations were repeatedly drawn. Yet, Nazish, who was born in this region and made of its salt, had been pushed out because of who she loved. It struck her as the cruellest injustice. She carried the grief of it wherever she went.

'Tell them now,' she said. 'Statement mein likho, I never wanted to come here. Woh tho halaat hi kuch aisey thay. I didn't choose this, this life chose me.'

'Sure, but let's start at the beginning. What was your childhood like?'

Nazish wrinkled her nose. 'Fine.'

'When did you realise you were different?'

'Kya?'

'Different. When did you first feel different?'

'Always. Even when you don't have words, don't understand emotions, you feel yourself different. Kabhi kabhi, when I was a young girl, main boht udaas hoti thi, depressed . . . thinking, feeling, I don't belong anywhere.'

'And when did you realise you were a lesbian?'

'Yeh lafz – lesbian – it came late. Main yeh kaise jaan sakti thi? Yes, I was raised in an educated house, but where I grew up these things don't exist. And before internet, how I could have learnt this? Lekin jab maine parha, I felt complete.'

'What about religion? Did you have any conflict with Islam?'

When the Home Office had posed the question, Nazish screwed up her mouth like she'd eaten something bitter. But she chewed on it, for Jamila's sake, turning to the window on her right, glimpsing the full, green crowns of the trees and the pale, cloudless sky.

'Kehne ko kuch hai hi nahin. Who I am is one thing, what I believe is another. I don't see conflict, jo marzi koi kuch kahe.'

At the end of the session, Nazish got up, but Jamila stopped her leaving.

'Explain something to me. You're obviously a well-educated woman. You studied English. You worked at a university. Why do you keep replying in Urdu? It's obvious you don't need it.'

'No, no, I'm bad.' Nazish scanned the floor as if she'd dropped something. Feigning ignorance was an old strategy of hers, shielding her from prying colleagues and family members, but what good was that to her here? She looked up at Jamila and decided to tell the truth. 'Kyun ke English is not mine. It's not safe for me.'

'What do you mean?'

Nazish zipped and unzipped her handbag.

'Oh, so you're giving me a nasty taste of how you'll behave at the tribunal?'

'I told you before. I'm. Not. Easy.'

'And I'm telling you now, I'm made of stronger stuff.'

On the day of their next meeting, one week later, Nazish woke up after noon. She was at the hostel the authorities had now allocated her to in Moston, miles from where she had once lived in Wythenshawe. The mornings kept eluding her, as did a decent night's sleep, but she didn't mind. Why would she sleep? For whom would she wake early? Alone in this country, her days became one.

She went to the park and sat on a bench. Squinting against the September sun, she watched joggers and young mothers, and pensioners carried along by their middle-aged children. Sunlight dappled her forearms. The full trees fissled, the thinnest branches beckoning to her.

She told herself that she was comfortable with this life of solitude. These assurances rang hollow, but there were moments that helped her to believe it. Several days ago, she got talking to the owner of a Pakistani takeaway. He offered her work. Last night, she went there and washed the pots and wiped down the kitchen, preparing it for service the next day. She left just after 2am, her feet and shoulders sore, grateful for some small purpose again.

The walk led her to the supermarket. She found the discount fridge empty apart from mashed potatoes, a joint of beef and cubed vegetables sweating in their packaging. Strolling through the aisles, she took note of the things she would buy with her first wage packet: fabric softener and loose-leaf tea and the jeera biscuits she used to eat by the dozen in Pakistan.

Later that afternoon, she made it to the office, where a tired-looking Jamila sipped from her mug. A packet of biscuits lay on the table, the orange packaging wrinkled, the plastic thread unspooled. A couple of the biscuits had toppled onto the dark wood.

'Go on.' Jamila held out the pack. 'Take one. Take as many as you like.'

'No, no, no, I can't.' Though she was raised to politely refuse such offers, she had skipped breakfast and her stomach betrayed her. Jamila slid the biscuits forward.

'Let's talk about home. Why did you leave?'

'Mere suqun ke liye.'

'Was there violence involved?'

Nazish rolled her eyes. 'Everything contains violence, Mrs Shah. It was psychological. Life or death. I had to choose. Kya mujhe aisey zindagi chahiye, with violence of all kinds, or do I give up and have no life at all? Kuch arsay ke baad, I chose another way.'

'Coming to Britain?'

'Yes.'

'How was life in Pakistan?'

'Kyun?'

'I need to know. You say that you came for your peace, freedom, so what was it about living in Pakistan that was un-peaceful, that left you feeling un-free?'

She gritted her teeth. 'I didn't say freedom. Not everybody comes here for their freedom, Mrs Shah.'

Jamila paused. 'OK. Peace, then.'

'It's a lot.'

'Nazish, if you only described your life how I need you to, things could be easier.'

'I want to do this another way.'

'I get that, but your story also needs to make sense. This is a game, Nazish. If you want to win, you've got to play the game.'

'But I don't want to play games. When I play, I always lose.'

'Well, we still need to clarify your personal history for the judge. Can't you see that I'm trying to balance what the system demands of us with you telling your story on your own terms? Isn't that what you wanted?'

Nazish looked from her hands to Jamila, whose mouth had tightened, her voice carrying a note of fatigue. Jamila was clearly a good solicitor, even if she had much to learn about the world. But too many times Nazish had fought alone. She couldn't afford for Jamila to grow weary and give up on her. Words spilled out of Nazish's mouth.

'My colleagues at university suspected me. Accused me of being in a relationship with another teacher. Somehow, they took pictures of us together, found letters we wrote to each other. They showed these to the administration, and we lost our jobs. Then somebody told my family . . . ' Nazish had refused to cry over the years, believing it a weakness, but now, suddenly, she was unable to stop the tears from coming.

When she looked up again, there was a glass of water on the desk and Jamila motioning for her to drink. She did so obediently.

After a while, she smiled and cast a look at Jamila, the look of a woman about to play a winning hand. 'Waise, I also understand this process, more than people think. I know what it wants from me. To receive asylum, I must criticise my country. Betray it. Tell them Pakistan is hell and this place is jannat for me. I'm not that stupid.' In the supermarket, post office, doctor's surgery, nearly everybody she encountered in Britain talked to her like she was an idiot foreigner, but she was nobody's fool. She snatched another biscuit from the table.

'I get it. But if you answer questions like this, we have no hope of winning.'

'I don't care.'

'But you do.' Jamila's pen pointed at her in accusation. 'Because you don't want to be sent home. Nobody wants that.'

Neither of them said anything. No, I really don't care, Nazish thought, glancing up at the ceiling, fighting to convince herself.

Jamila broke the silence. 'You know, I do understand all of this. The struggle to live an authentic life. More than you would think, actually.'

Was she a lesbian too? She looked glassy-eyed and earnest, and though Nazish couldn't understand why, she accepted that Jamila wasn't trying to manipulate her through a big show of emotion. Nazish read people too easily to know that.

'Chalo theek. This can be for you and me only then. Ek alag si witness statement.'

And so, over the weeks that Nazish visited Jamila, it seemed two stories were being told, two statements being written at once: the official one for the appeal hearing, and the unofficial one for herself. Nazish couldn't help her thoughts from escaping her mouth, though she was aware that Jamila selected only the most viable threads, weaving them into a statement that would help them in court. She chose not to dwell on this. It was enough that Jamila vowed to keep the final statement faithful. For Nazish, this promise was as precious as her grandmother's shawl, the one she wore now and played with while she spoke, gifted when she left Pakistan.

'Let's talk about identity. How you've expressed your freedom in Britain.'

'Kaunsi freedom? I'm not free, I am an asylum seeker.'

'But you attend different social and support groups?'

'Sure, lekin Pakistan mein bi, main logon ko jaanti thi. I had a community there too.'

Jamila leant forwards, fingertips pressed into the desk. 'But Nazish, this is part of the process. We must show them you're exercising freedoms you couldn't at home. We need to prove you're telling the truth. There's no room for doubt. They don't even accept that you're a lesbian, for God's sake.'

And, despite her promises to behave, Nazish leant forwards too: 'Aur main poochti houn, ke main yeh paise kidhar se lekey oun? I live on thirty-six pounds a week. Sometimes I have to choose, food or soap – or some other necessity. How they are asking these questions?'

But just as easily, she conceded Jamila's point and explained what living in Britain had provided her with: a place where, if nothing else, her sexuality no longer required daily management, where she could let down her guard and simply exist.

'Do you have a partner?'

Nazish clicked her tongue.

'Have you met anybody here?'

'Where I can meet them? How I can invite them to my hostel, a place I stay with twelve others? In Pakistan it was possible, lekin idhar yeh sab naamumkin hai.'

Jamila spent the next half an hour coaxing Nazish to talk, grasping at any lead. Nazish's high school days, her earliest friendships, but she crossed her legs and refused to talk. Only when Jamila brought up a gathering for LGBT refugees three months ago did Nazish allow herself a small smile. Warmth filtered into her voice as she remembered Fatou, the shy woman from Gambia.

'We exchanged numbers.'

Jamila waited for her to say more, but when she didn't, Jamila kept the pace going by changing tack. 'What about your girlfriend in Pakistan?'

'What you want to know?'

'Start with what she looked like?'

Suddenly, speaking about the past became easy. Beautiful Warda, with eyelashes as long as wild grasses. Who had kissed her, touched her in ways she hadn't been touched before, nourished her mind with recitations of Mirza Ghalib. Love had softened Nazish's sharp edges, helped her to embrace her own body and desire, dulled her constant urge to fight. She recalled them hiking to the crumbling temples of Tilla Jogian, bathing in the emerald waters of Katas Raj, drying off in the sun while eating packets of Slanty. Yet these memories were foreign now. After so long, it was like they belonged to someone else. What did love feel like again? She was too afraid to remember.

After the meeting, Nazish sat at the bus stop for a while. It was a mild day for October. She unzipped her handbag and found a box of jeera biscuits nestled inside. Jamila must have put them there. But when? She glanced back at the office in tears. Jamila understood that she was skipping meals to pay for bus tickets and hand cream.

She ripped the box open and scoffed a biscuit.

In the detention centre, it wasn't freedom of movement that Nazish had missed, but air – breezes, sunlight flickering along her skin, the powdery scent of violets in the park. When the enforcement officers grabbed her, she felt like she had stopped breathing. When they drove her to London, she held her breath the entire way. Some of the other women in the van wailed to themselves, some were trapped in an intoxicated stupor, some bartered with their gods. Nazish closed her eyes and waited for it to end. People entered the continent like this, hiding in lorries, squeezing themselves behind wheels. She had considered herself better, superior, for arriving through legal channels. But once captured, she understood that she was the same.

The detention centre had a dining room, day room, gym, library and laundry. The bedrooms were freshly painted, brightly lit, decorated with cheerful curtains and beech furniture. An idea of airiness, but ultimately synthetic. Nazish still didn't breathe, not for the three weeks that she was inside, sharing a room with a Congolese woman who had threatened to knife her by day and who had screamed for her mother at night. The indignities of that time would not leave Nazish for as long as she lived. She had plugged her period blood with tissue paper. Eaten potatoes and chicken nuggets and other processed stodge that left her unable to use the bathroom. Shivered in the cold with nothing to shield her but her grandmother's shawl and the clothes on her back. And not until she sat on the train that returned her to Manchester back in August, not until she made an appointment to see Shah & Co. Solicitors, had she dared to hold air in her lungs again.

She returned a fortnight later to find Jamila looking unsettled. Nazish skimmed the desk for snacks. Jamila passed her a box of mithai, and she set about peeling the thumbs of tape.

'I wanted to check if you're happy with the process so far?'

'Abhi tak, yes . . . but I didn't read anything yet.'

'There's one more thing. Something I've been holding back.'

'Go ahead. Pucho.'

'It's about your detention.'

Nazish's hands began to tremble. She pushed the box away and kneaded her thighs. She looked up. 'Sorry. Aapne kuch kaha?'

'I was just saying, we have to cover this in your statement.'

'Oh.'

'Are you okay? Should I wait a little longer before we get into this?' Jamila chewed on her bottom lip.

Nazish swallowed several times. 'I'm fine, go on.'

'I keep putting it off but I really must ask. Why were you detained in the first place? We may have gotten you out, but I never got to the bottom of that. They said you weren't reporting.'

Nazish reached for the shawl in her handbag and wrapped it around herself. She counted to three in her head, allowing herself some time to breathe. 'You want to know why I didn't report?'

Jamila nodded. 'It would help me to understand.'

Nazish took another breath. 'Were you ever woken from your dreams by men banging on your door?'

Jamila shook her head.

'Fajr ka waqt tha, still dark outside. I was sleeping after namaz. I heard banging on my hostel door, ek mard ki awaaz, shouting, "Open up, this is Immigration Enforcement." One by one, the girls in my room woke up. They were too scared, so I volunteered to open the door. The man put his hand on my chest. "Go get your documents. I need to see some paperwork." He snatched my registration card. "It looks like you're an immigration offender. You'll be coming with us." The girls were all staring at the floor. When he took me outside, not even one of them said goodbye to me.'

Jamila's eyes were wide. 'I'm so sorry, that sounds awful. But you didn't answer my question. What made them do this?'

Nazish let out a long breath. 'It—it was like protest,' she said. 'Reminder to them of my dignity. That I was asylum seeker, but still human. Ek insaan thi main.

'More than eighteen months ago, I claimed asylum. For a year, I heard nothing. My solicitor said wait for decision, so I waited. Maine khoob intezar kiya, attending my support groups, cooking, trying to survive on their money. Eventually, my friend told me to speak to my caseworker. Only she could explain the delay.

'Aur jab maine usko phone kiya, I find she's not there, she's on maternity leave, panch mahiney ke liye. I went crazy, screaming, I didn't care. I had been living miserable life. Not even life – I was on hold waiting to begin life.

'I decided to do things for myself. If they don't take my case seriously, I don't report to them. Pehla mahina, I don't go to their office, they do nothing. Second month, same. Third month, end of, they come for me. They give me refusal and transfer me to detention centre.'

'And what was it like there, in detention?'

Nazish's jaw tensed then slackened. 'Yeh log janwaron ka behtar khyal rakhte hain.'

Jamila came and stood beside her. 'Let me get you a cup of tea.'

Nazish drank as Jamila opened a window. The sound of revving engines filled the room.

'So, it was a protest. I mean, lots of people stop reporting, but I've got to admire your intentions, even if the Home Office had no idea. Still, I worry. What if you pull a stunt like this at the tribunal? I know you now, and I'm afraid. You're capable of anything.'

Nazish laughed. 'Mujhe boht ghusa aata hai. Sometimes I think, bring me a bed and a girl and I will prove my sexuality. It feels like the only way.'

'Don't even think about it.' Jamila lifted two pieces of barfi from the box of mithai and passed one to Nazish.

Once she had provided the last of her supporting documents, things went quiet. The statement had been agreed upon, the appeal bundle prepared. Jamila turned her attention to other cases until the day of the hearing on Monday 10 December. Nazish agreed to meet Jamila in town, close to the immigration tribunal. She waded through the crowds to reach her.

Jamila appeared momentarily confused. 'Wha-wow, look at you. You look amazing.'

Nazish was wearing a leather biker jacket with a white T-shirt, jeans and trainers. She had shorn her shoulder-length hair and fashioned it into a pixie cut. Carried on her shoulders was a studded leather backpack.

'Really?' She held onto those words, believing for a moment that she had just grabbed these clothes from her wardrobe, as if they weren't invested in meaning and risk and resistance. As if they were nothing more than cotton. 'Maybe it's too much, but I needed some change. Last night I was excited thinking, this is almost ov-er.' She sang the last word, jigging on the spot. In Pakistan, her look would have marked her out, made a target of her, but here she would appear as she liked.

Jamila examined her again. 'But you do look very different . . . '

Nazish frowned. 'What do you mean?'

'Couldn't it have waited until tomorrow?'

'Why should I wait? I spent my life waiting.'

Jamila stared at her for a moment, then nodded silently. Nazish zipped up her jacket, dishevelled her hair and walked towards the tribunal. But as it neared, she smoothed her hair down, tugged at her jacket, lifted the straps of her backpack.

Jamila caught up with her. 'Stop worrying, I'm here.'

Inside, Jamila went off to research the judge assigned to their case, leaving Nazish in the waiting area. A thousand times, a feeling in the pit of her stomach told her that it wasn't too late:

she could still run to the bathroom, wash her face and take off her accessories, lift out the old cardigan and shawl from her backpack, and a thousand times, she dug deeper into the chair.

Jamila soon reappeared beside her. 'Do you trust me to do what's right for you?'

'Why? What did you hear?'

'Bad judge. She has a reputation with LGBT cases.'

'What you mean "bad judge"?'

'Not favourable to us. Bland enough in person but stings you in the decision.' She saw Jamila hesitate before continuing. 'I hate to do this, but it's how the game works. We don't want a bad judge *and* a crappy Home Office Presenting Officer. A bad judge can break a case. But if you were feeling unwell, we could ask for the case to be adjourned, pray for a better judge next time?'

'Whatever is going to happen, I want it to happen today.'

'I'm telling you, I think you should be ill. This isn't going to work.'

'I know and I don't care.' Nazish had been hiding her entire life, ever since the seventh grade when she lied to her friends about finding their Urdu teacher so beautiful it made her stutter.

Jamila gripped her knee. 'I'm not joking, Nazish. We could lose. Please tell me you're feeling sick.'

Heat rose up her back. She brushed Jamila's hand away. 'Don't you understand yet? I have to do this my way. Go, if you want, but I will stay.'

The judge sitting opposite Nazish had thin lips set in a miserable line and dead birds hanging from her ears. She complained of not receiving their bundle of documents before the hearing. Luckily, Jamila had a spare copy.

The Presenting Officer was as callous as Jamila had warned – this tiny man with a receding hairline and outsized confidence, who prowled around the courtroom like he owned it. 'That's fine, Ms Durrani. I don't need any more,' he said, cutting Nazish off after every question. 'Ma'am, the Appellant came to the UK in April 2010, but didn't seek asylum until six months later, when her visit visa was due to expire. A genuine refugee, somebody honestly seeking protection because they feared persecution, would have applied at the earliest possible opportunity.'

Jamila got up. 'Ma'am, how can somebody claim asylum if they don't know the provision exists – if they've never heard of the concept before, least of all on grounds of sexuality?'

'The Appellant might have indulged in same-sex sexual activity in the past, but this does not make her a lesbian. She has had no romantic relationships while living in this country, has made limited use of lesbian groups, venues and services . . . ' The Presenting Officer moved his hand through the air as if to suggest an abundance of these services.

'Since when did intimacy define sexuality?' Jamila continued. 'And since when did sexuality determine our interests or the company we choose to keep? Ma'am, many of the arguments expressed by the Presenting Officer today reflect an understanding of sexuality better suited to the past. A person can be a lesbian without being in a relationship. A person can be a lesbian and fail to socialise with other lesbians – though it's worth noting that my client actually has. What matters is that my client has provided a detailed and consistent account of herself, the development of her sexuality, and her life in Pakistan as a woman concealing her identity to stay safe.'

The Presenting Officer pointed to individual items of Nazish's clothing: 'The Secretary of State believes that the Appellant has presented herself today as a lesbian solely to establish a claim for international protection. It's the most cynical way of gaining status in the UK.'

Jamila sprang up, unmistakable fury in her voice: 'Ma'am, this really is the most misguided—' but the judge turned to Nazish.

'This is something you should answer, Ms Durrani, because you haven't yet and I'm not sure I understand. Why has your appearance changed so dramatically from the photographs you provided? It does seem like you have modified yourself to appear more like a lesbian.'

Nazish looked ahead, startled. She had been sitting on her hands, turning her head left and then right. Her life had been floating down the river while she was stuck watching it from its bank. She freed her fingers, blood flowing back into them, and straightened up. 'Tell me something,' she said, addressing the courtroom. 'What does a lesbian look like, dress like?'

The judge repeated herself. 'I am asking you, is this who you really are, or did you alter your appearance for the hearing today?'

'And I am asking you, what does a lesbian look like? I am not different because I'm dressed like this, it is part of the same identity. I did this to express something of myself. To tell my story, share more of who I am. Is that a problem?'

Nazish turned to gauge Jamila's reaction. She half expected to be scolded for acting out. This was probably the first time Jamila had witnessed one of her clients refusing to concede. But Jamila's eyes were on fire. She was glaring at the judge, who had glanced down to consult her papers, demanding an answer from her.

The judge eventually raised her head. 'No, it's not a problem. Sharing your story with us is the very purpose of the asylum process.'

At the end of the hearing, the judge explained that her decision would be communicated to them in writing. Nazish felt oddly calm – she had done her best – but she glanced at Jamila for confirmation. 'How did that go?'

Jamila stood up, started packing. 'Given the circumstances, good.'

They were ready to leave when the judge spoke again. 'Do you have an umbrella, Ms Durrani?'

'Huh? Me? No.'

'Well, you'll need one in this country.'

The judge looked to the large windows on her right. It was beginning to rain outside.

Nazish clutched Jamila's arm. 'What did that mean?' she whispered. 'I won?'

'Nothing. Don't pay any attention to her.' Jamila sorted the papers in her bag.

She locked eyes with Jamila, who shared none of her elation. 'It's raining, Nazish. It's an umbrella. Let's wait for the decision. In this country, it's always raining.'

Seven

Jamila's head started pounding as they left the tribunal that Monday evening. Nazish was too happy to notice – she skipped in the rain, laughing at the Presenting Officer's bulbous nose and windburned skin. 'I want to travel when all this is over,' she said, as they sat down to hot chocolates in a café, Christmas lights gleaming in the flagstones around Piccadilly Gardens. 'I want to see the pyramids, the Ayasofya, the Great Wall of China. I want to help other refugees like me. I want children.'

Jamila listened quietly. Yes, the judge had referenced the rain and told Nazish to buy an umbrella, but Jamila dared not trust it. Too many of her appeals had been decided on a whim, too many times her faith and hard work reduced to foolishness. The sides of her skull were being squeezed by an invisible vice, she needed to go and lie down, but she ignored the pain. Nazish had been a magnetic client, challenging and inspiring to work with, she wanted to stay around that energy a while longer. Only when Nazish ran out of questions and her eyes began to droop did Jamila take the chance to leave.

She drove home and went to bed, but the pain was sharper by morning, daggered her eyes. She was in no state for work, but what could she have done, called a locum? There was nobody to step in. She headed into work as usual. The sun was absent from the sky, a mist rising on the horizon, a white band that grew thicker as she drove south.

Before lunch, her father passed through the office. Catching her wincing at the sound of the telephones, he said, 'I don't know why you insist on suffering. Take something.'

She wasn't opposed to medication, nor was she a martyr as her employees might have expected. She simply hadn't found the time to take some tablets. Nonetheless, she found it hard to believe her father cared, not when he strolled out to meet a friend. She tried to eat, managed only a couple of forkfuls of salad. Making her way back through the staff area, she told herself it would be over soon. She just had to get through the afternoon. Then she could go home and sleep the migraine out of her system.

She stopped some way behind the reception and pressed her head with her palms.

Babar was speaking to a client there. 'I'm sorry, but a few people have appointments ahead of you. Because you didn't book, I'll have to send you in after them.'

'How long is that?' a voice barked back. She strained to recognise it through the agony.

'I couldn't say. Every client is different.'

'Well, I can't keep waiting. My time is very precious.'

Babar's shoulders stiffened. 'You should've made an appointment then.'

Babar was lucky her father wasn't around. He understood better than anyone that clients were consumers and needed to be pacified, or else they behaved even worse. Babar would have gotten an earful. She stood on her toes to get a glimpse of who he was talking to.

'It's Mr Khemiri. He arrived before lunch,' said Rubel, who had shadowed her from the kitchen and observed the scene from a safe distance. 'He's been calling all morning, driving us crazy.'

After a four-year wait, the Home Office had determined Hassan's asylum claim. Following a crude summary of his case, they had provided their rationale for denying him. All it took was for the caseworker to find one small discrepancy. Just one to unravel the case. After that, each subsequent discrepancy – no matter how tiny or inconsequential – hit harder than the last. The conclusion was resolute: *It is clear that you lack knowledge about the Democratic and Social Movement party (Mouvement Démocratique et Social) in Algeria, of which you claimed membership. Consequently, it is not accepted that you are a genuine refugee . . .*

Refusals of this kind were difficult to challenge – an entire system geared towards rejection, unable to accommodate doubt or contradiction, always convinced that the claimant was lying. She would read such refusals and, feeling about as useful as a plastic bag taped over a broken window, try not to let her frustration transform into a crisis of confidence.

'Are there people waiting before him?' she asked, gauging how much time she had before she had to deal with him.

Rubel smirked. 'You scared, Mrs Shah?'

'Don't be silly.' She tutted, went into her office and swallowed some painkillers.

Several clients and one hour later, Hassan trooped in with a friend. Jamila slapped her thighs in preparation. The friend was a barrel-bellied man with pierced ears and pockmarked skin. He wore running tights and a black vest, looking like a cross between a ballet dancer and wrestler. Her clients usually brought their friends along to advocate for them whenever they were worried about their case, or to intimidate her when unhappy with her service. Like a police detective, the friend sat on a chair and bent forward, imposing himself on her desk and inspecting her.

Hassan towered above him, his face beaten with distress. 'You really hurt me today, Mrs Shah,' he said. 'Why did you keep me waiting? Did you not see me? Am I not your son?'

'Son?'

'I'm like your son.'

'I'm happier childless, thanks.' She mustered a smile. She and the bad penny were the same age. 'What can I do for you? Are you ready to submit an appeal?'

He scrunched his face. 'God, you don't listen to a thing I say. You say you do, but you don't, you really don't.'

His voice was hoarse, a hammer to her brain. She took a final cold sip of coffee and drew upon every last drop of caffeine in her body. 'Okay, tell me, when didn't I listen to you?' She had called him personally to deliver the news of his refusal, listened to him raging about the 'stupid' caseworker and the 'stupid' system and the 'stupid, messed up' decision. She had calmed him when he threatened to slash his wrists on his next visit to the reporting centre, offered to submit his appeal for free when he said he had no money. What more did he want?

'Why you keep talking about appeal? I don't want appeal, I want my visa.'

Her voice adopted a note of incredulity. 'I can't just make them *un-refuse* you.'

'They did in my friend's case.' He gestured towards his friend, who opened his mouth to explain.

Jamila raised her hand. 'Every case is different.' Hassan knew this, but no matter how often she stressed this to him, to any of her clients, it didn't take root in their minds.

'Don't you remember the issues in your refusal letter?' she continued, swallowing her irritation. 'I explained them over the phone. The Home Office thinks it will win this appeal and, even though I don't agree, I can see why. It's a credibility issue. You gave them reason to doubt you.' She had discharged her duty, statemented his case, tried to smooth out the inconsistencies in his story. But what he had said at the Home Office interview she could not control. It was his story, anyway, she a mere conduit.

His bottom lip jutted out. 'No, they don't stand a chance.'

'But they do, my friend.'

His arms sprung out from his sides, one cuffing the bookcase. 'This is the problem, man. You don't listen. You say you are, but you're not. All of you are the same.' He turned and flopped against the bench as if winded.

She switched her attention to his friend, arching a brow. 'All us what? Solicitors? Women?' She wasn't being flippant. Any time a client misbehaved with her, she couldn't help but wonder, would they have done the same with her father?

The friend blinked several times. 'No-no. He's just stressed, you know? No status, no job, three children.' His voice was high-pitched and uncertain.

She didn't respond. Her vision was beginning to blur. The pills weren't kicking in hard enough. 'Fine. I'll write to the Home Office and tell them whatever you want. Are we done now?' She blinked several times to clear her sight.

Hassan slowly turned back. 'Do what you think is right, Mrs Shah,' he said sheepishly.

She flung her hands in the air. 'Do what I think is right? I already told you what I think is right, but you don't care. You have this silly idea that you can force the Home Office into withdrawing its decision. Fine – you obviously know better.'

Straightaway she regretted opening her mouth. Hassan's face drained of colour. 'Why would you say that, huh? You know the situation I'm in.'

She looked down at the three paper clips in her hand, which she had been weaving together and then separating, transferring the heat inside her to the thin cold metal. It wasn't his fault, she reminded herself. Hassan was suffering as her other clients suffered, under a system that kept them in limbo for years, dangled the promise of a better life as long as they remained patient, then snatched it all away. But her mind fluoresced with thoughts of how difficult he was, how many demands he made, how nothing she said was ever quite good enough. She put the paper clips on the desk and said, with as much authority as she could muster, 'Okay, but Hassan, if you want my help, you need to stop behaving like this. It's not acceptable.'

Stern but reasonable: she banked on this silencing him. Instead, Hassan exploded. 'No, this is not acceptable! You are not acceptable!' He paced the room, waving his long, bony arms, his scarlet ears twitching. 'I am sick of this office, of everybody around here!'

'Listen to me, Hassan. I'm on your side.'

Swinging around, he grabbed a book from the shelf and made to throw it before pausing, lacking conviction in the final moment. She appealed to his friend for help, who shrugged and tapped the side of his head. 'Crazy,' he whispered.

She couldn't respond. Hassan's voice had grown distorted. Since before they had arrived the nausea had been welling up in her stomach, but now it threatened to spill over just as Rubel appeared at the door.

'What's going on?' he asked.

'Hassan, I think it's time for you to go,' she managed to say. He didn't hear her. She clutched her abdomen and spoke louder: 'I mean it, find another solicitor.'

Instantly, his voice fell. He knelt and placed the book gently on the floor beside him then inched over, crouched, almost collapsed on the crumb-ridden carpet. 'Please don't say that, Mrs Shah. I'm sorry.'

His friend cried out, 'It's hard for a man like him. No money, no job, three children—'

The prospect of Hassan attaching himself to her feet made her recoil. She couldn't imagine forgiving him, not like this; she didn't want him anywhere near her. 'Honestly, Hassan, I feel really unwell. Every time you come to my office you cause me trouble. I can't take it anymore.' The room began to spin.

'Please, Mrs Shah—'

She twisted her knuckles into her eyes and heard only Rubel saying, 'You need to leave,' and Hassan murmuring sadly, 'Really, I'm sorry.' When the door clicked shut, she brought the dustbin to her knees and rested her head against the desk, cushioned by her arms.

Seconds later, bile spewed out of her.

Eight

When she came to, she sensed other people in the room. She heard whispering.

'Should we wake her?'

'No, she's tired.' Rubel, she thought.

'But how much longer can we stay?' Babar, itching to get home to his wife and kid.

She raised her head and scrubbed her eyes. Her face was clammy. A sour smell lingered in the room, cut with cheap air freshener. The front shutters had been pulled down, lights around the office switched off. The two of them had assembled opposite: her jury, ready with its verdict.

'I sent the clients away,' Babar said.

She stared at the clock: almost 6pm. How long had she been asleep?

'You're working too much,' Rubel added.

Her head was still throbbing. 'I should call Hassan. Apologise.'

'You didn't do anything wrong.'

She stared at them, struggling to agree.

'Let us lock up tonight. Go home and rest.'

She did as she was told. But lying in the dark that night, throat stinging and head numb, she swam in and out of sleep. She had never shouted at a client like that before. She had betrayed her father's legacy.

Early the next morning, she called Hassan.

'It's fine,' he announced before she said anything. 'I am a big man. I forgive you.'

'Err, okay. Thanks.' But it wasn't his forgiveness she wanted. She cleared her throat, her desire – if she was permitted to have one – becoming clear to her. 'I've been thinking, and I really believe you should start looking for another solicitor. We're not a good fit.'

Hassan was quiet for a moment. 'No, Mrs Shah. I can't. I started at your office, and I will finish there too. Whenever I come, I feel God all around me.'

She stared at her hands.

At the end of the working week, Jamila gave in and drove to Chorlton. Her sister had tired of her excuses and demanded that she show up for dinner, but Jamila had also found herself in the rare state of wanting company.

The weather was bleak: cold, foggy and starless. Most of the shops along Wilbraham Road were shuttered apart from the neon-blue streak of the fish bar. Jahida's place was covered in flood lights, ivy growing up the side of the house. The shape of it on the bricks was like a wolf, half-heartedly howling at the moon. Jamila rang the bell and waited.

Jahida was the pretty one. The one who had the fortune of looking nothing like her parents – of being her own person entirely – while Jamila was stuck resembling them both. She was taller, with graceful cheekbones and an acid tongue. Her incredible figure allowed her to wear all sorts of flowing fabrics in her favourite pastel shades without worrying about proportion. Indeed, when she opened the door, she was still dressed in her work uniform: wide-legged, blush pink trousers and a cream chiffon blouse with sleeves like bat wings.

'Sorry, I'm late,' Jamila said, embracing her sister.

'Let me guess, work?'

Jamila smiled painfully. 'Where are the kids?' The house was unusually quiet.

'Nadeem's putting them to sleep.'

'How are they?'

'A handful. How's the office?'

Jamila gave an empty laugh. 'A handful.'

She followed her sister to the kitchen. The house had been renovated recently and looked like an expensive showroom. The muted walls, beige carpets and grey kitchen cupboards weren't to Jamila's tastes – not with a room fragrance so astringent it smelled medicinal – but she couldn't deny the attraction. It was the kind of sober, middle-class living that Jahida had always aspired to.

Jahida wasted no time in loading their plates with food from reheated containers. She knew that Jamila liked food but ate poorly. Rotating on her heel, Jamila looked for something to do. 'Is paaji not eating with us?' Only two places had been set around the dining table.

'He ate with the kids.' Jahida led them to the table and sat down to eat.

The food smelled heavenly: rice, lamb and okra. Jamila couldn't remember when she'd last enjoyed a home-cooked meal.

'Now, tell me, what's going on with work?' Jahida knew, had a nose for disaster.

'It's one of Dad's old clients. I can't handle him. He calls me all the time, and every day it's a different problem and it's rarely one I can solve. This time he'd heard that the Home Office can back out of an appeal and grant the client if it thinks it's going to lose, so he demanded I make the same happen for him.'

Jahida licked the back of her spoon. 'I can't believe you chucked a client out. Well, I can. You loved your tantrums as a kid. Remember when you scratched Dad's ears outside the museum? Made him bleed? He hasn't forgotten.'

That incident was legendary, brought up any time she spoke up for herself. Any time she drove off course from the path they had laid out for her, they branded her a troublemaker. Sure, every family needed a villain, but with all that she did for them, could it stop being her? Even just for a moment?

'I was hoping for a little more sympathy, to be honest,' she said.

'You're the face of the system for these people. What do you expect?'

It struck her as profoundly unfair, mutating into the monster that she was battling on her clients' behalf, a scene in no video game she had ever played before. Still, it was easy for Jahida to pontificate. She couldn't do this job. Couldn't handle being this close to the Home Office. To hate something that you knew so intimately it devoured your weekends. To hate something because it lived inside your head, because you had trained yourself to follow the contortions of its policy.

'Anyway, we know the problem is you,' Jahida added.

Jamila dropped her spoon. 'Oh, here we go again.'

'It's your way of working. So obsessive. When will you start thinking about yourself?'

'So you want me to start rejecting cases? "Sorry, I can't do this, I'm on a break."'

'Why not? Look at you. You're so burnt out I'm not surprised you went for him.'

'Burnt out?' She didn't feel *that* bad. Jamila pretended to be affronted and looked away. She stared into the garden through the patio doors, the lawn studded with amber torchlights. This wasn't the evening she had come here seeking.

Jahida took her arm. 'Seriously, though, let's go away somewhere. I'd love a break too.'

Jamila saw from her tired eyes sparking that Jahida was already dreaming up destinations. She pulled away, picturing the bedlam that would greet her upon returning: a threadbare list of clients and a stack of complaints from her regulator. 'Mum and Dad would go apeshit.' It was not like she could afford another solicitor to help her. If she couldn't handle the office, they would have to close.

'I've told you before, they're not like that.'

'You mean, they aren't like that with you. You're the good Pakistani girl. You got married and had babies. We're not the same.'

'It wasn't as easy as that for me. But who says we've got to be the same? You want to focus on the family business, fine – I'm just giving you some perspective.'

'I'm preserving it for the next generation.'

'Why bother, though? We don't know what the kids will want to do when they're older.'

It rattled Jamila that her sister never acknowledged one fundamental truth: that Jahida was free to live as she wanted because Jamila had taken on the family burden, staked her entire future on the family legacy. A legacy that began at the knitwear factory where her father had once worked as a machinist, then moved to their living room where he first began his business. Jamila pictured herself at that desk as a child, her fingers hooked around the telephone cord. The office lay at the root of everything: who they were as a family, the place that every subsequent generation would come from.

Jahida sighed. 'Don't you want all this, Jam?'

Jamila wrinkled her nose. 'All what?'

Jahida gestured to the room.

'God, let's not do this again.' Jamila picked up her spoon, scooped rice. All this wasn't very much at all.

'Come on, now. That next generation stuff was a Freudian slip. Zak was three years ago now. Didn't you think you would be sorted?'

People seemed to think that relationships were all that occupied her, but lately, Jamila could only consider a partner in the abstract. Such a distant prospect, it was surprisingly easy to ignore. Easier still to assume that it wouldn't happen at all, that she had paid a price for inheriting the business. 'Why would I think about this stuff? Everything I need I can give myself. Pakistanis are so marriage obsessed.'

'Everyone is.'

'Maybe Mum and Dad put me off.'

A convenient excuse perhaps, but those memories of their parents' arguments, back when Jamila and Jahida were children, still burned away in her mind. Whenever they had exhausted the gamut of insults and accusations, her parents would retreat to their trenches. Jahida would take advantage, chatting for hours on the phone to her friends. But Jamila couldn't stand the tension. With a headache blooming between her temples, she tightened her mother's scarf around her head and carried missives back and forth. Desperate to broker a truce, she couldn't rest until she had dissolved their divides.

'And look how good they are now. Anyway, forget marriage. What if I set you up—'

'No, baj. I don't want your help.' Delivered more frigidly than intended, her voice shrill, but she didn't care. Why did talk always turn to men? Why couldn't they remain in the background where they belonged? The thought caused the edges of her mouth to curl in amusement. She hid it from her sister. Just as she hid the fact that, though she and Zak had lasted no more than eight months, she was yet to move on from that failure. She had tried to have it all and bombed.

Afterwards, Nadeem joined them in the living room for tea. They talked about the restaurants they'd been to, films they'd watched, books they'd read, but Jamila hadn't been anywhere, she hadn't watched or read anything. She couldn't remember when she had last gone out dancing, returning home in the early hours, sweaty and exhausted with her eyeliner smeared. She had nothing to offer.

Only then, observing Jahida on the sofa, so close to Nadeem that she was almost sitting on his feet, did she wonder how others had managed it. How had they maintained relationships without losing some essential part of themselves? With the image before her, it was hard to deny: she wanted a partner of her own. Someone to share secrets and burdens with. Someone to occupy the silence with her. And, for a time, it had been real.

A whimpering emerged from the baby monitor. Nadeem went upstairs and returned with Halima attached to his hip, her fine hair stood up in the shape of a question mark. Jahida unbuttoned

her blouse and breastfed. As Halima gurgled, Jamila stared with
wonder. How dependent they were at that age, how utterly useless.
It was only in the last few weeks that Halima could hold her own
head up. Her sister never complained, took to motherhood like
man to religion, rhapsodised about it as some clarifying, mystical
experience. But surely it took its toll?

Jamila tried to imagine a child of her own. Countless aunts
had told her that a woman without children was blind. But the
idea of playing host to a creature growing inside horrified her.
The world already tried its damnedest to reduce her to her body,
her biology, her gender. Her clients were responsibility enough.

At the end of the night, Jahida followed her into the hallway.
'Babe, have you ever considered the effect this office has on you?
Listening to those harrowing stories, taking on their expectations.'

'We're supposed to spend our lives fighting for justice, Dad
used to say to us.'

Jahida touched her cheek. 'You are your own worst enemy, Jam.
I keep telling you, chill out, live your life, people will understand.
You can't serve others when your own bowl is empty.'

If only it were that simple.

Jamila bagged her feelings, as she had learned to do, and
embraced her sister. Beneath the expensive silk chiffon, the bones
in her back were angular and sharp.

Nine

That Sunday morning, Jamila lay in bed and wondered if her sister was right; that her work was full, but her life was not. Jahida hadn't used those words exactly, but it was what she had meant. Delivered in that calm, almost detached manner of hers, the assertion had thoroughly disturbed Jamila.

Over the weekend, she grew determined to prove it wrong. Her life could be full if she wanted it to be.

She began by taking herself for a walk. It felt like the thing a healthy person did. She went around the block, past the old Moorish synagogue, watching the cloudy sky, trees shocked still by the cold, their occasional shadows on the asphalt, and asked herself what people did on their days off — what she used to do. Time stretched ominously in front of her.

She would bake, she decided in the end, thinking of the apples in her fruit basket, unsalted butter in the fridge, of the sweet cinnamon her mother had brought back from Sri Lanka last year, how those thin, rolled-up tubes stood in the jar, begging to be used. And, while the cheesecake was in the oven, she would pick a book from her shelf, arrange herself on the sofa and finally read.

For the rest of her walk, Jamila was taken by this plan. But returning home, she slowed. The house was dark. So empty and cold. The idea of being there, for the entire day, suddenly filled her with dread. She wanted to stay out longer, or maybe to visit someone – she couldn't go back there. She tried to sever an automatic pull towards the office, or to the files she had brought back for the weekend. She couldn't do that either.

As she weighed up taking another round of the block, a voice called out to her. She looked up, ahead. Her parents were standing at the mouth of her driveway. They waved and held plastic bags opaque with condensation. Jamila's heart lightened as she quickened her pace.

'What are you guys doing here?' she said when close.

'You're so busy these days, we decided to come to you instead,' her mother replied.

Jamila embraced her tightly, and then her father. She was so glad to see them, she rushed to unlock the door.

Her mother stomped into the hallway and X-rayed the floor. 'Where's that snake of yours?'

'Bertha doesn't just roam about the house, Mum. She's in her tank,' Jamila said from behind.

Her mother shivered. 'Well, keep it away from me.'

Her father mimicked her, and Jamila laughed. She would bring Bertha out when she wanted them to leave.

Jamila squeezed past her mother and dumped as much rubbish as she could find in the kitchen, hiding the rest from her mother's eyes. She seated them at the dining table that had never managed to entertain guests and laid out plates, glasses and cutlery. She took their bags and unwrapped the packages and served the halwa puri they had bought from Anmol.

'How are you?' her mother asked. 'Fine?'

Jamila stuffed her mouth with food and nodded. Yes, she was fine now.

'What shall we do today?' her father said.

She shrugged. 'I was planning to stay home and bake.'

'I can work on the house if you like.'

She had not done anything to the house in a while. Her framed photographs and artwork were stored away. He could help her to hang them up.

Once they had finished eating, her mother sent her upstairs to shower while she washed the dishes. Jamila tried to protest – they were her guests – before giving way. There was something about being their youngest daughter that she had not completely relinquished. Away from Jahida, she became the sole object of their affection.

When she returned, a towel wrapped around her hair, she found her mother sorting through her fridge.

'I had to,' she said, spotting Jamila at the door. 'There was a bad smell inside.'

Her father sat in the living room with her toolbox next to him. His head made small, mechanised movements, like the birds in the garden, as he examined the walls and skirting boards and scribbled in his notebook.

It surprised her sometimes, the tenderness with which they treated her, even when she had neglected them. Jamila smiled to herself, then went upstairs to dry her hair.

She and her mother began making the cheesecake near midday. How pure it felt to work foremost with her hands. How monastic. She crushed the biscuits and baked them with butter, mixed the cream cheese with vanilla, eggs and sugar; her mother peeled, cored and chopped the apples and braised them over the stove.

The sun shone through the house; it felt warm and full. Jamila stared idly into the garden and wondered what John was doing, where Nazish was and what time Hassan would call today.

That was when her phone rang out from the living room.

She ignored it, afraid that she had summoned Hassan by means of telepathy.

'You should get that,' her mother said.

She didn't move. Something had lodged itself in her throat, like a fish bone.

Her father entered the kitchen, holding her phone like it was a delicate antique.

'Mrs Shah! I need to see you now.' Nazish's voice was high-pitched and breathy, unlike she had ever heard it before.

'But we're closed today—'

'I'm on my way to your office.'

Her gaze fell over the ingredients sitting in three bowls on the countertop. Whatever it was, she wouldn't go. She couldn't have her sister proven right.

A hand took her elbow.

'Go. I'll handle the rest,' her mother said.

But it was her day off. She suppressed the urge to cry.

As she drove to the office, she couldn't help thinking back to when she was a little girl. How her entire childhood had been dominated by the demands of their work. Every week, her father made promises about the wonderful adventures he'd take them on at the weekend. She and Jahida loved to alternate between swimming, shopping and the fancy park in Cheadle. But on too many Sunday mornings her father pronounced that he needed to pop to the office for an errand, swore that he'd be no more than a couple of hours, assured them that he'd not forgotten – there'd be plenty of time for adventure. And too many times, the appointed hours would pass, their mother would piece together their jigsawed hearts and the two of them would sit in a corner and sulk for as long as they could withstand his bribery.

Nazish was waiting outside the office, pale and shivering. 'They detained her. How they can do that? She followed every rule.'

'The Gambian girl?'

Nazish nodded and wiped her cheek. Hate seeped from her eyes.

Jamila led Nazish inside and embarked on a hauntingly familiar routine.

Night was falling when the work finally released her, the sky clear and cornflower-blue, the clouds translucent and curled like smoke. She was tired, but eager to make the most of what little Sunday remained. From the office front door, she turned the corner, hurried along the alley to her car, then stepped on something soft.

Instantly, she knew. 'Oh, for God's sake.'

She keyed the torch on her phone, flashed it on the ground and lifted her shoe.

Was it animal or human?

Half an hour later, she tried leaving the office again. The crows were squawking when she parked outside her parents' house, loudest when the light was being leeched from the sky. Some of them pecked at the remains of a takeaway. When she crossed the street, most flew to the safety of the trees. One hobbled in the opposite direction, like a proud pensioner. It stopped part-way and glared at her, before limping on.

The front door purred against the thick pelt of the carpet and her mother appeared in the doorframe. Jamila studied her from head to toe. 'You're so dressed up.'

Her mother was wearing that favourite salwar kameez of hers: navy, with silver kadai around the neckline, peach embroidery at the hem. The floral fragrance of her perfume filled the hallway; the expensive kind, reserved for special occasions, revealing its layers over time.

'Your dad's taking me out for our wedding anniversary,' she said, with none of the unease that coloured Jamila's childhood, when her mother shrunk her neck before her children's questions about their relationship. With Jamila in charge of the office, her parents had the time to get to know one another again – over leisurely lunches and dinners, visits to stately homes. 'We're going to a new place in town. You're coming – we hardly caught up this morning.'

16 December. Of course. Jamila had forgotten their anniversary. Before she could reject the invitation, she was tugged into the living room. The television was on, the sound low. Mangled voices hovered in the background. She fell onto the sofa.

'All your work done?' her mother asked.

'Hmm.'

'You missed your sister again.'

'It's fine, I saw her the other day.'

Her mother reached for the bowl of chevda on the coffee table and dropped it into her lap. Jamila took a fistful and crunched; her right knee bobbed up and down. 'What time are you going out?' She ran her tongue between her lips and gums, loosening the mushed gram clumped there, searching for a reason not to join them.

'Your dad is upstairs getting ready. I'll tell him to hurry up.'

'No, I'll just finish this.'

'You'll ruin your appetite.'

Her mother rose to call him, but Jamila latched onto her arm. 'I said I'll wait.'

She funnelled more of the chevda into her mouth. Her lower jaw felt tender. It may have been the incessant crunching but the discomfort, she realised, had been there all afternoon. She dusted the chilli and salt from her hands, pushed her fingers into the points where the upper and lower jaw met.

'What's wrong?'

'Nothing.'

'I can see the tension in your face.'

Jamila felt the frown whittled into her cheeks. She placed the bowl on the coffee table and bounced her knee again.

'Tell me,' her mother said.

'Oh, I'm just tired. Frustrated.'

'Frustrated?'

'All I want is one day – just one Sunday – that's completely mine.' The last one had been over six months ago, pottering about the garden in the sun, picking early raspberries from the bramble that mounted her fence. She had spun the blended fruit into a raspberry mousse cake, then watched the Olympic opening ceremony with her parents.

Even on Eid, she had come into work. 'I'm losing my weekends. I have no life.'

'That's how life is, meri jaan. That's how it is to run a successful business.'

'But aren't businesses supposed to make your life better? This is endless.' She got up and walked over to the fireplace, and her legs soaked up the heat of its flames.

'Well, what can we do? That place is your father's – it's his life's work, his legacy. We can't just close it down.'

Her jaw started to throb. 'Did I say we should close it down? I'm telling you how I feel.'

'And I'm glad you're sharing that with me. But what do you want me to say? Speak to your dad.'

She caught the steeliness in her mother's eyes, almost imperceptible, but it matched the hard edge to her voice. This was why she suppressed her feelings and kept her thoughts to herself. She stepped away from the fireplace, grabbed the television remote and flicked through the channels, settling on some banal cookery show about a white man discovering recipes in the Middle East.

Her mother lifted her crime novel from the table and resumed her reading.

Footsteps creaked on the landing. They went out into the hallway. Her father gipped the handrail as he descended, pausing on each step. He was only fifty-eight years old. He dyed his greys every Sunday and power-walked every morning, but she had never seen him so frail.

He glanced at her and smiled. 'I thought the house smelled sweet.'

Upon reaching the bottom, her mother hit his arm. 'No, that's me.'

He laughed and placed his arm around her shoulder as she struggled. 'Stop it.'

Jamila ran her knuckles across the radiator, its dimples hot and smooth. 'I think I'm going home.'

'Chal aaja. Spend time with your parents for once,' he said. 'Me and your mother were married thirty-four years ago today.'

Her stomach called out. It seemed easier to go along with it.

Nawaab was heaving when they arrived, filled with Christmas parties and Pakistani families drawn to the economy of an all-you-can-eat buffet. Through her father's connections, they got a table quickly and headed to the food. Jamila towered her plate with various salads, meats and fried foods, then sat to eat in silence. Noise from the other tables thundered over them.

Her father cast sideways glances at her mother. 'What do you think of the pakodas?'

Jamila acted as if she had only just noticed them. 'Nice.'

'You'll have to try mine one day. Didn't I tell you I'm a better cook than your mother?'

'So why did you leave the cooking up to Mum all these years?'

Her father laughed and started to say something, but then stopped himself and looked at her mother, who was no longer eating. She grimaced as if she had indigestion – as if she couldn't eat a mouthful more until they had spoken. 'I think you should tell him,' she said.

'Tell him what?'

'Tell him what you told me.' She turned and delivered the blow. 'Your favourite daughter isn't happy.'

Jamila's gaze tumbled to her plate. They always did this, her mum and Jahida, treating difficult conversations like plasters over delicate wounds, to be ripped off in one pitiless swipe. She ate with her hands, sinking her fingers into a potato, then into a piece of chicken, cherishing how easily these two things yielded to her.

Her father tried to draw her out with that placid, sing-song voice he reserved for their most challenging clients. 'Yes, tell me, darling. What's the matter?'

'Can we eat in peace before we get into this?'

She chewed slowly, not letting her gaze leave the table.

Between courses, they didn't move. Her half-confession hung in the air between them. She kept her eyes fixed on the bones they had picked clean and dumped on a plate in the middle of the table, summoning the will to begin. She took a deep breath, then glanced at her father.

'I can't do this anymore.' The words took her by surprise, but it was the truth.

83

'Do what, my darling?'

'I can't keep on at the office like this.'

'You're fine. You're tired, all you need is some sleep.'

'I've abandoned everything to make a success of this job, I'm not fine.'

'This is what it means to be devoted to your profession. I did it for all those years and did you hear me complaining? No. I used to wake up in the middle of the night with clients calling me for help. Whenever we were getting audited, I'd head back to the office after dinner and examine files through the night, come home and sleep for three hours before getting up for work again. I did that for you and your sister, so you could have the kind of life I didn't.'

And yet she was living the kind of life he had chosen for himself and, later, for her. The kind of life she had always hoped to avoid. A life entirely without dreams or aspirations, only more work.

Her father moved away from her. She slid a hand across the table.

'Dad, I'm turning thirty next year. I'm too young for this kind of pressure. I don't deserve it. Nobody does.'

He turned back, baring his teeth. 'So, what then – we should just close the office down? Try to understand, Jamila, how much that place means to us. I ran this business for twenty-five years and you can't handle it even for one? How are you going to cope with the rest of your life? Try to take this seriously. Sometimes I think you don't take your commitments seriously enough.'

There it was: her father's favourite move. Every time she shifted under pressure, every time she expressed a desire that didn't conform to the plans he had created for her, his criticism was that she lacked seriousness. She wanted to jump out of a window.

'That's unfair, Dad. I'm sweating my guts out in the office and all you can say is I'm not dedicated enough? Maybe ask Jahida, who thinks that I'm run down and obsessed with work and can't switch off. I'm starting to think she's right. I *am* obsessed, thanks to you. I can't think beyond what you expect of me.'

'No, you're unfair, Jamila. We've worked hard and now, when it's our time to enjoy our lives, you don't want to take your responsibilities. Where has all this come from? I thought you were happy.'

Jamila stacked their empty plates, then went to the buffet for a main course. She'd made the question of happiness clear enough. When she returned, her father placed his hand on hers, relaxing the muscles in his face that were pulsating just moments ago. 'Maybe you need another holiday. You could go somewhere hot and sunny, maybe visit your uncles and aunties in Pakistan?'

'I don't need a holiday—'

'It could be my gift—'

'A holiday isn't the solution to my problems, Dad. Can you gift me time?'

Her mother rushed to his aid. 'You're not understanding. Your father is trying to help you.'

She glanced at her parents. You couldn't pass a needle between the two of them.

He nodded and squeezed her hand. 'Why else do I come into the office? I come in to see if my daughter needs help with a case, if she wants a cup of tea, if she's had her lunch on time. What else can I do?'

'That's not true, but fine. It isn't what I need from you. I'd rather you understood the impact this job is having on the rest of my life. I can't breathe – I'm never allowed to, not for one minute. With our clients, with immigration law, there's always one more thing. I can't even think about meeting someone—'

'Just say the word and we'll find you a match?'

'For God's sake, no! I gave up a perfectly good—' She stopped herself. Relationship. I gave up a perfectly good chance at happiness for you. She had always kept Zak from them, never even mentioned him in case they disapproved of his tattoos and his desire to emigrate. Even now, she felt too humiliated to share her grief with them. This reminder of it only threw her into despair.

She paused and hauled herself out of it. 'What I mean is, I never go to the gym, never see Maryam and Samir. I feel awful ignoring them, but I tell myself it's for a higher cause. I rarely, if ever, get an evening to myself. I'm a human being, Dad, not a robot. Why must I live the way you did?'

He turned to her mother with a look of exaggerated sadness. 'No matter what we do, it's never enough. Give birth to them, raise them, get them to this point in their lives and, somehow, it's our fault. It's my fault that I built a big business for her and gave her the security of being her own boss. Maybe if she had to struggle like other people do, she'd be more grateful.'

Her words were being twisted. She let out a shriek. The noise of the restaurant dropped several decibels, but Jamila didn't look around once. 'You didn't give me security, Dad. You gave me a noose!'

'But I don't understand, you chose to do this?'

'No, I *never* chose this. You groomed me for it. You kept telling me how good it would be. I would inherit a ready-made business, I would have security, I would be my own boss—'

'And were we wrong to say that?'

'Yes, you were, actually. Because, now that I'm saying it's too much, all you care about is yourself. I knew it was a bad idea to talk to you.' She glowered at her mother. 'To either of you. It couldn't have gone any other way.'

'Don't speak to us like that. We're still your parents,' her mother said.

Jamila held her knife and fork in her hands. But seeing how impervious their faces had become, she dumped them onto her plate and got up, tears building in her eyes. 'I'm done.' She left the restaurant and hailed a taxi home.

Jamila woke up on her sofa, her hair a sea of waves. A trail of drool ran down the side of her chin. She sat up and wiped her mouth, then glanced at her phone: it was past ten o'clock. She had slept for two whole hours.

Slowly, the conversation returned to her — the fatigue too. For too long she had been ignoring her numbness and exhaustion, the lingering worry that she wasn't right for this job.

She had tried to escape it once. Aged twenty-four, she had won an internship at the European Court of Human Rights. She moved to Strasbourg, where she worked on minority rights and bought herself a bike, hoping to stay on when the internship was complete. But right when they offered her a job, her mother called and said that enough was enough: her father had developed an arrhythmic heartbeat and needed her back in the office. And Jamila, who'd had nightmares of losing her parents ever since she had observed her father's work as a child and realised that some parents were snatched from their children, fell in line and rushed to be beside him.

Over time, she concluded that the window for change had passed. Her training had locked her into a reputable career as an immigration solicitor and she was ungrateful for wanting to pursue anything else. But in quiet moments, she fantasised. About running away and joining a cookery school, teaching English in Japan, opening a teashop in Istanbul.

Scrolling through her phone, she landed on his profile again. Zak was the one who had listened to her. Who had offered a way out. Who had held her hand in dessert parlours and insisted that her desires mattered. And now, though she wrote *Hi* and pressed send, she rubbed her chest and wondered how to go about finally mourning his loss.

The doorbell rang.

Her mother glared from the other side of the doorway.

'You calmed down yet?'

Jamila left the door open and returned to the living room. Her mother disappeared into the kitchen. A minute later she emerged, holding a bottle of oil in one hand, a glass bowl in the other. She scowled. 'You might think you can speak to us in whichever way you want, but I still came to check on you.'

'I didn't ask you to.'

Her mother shifted towards the landing. 'Oh, so should I go?'

Jamila wasn't sure what she wanted, what was the right thing to do. If she rebuffed attempts at a reconciliation, perhaps it would not come again. The resulting silence her mother interpreted as consent to march into the room. She thrust the bowl at her. 'I finished the cheesecake for you this afternoon.'

Jamila took the bowl. The cheesecake looked light and creamy, not at all overbaked.

'Sit on the floor so I can oil your hair.'

Jamila stretched out her feet and felt for the ground. She sat cross-legged on the floor, resting her back against the base of her sofa. Her mother sat on the sofa, her legs caressing Jamila's shoulders. The bottle's metal cap made a light scratching noise, releasing the pungent smell of mustard oil. Her mother collected a small amount in a cupped hand, then rubbed her hands together. It made a slippery, leathery sound.

'Do you remember when you were young, how I did this for you and Jahida every Sunday evening? I would give you both a bath, then oil your hair and sit you in front of the fireplace. You used to love it,' she said, her fingers feathering Jamila's hair.

Jamila considered the time she had stuffed a tissue into its flames, almost setting the house alight. 'I remember.'

'And look how healthy your hair is now – how thick. I did this. Feeding your roots. It was my investment.'

Her greasy, fleshy palms massaged Jamila's scalp. Jamila closed her eyes and gave in to the undulations. She felt like a mound of clay on a wheel as her mother moved down to her neck and shoulders, thumbing through the bumps and air pockets trapped there.

'Your father loves you,' her mother said after a while. 'He can't live without you.'

Later, when her mother picked away the nest of loose hairs, she tried again. 'Your father's really upset. He can't bear to see you unhappy. You know he's had a hard life.'

Jamila opened her eyes, feeling like several millennia had passed. 'It doesn't matter, I wish he would listen.'

'He was trying to. You didn't need to scream.'

'Don't exaggerate, Mother, I did not scream.'

'What do you want from us?'

'I want to feel heard. I want to know that you're helping me to work these problems out. This isn't about the office, or my career, or Dad's legacy. This is about me. My happiness. There has to be another way.'

It took some time, but eventually she heard a sound come from her mother's throat – softer than a grunt, more guttural than the kind of 'hmmn' that glided across her chest. Her hands returned to Jamila's neck and shoulders, pressing them like she was bringing lumps of clay together.

'Come home with me tonight. I'll make you a nice breakfast before work.'

She had to get to Friday. Only five days until Friday. When that day came, she wouldn't open on Saturday. She'd spend that day on herself. Quinces were in season. She had seen crates of those yellow spheres at the Turkish supermarket. She would poach and preserve them, use some in a cheesecake. While it baked, she would read a novel, and then, in the evening, sprawl across the sofa and watch trash on the television. And she'd eat one slice, maybe two, of a cheesecake filled with the fragrances of quince, vanilla and honey, crunch from pistachios and a kadayif pastry base. She'd do all that, she thought. She would. She would.

Jamila rested a cheek against her mother's thigh.

'Will you warm me some milk before I sleep? My whole body's aching.'

Her mother stroked the top of her head. She was smiling. Jamila couldn't see it, but she knew that she was. 'Get into bed and I'll bring it up.'

Her mother disappeared into the kitchen. Jamila went upstairs and slipped beneath the covers. She looked out of the window, at the pitch-black sky, the stars smothered by pollution. Between the plaited branches was the moon, the thinnest whitest crescent leaning against a twig. She watched it for a while, running her fingertips through her hair, rubbing the oil into her hands. Christmas was coming. A tiny light switched on inside her.

Ten

Jamila wanted a quiet Christmas, the holiday to herself. When, on Christmas Eve, not a single client had visited all morning, she closed the office early, drove straight home and got into bed. She didn't leave it for the rest of the day. She filled the time with festive movies and a takeaway, then slept until her body could take no more.

She woke the next morning determined to grow content in her own company – and Bertha's. After a slow breakfast, she trekked to Kersal Wetlands. She peered into the houses that lined the way, seeking out their decorations and gathered families. Her own family had gathered too, on the other side of the city, and her uncles, aunts and cousins were joining for a big Christmas lunch – but she wasn't attending.

She took handfuls of sweetcorn and peas and tossed them at the mallards, moorhens and geese paddling in the river. She seemed to be the only human in the park and was glad to watch their bickering. As they ate, she felt the silence descend upon her, and the swell of her solitude, which she tried to embrace. The wetlands were vast, the city's skyscrapers far away, but she didn't last long before leaving the park with a bag still full of lettuce.

She returned home for her music, the television – something to do. But as she ignored the calls and texts arriving from her family, she began to feel hollowed out from the inside. Her mother might have attempted to broker peace, but in the week since their altercation her father had not called at all. For as long as he failed to address her unhappiness, she would not see nor speak to him. She could not allow things to go back to the way they were. She had more at stake than he did. And yet, skipping Christmas struck her an act of profound self-harm. Her family were celebrating together with a lavish meal, but she had buried herself inside to eat alone.

What did it mean to have a full life? she wondered. All she had known was to strive for whatever was expected of her. Get educated, get qualified, get into work, take over; nothing else mattered. But it did matter, she knew now. Because the life she was living was lonely. She couldn't admit that to anyone – it had taken long enough to admit it to herself – but it was no life at all.

Maybe the answer was to quit. Admit that the office had defeated her and bow out with the little fight she had left. She tried to imagine what she could do instead. A master baker, a video-game developer – every idea felt like a fantasy.

At around noon the next day, her phone buzzed on the table. It felt like so long since she had spoken to someone, she decided to answer it.

'Pack a bag, we're going on a trip.'

Jamila looked out of the window in bewilderment. 'What are you on about?'

'I'll be there in twenty minutes.'

'But wait, where are we going?'

The line went dead. Jamila stood up and stared at the kitchen – crumbs on the floor, dishes in the sink, the basket of washed clothes ready to be folded and put away. This was insane.

She skittered into the living room, then up the stairs, where she sat on her bed and tried to think clearly. She pinched her lips. She didn't know how long they were going for or what she would need; she hated the feeling of being surprised.

True to her word, twenty minutes later Jahida's car was beeping outside. Just enough time for Jamila to shake off the temptation to refuse her sister, pack a few clothes and feed Bertha. She tossed her rucksack into the boot of the car and climbed into the front, where her sister smiled from the driver's seat. 'You didn't need to pack so sparely. We're not going camping.'

Jamila shook her head. 'Just shut up and drive.'

Jahida laughed and eased away from the kerb.

'So, where are we going? You need to tell me, I'm not a child.'

Jahida didn't reply.

'Well? I hope you've not gotten carried away, I didn't bring my passport.'

'That's okay.' Jahida's voice was sunny and unperturbed, mocking her.

'Fine, you can have your fun today, but I need to be at work tomorrow.'

'No, Jamila, it's Christmas. One of your staff can put up a sign.'

Jamila glared at her sister, to no avail. They were heading out of the city. Trapped, Jamila turned to the radio, twisted the dial, couldn't settle on a station. By the time Jahida shouted at her to leave Pink Floyd alone, they were on the M61, hurtling away from the hill towns. The land became flat, populated by anaemic clusters of emaciated trees, the sky like a slate roof. Jamila looked up patisserie courses on her phone.

'I'm proud of you, you know?' Jahida said, staring straight ahead.

Jamila scrunched up her face. 'Please don't do this.'

'I'm serious, you did good.'

Jamila concealed the smile growing on her lips. 'Why can't we be the sort of family that keeps secrets?'

'What happens now?' Jahida asked.

'I don't know.'

'Well, what do you want to happen?'

'For you to focus on that car trying to overtake you.'

Jahida rammed her foot on the accelerator. Soon it became obvious where they were heading, but Jamila said nothing more, not even when the signs confirmed her hunch – white pictographs advertising the tower, the piers and pleasure beach.

The car climbed up a multi-storey car park behind a red-bricked building on the North Shore – a hotel of dark furnishings, faded glamour and eucalyptus disinfectant. Their room was similarly timid: limp curtain swags festooning the window, amber stains on the gold bedsheets, a thin pleather headboard stapled to the wall. They unpacked before heading downstairs for afternoon tea. Jamila ignored the worn patches in the jewel-toned carpet, the chandelier missing several bulbs. The patisserie looked shop-bought, but she ate it anyway. Heat from the fireplace ruddied their cheeks.

'So, why are we here?' Jamila asked.

Jamila watched her for a few seconds. 'You know why.'

'No, I don't.'

'Then you're dumber than I thought.' Jahida looped her forefinger through her teacup and stared out the window. Her face was relaxed and inexpressive. The sand and sea and sky were the same impervious layer of brown.

Of course Jamila knew why. She simply wanted to hear those reasons articulated in the open. She lodged a macaron in her mouth and went back for another. A knowing look passed between them and smiles so slight they would have been undetectable to others.

'Fuck, it's freezing,' she yelled when they ventured outside.

Jahida couldn't hear through the hat, hood and scarf she wore to protect her ears, and the wind rumbling along the promenade. They walked, or rather, were propelled forward, while latched on to one another. The sand looked smooth and hard; the sea spiked and bristled against the elements. Most of the shops were closed, the theme park too. The empty wooden rollercoaster was a sad sight beneath the foaming ochre sky. Like the hotel, it had come to prominence in a different time and subsequently fallen into disrepair.

They took cover in an empty arcade, troubled by the lack of bodies and the lurid colours and music so loud the place had an unhinged quality. But they stayed, pushing two- and ten-pence coins into the slot machines, praying for reward.

'Remember how Dad wouldn't let us play on these? We had to beg him for a bit of change,' Jamila said.

Jahida shrugged. 'I brought my own change with me.'

Jamila rolled her eyes and walked away. Jahida couldn't have been more obvious. But she was right, of course. It was a question of courage. Jamila took a coin from her pocket and jammed it into a different machine.

In the evening, they tried again. They walked the golden mile in pursuit of the Blackpool illuminations. The wind had mellowed, but the temperature had dropped and the air knifed bare skin. Lights tiered the horizon, row after row: lanterns and sea creatures and cheap party decorations. Hazy memories of their childhood visits returned, which they traded over a fish dinner. Jamila doused her chips in too much vinegar and, when she inhaled the steam, her nostrils burned.

'I want to stay a couple more days,' she announced suddenly the following morning.

They were packing in their room after breakfast. Jahida lifted her head from her suitcase, looking like she couldn't quite believe what she had heard. 'What about work?'

'It can stay shut for another day or two. It's almost the weekend anyway.' She had already texted the staff.

Jahida's surprise gave way to softness. 'I'm proud of you.'

But when Jahida climbed into the car and drove away, reality hit Jamila. She was all alone, on a trip she hadn't organised, in a hotel far from home. Her toes grew cold. She went inside and extended her stay with reception, then returned to her room and got into bed. She lay there for hours reading, building the courage to head outside, if only for an hour at least.

When she did, she immediately sought the company of the sea. The waves thrashed and the sand was packed tight and hard like concrete. As seagulls shrieked in the sky, distressed by the lack of tourist off-cuts, she filled time inspecting the shoreline from a distance and taking pictures of the rivulets and creeks. The air smelled stale and sulfuric and left traces of salt on her face.

The second day, she stayed out for longer. She returned to the sea and walked from pier to pier, and then into town, finding somewhere quiet to sit. She read as she ate in a café, ignoring the eyes of other customers. Later, she encouraged herself to put her book down and sit with her thoughts, even smile and watch the customers back. This wasn't so bad, she thought, she could do this. Take time away from the office and spend it by herself. And when she struggled, she would learn. Sometimes bones had to be broken again to be reset.

Part II

Eleven

Babar

Surely, the flat was big enough for them?

Babar stood in the doorway, surveying their bedroom. A small window to the left, a scuffed white dressing table to the right. In the middle, a large bed with its springs intact and his four-year-old, Ariba, sleeping in it. It could be bigger, yes, but there was nothing he could about that now. That morning, he had extended their tenancy.

And, with eighteen months on the contract, he could start making his mark. He'd already planned to revive the grubby walls with a coat of paint. Calypso, it said on the dusty tin he bought from the DIY shop. It would do. And when he found time he would replace the carpet, which scoured the soles of his feet like wire wool, and the tattered headboard and the torn blinds.

For the last three months, Babar had loved not sharing a bathroom with his in-laws. The kitchen allowed him and Habeebah to cook as they pleased, flirting with Western food like spaghetti bolognese and shepherd's pie, satisfying no cravings but their own. Finally, they had a living room where they could relax by themselves. Without the pressure of living under someone else's rules, he and Habeebah no longer argued about how much he contributed to her parents' bills or the hairs he left on the bathroom floor. Every day, Babar counted down the minutes until he finished work and, when he got home, he kicked off his shoes, changed into an old salwar kameez and lay on a faded kilim in front of the electric fireplace. Ariba played around him. Smells of dinner wafted in from the kitchen. He had achieved something his older brothers in Pakistan hadn't: he was the master of his own home.

Ariba started to suck on her empty bottle. Babar moved forwards and removed it from her mouth – she grimaced as if she were about to cry, then settled. He placed the bottle on the dressing table. Beneath it they had stacked their recent purchases. Yes, the new baby would have Ariba's hand-me-downs and, yes, their family and friends would gift new clothes, but in their excitement, he and Habeebah kept shopping for more. They bought things they hadn't expected to need the first time around: a changing mat, bottle steriliser, an infant tub – Babar checked them off his mental list. They'd bought things his brothers would have mocked as frivolous, but were too cute to resist: crocheted blankets and polka-dotted bibs and expensive woollen mittens. Habeebah's parents offered a pushchair that seated both children; her elder sister Parveen promised a cradle. But where would they put the cradle? Perhaps the dressing table would have to go.

An argument erupted outside. Babar spread his fingers through the blinds and watched two men squaring up in front of the chicken shop. The neighbourhood was turning, some said. He frowned at its latest intrusion. He closed the window, shutting out the noise and the smell of old cooking grease, and went into the living room.

Habeebah lay on their ugly brown sofa, watching an Indian soap. 'I think the dressing table should go,' he said. 'We'll put the cradle in its place.'

Habeebah stared at him. 'And what will we do with our things?'

'But the legs are broken. We can get a new one.'

'Don't waste money, fix it. We'll move the bed.' She turned back to the television.

Babar sat and squared her thriftiness with his love of nice, new things. He followed the picture for a while, the sound low to avoid disturbing Ariba. It was a typical 'saas-bahu' tale: the conniving mother-in-law, the anxious daughter-in-law, the hapless son caught in the middle. He rolled his eyes, but Habeebah was engrossed: elbow planted on the armrest, chin balanced in the base of her palm, other hand resting on her stomach.

'Yeh kaunsa drama hai?'

'*Diya Aur Baati Hum.*'

Babar considered the title: *We Are the Lamp and the Wick.* They were the diya and the baati too; Ariba and the baby were the oil that kept them burning. He gazed at Habeebah curiously. Living in Britain, far away from his family in Pakistan, his parents couldn't interfere and, now that they had moved out, her parents couldn't either. Their life was free from petty television drama, and yet she continued to pine for it.

'Put the BBC on for a while,' he said.

'Why? There's nothing on there for us.'

Her face was pale and dry. The pregnancy draining her. She vomited most mornings, though the GP assured her, as he had when they were expecting Ariba, this would lessen with time. Five months in and it hadn't. He took Habeebah's swollen foot and began massaging.

After a while, she stretched her other calf across his lap and Babar pressed that foot too. Yes, their life could be good. Not that it wasn't already. But if they stayed on this path, it would only get better. Better than his brothers' broken lives, stuck in a single, stifling household, working endless hours as motorcycle mechanics. Who handed their salaries to their mother at the end of every month, unable to make even the most basic decisions for themselves – what to eat that night, which school to send their children to. His brothers had always ridiculed him, his soft hands and bookishness, his constant dreaming. But he was his father's hope. So, when it was time, he and Habeebah would move to a bigger place, a place with more than one bedroom, a whole house where their children would each have a room of their own. He cracked his knuckles and mulled over colour schemes.

A month later, Parveen delivered the cradle and Babar spent that Sunday afternoon assembling it. He stepped back and admired his handiwork.

'It looks good, no?' He turned to Habeebah, who watched him from their bed, which he had moved closer to the window.

'Didn't I tell you it would work there?'

Babar gave her a wry smile. 'Haan, meri jaan. Everything you say is right.'

'Then don't forget to speak to Mrs Shah tomorrow. We only have a few months left on our visas. All this effort, and we might have to beg your brothers to take us in.'

He hesitated. 'No, Bebo, I can't. She's been having a hard time. It wouldn't be fair.'

'Why not? She's your boss. If anybody understands our position, it's her. I know she'll say yes. Just ask.' Habeebah got up to make them some lemonade.

Babar listened to the police sirens outside.

His desk was swamped with work. Over the weekend, Jamila had assigned him another eight files, each one labelled *URGENT* with a yellow Post-it.

She used to deal with these matters herself: helping clients source their supporting documents, informing them that their applications had failed and required an appeal. Those conversations took forever – 'Please, can I bring the documents after the deadline? Please, can you write my story? Please, why don't you make the Home Office accept my case?' Then, a few days into the new year, the announcement: Jamila was spent. Sick of working herself into the ground. Both he and his fellow paralegal, Rubel, realised that things were about to change. Soon after, more and more files began appearing on their desks, more paralegal work with complex instructions and printed samples clipped on. Jamila began scoring Babar's letters to the Home Office with red ink, which left his face a similar colour, but he corrected them, thinking of his babies.

He role-played their conversation as he worked, mouthed sounds instead of words that eluded him. He tried calling other solicitors first. None of them picked up – it felt like a sign. Before lunch, Jamila called him to her office. His chance had come. But how to phrase this request? The idea of speaking to her freely made his backside sweat. Among his colleagues, he alone was intimidated by her brisk demeanour, her power over him, her dislike of small talk. She was always laughing with Rubel, gentle with Sadia, reverential with her father. He longed to make her laugh.

And how exhausted had she been really, he wondered, walking to her office. Today, like every other day, she had dressed in a suit and straightened her hair. No matter how busy the office got, she saw to her clients cheerfully and left the real work to him and Rubel. Yes, there was that afternoon before Christmas when she threw up in the bin and passed out on her desk, but maybe she had eaten something suspicious. Anyway, she'd had the holiday to recover.

He slid back the door to her office and found two clients standing over a vast pot on the desk. It was made of steel and had a heavy lid. He recognised the couple: Mr and Mrs Singh had recently won the right for Mr Singh's eighty-year-old mother to visit from Delhi. The couple had often sat beside him as he drafted their letters to the Home Office. They promised to feed the office when they saw success, and here they were.

'Babar, will you help Mr Singh take the food to the kitchen?' Jamila asked.

He made a beeline for the smaller bowls containing salad and raita, leaving the heavier biryani pot to Mr Singh. He led the way to the kitchen, before guiding Mr Singh to the exit.

'Thank you again for everything. Not even in her dreams had my mother imagined she would visit England,' Mr Singh said.

'Sure, any time,' Babar said, eager to get back. He was in danger of losing what little courage he had scrabbled together.

When he returned, Jamila held out a shiny red box.

'They left this for you. For your hard work.'

Mithai? For him? Babar flushed with delight. Clients rarely recognised their efforts as individuals, preferring to reward Jamila alone or the office as a whole. Both were the same essentially, since Jamila shared whatever she received.

'Thank you.'

'You deserve it.'

He found himself bowing. As he walked towards the door, he stopped himself.

'Was there something else, Babar?'

He sat down across from her.

'Mera kuch karo, Mrs Shah.' He ran a bitten thumbnail along his teeth. This wasn't how he had planned it. He was a helpless boy at the mercy of his brothers again.

'What do you mean?'

'My visa is ending soon.'

It seemed like more than three years ago that Babar had come to Britain as a naive accountancy student. So much had happened since then. His father losing control of the loan repayments, the loan sharks threatening to kill him. Babar's brothers blaming his ambition. When the monthly money transfers dried up, he was just a year from completing his ACCA exams and desperate to finish. He couldn't forget slugging himself from business to business handing out CVs; how Jamila and her father were the only ones willing to take him on.

She had saved him. He had devoted himself to her after that.

'What about a student extension? You could return to university?'

He shook his head. He had started off by helping with Jamila's bookkeeping, using his salary to provide for his family and settle the debt back home. But two months into the job, when it became impossible to balance university, work and parenthood, he'd had to abandon his course. 'I can't afford to. Not with the baby coming.' He hoped she would feel the weight of his responsibilities. But when it left no impression on her face, resentment swirled in his stomach.

'And how old is Ariba now?'

'Four, almost five.'

'Right. So, you can't apply under the seven-year rule yet. Hmm.'

'Kuch aur socho na, Mrs Shah. If anyone can find a way, it's you.'

She removed her glasses. A pained expression had come over her face.

'Babar . . . I don't think I can give you the time you need.'

He began to sweat.

'You know what's been going on around here. It's just . . . I need to establish some boundaries.'

Babar couldn't absorb anything. Despite his hard work and dedication, she had 'established some boundaries'. His mind began to race, imagining where this path led him, each destination more nightmarish than the last – jobless, homeless, detained, deported. He conjured his brothers' wooden words of sympathy, his father's humiliation, his wife's regret at marrying the weak one. And what would become of his children?

'Imagine I took on your case and came up with a strategy. What if it didn't work out? What if you were refused? Could we stay on friendly terms? No, you'd blame me for ruining your case, your future, maybe.'

'But you're my family. Iss mulk mein mera aur kaun hai?'

Indignation prickled his scalp. Jamila had helped countless people, members of staff as well as clients. She had assisted Sadia with her husband's visa; assisted Rubel with his. Even when she didn't want to take on a case, if the client begged hard enough, she caved in and grumbled afterwards. He closed his eyes and dug the weight of his body into the chair. He wouldn't let her do this, eviscerate the life he was building. He was even prepared to pay.

'Really, I'm sorry.' She bit her lip. 'I'm not saying I won't help you. It's just—'

The room filled with a thrumming sound. A deluge of hailstones falling from the sky, some hammering the window then sliding down, half-melted.

He couldn't bear to look at her then, casually leaning back in the chair, like she had knocked back a man trying to clean her windscreen at a traffic light.

Suddenly, she bent forwards and began rummaging through her drawer. 'Here, take this.' She handed him a business card. 'Gemma's my friend from law school. I'll call in a favour and get you a discount. You'll like her, she's brilliant. And with Gemma I can keep an eye on the case, discuss strategy and she won't be offended.'

Babar slipped the card in his pocket and left the room.

Rubel was standing outside. 'What did she say?'

Babar shook his head.

'Oh, yaar.' Rubel slipped an arm around his shoulders.

'It's fine, I understand. I'd have done the same,' he said, with a feeble smile. But had their roles been reversed, he would never have refused her. The strong uplifted the weak, it was a duty laid out by God. Instead, she had shown him he was worthless.

Habeebah was waiting by the door when he came home that evening. She took his bag and, as he embraced her, he smelled the perfume of the day's cooking mixed with the acid tang of vomit. He looked inside for Ariba, who was sitting two feet from the television, watching cartoons.

'Ariba, sit back,' he said.

'How was your day?' Habeebah asked.

Babar removed his coat and shoes and went into the living room. He stopped by Ariba, picked her up and placed her another two feet back before falling onto the sofa. 'Long. Boring. You?'

Habeebah sat next to him. 'Same. At least you got to stay out.'

He took her hand and kissed it. 'What's for dinner?'

'Palak gosht.'

'What time are we eating?'

'In a minute, but tell me first, what did she say?'

'Who?'

'You know who. What did she say about helping us?'

Babar removed the business card from his pocket. It had sat there all afternoon without him looking at it once. Soft and embossed, the card looked and felt expensive, shining beneath the overhead lights. 'She gave me this,' he said, passing it to Habeebah.

As she took in the details written on the card, Habeebah's eyes widened. 'You mean she said no? But she's your boss and idol. Your friend.'

He shrugged.

'She's the best, you said. You don't trust anybody else with your case. Doesn't she care?'

'I don't know.'

'What about your job? You can't work for her without a visa.'

'I said, I don't know!' He couldn't bear the question, nor the reediness of his voice.

For as long as her cartoons occupied Ariba, they discussed options. He half listened as Habeebah talked of preparing the application themselves with the experience Babar had accumulated at the office. Of living without a visa and waiting until Ariba turned seven. Of cutting their losses and returning home.

Habeebah rubbed her stomach. 'Well, I can't live with the uncertainty. Not in this condition. You'll have to ask her again.'

Babar felt lightheaded and unsteady. He went into their bedroom and lay down.

Through the rest of January and into the first weeks of February, he began staying late to get ahead in his work. He used Friday evenings to work on the accounts and took over the office stationery order. At lunch he regaled Jamila with stories about the funny things Ariba said and did: declaring her wish to marry her schoolteacher; pushing the boys in the playground who hogged the swings; asking if they could get a kitten when Habeebah (who was allergic) died. And when this failed to alter Jamila's mood, he found himself arriving to work late, withdrawing from lunchtime conversations, dawdling between tasks. He stole pens and reams of paper from the stationery cupboard. He used doctor's appointments as an excuse to browse the stalls in Longsight Market. The clouds grew progressively darker and heavier, the same colour as the tarpaulin roofs being slapped by the wind. He ran his hands along bolts of fabric, bright as sticks of Blackpool rock, unable to separate himself, seeing no point in returning to a place where his position came after their clients'.

One morning, she called him to her room.

'I just spoke to Gemma about your consultation with her. She mentioned your in-laws – your mother-in-law's got respiratory problems, right? Father-in-law's in a wheelchair?'

'Right . . . ' he said suspiciously.

'She suggested an application as your mother-in-law's carer since Habeebah is responsible for them anyway. Your sister-in-law has early multiple sclerosis, so she can't help. You'd potentially move back in with them. She'll submit the application before your visa expires. I think it's a good idea. You can keep working for me without any issues.'

Babar had held his head in his hands yesterday, when Gemma recommended they give up their flat. A necessary compromise, she had called it, and he had lost what little hope remained.

He sanded his fingers against the edges of the desk, refusing to look at Jamila.

'And you called me here because . . . '

'You can start getting your stuff together. Proof of your mother-in-law's illnesses and need for care; proof there's nobody else to look after her; proof that you're doing the caregiving already and she can't manage without.'

Why was she doing this? Pretending to care when she didn't. What did she stand to gain? He stared at her. 'If it matters to you so much, you could just deal with the case yourself.

'Babar, don't. I'm trying to make some difficult decisions here. I'm doing what I can.'

Her mouth tightened. The danger of being fired became all too real again. He scampered out of her office.

Babar spent the rest of the afternoon reading about visa applications for carers. At four, Habeebah called to say she was going to the hospital with her sister. Nothing to worry about, just the same discomfort she'd been feeling in her stomach for the last few days. Again, Babar only half-listened. He agreed to drop into his mother-in-law's when he finished work, pick up Ariba and some food. He mentioned it all to Jamila when leaving an hour early.

That evening, Babar was standing next to his bed when the phone rang. He had tucked Ariba in and passed her a bottle of milk. Almost five years old and still she took a bottle to bed at night; Habeebah refused to wean her off. Ariba balanced it in one hand, curling her soft brown hair with the other. It amused Babar how intently she watched him while playing with it. Wherever he moved, her eyes darted to find him.

Babar retrieved his phone from the dressing table and walked into the living room. It wouldn't take long, he knew, before Ariba followed him there. He'd have to put her to bed all over again.

'No news yet, Mrs Shah.' It took hours at A&E all without phone reception. Had Habeebah been seen to? He lowered himself onto the sofa, resting on its outer edge. In the kitchen, the radio alternated between snatches of old Bollywood songs and static. 'Sure. Soon as I hear anything, I'll let you know.' Errant pieces of Lego were dotted beside the coffee table. They must have escaped him when clearing up after dinner.

'You don't think . . . maybe you should have gone with her?' Jamila said.

'Somebody needed to stay with Ariba,' he replied irritably. Ariba appeared at the door, ran in and climbed onto the sofa. Her face fell onto the velvety armrest, sucking forcefully on her bottle. 'She went with her sister.'

Babar cut the call and reached over to collect the errant pieces of Lego, his knees dropping to the carpet. Jamila's name on the call had surprised him; he almost hadn't picked up. Habeebah would say how kind it was, but anyone could call. She'd had a real opportunity to help them and refused it.

He felt a sharp thump to his ribs. Ariba stared back innocently. He stroked her cheek as she smiled, releasing the pressure around the teat with a kissing sound.

Babar reached for the soles of her feet. 'Chalo choti-ma, my little monkey. Bedtime.'

'No, Baba, don't,' she giggled, kicking his hands away.

'Bed, I said.' He scooped her up and brought her to his chest. Her nimble fingers searched for loose hairs at the back of his skull. Curled, twisted and pulled until sleep had claimed her.

He lay with her on the bed for a while, watching her chest rise and fall. Still no news. Maybe he should have gone with Habeebah, after all. He went into the kitchen and switched off the radio, grabbed two pears, a plate and a knife, then sat in the living room eating and watching the highlights of a cricket match. On an old envelope he listed the documents required to support their application – the keys to the house that eluded them.

He didn't need Jamila. He could succeed without her.

At around nine, the call came from the hospital. Parveen. The doctor had finally checked Habeebah. She didn't know how to tell him. The baby was dead.

Under the torrid glare of the hospital lights, Ariba slept in his lap, fingers knotted to her scalp, her breath smelling of stale milk. Babar wiped his face with a handkerchief. His mind was a mess.

This is not your life, Babar told himself. This is not happening to you. He looked up from his feet to see that it was. It was his daughter cradled in his arms. His wife resting on the hospital bed with her eyes closed, face swollen from crying. His family and friends looking morose in chairs around the room, searching for words of comfort, snatching these quiet moments to make sense of it all. Rationalise disorder and pain, attach a narrative to it and the appropriate significance.

A knock on the door, a hand on his shoulder. Babar turned to look.

'As-salamu alaykum.'

'Wa alaykum as-salam.' He vacated his chair for her.

Jamila entered and approached the hospital bed. She whispered something to Habeebah, who was unresponsive. She took Ariba from Babar and sat down.

Habeebah's mother filled the silence with an orchestra of sniffles and wails. Occasionally, she wiped her nose with her dupatta and repeated, 'Hai Allah, why did you have to do this to my daughter? Whatever did she do to you?'

He knew that she was in shock – that she, too, was processing her loss – but he despised the noise and, by extension, her. Unfair, but he wished God had taken his mother-in-law instead.

Parveen addressed Jamila: 'The doctors took her straight in for testing. They checked the baby's heartbeat. There wasn't any. He'd probably been dead for a few days. That's why she was in all that pain.'

Babar winced. Every word, every sentence burst through him like a hot poker. He had seen the baby when he got to the hospital. A boy. Mohsin was the name they had chosen. With reddish skin like the inside of a papaya, soft down on his head, toes tinier than teardrops. Loneliness swept over him. He wished his parents were here, his brothers and their wives too. He longed to hear their voices. In his pockets, his hands tightened into fists.

'All this is up to God,' his father-in-law intoned. 'He does what He wants and we have to trust Him. Who knows, maybe there is some hidden benevolence in this?'

Babar slipped out and headed to the bathroom, splashed his face with water. He couldn't agree that something good could come from death, from a life ended before it had begun. From the vending machine he bought a milkshake, discovering his thirst as he drank, submitting to it. There wasn't a thing he could control. Not even the borders of his home.

Wednesday 20 February. In the office of Southern Cemetery, Babar completed the paperwork, then stepped out into the bitter air. The sky was bright and unending. The soft, uneven pathway was filled with tire marks and brown puddles, reflecting splinters of tree, cloud and sky.

It had rained all night. He had heard water dripping onto the asphalt outside while speaking to his parents on the phone.

'We lost the baby,' he said to his mother.

'Hai Allah. What happened?'

He struggled to find words of explanation.

'Mera puttar, don't cry. Allah di marzi,' she said.

Unborn children – those that never took a breath in this world – were not given proper funerals, his brother declared. They didn't need them; they were pure. Though he said nothing in response, Babar objected and, once again, gratitude permeated through him – even as he craved their company – for the distance between them. He and Habeebah would decide how their baby was laid to rest and no elder could tell them otherwise.

The mourners had parked their cars on the other side of the pathway and waited solemnly beside them. Habeebah's family were there, though Habeebah herself had chosen not to attend. Couldn't bear to, she'd said. She stayed at home with Ariba. His other family, the office family, Jamila and Rubel – a heavily pregnant Sadia having tactfully stayed away – stood close by. He went over and greeted everyone.

Later, a man led them to the burial spot. Babar lifted a small casket from the car – so small, no bigger than his forearm – and walked to the green patch by a young cherry tree. The earth yielded, squelching beneath his feet. The man, short, hairy, ginger, his overalls covered in dirt, removed a plastic cover and stepped into the open grave. Four tiny caskets were stacked on top of each other, the babies sharing a grave with a new set of peers. He took the box from Babar and slotted it in.

'Once the grave is full, we'll fill it up with soil, but you can take a little now,' he pointed to the mound of dry earth nearby in a wheelbarrow, 'and sprinkle it over.'

Babar turned to his father-in-law. 'Would you say something?'

He nodded and rolled his wheelchair forward, held out his hands. 'Praise be to God, Lord of all worlds. The Compassionate, the Merciful. Ruler on the Day of Reckoning. You alone we worship, and You alone we ask for help . . . '

Babar brought his hands to his face; the mourners fanned around the grave did the same. He grabbed a fistful of earth and sprayed it along the casket. The mourners followed, then offered their condolences again.

'You will get through this,' Rubel said, patting his chest. 'Whatever you need, I'm here.'

'Allah will bless you with more children,' his brother-in-law said.

Jamila offered no words, only a tight embrace, palms spread across Babar's back. Babar accepted it gratefully. Words were superfluous in the end. As if directed at him through glass or water, they lost coherent meaning.

The mourners drifted back to their cars. Babar tried walking, but he slipped and toppled over, unable to feel his legs or his feet. Two people pushed their hands beneath his arms, reaching for his shoulders, just before he hit the mud. Rubel and Babar's brother-in-law. They caught him, hauled him up and pulled him to their car, leading him over the wet earth. But a small hole in the ground and the tiny coffin resting inside it kept pulling him back.

The white thread of dawn pushed through the black velvet night. As a solitary bird issued its morning song, Babar lay awake thinking of all that the day would demand of him.

He found himself rising early to pray. Why? He wasn't especially religious, and now he was deep in a quarrel with God. But prayer was all that he knew. In God's word, he found shelter. And slowing down his prayers, inhaling the Arabic and pushing it down towards his core, temporarily numbed him.

'What are you doing?' Habeebah's voice was nasal, monotone.

'Namaz.'

'Why? What good will it do?'

Saying nothing, he prayed. Then he folded the prayer mat – ignoring the bibs, clothes and baby monitors beneath the dressing table – and returned to bed. It was customary to follow each prayer with a dua, a more personal supplication to God, but Babar skipped it. No, he thought. I won't give you that. I have nothing more to say to You.

Babar returned to work the following day. For the next week he sat at his desk, typing letters to the Home Office. Every few minutes his mind attached itself to other things and the words blurred together. How quickly the world moved on. How effortlessly it progressed without him. Time lurched forward, always, but he couldn't anymore. He was frozen, the grief fused to him. He considered leaving – returning to Pakistan, to the comfort of his brothers, or perhaps to a city far from them all. What was the point of being here? This country had hurt him, would always remind him of what he had lost, what it had stolen from him.

Jamila called him to her office.

He pressed her as soon as he sat down. 'What do I do now? Where do I go?'

'You could take some time off to grieve, like I said.'

He wasn't interested. 'You could help me.'

'But Babar, I am helping—'

'You could decide whether I leave or stay.'

'Don't be silly,' she said. 'I'm not in charge of your destiny. That's you and that's God.'

As she set her mouth, Babar tried to picture her struggle with the office workload, working late and processing files and distributing them between their desks.

No. This wasn't suffering; she couldn't begin to imagine how he was suffering. This was melodrama. He looked at her with contempt – her tiny mouth, her heavy frame, the illusion she projected of tireless, boundless altruism. She had thwarted even this tiny request.

Jamila sighed. 'Look, are you unhappy with Gemma?'

'No, not Gemma, but—'

'She's finalising your application to send next week. I'd only be doing the same.'

Babar threw his hands up a little and slapped his chair. How could she not understand? This had nothing to do with Gemma anymore. His whole life had imploded.

She advised him to finish what he was doing, go home and rest.

Once the application was submitted, March grew quiet. Babar became occupied with other tasks. He negotiated a break on their tenancy and returned to living with Habeebah's parents off Wellington Road in Stockport, where Habeebah took to her bed, leaving only to retrieve Ariba from school. He urged Habeebah to take walks with him for her health. Only on Ariba's fifth birthday did she agree, lighting the candle on her cake, joining them afterwards in Cringle Park. She watched with a distant look in her eye as Ariba rode the carousel, pushed a boy off the swings. Babar firmly held onto his wife's hand.

Then one evening, more than a month after the funeral, Babar returned from work to find a brown A4 packet waiting for him. He knew what it was going to say before he had even opened it – it was almost cruel how quickly their reply had come. Even so, he tore at the flap and read the pages, printed in black and white. When he had finished, he walked quickly out of the house and ran back to the office.

He caught Jamila in her car, manoeuvring out of the car park, the office shutters pulled down. He flailed his arms in the alleyway. His chest was heaving.

Jamila wound the window down.

'What's the matter? What's going on?'

'They've refused me, the bastards refused me,' he said, between breaths. His legs and stomach ached; the back of his shirt was soaked.

'What did they say?'

'The usual. They think Habeebah's mother is fine.'

'Jump in.'

Jamila called Gemma as Babar got into the front passenger seat and pulled on the seatbelt. He felt sick. The drubbing of his heart sounded in his ears.

'Right. She's waiting for us.' Jamila reached into the back and grabbed a bottle of water. 'Drink this and get your breath back. Stay calm. We're going to sort this out.'

He grabbed her hands. 'Mera kuch karo. I can't go back. You know why.'

Leaving was unthinkable. He had a child buried in this soil.

'I know. And we're going to get you over the line.'

Line. Yes, it was a line. Not the end of one, but a boundary all the same. The death of his child had created a new kind of border, one that enclosed his life and bound him to this land.

Jamila put an arm around him. His head fell onto her shoulder. After a minute, she pulled away. 'We're going to get you over that line,' she repeated, moving the gearstick into first.

You could have helped earlier. You could have avoided all this, he wanted to say. 'What will happen now?'

Jamila looked at him. 'It's going to be okay . . . I promise.'

She released the handbrake and the car lunged forward. They pulled out onto Kingsway, turned left for Burnage Hall Road, then Burnage Lane, continuing along Slade Lane until they drove along Stockport Road towards town. They passed the Pashtun takeaway that sold Habeebah's favourite chapli kebabs, the public

library where they once borrowed books for Ariba, the flat above
the fried chicken shop where he had dreamed up colour schemes,
planning their upward trajectory. And, as they left these beacons
of his old life behind, Babar swigged from his water bottle, trying
to believe Jamila.

Twelve

On a Wednesday evening in the middle of April, Jamila watched with satisfaction as her last client left the office. It was 5:45pm; Babar and Rubel had left for the day, Sadia had recently gone on maternity leave. She got up, stretched and admired the eerie office silence. Then she switched off all the lights and heating, eager to disappear before a client blackmailed her into staying.

An arctic wind blasted in from the front door, followed by a frantic rapping against the glass. A nasal voice called out: 'Mrs Shah, where do you think you're going?'

Jamila's stomach dropped. She withdrew into the staff area and hid behind some machinery. She hoped that the client would leave of their own accord. Couldn't they tell she was closed? But the rapping continued, its doggedness infuriating. Eventually, Jamila rose from where she had crouched by Rubel's computer, forsaking the safety of the dark.

Hassan had pressed his face into the reception window, searching for any trace of life. Jamila shook her head as soon as she saw his thick, indignant eyebrows. 'I'm sorry but you'll have to come back tomorrow—'

'No, no, no. This is no good for—' Hassan's voice boomed, then broke. He turned away from the window, coughing and spluttering, a box of eclairs shrouding his mouth. Jamila stepped back from the counter and covered her face with the nearest envelope, though the slit in the glass really was too small to contract anything.

'Should I get you a glass of water?' Jamila asked, guiltily.

Hassan hacked away and didn't answer.

'I thought you were open for as long as we needed you,' he said when he had recovered. He wiped his eyes with a clean white tissue, fluid glistening at the bottom of his nostrils.

Jamila felt a squeeze of empathy towards him. But for the umpteenth time, she pointed to the opening hours stickered above the counter and called attention to what her clients ignored. 'No. Not unless it's an emergency. Not anymore.'

'I need an update on my file. It won't take long—'

'Come back in the morning and we'll talk for as long as you want.' She felt silly pushing back over a small task, but he was sillier still for trudging in when he was sick. Always, he refused her service as she offered it to him. He preferred taking two buses in the cold, when she could have updated him over the phone.

Hassan fired her a dark, dismissive look. 'Allah bless you, Mrs Shah, but I'm very disappointed.' And before he surrendered to another coughing fit, he spun around and stalked away, jamming the front door against the welcome mat.

Dry leaves scuttled across the road like fleeing mice. Shame and unreason bested her sense of achievement. She could have looked up his case – it would not have taken that long – nevertheless, Jamila grabbed her bag and moved towards the alarm. She was about to key in the code when she jumped at the door creaking at the back of the office, followed by the sound of footsteps approaching.

Babar poked his head around the photocopier.

'What are you still doing here?' she asked, unclenching her muscles. 'You scared me.'

'Sorry, I was in the toilet,' he said, sheepishly.

'I almost locked you in.' He had been in there for a while. Was he hiding, hoping to catch her alone? They had talked a lot in recent months. She'd had more than her fill.

'The barrister just faxed over Hassan Khemiri's appeal grounds.'

Hassan's appeal hearing had taken place at the end of February. It had been a difficult experience, which was confirmed when the judge's determination came through, a few weeks later, and found he was an inconsistent witness to his own story. When Jamila delivered the news, he threatened to empty her bookshelves until she promised to send the decision to a barrister, at no extra cost, and find the grounds to appeal again, arguing the judge had misapplied the law. Despite knowing this, Babar had held onto the grounds all this time.

She read the grounds while worrying about how she would explain this oversight to Hassan. The papers were still warm and carried the fresh, almost burnt smell of ink. Babar watched closely, like an official testing her literacy.

A slow, sinking feeling moved through her.

Babar stepped forward. 'It's bad, isn't it?'

'No, not bad.' She kept her voice light, though she hardly convinced herself.

'The court will reject him.'

'Send it anyway.'

'A lost client is dangerous. Don't you always say that to us?'

Babar stood confidently, hands in his pockets, hips pushed forward. Only a few months into working on more advanced cases and already making pronouncements on their viability. It would have amused her if she didn't fear he was right: the grounds weren't enough to save Hassan.

'It'll be fine,' she said, trailing the sensation of Babar volleying her words back at her. Bold or grating, she couldn't decide. From the ashes of this case, she would build Hassan Khemiri another one. Build it around the activist from his political party who had just been found murdered in Oran, or build it around his children. Lose a life, like in her computer games, and resume at the nearest checkpoint. That is, if the system didn't tire of him before she had the chance.

'I guess some people don't really matter, do they?' Babar muttered to himself.

The comment startled her. Given how much she had done for him, it was certainly daring. 'Did you want to say something?' She angled her head towards him.

'Me? No, Mrs Shah.'

She watched him inspecting the reception, feigning an indifference he clearly didn't feel, and sighed. She understood his vulnerability, his strange investment in Hassan's case; he was awaiting a date for his own hearing. But there was no time to unpick this, she really had some place to be. 'Good. Because, Babar, I thought you trusted me. I thought you trusted nobody else.' She smiled, hoping to induce the same in him, an easy truce.

He bolted his mouth and grimaced.

Jamila considered the lines carved around his eyes. The desiccated quality to his voice. The unwashed reek that had begun to waft from him. How grief guillotined his laughter and censored him. Once the first to play practical jokes, singing Punjabi songs as he worked, sparking discussions about the future of Pakistan over lunch, all he contributed now was this refusal to smile. She reached for his shoulder. 'Maybe you do need some time off—'

He jerked away. 'No, work keeps me busy. If only Habeebah could do the same. At night, she cries a lot.' He paused for a beat, held her gaze. 'She worries about our future.'

Jamila nodded slowly. She had tried to maintain a healthy distance from his case, but his grief had awakened a new level inside her, a willingness to look the monster in the eye again and fight to ensure that the baby buried in cold English soil wouldn't be alone – even as she wondered how to do this without it depleting her. 'I've got your letter of support written out just here, actually.' She strode towards her office.

His eyes graced the page for no more than a second. 'It's good.'

Jamila moved decisively towards the alarm. Babar was no innocent – he knew the realities of this work. He may have looked at her like she was a prophet or mystic or magician, but what he really wanted — for his baby to live again — was not something she could give him. Briefly, she glanced back. Babar's head had fallen limp, revealing the bald patch spreading over his crown. It speared her.

She caught the echo of an earlier evening then, some three weeks ago. When Babar's determination had arrived and he had motored his way to her, wheezing and dripping with sweat, and she had hugged him and stroked his head, then driven him to Gemma's office. Inside, with Gemma studying the letter, he turned to her, his mouth taut, his eyes mean and small. 'It's your fault. You did this because you don't like me. You want to separate me from my son. You were jealous of me and hated my happiness.'

Then, as it did now, her skin had tingled then numbed. He had made her feel cruel for pursuing a trivial change for herself, in denial of his suffering. Foolish for charging after it even as it threatened to lose her an employee that she herself had trained. All she wanted was a break, a renegotiation, before things got truly dark. But she was never allowed that. Never allowed to complain. Never, ever allowed to come first. She had tried to prioritise herself, for the first time, and now a baby was dead.

The sun had set by the time she got into the car, but it didn't matter. There was plenty of light left in the sky and that triggered an uptick in her mood. Though spring had come late this year, there were new leaves on the trees and crocuses lingering on the ground. Even the winter-refuging ladybirds had migrated from her bedroom. The magnolias, however, had refused to cede. A persistent cold front had left them suspicious, their cream-coloured buds fat and hard, like ivory bullets.

Jamila bumped towards town. A week of ice, at the beginning of April bizarrely, had created new potholes in the road and tarmac crumbled beneath her wheels along Birchfields Road. She listened to the radio as her thoughts rolled back to work. How clean her office was now. The cleanest it had ever been. It was the first thing she had done when returning to work after Christmas, imposing herself on the office to curb her father's reign. Though he had retired over a year ago, his influence loomed large. It had never occurred to her before that she could question his philosophies, just stop running the office in his image and instead build it in hers.

She began with the small things: moving the successful files that once lived on the floor beside her, rehoming them in an empty cabinet; clearing the shelves of her old Thank You cards, dumping all but her favourites. The last half hour of every day she reserved for sorting through the files on her desk. She knew that establishing real and lasting control over her business would take more than imposing order where there was once chaos, so she tried to accept her limitations. She farmed out the post to Babar and application forms to Rubel, proofread letters as they came to her rather than taking them home, recognised when there wasn't enough time to squeeze in another consultation. She stopped coming in on Saturdays. Gradually, her heaviness was lifting. But on the days she forgot and went back to her old ways? Water pooled around her ankles.

The appointment she had booked was with herself at the gym. Three times a week she came here – she pulled on a navy vest and leggings, plugged in her headphones and walked out to the sound of screeching guitars. She left the toils of the office behind her.

The equipment room was a palace of mirrors. Cold air jetted out of ceiling vents, pushing a stale, faintly sour stench around. Her eyes moved between her favourite pieces of equipment, planning a route between them, one unbroken line connecting the dots on a page. She hopped onto a treadmill and thumped a series of buttons, layering speed, then an incline. No point in starting slowly when she loved to dive straight in.

The first kilometre was easy; her breath barely broke. She upped the speed and extended her stride, face fixed on the timer. Soon the distance would hit her legs. Soon the metrics of success would be redefined again and again – depending on how she tired she was, how determined, how the parallel blisters on her big toes behaved beneath their pink, fibrous plasters. Depending on whether her mind or body won out in the end. But, for now, she considered nothing beyond her ambition. Could she clock her first kilometre in under six minutes? Her second in under twelve?

She felt it, just as she reached the halfway point. A dull stitch crawling from under her ribs. She sought to contain it, control it, pushing it up like a ball of electricity, out through her nose with her breath. She told herself she was strong. Powerful. She had done this plenty of times before. Made a pact with her body to get her to the end of the line.

The repetition of these words – strong, powerful, resilient – conjured a face. A gaze. Samir's gaze, when she had finally met him and Maryam for dinner in Chinatown last Friday. It had drilled into her so much that she'd crossed her arms and hunched· over the table.

Samir was a giant, with a square face like a postage stamp and a lip ring. 'You look incredible,' he said, his eyes not moving from her body.

'You know I live to please,' she laughed, hunching her back even further.

It didn't matter that Samir was gay, she had wanted to terminate the endless commentary on her body. Her body was a cage, she wished to escape it. But now, as she looked up and stared into the mirror ahead, her face red and saturated, her breath ragged, she wondered if Samir was right.

Forsaking all illusions of grace, she grunted through the last 100 metres, then stumbled off the treadmill. Legs leaden with lactic acid, she doubled over and recovered. She'd managed two kilometres in twelve minutes and three seconds. Not bad, but not the record she wanted. She mounted the nearest cross trainer and loaded up her settings, swinging her arms smoothly, with the moderate force of an old locomotive.

The dinner had been far more uncomfortable. When she arrived, Samir and Maryam were already sitting beneath the canopy of the Try Thai bar, chatting and laughing. Jamila found herself on the outer edge of a circle, looking in. She hadn't imagined they would become closer in her absence. It took some degree of determination to walk over, especially as her instincts compelled her to leave.

Things didn't immediately improve. Of course, she had expected some discomfort, and rightfully so – she had disappeared for almost a year – but the bursts of hostility she caught on their faces as she explained her absence, slotted between tight embraces and rising intonation and strategic sips of lemonade, had surprised her.

'Theek hai, na. You were always quite inconsistent,' Maryam said, touching her dyed blonde hair, her girlish perfume a reminder of their youth.

'Any time you got overwhelmed at university you'd disappear on us,' Samir added.

Jamila proffered a lengthy apology, acknowledging her flaws while retaining a note of bitterness. Neither of them, her two oldest and closest friends, grasped the degree to which she had felt buried. Even a text message, a few words to let them know she was alive, had required superhuman strength.

But, as they caught up, that bitterness turned to regret. She had missed out on so much: Maryam was engaged to be married; Samir had moved in with his partner and was studying for a PhD. Of course, there was envy; their lives had unfurled with the momentum of a roll of fabric, while every freedom she'd had to claw for herself.

But as Samir had them in stitches with his impressions of his supervisors, she was reminded that she had missed them too: the ritual of regularly meeting, eating Thai food, reminiscing about school and university, watching movies and going out dancing. Over the years, they had grown apart several times, amassing different tastes, experiences and politics. But, like strangers at a party, the rotation of the world, of people, had its way of reuniting them.

'What about you? Any movement on the relationship front?' Maryam asked then.

Movement. Maryam thought of little else. As if them all following the template of settling down with partners and children was essential to the life that she envisaged for herself. Jamila shook her head.

Maryam stared through her. 'Really? You've not met anyone you've liked at all?'

'Do the men in my gym count?' She pictured their huge chests and pencil-thin calves. They pawed at one another while working out, posed and took photographs, their movements charged with eros. Most evenings, she was the only woman in the gym, aside from the diminutive hijabi who occasionally visited with her much larger husband. Even then, it was no place to meet someone. It was a wildlife documentary – a safari – and she watched with bemusement.

'Have you heard from—' Maryam began.

'Zak? Last I saw he was hiking around Vancouver with some blonde.' As expected, he had seen but not replied to that message of hers. Then the pictures appeared on social media, the two of them arm in arm, cheek to cheek, impossibly perfect. Jamila had choked on her devastation and found the clarity to block him.

'Do you wish you'd—'

'Actually, can we change the subject?' It still hurt to think about him. Not even one tiny response to her message? Jamila caught the waitress's attention for a drink.

Maryam and Samir weren't convinced by her answers about relationships. Again and again, they circled back to the topic like they could coax something more from her. Soon, it began to grate. She was not tiny, thin and passive. She had never commanded male attention like either of them. Even the ones that did approach her either assumed that she had no ambitions beyond her degree or was betrothed to a cousin in Pakistan. It was being overlooked at university that had made her withdraw from love in the first instance and place no value on beauty but invest it all on her mind.

It occurred to her that neither Samir nor Maryam had ever remedied this by setting her up, not even in these last three years of singlehood, and they had plenty of friends. In fact, Zak, an aberration, had happened on a night when neither of them were around. And yet, rekindling these friendships struck her as a step forward. There was no denying the work she had to do, but old friendships were vigils to the past – and perhaps torchbearers of the future she wanted.

She finished her workout and prepared to go home. She planned to shower and eat, read and sleep. But walking towards her car outside, a white van caught her attention. It drove steadily along the main road, billboards stuck to either side of it. *In the UK illegally? GO HOME OR FACE ARREST. Text Home to 78070*. She watched it disappearing around a corner and onto the nearby estate.

Thirteen

Sadia

He always packed his bag for work. This Sadia established early on in their marriage. A culture of dependence she would not feed, could not risk him becoming one of *those* Pakistani men, the ones they all knew – the ones who needed their wives to wipe their backsides.

She blamed mothers. Women that bred insatiable little emperors. Wives spent their lives trying to beat it out of them. But when Akbar's mother discovered him in the kitchen one day, standing over bread and baingan bharta – with Sadia watching him put this lunch together – she was left counting her victories.

Glossy, crimson nails shielded her mother-in-law's petrified mouth – 'Ha Allah, yeh kya ho raha hai?' – before she elbowed him aside and took over.

From then on, Mummy's boy strapped her lunches to him. His rucksack high on his back – sat so high, strapped so tight, Sadia could have sworn he was waiting for the bus, ready to attend school again.

He always walked to work. Sometimes they left the house together. From the very beginning, that walk betrayed him. In that empty face and those unburdened shoulders, in eyes and feet he barely lifted from the ground, Akbar revealed his absence from this world.

In those early days, Sadia found reasons. In those early days, she understood. Perhaps he prefers another world, she told herself. The world inside his head. But, as time passed, that walk symbolised all that she despised about him. How it exposed his wish to disappear, even when they were together. How he failed to see beauty even when she stood right in front of him.

This was not a forced marriage. She was not taken to Pakistan, divested of her agency, her passport held hostage until she agreed. Akbar did not choose her, nor did her parents choose him. The decision was all hers.

Did he remember when they first met in Lahore? The day Akbar bundled into her home with his parents and extended family in tow? Uncles, sisters, grandparents – everybody wanted to be consulted. The air grew heavy, but air tended to become that way when futures were subject to negotiation. Did he recall – as their families chatted after lunch – his mother suggested she and he talk in private?

Sadia stared at her father.

'Why don't you go next door?' he suggested. 'Ask all the questions you've got. It's you two spending the rest of your lives together, not us.'

A sympathetic laugh fluttered around the room.

She was no fool. She knew what she was supposed to do. Gawp meekly at the carpet and defer all questions to him. And maybe she'd have considered it had Akbar been different. Those first minutes alone, he was as still as a tomb. He looked past her towards the television, as if a programme reached out to him from beyond the black screen.

Sadia took advantage. She stared him up and down, twice, three times – four times for completion. Her gaze was as thick as it was brazen – it had to be: he had withdrawn his – and it permitted a thorough examination. Of his full lips, his quivering expressions, the space his body took on the sofa. Of his strong nose, heavy jawline, the delicate brow-bone. How tightly interlocked were his fingers, how broad his shoulders, how sweet the little paunch. When he finally felt the weight of her scrutiny, a scarlet flush travelled up his neck to his forehead and she observed it with pleasure – the way a cat tortures its prey, clawing at it, then letting it run, only to trap it once again.

There in that room they were to knit and loop the first stitches of their life together. But they could not fashion stitches from his reserve. She stared right at him when she spoke, willing him to meet her there. Her chest thumped as she adopted an abrasive tone. 'Don't be expecting me to sacrifice my career for you. Whatever happens, I'll keep on working after marriage.'

She waited for his eyes. They fell to the floor. His face remained there, pinned, even when he replied, 'I have no objection. I will do my best to make you happy.'

Everything sounded better in Urdu. In this poetic, majestic language, his statement sounded romantic and profound and deferential. And it was enough. All that she held in her hands as they walked back was a promise that in English sounded trite. So much rested on this perception of his kindness, dignity and deference; in the way he nervously sucked in air after he had said this; in just an impression that she had of him. Sadia threw back the door to find their families strung together in delicate unity.

Her father asked if they were happy to be married.

'Ji haan,' he said slowly.

She moved her head ever so slightly to indicate her assent.

He was a lawyer, they told her. They said he had an MBA. So, months after their wedding ceremony, when Akbar joined Sadia in Manchester from Pakistan, his seamless slotting in at another immigration firm made her ribs ache with pleasure, at how their life could grow and blossom. She joked about viewing the firm as her rival, but he spoke of it with such awe. He clearly believed it was some sort of sanctuary, a holy shrine where the disenchanted came to transform their lives. His boss, Mustafa was its shaman.

She insisted that they visit each other's work. Honestly, she wanted him to know what she did there. With this knowledge, she hoped to grow closer to him. Did Akbar remember his first visit to Shah & Co.? How he pottered behind her, on a tour that ended at her station? Hers was the reception desk, a fortress of paper files curved round the perimeter. That day, Mrs Shah had been too busy to offer more than a terse greeting.

She hadn't liked what he had seen then – seen through an outsider's gaze. The office was small and untidy. Every empty space had something crammed into it: containers of archived files, copier paper, used printer cartridges. The waiting area was permanently blockaded, with clients dribbling out the front door or over towards the toilet. Sadia found it stifling. But, begrudgingly, she came to acknowledge that there was also something beautiful in that dirty waiting room, where the dustbin overflowed. It was the chorus of hopeful voices chattering excitedly in different languages. Screams of delight came from Mrs Shah's office from clients who'd succeeded. When her devotees had failed, she promised to keep fighting. It was a temple. A Sunday school. A community centre. Akbar's reverence of his boss had been a mystery, but with time she understood: the work had a spiritual dimension. If Mustafa was a visionary, then Mrs Shah was too.

But, upon visiting Akbar's office, Sadia was blindsided to learn of his role. Sure, any role was better than none and, sure, Akbar had the space to operate at his own unique frequency. But a clerk's job wasn't the same as a lawyer's. He would never earn a lawyer's salary. It was admin, at the bottom – dispensable, trash. A cold feeling padded the hollow space inside, like somebody had taken her dreams and crushed them beneath their feet.

Every day after work, he ventured towards Shah & Co. to collect her. He hopped on the bus, couldn't drive. Said that his eyes wouldn't sit still, as if his vision was a naughty child.

Sadia pictured his body falling into the rhythm of the vehicle, plunging back to his natural state. His mind empty, his jaw slack.

Slipping out through his meaty lips, an inch of his tongue, resting, sunbathing. When she emerged from the double doors, she'd find him staring into the distance. She greeted him loudly and, without fail, he grabbed her bag and carried it.

On the bus home, or in cafés and restaurants, they spoke about their day. It had not been so easy to loosen that part of his mouth, the part that confessed the mundane. But Sadia was patient. She worked at it. She showed him the way. With her encouragement and example, he soon nurtured words in his mouth like they were pea shoots, tender and young, and she toiled in harvesting them.

'One client caused a scene today,' he once began. They sat nursing tea in the window of a café. Freelance workers jabbed at laptops. The air was perfumed with freshly ground coffee.

She reached forwards and prodded him. 'Acha, kya hua?'

'Kya bataoun, bas, she was shouting and screaming.'

'What was wrong with her?'

'Beysabr thi both. She walked in and wanted to be seen straight away. Itna shor machaa rahi thi and the reception was full of clients, so we just sent her through.'

'But why?'

'Mustafa asked us to. Said she was troubled. Distressed. Koi bimari hogi usko. But the clients got angry, so then we had another problem.'

'What was her story?'

At this point, he adopted a solemn expression. He removed his flat cap and wrung it. As he spoke, his eyes lost focus and Sadia knew he was surrendering to the woman's memories.

'. . . The local mafia demanded that she pay a tax for her market stall, but she couldn't afford it. When they came for the last time to get their money, they emptied her shelves, took her to the back and doused her with petrol . . . .'

On the rare occasions that Akbar shared such stories, she would wait for him to return from the places he'd been taken. Then she would slide her hand across the table – or along their legs if they were sitting on the bus – and encase his hand tightly within hers. They would stay like that, quiet and still, until he was ready to move again.

He walked with her to the front door of their home. They always crossed the threshold as one, but this portal stripped them – melted the glue that bound them – and they separated on the other side.

Akbar was pulled into the orbit of his family – the half that lived here in Britain. Sadia dashed to their bedroom. They remained divided like this for the rest of the night. Sadia developed a routine, peeling off her work clothes, scrubbing work debris from her face. She slipped downstairs and prepared something quick to eat. Curled up on the bed, she pushed food into her mouth, the television her companion.

He wasn't alone. He ate with his parents and sisters. She heard every crunch, every slurp, every smack of his lips. She heard his mother inserting herself into every part of his meal.

'Akbar, try the yoghurt. I made it at home.'

'Akbar, take another chapati. The one in your hands has gone cold.'

'Akbar, don't forget the aubergine pakoras.'

He barely looked up from his plate as he cautioned her: 'Ma, when I want something, I'll take it'.

Was his mother made of silicone, the way these warnings slid off her? A minute later, she would reach for the lassi jug, the salad plate, the pickle jar, and say with her head lopsided, her voice cotton-soft: 'Akbar, shall I give you some?'

A dull thwack on the table. Brows knitted as one. Akbar would turn to her and snarl, 'Ma. I just told you. I'll do it myself'. His voice reached up through the floorboards.

But his mother would snap back, 'How dare you talk to me like this? Who do you think you are? I only left your brothers behind because you couldn't manage without me.'

Sadia wondered if this was what she had to look forward to, his behaviour towards his mother an indication; if it was just a matter of time before he turned on her?

After dinner, they collected across sofas. Akbar and his parents and sisters sitting there shelling peanuts, peeling lychees, popping dry figs into one another's mouths. They whispered as they snacked, digesting meals with more food. Sadia yearned to join them, but by then she had learnt better. Should she traipse downstairs and pull open that door, a hush would descend, as one of them hurried to initiate another topic, another conversation, something to draw her to distraction. A second too late, however, for she had understood: this was a private family moment. Only when she peeled herself away did the chatter resume, and so those constricting silences she filled with more television and more texts to her friends.

Get back downstairs. Sit among them, you idiot, her schoolfriend Khadijah once instructed.

What's the point? I've tried too many times.

He would sidle in near midnight. Their room was dim. A solitary circle of light pooled against the far wall. She had fallen asleep, her body pushed to the end of the bed, holding herself together.

But she woke up then and tracked his movements with half an eye. How he changed into tracksuit bottoms and an old T-shirt, and gingerly folded the outfit just worn. How he strolled to the bathroom, brushed and flossed, and returned with water dripping from his chin. Sadia's secret vantage point left her dizzy, failing only when he slipped into bed beside her and reached for her shoulder – always her shoulder, not her arm, her foot, her waist – pulling her back into his orbit. She could even have timed it.

Beneath this, she knew, lay contentment with the order of things. The way he saw life arranged into boxes, one per occasion, never to be opened otherwise. He'd enter, open the box labelled 'lover' and become eager, devoted. She watched him transform, a gem beneath light. His face, round, full, dimpled, glowed like the moon. There were times when exhaustion owned her body, and she would take him in her hand. In the mornings, she'd push him to the bathroom ahead of her and bring that hand to her face, taking in the salty, sweaty fragrance implanted on the webbing between her thumb and forefinger, where she had held him firmly, when her fears seemed weightless. On other occasions, he would fall beneath the sheets without prompting. A shiver would sink through her, like she was continents becoming one again.

Across the world, societies demand that women sacrifice. Pakistani culture is no different. When marrying, women are taught to sever ties with their past. Sadia never questioned this – saw no reason to. If anything, it warmed her heart. To marry, as other women married, to invest as other women invested, to sip and dip into milk and honey as the women around her, she was merely following a lineage. But the idea that Akbar's home was hers forever and the one in which she grew up in now foreign, this caused her hopes to wither.

Yet, she tried. She believed. Sadia moved in with his parents before the henna on her hands had faded. The months before his arrival from Pakistan, she hoped to spend building relationships with her new family. Fidelity would bring her closer to her mother-in-law, solidarity with her sisters-in-law. Her father-in-law would cherish her like a daughter, so that if ever Akbar tried to oppress her, Sadia would have a champion.

Indispensable, that's what she decided to be. And there were so many components. There was assuming responsibility for his mother's healthcare. Speaking to his brothers in Pakistan every week. Watching the Pakistani news with his father, shaking their fists at the state's political and moral decay. Devoted to his sisters, she took them for facials and lunch, sometimes a Bollywood movie at the weekend. Each time, she thrust her credit card forward. Each time, she took the hit.

They prepared Akbar's visa paperwork together. She kept at it, even after his application failed three times and she was left wondering how the clients at work managed with being told that their marriages weren't 'genuine' enough. If she hadn't met the financial criteria, he'd never have made it to this country. But long after the gloss on their nikahnama had scuffed, Sadia went to his mother and handed her a cup of tea. 'I've been feeling really homesick lately. Ammi Abu ki boht yaad aati hai. Can I go visit them?'

It was a humid August afternoon. Akbar's mother took Sadia's hand. 'I used to get like this too, especially in the early days. Stay for as long as you like, my dear. I'll never stop you.'

Akbar – Sadia's thoughtful, chivalrous Akbar – accompanied her on the bus. Every gentle graze of his body sent an onerous charge racing through her. She snuck glances at his full belly and hollow eyes, weighing everything that he had given her against all that he could not. When Sadia shut the door to her parents' house, she announced a decision that nobody would reverse: she wouldn't go back.

Two nights of tumult. Her father fought; her mother secretly gave her support. In the cold shock of her childhood room and its single bed, sleeping without him for the first time in months, demons feasted on her emotions. She hankered for his solid form lying next to her. But what was the point when she would only have access to half of him?

Finally, when her father grew weary, Sadia dialled Akbar's number. She hung up before it rang, alternating between the living room, the kitchen, her bedroom, leafing through their wedding photographs, eating whatever she thought would loosen her throat.

'Akbar, it's me.'

'Sadia, kaisi ho tum? How are your mum and dad?'

Her pounding heart skipped. That disembodied voice – a voice that did its best to hide so many insecurities – she couldn't pretend it meant nothing to her. Her stomach was collapsing in on itself, but she pushed on. 'Akbar, I'm not coming home.'

She breathed in deeply. Relief was coming, she knew it. The secret that was stuck there, jabbing away from the inside, she could feel it subsiding.

'Do you want some more days with them?'

'No. I'm not coming back. At all.'

'Never?'

'I can't live in that house anymore.'

'But what happened? What did I do?'

'Akbar, just leave me alone.'

'Please, tell me. Maine kya kiya?'

She hung up, tears wetting her kameez.

Later, he lay on her bed and tried to describe it. Inside him, a bell had tolled. Solid and unrelenting, it tolled and faded, tolled and faded again. He had to do something before it was too late.

Akbar had leapt up the stairs, taking two at a time. Into the open mouth of a purple case he threw shirts, knitwear, underwear. The rest can wait, he thought, the rest he would come back for. Five words, he hummed, five words his momentum: I need to be there.

He stood opposite Sadia's house, jaundiced beneath the light of a lamppost. From the darkness of her bedroom, she peered at him in surprise. The last thing she had expected was for him to turn up here. Her thrashing heart revealed its hand, but Akbar, washed out by that yellow sea, was inscrutable.

Was he worried about community? Did he fear the emasculating power of their words, if they learned he was to become a ghar-jamai, a man who lived with his in-laws? As he stood there, was he weighing up the pros and cons, calculating if she was worth it – or was it a question of courage?

He pushed past the gate and knocked on their door. Her father went to open it. Sadia ran down the stairs and slipped in behind him.

'What do you want?'

'Uh . . . Sadia . . . '

That was all it took. Her father's shoulders rose to his ears, but she arranged her fingers along his collarbone. 'Abu, just let him in. Send him upstairs.'

When the gap opened up and Akbar took those heavy-footed steps inside, did he turn back from the front door to consider the opportunity of that endless black sky, which still offered to wrap him up in its protective cloak and transport him back to security?

He sat on the bed, every inch the bride anxiously awaiting her wedding night. Sadia recalled their first meeting. This time, she decided to handle things differently. She positioned herself in front of him, hands on her hips, a pose she could have held until dawn.

Akbar lifted his head to find her. 'I am here to take you home.'

'Akbar, that isn't my home.'

Silence. Then: 'I will stay wherever you choose.'

'Well, my place is here. This is where I want to be.' A rush of emotion pumped through her, much of it new, but sweet and addictive, and it led her towards him. She stroked the back of his head, the short hairs soft. He took her hand and sat her down beside him. Her arm cradled his neck, her head on his shoulder, his hand sneaking around her waist. He pushed her back and she lay with him in this state of entanglement.

Over the next few weeks, Sadia wondered if a change of environment, of focus, of circumstances could be the palate cleanser necessary. They moved to a flat of their own. It was far from his parents, in Hulme, but a short walk from hers. It had two generous bedrooms and a dinky alcove for a kitchen. When they moved in, the entire building had smelled of damp and old people, so she floated through the rooms waving sticks of agarbatti. She used her savings to buy furniture. She started cooking again. In that space – on a street lined with trees and children riding bicycles until dark – she cautiously allowed her hopes to unfurl, petal by petal, digit by digit, minute by minute. The longer it lasted, the more she allowed herself to believe that he could still bloom into the model husband.

'If this marriage has a future, Akbar, it's going to need a lot more from you. Take responsibility for yourself, for us. Could you pay to run this household without my help? Could you provide for your kids if we had them? These are things you need to think about.'

She had him leave Mustafa's office. Working there made him complacent, would get them nowhere, and it terrified her to think he would never aspire to better.

But he tried. She could see he was giving it everything. In the evenings, he waited tables at the local Indian. By day, he made applications for positions she had bookmarked. These were jobs befitting his status, jobs that suited his skills. She scoured for employers that wanted degrees in law and business, which offered hefty benefits and scope for career progression. He took on positions in factories, supermarkets, warehouses, lasting no longer than a few days each.

On weekends, he woke near midday. They stole hours in Salford Quays before work hauled him in. They walked along the canals and squinted at their metallic shimmer. They laughed as their hair danced, puppeteered by the wind. They admired the Imperial War Museum, the aluminium shark – a sharp fin jutting out of the graceful slope of its back. Occasionally – just occasionally – they held hands, shy fumbling with what other couples found so instinctive. She would think that she loved him.

One Saturday morning in January, a pure-white light beamed into their bedroom. Sadia lay back on the bed, watching the rise and fall of her stomach, then glanced out of the window, the trees shuddering as a violent gust ran through them. Akbar slid out and into the bathroom.

She contemplated the changing state of their street. During the late spring and summer, the parallel rows of trees that went back as far as the horizon would birth a verdant emerald canopy. Her heart shivered with joy whenever she stumbled upon these streets as a child, where she could walk beneath the meeting place – the point at which the branches and leaves converged from both sides.

On that particular day, though they were deep in the throes of winter, the image was no less arresting. She saw trees that defied seasons, their arms full and golden, stubbornly clutching fistfuls of leaves. Light shone through the intricate weaving of branches and stems, black and blue and green and gold. She spied trees that were naked – spindly black shadows against the endless white sky. Their coiling black forms possessed a quiet, elegant dignity. It was the knowledge that spring would return soon. Even with the trees that were some place in between – semi-dressed, balding – wherever she looked, there were – even on days that were cloudy and grey and wet – reasons to be hopeful. If only she felt the same.

She threw back the covers and slowly got up, making their bed, straightening their sheets, each task rendered more cumbersome by her growing belly. Akbar's clothes smelled oily, of karela stuffed with mincemeat – the meal she had cooked the night before. She dumped the clothes in the laundry basket and made her way to the kitchen.

It was not that things became clearer – they were never clear and, in the messy aftermath, clarity was a thing that kept on slipping through her fingertips. Even now, Sadia returned to that period in their lives and contemplated the virtue of her decisions. Those decisions were like the Pennines – peaks that surrounded her, but remained a fuzzy shadow on the horizon. She hoped to get there, one day, to the summit of all knowledge.

Akbar came back from a late shift one night to find his suitcase sitting in the hallway.

'What's this, Sadia? Mera bag udhar kyun hai?'

She clutched another bag in her hands. It landed by his feet. 'Go back to your parents.'

'But why? What have I done?'

'Kuch nahin. You've done absolutely nothing, and that's why you need to leave.'

Hot air tumbled out of his body. But, as with all things, he accepted this new turn. He lifted his bag, pulled the handle from his case and shrugged out of the door.

In the days, weeks after, her mother and father fielded phone calls – those trying to smooth over this temporary bump, and those seeking information of who'd done what to whom and why and how, and what would happen next. Relatives phoned with bouncy, mischievous voices, claiming that Akbar's parents had only sought this match because they wanted him closer to them in Britain. Now, with his visa secured, they could marry him off as they pleased. She didn't listen to gossiping families that organised like government ministries and tried to control what she could do. It was over. There could be no amnesty, of that she was adamant, despite her parents' pleading. There would be no more compromise.

She came too, the last person Sadia had expected to see – Mrs Shah perched on her doorstep, dressed in a cheap salwar suit, looking like she had no right to be there.

'His parents asked you to come, didn't they?' They were her family friends.

Jamila fiddled with her dupatta. 'Uh . . . no?'

For as long as Sadia could remember, Jamila's father had been a leader in their community. People had flocked to him with all sorts of marital problems. Her father was careful with this responsibility, had honed his wisdom over many years, but, when Jamila took over the office, she began offering her half-baked opinions to anyone who would listen. Sadia would accept no such thing.

She let Jamila in. They sat in the lounge, drinking tea.

'I wanted to talk about Akbar,' Jamila began.

'You're not married, are you?' Sadia asked.

'No—'

'And you've never been married before, have you?'

'No—'

'So why do you think you can come here and lecture me now?'

Jamila's cup rattled against her saucer. A few moments later, she tried again, caution in her voice, but also a good deal more determination. 'But I was in a relationship, you know. People think

I'm frigid, but it lasted a good eight months. His name was Zak, Zakariya. He had a beard and tattoos. We met at a heavy metal night in town.'

'You, a metal head?' Sadia almost laughed in derision. There was no way that Jamila went clubbing, just as it was categorically impossible that she had found a man to want her.

'He was a socialist and he'd take me along to his protests and meetings. We'd hide away in galleries and museums and talk for hours. He'd tell me that I was wasted in my job and could do just about anything else.'

'What was wrong with him then?' Surely he was as defective as Akbar.

'I look back now and think my parents would have been fine with him. They would have loved that he was an engineer and fluent in Urdu. But when Zak started talking about meeting each other's families – when he said that he wanted marriage and children and to emigrate to Canada and have me join him there – I shut it down. My parents needed me. I was afraid of being a frivolous person in their eyes. The office needed me. The work felt important and made me noble. I couldn't have nice things. I regret that now.'

Jamila closed her eyes. She looked as though she was pouring that regret into a bathtub and forcing herself to lay in it. Sadia was too stunned by what she had heard to respond. The story clashed with the frosty image she had conjured of her boss in her mind.

'I'm sorry if I annoyed you by turning up here,' Jamila said. 'They asked me to come, but I wanted to see if you're okay too. And if I can share anything it's this: so much of life begins with an act of imagination, then a conjuring, and I let mine fail me. I was afraid of the work involved. I don't want you to make the same mistake. Akbar is a good man—'

'But good is not enough. You know his abilities.' Jamila had gotten him the job at Mustafa's.

Jamila bit her lip. 'And that's okay too, to know the work demanded of you in a relationship and reject it. Everybody wants to have it all, but it's always women who are expected to give more up. Only you know the level of self-sacrifice involved.'

'Too much. I can't anymore. I won't.'

'Then I'm on your side.'

Sadia took this strange encounter as licence to press on with her separation. She grieved through her mother's cooking, in rice and meat and cakes and, oddly enough, in the vegetable curries – karela and tori – that Akbar adored so much. It was a strange mourning ritual, seeking the kitchen's grace, weaning herself off him with every meal. She couldn't quite understand it.

The calls stopped eventually. That was when the divorce papers fell onto their doormat, when Sadia made it clear to Akbar's family that she was not playing. In May, she gave birth to their daughter. He paced the length of the corridor outside her delivery room, waiting for news. His parents sat there too, moving their lips in prayer. Sadia let him choose her name. He settled on Maliha. It was an act of contrition.

At some point, when her visitors had gone, Sadia sat up and looked around. The hospital ward was huge. Nearly all the women still had their partners sitting beside them. Only she lay there alone. It was then that she felt this great wellspring of despair, like the walls were coming for her, would close in and squash her – like she had done everything wrong.

That's when she snuck in. Mrs Shah. Five minutes before visiting hours ended.

'Why are you looking so sad?' She took the baby and sat down.

'It's just . . . ' Sadia sniffled. She couldn't begin to articulate her fears, how ill-equipped she suddenly felt.

'Chin up, you're going to be fine.' Jamila played with Maliha, lifted her up and whispered to her like they were co-conspirators. 'I'll be glad when you're ready to return to work, we're run ragged without you.'

Sadia looked over and encountered something surprising: a softening in Jamila's armour as she held the baby, an interior unbolting – a change so slight and imperceptible that even Jamila herself may not have recognised and certainly would have fought to deny.

Sadia smiled and glanced outside at the bright blue sky, thinking about unwrapping her daughter's fists later and searching for her luck line. She wanted to believe that Maliha's life would be better than hers. She wanted to believe that her choices would be different. She pictured that life laid out before her now, a life without interference, without sacrifice, without compromise. In a sunny room filled with fruit and flowers that was easy to imagine for a while.

Fourteen

Once they were home, Jamila continued to visit Sadia and the baby. Sometimes, she arrived at Sadia's flat with two pieces of a pie she had baked the night before. Other times, it was some quickly made pasta. She held the baby and drank tea while Sadia took the chance to nap or shower and, when she returned, they ate together and talked.

'How are things with Akbar?' Jamila asked on one such evening.

'He's coming round to see Maliha tomorrow.'

'How are you feeling about everything?'

Sadia cast a long, pained glance towards the kitchen. 'I'm glad he's not here. I might be alone, but at least I'm not so stuck anymore,' she said. Something resembling peacefulness settled on her face.

'You're so lucky to be in that headspace. To find things difficult but have no regrets. I have so many regrets,' she said, thinking of how Zak continued to haunt her, despite her attempts to dislodge him from her thoughts.

'But you never really decided, love. Those decisions were about pleasing everyone else. Maybe it's time to make some new decisions. Ones that are totally for yourself.'

Those words stayed with Jamila. In the aftermath of the ending of something treasured, it was somehow too easy to live with regret. It took greater courage to accept pain as an inevitable consequence of living and to strike forwards anyway – only making better decisions this time.

She continued to think about this when she returned to her office after lunch one Monday afternoon to find guests already waiting inside.

'He saw it too,' the first guest said, cracking a monkey nut between his teeth. 'The van.'

She stopped at the door. 'The "Go Home" van?'

Her father was sitting on the other side of her desk with his best friend Saeed. They were shelling monkey nuts and tossing the kernels into their mouths. On the back bench a young man stooped over his phone. He had what looked like a playing card tattooed on the back of his right hand. His black shoulder-length hair fell in perfect waves – Jamila could never get hers to look so good – and obscured his face.

Her father hadn't been to the office since December. After their argument, he had refused to speak to her until she apologised for her disrespect and, despite her mother's mediation, insisted on playing the victim. She ignored his demands and used his absence from the office to press on with her mission instead.

'Not on our street, but the main road, yes. We saw the van a few times,' Saeed said.

Shortly after, Saeed had caught his restaurant staff whispering in the kitchen. Some had their papers already and wouldn't be intimidated. Some were still waiting. Some talked in quieter voices of leaving for Paris, Hamburg or Vienna, where they had relatives, where conditions weren't as hostile. Where it wouldn't take as long to become legal.

'So did I.' But since her parents shared everything, her father obviously knew that. She hadn't stopped smarting over what she had seen, an image it had taken her a while to absorb: a uniformed officer, the Home Office logo, a pink fleshy hand clutching silver handcuffs.

106 arrests last week in your area.

GO HOME OR FACE ARREST.

Her apprehension had grown tendrils. They climbed her organs as she sat before her laptop that evening trying to find out more. Was it a private enterprise or the start of a new draconian policy? Though she found nothing online, the words sat in the air, stinking of fish, repeating in her ears even as she turned up the sound on the television. Go home? Home wasn't an answer, a destination – it was the start of a question.

'If all my staff leave, I don't blame them,' Saeed said.

'No, it shouldn't come to that. If I can help—'

Her father interrupted. 'Well, your uncle didn't come to chat. He needs you.'

For Saeed, she bowed her head. 'Sure, Dad. Anything.' Across the desk, her father and Saeed had built little mounds from their dimpled peanut shells. Red silk skins clung to their shirts. Dust sprinkled their jackets. 'What state have you left my floor in?' she asked, handing her father the dustbin.

'It's fine.' He took the bin and grinned. A glimpse of his old self. A glimpse into what perhaps lay unsaid on his tongue. She returned his smile and continued smiling, even after he had stopped. 'Listen, we've come about the boy. It's a citizenship case,' he said.

Saeed glanced over his shoulder. 'This is my nephew, Khalil.'

Jamila wondered if her father would stay for lunch. She had roasted some chicken if he wanted it. There was more than enough for two. One smile and she had half forgiven him.

Khalil raised his head. She took a good look at him. He was handsome, a facsimile of his uncle. They had the same narrow forehead, the same high cheekbones – though Saeed's cheeks had begun to slacken and sag like a dog's ears – the same full, rounded lips. They shared the same absentminded tendency, she noticed, to hide their top lip beneath their bottom.

Jamila reached for her notebook and a pen. 'How old are you, Khalil?'

'He's twenty-one,' Saeed said.

'What's your immigration status?'

'He has indefinite leave to remain. We were refugees. I came from Afghanistan in the early eighties, after the Russian invasion, then my sister came afterwards, through Pakistan, when the boy's father died in the civil war. His mother suffered too much for him.' There was a note of pride in Saeed's voice that gave Jamila pause.

'And Khalil?' she asked.

'He stayed in Peshawar until he was five.'

She jotted this down, as her father took over. 'I told them it was a simple, straightforward case. Khalil has indefinite, his mother had asylum, he's spent most of his life in this country. No reason to worry.'

Was he showing off? Definitely. Before a best friend, she recognised the impulse. But then he shifted into Punjabi, crossing his legs and sighing: 'Your consultation takes so long, no wonder you're always tired. Look at me, I can diagnose a problem like this.' He clicked his fingers to an urgent rhythm.

The comment stung. Saeed and Khalil were primarily Pashto speakers, but had they understood? Jamila stopped writing and stared at her father. She considered a piquant retort to remind him: he couldn't be this familiar, they had not yet reconciled. But there were outsiders present. Watching. If she reacted, he would only add it to his list of grievances against her and he deserved no such gift.

Instead, she dissolved her smile and focused on proving him wrong. All her questions were directed at Khalil, and all were answered by Saeed. (Would somebody, please, let the boy speak?) He was an unremarkable child with a stutter. He had performed badly at school. But a foundation year in science had been transformative. Something had clicked and he'd done well, securing a place to study Mechanical Engineering at Sheffield. He modelled part-time for fashion magazines.

The more Saeed talked the higher Khalil's phone moved from his lap. At one point, Jamila glanced over and saw that his face had been lost to it entirely, positioned so close the blue glow on his cheeks matched the dark bluish white of the sky outside. She considered ways to bring him into the conversation – he was, after all, the client – but her father jangled his keys in his pocket. 'What does all this have to do with anything?'

'I thought you told me every detail counts?' she asked innocently.

He spat out a piece of peanut skin and didn't respond.

Jamila pressed the side of her pen against her smiling lips. 'Anyway, the Home Office fee is £851, but, of course, my work will be for free . . . ' She paused to let Saeed or Khalil dispute this.

'Thank you,' Saeed said, bowing his head.

'Sure, no problem.' That was probably the right thing to do. She hoisted a bulky red file into her lap, which was stuffed with guidance for clients, templates and monthly updates on immigration legislation. 'I'll give you a list of documents—'

'Your daddy already told us what to bring.'

Her father closed his eyes imperiously. 'Call your boys and start the application. No wastage of time, please.'

Nothing had changed with him at all.

Once more, she repressed the urge to say something, lifting her phone as he held court: 'And I already told them about their mistake. "This is a very big error, not to apply for citizenship earlier. Home Office policy is changing all the time. Who knows what can happen tomorrow?" Didn't I say, my good friend?'

He slapped Saeed's thigh, who laughed generously. 'Yes, sir. You did.'

She waited for Rubel to come and take them, ignoring the men, who were quiet now, aside from the odd fracture of a monkey nut.

'Your daddy's really proud, you know? He's always talking about you,' Saeed said.

Jamila smiled at Saeed, but avoided her father. His need to demonstrate his superiority was pathological. What wisdom did he have to offer here that she didn't? What was the point of this pride if he gave her no room to be?

Rubel's fingers tapped on the door. His suit jacket was all buttoned up, his shirt collar starched stiff, but there was an ease about the way he carried himself into the room, stroking the blank file in his hands. He nodded at her father, primed for an introduction.

Oh, to be so carefree and confident. 'Before we get the application started, is there anything I should know about your past? Any criminal convictions, any speeding tickets, any contact with the police?' Jamila asked.

'No, Jammu. He is completely clean,' her father said.

She looked past him to Khalil. 'It doesn't matter how slight or insignificant, is there anything you can think of?'

For a moment, Khalil stared blankly. Then he slowly shook his head.

Jamila hoped that this was the last she would see of her father in the office. Having facilitated an introduction for Khalil and Saeed, she prayed he would return to his life of long walks and lunch dates with her mother. It had taken all her strength not to react to his provocations. In diminishing her father in front of his friend, she would only end up diminishing herself.

But a week later, he was back. It was the last Tuesday in May. The mornings were still unsettled: occasionally mellow and bright, then cold, windy and wet. Jamila got to work early and gave the central heating a quick blast to heat the office up. Soon after, her father's voice resounded in reception – 'Good morning, friends!' – and he spent what felt like an eternity greeting and catching up with her clients. Then he strolled into the staff area and struck up a conversation with Rubel.

Like news of an infiltrating soldier, his presence disturbed her. What did he want? What was he saying? How dare he turn up like this. Seething, she pressed her ear against the door and tried in vain to counter-surveil. When he finally vanished into the kitchen, she logged the time he had spent distracting her staff.

Clients came and went. He fell out of her mind. She snatched spare moments to review the tabs saved on her phone. A railway arch for sale in Cheetham Hill, empty shops in a converted mill, the cost of a food truck and its associated licences. She continued to indulge her fantasy of starting a food business, of switching to an industry with much lower stakes.

Before lunch, there was a knock on the door. She swung back in her chair.

'Can I come in?'

She flipped her phone over. 'Sure, why not?'

'I just thought I might need your permission first.' There was trouble in her father's eyes and a sly curling of his lip. He carted in a mug full to the brim with tea and sat on the back bench, his left arm stretching along the windowsill.

She said nothing of the proprietorial way he sat. Instead, she waved a packet of garibaldis from her drawer.

He leapt at them, then, catching himself, retreated. 'It's cold outside, no?' he asked, his demeanour cool.

Jamila coached herself in silence. There was no duty to speak, no need to further a conversation. He was the one who had arrived without warning. She tried to enjoy the upper hand.

'Everything okay?'

She nodded, biting her lip.

'Good.'

'Good,' she said. 'You?'

'Of course.'

He sipped his tea and glanced out of the window. Pressure inflated a castle inside her. She grabbed Rubel's letter and started reading. But her father's slurping soon invaded her thoughts, his cinnamon scent coating her nostrils, his judgmental stare like a hand on her head. She needed to know the purpose of his visit, or, better still, have him leave without saying anything at all.

'Have you sent Khalil's application then?'

She looked up. 'No, not yet—'

The cordial, almost ingratiating expression on his face transformed into a snarl. Hair that was tucked behind his ears came loose and shook like a mane. 'This is my best friend's nephew. They are counting on me. Why don't you understand?'

It aroused something inside her. Something yellow-eyed and trumpet-nosed, something slimy, scaly and green, something that had been gliding beneath the surface all this time. She snapped her teeth. 'Yes, I get it, I'm not an idiot. But some things need to be finalised. Would you prefer that I sent it before it's ready?'

'Why is it taking so long then? I know why, you're always closing early and lazying about at home. I would have finalised it already.' He said it with such distaste, it was like she had to abandon herself to be successful, worthy – good in his eyes. She had to put in the hours that he had, treat life as something to be lived for others, like he had.

'Why would you say that?' It was a familiar line of attack, but she couldn't believe that he was pursuing it after their last big conversation.

'It's my friend's case,' he said indignantly.

But she knew the real answer – every decision that she made in her life undermined the decisions he had made in his. She raked her fingers through her hair. 'I can't believe you sometimes. I never ask for much, but you? Take take take. Assume that I owe you everything. Even my free time.'

'You didn't ask because I gave you everything. You're so outspoken with me now because of how I raised you.'

'No, Dad. You raised us to listen to you. Be obedient to you. Both of you did.' Jamila swallowed hard. The volume of her voice had steadily risen. But so what if her staff were walking past her window to catch what was happening inside? She was no more than a receptacle of his dreams; not a daughter, but an heir – an automaton built only to serve the needs of his empire. 'I never learnt to give myself what I needed. Not for one second could I think—'

'And what did we give ourselves, eh? Everything we did was for you two. Maybe if you had a family – a husband, a child – you would forget these silly ideas you have. You wouldn't be so selfish.'

She stifled a scream. 'Selfish? But I am married, Dad! I ended up marrying your business. And I gave up something for that. Someone – I gave up someone really important to me because of you.'

He stopped as he was about to drink from his mug. 'What? Who?' He studied her.

Jamila's voice dropped. Unadorned, the truth pierced her chest. She had to speak quickly, bury the issue to stop her father from reading her face. 'It doesn't matter. Someone. The point is, I'm a woman, Dad. You might have forgotten. You had Mum dealing with everything at home, but what will marriage solve for me? What will it give me but more work, more expectations? You have no idea.'

Her father volleyed her words back with a hand, like they were too much to process. Then, a moment later, he nodded. 'Okay, fine. Come for dinner and we'll talk.'

'You won't disappear on one of your walks again?'

He had done it every time her mother invited her to dinner. Getting up as soon as she arrived, pouting and waving from the front door, no matter the weather. Her mother would call behind him, 'How long can someone stay angry at their daughter? I'm telling you again, stop this. You're a grown man.'

It was a blow in the beginning. His refusal to address what lay at the base of their quarrel left her wondering what her grandmother had eaten while pregnant to give him such stubborn blood. But, as with all mistreatment, the longer their disregard of one another dragged on, the easier it became to endure. Her mother maintained that he would fall out of this, so Jamila continued visiting for meals and bumped past him whenever he passed her in the hall.

There was a knock on her office door. An ecstatic-looking face appeared in the crack, then bounded in laughing. 'Salam, Mrs Shah, Mr Shah.'

It was like the sun had entered the room.

'Nazish,' Jamila brightened and sat up. 'Come in, sit down. Such brilliant news, no?'

'You fought for me, Mrs Shah,' Nazish said.

'We did this together.'

'All I did was cause you problems.'

'Both of you were patient and worked hard,' her father said.

Suddenly, he was smiling the kind of smile that had been missing from his face. A smile that she had missed on a cellular level. Jamila glanced at them both and absorbed how tenderly they were looking back at her. 'Honestly, this was such an important case to me. I won't forget it,' she said, her throat filling with emotion. This was much more than a case: she had watched Nazish fight to live life on her own terms.

Her father offered to photocopy the documents and give them some time together.

'There's quite a bit to do now. Call social services and apply for your National Insurance number, start looking for a place to live. You have twenty-eight days in your asylum accommodation before you must vacate. A refugee organisation might help you to find somewhere—'

'My support group is already helping me,' Nazish said.

When Jamila handed the visa to her, Nazish kissed it and held it to her chest. 'I can start my life again, Mrs Shah. Finally, I can live. I can do anything I want and stop being afraid.' Her voice quivered.

Jamila passed her a tissue, which Nazish took with a shaky hand, and brought one to her own eyes. It was why she did this work. 'Have you decided what you'll do next?'

Nazish sniffled. 'No.'

'Well, you might not want to – this place probably isn't good enough, given your experience of teaching at university – but I do need someone to control my front desk. It's only maternity cover, but I've had four agency receptionists quit on me. Four. I really could do with someone reliable.'

Nazish looked like she had emerged from a wreckage.

'I mean, you don't have to. But it could give you some stability. And if you liked it and progressed, we could talk about—'

Nazish grabbed her hands. 'No, Mrs Shah. I want to, I want to. I was just thinking, I can't believe. So many of my friends told me that time after grant of visa is like climbing out of one cave and falling into another. But you saved me. Again.'

Jamila felt herself blush. 'No, it was God.'

Her father returned with the documents, which Nazish placed in her backpack before leaving to share the news with her grandmother.

'I'll call you about a start date.' Jamila waved goodbye, then fought the urge to move on. An almost impossible case won. She wanted to hoard this success like an expensive ointment, massage it slowly into her skin, prolong the ritual of it. Each of their meetings uncoiled in her mind. Nazish was one of the toughest, smartest, most startling people she had ever encountered – tough but emotional, completely one of a kind – and yet her real challenge was only just beginning. As colleagues, she hoped some of that nerve would rub off.

Her father took his place on the back bench again. 'You look very happy.'

'I am,' she said, smiling broadly.

'And what was that about a "start date"?'

'I offered Nazish a job.'

He lurched forward. 'You did what?'

'I need a receptionist.'

'But you don't know anything about her.'

'What do I need to know? She's capable, determined—'

'You don't even know if she can type.'

She slid forwards in her chair to meet his gaze. 'Could Sadia type when you hired her? No. I was there. She'd barely finished school. But all you knew was that she was your friend's daughter and you had promised to give her a shot.' The day Jamila took her concerns about Sadia's inability to type or construct even the most basic letter to her father, he had dismissed her and told her to train Sadia herself. She had held it against them both ever since.

He assumed a slow, condescending tone. 'I'm trying to help you. There's so much you don't know about running a business.'

'But you could just let me learn. You could just let me do things my way. And if I make mistakes—'

'I should let you destroy what I killed myself to build? One complaint from the regulator and you'll come running to me faster than a djinn's fart.' He snorted with laughter.

Heat bounded off her cheeks. 'Oh, really? But I thought you wanted me to succeed you? I thought you didn't trust anyone who wasn't family? If you can't let me run this office my way, maybe you should find a replacement, or, better still, do it yourself. Or, you know what, maybe I'll sell it – everything is in my name, after all. That would be fun, wouldn't it?' She gave him a sadistic glare.

'You're crazy.' He shook his head, looking like he wanted nothing more to do with her.

'Oh, no, I'm very serious, Dad. You promised Mum that you would change. All this time, I believed that you were trying. But you're the same as you've always been. So now you decide: either you go from here, or I do.' She meant it. She would disappear. If there wasn't a room in her life that was hers and hers alone, she was better off withdrawing from it entirely.

Fifteen

Her father fled the office like a lion fleeing a stotting gazelle. The image amused her: his bent spine, shocked face, white-knuckled grip of the door handle. The sad jangle she caught of the nuts in his pocket. But with their argument rebounding in her ears, she stilled herself. Her father hadn't responded to her threat to sell the office and leave, but it didn't matter. He had retreated.

And as the sun's presence in the sky stabilised, gently baking the city, Jamila used this retreat to continue expanding her life as she had been. Over the next few weeks, she closed early and headed to the gym, met Maryam and Samir for dinners, visited Sadia and the baby, and sat with herself at home and worked through the books on her shelf. Nazish became a part of her social life too, over hot chocolates and walks across Tandle Hill and Holcombe Moor, agreeing to never speak about work. Every minute, every evening to herself – every plan that went fulfilled – was a victory, a resistance against her father's demands. As though the cord that bound her to him had begun to slacken.

Then, one dreary Wednesday in June, Khalil turned up. As Rubel unearthed the file she had allowed herself to forget, she was curious as to why he had come unchaperoned – though not enough to let him jump the queue and mess up her system.

'All right, so I think it was August last year when it happened. I'd just got my foundation year results back. In a couple of weeks, me and my mates were heading to different universities. We wanted to go out one last time. We hit the bars in the Printworks that Saturday night, about ten, maybe fifteen of us from the same year in college, and a few from the year below. We had a fair bit to drink. We didn't think we'd see each other for a while, so everybody kept buying rounds.

'About eleven o'clock, we headed to a club in Deansgate Locks. Missoula, you might have heard of it? We spent the rest of the night there, drinking, smoking, dancing. Inside, this girl I'd liked for ages finally got with me. Then, at about three in the morning, we decided to leave together and sneak her into mine. We went outside for a taxi when some girls in the smoking bit started on us.

'"Get a load of them, smooching over there. Look at her, kissing that Aladdin. Little Sinbad the Sailor." Then one of them then called over, "Get a room, you two. You're disgusting."

'I was wearing my embroidered waskat with a T-shirt and jeans. My girlfriend, Hannah – yeah, she's my girlfriend now – told them to go fuck themselves, but things kicked off. Suddenly, they were screaming, pushing the barriers, which weren't even that high, only up to their waists or so. Of course, we shouted back. We were drunk, we didn't know what we were doing. And I'm not going to let somebody talk to me like that in front of a girl I like. Then one of them took it too far. Started calling me a camel rider, pretending to speak fake Arabic while riding one, or whatever. She climbed over the fence and got right in my face. She knew what she was doing. She wouldn't stop, and her friends just stood there laughing. At some point, I lost control and slapped her. It got to me, I guess. And, like I said, it didn't help that I was absolutely hammered.

'But it turned out there were police nearby. Her friend went and got them involved, accusing me of threatening and beating them. I told them my side of the story, and they gave us all a warning and told us to go home. Me and my girlfriend ended the night sobering up in a takeaway. I couldn't get over what had happened. I felt like I was the one who had been slapped. But Hannah told me to forget about it, so I tried. I never heard from the police again.'

Jamila's mind started droning like an old computer, converting the sounds she had heard into units of meaning. Khalil was striking. Cedar-smelling. His hair had been scraped back into a greasy ponytail and several loose strands framed his face. It had been a surprise to hear his voice too, which was tremulous and breathy to start. But, as he talked, it grew deeper, a rasp adding to what was already clear and appealing.

'It's been on my mind ever since you asked if there was anything, uh, criminal' – he squirmed as he said it – 'about my past.'

A part of her wished that she hadn't asked and didn't need to. But she did. In the last twelve months, the immigration rules had changed, ramping up restrictions on who could work, who could appeal, who could rent a house; how long they could live here, which tests they had to pass, which walls to climb. Fines and sanctions if the restrictions were broken, the forms had tripled in size and so had the work – when each form took hours to complete was it any wonder that the job had bested her? The aim of all of this, according to authorities, was to create a 'hostile environment' for illegal immigrants. Deter them from coming over or wanting to stay. It meant that aspiring citizens had to confess their sins in the application forms and hope that a twenty-year-old caseworker, trained for all of three weeks, believed that they were worthy of redemption. A speeding ticket? A parking fine? Crimes against humanity? The state needed to know.

For Jamila, it was a promotion of sorts, albeit one she had never asked for. Like a court judge she was expected to sort between good and bad, the right and the wrong sort of immigrant – who had the right to make an application and who didn't. She had to determine whether Khalil (who had never been an 'illegal' immigrant) met the criteria for citizenship – criteria that rested on good behaviour. But who was she to draw the line on what was 'good'?

Khalil stared expectantly. Dust motes travelled through the air, their presence illuminated by the clouds breaking and sunlight forcing its way into the room. Jamila tried to formulate a response.

'So, you actually hit this girl?'

He winced. 'Slapped – yes. But I wouldn't call her a girl. She was older than me. In her late twenties, at least.'

'All the same, you're a grown man.'

'You make me sound like an abuser.'

She glanced down at her notes, chastened. He was quick. She reminded herself to act like a good solicitor and examine the story from all angles, like a rabbit gripped by the ears – this was the professional thing to do – before deciding upon a course of action.

She looked at him again.

He didn't seem particularly remorseful.

She was in her late twenties too.

Khalil's backpack rustled as it slipped down his knees. He picked it up and leant forwards, at an angle, his shoulder and backpack aimed at her like a rifle. 'Go on, what would you have done?'

His directness jarred against the courtesy she expected from him. This was, after all, their first proper conversation. He had given no indication of bad manners at their first meeting. 'In the same situation?' Not that. Anything but that, no matter how loud and provocative the girls had gotten. 'I would have walked away.'

'I thought a lawyer like you would understand the power of their words.'

She shook her head at his naivety. It wasn't that she underestimated how deeply words could wound, but that she had been raised by parents who distrusted the world, parents who knew that, when choosing to react, they always had much more to lose. It was why, to this day, she was nervy when out until the early hours. At weekends, the city centre was a tinderbox, patrolled by drunk young men itching to fight. Her brown skin and feminine frame marked her out as easy prey, even with Samir promising to protect her. But Khalil didn't understand this – or maybe now he did, but couldn't admit it.

'I wasn't thinking, okay? One minute she's humiliating me in front of Hannah and the next minute she's holding her cheek. I've never gotten into trouble before. I'm not that kind of person,' he said.

She believed him – his eyes were as clear as cellophane – but a measure of disquiet remained.

'We should probably discuss this with your family,' she said.

A curtain of surprise swept over his face. 'You think it'll hurt my case?'

Maybe it needed to, given what he had done, for Jamila to continue believing in the existence of justice. An eye for an eye, especially when David fought Goliath. 'I think it would be useful to get their take on this.' She could make it their problem – her father's problem, despite not wanting him back. She could let them make the essential decisions in this case while she focused on staying well.

Khalil dug up the grit in his voice. 'No. You saw what my uncle was like. I want to deal with this myself. Speak for myself.'

She paused to consider him. This, despite her reservations, she understood. Wanting to be treated like an adult. Responsible for your own destiny. 'Do something for me, then. Visit your local police station, see what they have on you.'

His mouth fell open. 'But it wasn't that serious! The policewoman said it was a verbal warning. It wouldn't appear on my record, no one would know . . . ' He scrambled to his feet. 'Do we need to tell the Home Office? Maybe we don't tell them.' For such a lofty, broad-chested young man, he looked small.

Jamila closed up like a sea mollusc. She didn't want to share her thoughts with him, hadn't settled on representing him. 'I'm not saying that it's serious. I just can't submit your application until I've seen the documents. Bring me whatever the police have, and we'll take it from there.' That would buy her some time to decide.

Khalil lifted his backpack and lumbered out. His shiny, scared-looking face guilted her, but it was also easy to let him leave. He had hit a woman. With all his male strength. She couldn't excuse that. He was, in effect, her father's charge. She wouldn't do it, didn't have the bandwidth to deal with Khalil and all these new complexities. She would say no, like she had done with Babar. No, this time to her father.

And yet, in quiet moments, over successive days, a dilemma cloaked her. Though she felt uneasy about what Khalil had done, there was no precedent here, no reported case and, critically, no suggestion that he had broken the law or disrespected Britain. All she had was the guidance that she loaded and re-read several times: *To be of good character you should have shown respect for the rights and freedoms of the United Kingdom, observe its laws and fulfilled your duties and obligations as a resident of the United Kingdom. Checks will be carried out to ensure that the information you give is correct.*

During client consultations, she found herself scrutinising the questions on the form. No, Khalil didn't have any convictions. No, he was not a terrorist or a war criminal. He had slapped a girl while drunk, but there was no space in the form for this—

'Are you even listening, Mrs Shah?'

'Huh?' She looked up.

Hassan was staring at her, ears red, nostrils flaring. A crisp-crunching little girl sat shocked beside him. 'I'm talking to you about my appeal. Have you heard anything? It's been months.'

Jamila bit her lip. 'Sorry, Hassan, I'll send the courts a stern reminder today.'

Hassan muttered darkly to himself.

In the evenings at home, with Bertha writhing in her lap, Jamila weighed the case, its moral complexity and connection to her father against the hostile policy and muddy guidance. On the one hand, she appreciated Khalil's desire to step outside his family's realm of influence, but, on the other, she worried that his case would undo her attempt to step outside of hers. When she smelled smoke billowing from her cooker as she researched another part of his case – the chicken sizzling like a lump of coal in a barbeque – she realised she had to do something. The dilemma was threatening to envelop her entirely.

Sixteen

Saturday afternoon. There was so much to do. She had a talent for clutter and none for domesticity. Armed with a duster and some antibacterial cleaner, Jamila went from room to room, dusting and spraying and, later, wiping.

Expectations were high, even if they were mostly her own. She still had no idea what her friends made of her. After their first reunion, though she had always been busy and aloof, they now seemed to consider her a bad person for it. She continued to meet them anyway, suggesting dates for dinner, coffee and movies. Some of their old camaraderie returned, but it rarely felt as easy as being around Sadia or Nazish. Whenever Samir and Maryam brought up events from when she was absorbed in her own problems, she was left watching and smiling inanely, and wondering if the gaps that had opened between them were simply too great to close.

And yet, with her heavy metal radio station yowling over the vacuum cleaner, rising like a ball of hair twisting up its pipe was a wish to host the perfect evening, in the perfect setting, to please her friends and try to make up for her absence anyway.

She was easily distracted. In the bathroom, she cleaned the toilet, then deemed it essential to scrub the black mould growing between the shower tiles. In the living room, she sorted through stacks of post and treaded time by revisiting the Thank You cards she had brought home and never filed away. She grew distressed at the bad, vegetal smell coming the kitchen and emptied the recycling bin, one hand beneath the heavy compostable bag, fingers wet with juice, worrying that the smell would remain, an uninvited but overbearing guest.

When she looked at the clock, it was almost 5pm. Samir and Maryam were arriving in an hour. No time to shower or cook as she had planned, but just enough to assemble a dessert out of some cream, fruit and madeira cake, then pick up a takeaway.

Outside, the city was beautiful. The sun shone, trees were silhouetted by magpies, buddleias waved their honeyed scent. Jamila rushed to the shops and wondered what she could have achieved with a better use of her time.

The takeaway order she had called through was ready. She grabbed it and popped into the newsagent for milk. By the fridges, the community noticeboard had flyers about Qigong lessons for the over seventies, a missing ginger tabby named Squeak and a course on hydroponics, but it was another flyer that caught her attention:

106 ARRESTS LAST WEEK IN YOUR AREA.
Text Home to 78070.

She ripped it off and balled it into her pocket.

Samir and Maryam were waiting in the driveway, holding limp bags of popcorn, thick slabs of chocolate and wine. There was a fullness to Samir's embrace – a warm 'mmm' sound escaped his mouth as his hand moved in circles on her back. Maryam's hug barely classed as one. She clasped Jamila's arms and kissed the air.

Samir wrinkled his nose as he passed through the hallway. 'Your place is a bit rough and ready, isn't it? Smells like my nan's bathroom.'

'It's a work in progress,' Jamila said, her smile fixed but flattening. She shouldn't have used Jahida's rose diffuser.

'It was a work in progress back when you were thinking of buying it.'

But the progress was visible to her – really. She had bought the most beautiful velvet sofa with a scalloped back, then uprooted the carpet to discover floorboards that only needed a little sanding. The walls bore a tiger stripe of her swatches – Paeony, Poppy, Terrapotta, Sunstar – though the colours weren't siblings, not even cousins, since Jamila couldn't decide on an aesthetic that represented her. Stripped-back and minimalist? Dark and cocooning? Contemporary and eclectic? She could make a case for each one.

'You're serving very chaotic energy right now,' Samir said upon viewing the lounge.

'Sure, Samir. Tell me about my dark chakras.'

'Oh, yes. Very dark, very disturbing. Muddy colours everywhere.'

Maryam protested. 'Come on, Samir. She's doing a lot better now.'

'No, you're right, but I can't help what I see. I see an absence of solar colours. I see negative energy, depleted energy.' He turned his mouth downwards, like a sad party clown.

'Well, you should have seen me six months ago.' And with a short laugh that ended too abruptly, Jamila retrieved the plates, glasses, cutlery and juice that she had left on the kitchen counter. Kneeling by the coffee table, she smarted from the comments and questioned whether inviting Samir had been a mistake – he was always too forthcoming with his opinions – before opening the containers of food.

'Don't listen to him, na. This place has loads of potential.' Maryam shoved Samir, who looked at her as if he had done nothing wrong. 'Your kitchen is amazing.'

Jamila looked up and smiled. 'When did we ever listen to him?'

Maryam laughed.

Buoyed by that moment of solidarity, Jamila filled their plates. She returned to the kitchen for napkins and soy sauce, bowls for the popcorn and crisps, Jaffa cakes. Sweat pearled her brow. A shift in scenarios, but serving people all the same – it was where she felt at home.

'This is good,' Maryam said.

'Really good,' Samir said.

'How's work?'

She remembered the flyer. Jamila teased it from her pocket, smoothed it out against her thigh and placed it on the coffee table. They edged forwards to get a look.

'What the—' said Samir.

'Where did you find it?' Maryam asked.

'At the newsagents,' Jamila said.

'In your area?'

'On the community noticeboard.'

Samir shook his head in astonishment. 'I can't believe they're rounding people up and deporting them. They're fleeing for their lives, for God's sake, just leave them alone.'

'Yeah, but they're not all innocent, are they? Some of them are criminals hiding away, some of them aren't even real refugees,' Maryam said.

Jamila caught Maryam looking at her. For what, approval? This early into her evening, she gave it to her. 'I suppose that's true. The idea that all immigrants are victims is just as dehumanising as assuming they're liars and criminals. They're good, bad and ugly, just like the rest of us.'

'How do you feel about it all?' Samir asked.

Jamila sat back to absorb the scale of the question. 'I don't know . . . They've always done this, it's just the tactic of billboards and flyers that's new. And of course I agree, it's crass and invasive, but is that the only reason we're angry? That it's become all too public?' Not for the first time, she thought about how strange borders were. For fear that she might find herself complicit in their enforcement, she had rarely considered them in much depth. The idea of drawing lines across land, some completely arbitrarily, of containing some people and shutting others out. The idea that one person could say to another, 'No, you cannot live here,' when who among us owned the land we live on − truly owned it outright? And who was responsible for the wealth and stability attached to it?

She remembered Khalil then, and decided to share his case, careful to omit any identifying details.

Samir shrugged upon learning of the slap. 'Well, you can't blame him, can you?'

'Can't you?' Maryam twisted her torso around to confront him.

'Maybe I'd do the same if someone was racist to me.'

'Are you serious? What he did was disgusting. He's a woman beater.'

Jamila observed her friends. Samir was composed enough, but Maryam looked distraught, like she had felt the full force of the slap herself. They both stared at her, waiting for her to arbitrate, but Jamila empathised with both of their views. She didn't want to align herself with either.

'Do you know that I hit a boy once?' she said eventually. 'Back in primary school – Maryam, it was before you joined us, I think. Whenever I played football with the boys, there was one who would call me a girl, a sissy, and insist that I wasn't good enough to play with them. One day I got sick of him. When I missed a shot at goal and he berated me for kicking like a girl, I went over and punched his nose.'

Samir was dousing his plate with soy sauce. 'What? I don't remember that at all.'

'I didn't like being called a girl. He ran away bleeding.' A smile formed on her lips, though the incident had been traumatic. Not only was she suspended from school, spoiling her perfect attendance record, but her parents had taken away her comic books and video games. It had taught her a valuable lesson about justice, she realised then. Justice that you clawed for yourself when the world refused to hand it to you.

'Haan, but that was a boy, Jam. Your dude hit a girl. A girl. You can't be thinking of representing him,' Maryam said.

'Because that would violate the laws of feminism or something?' Jamila asked with a dry laugh. 'He made a mistake. Even the most prolific serial killer has the right to a lawyer. It's how the system works.'

Maryam glanced down at the coffee table. Her pale face had grown increasingly coral coloured. Jamila and Samir's eyes met. They had always known that Maryam was different from them. She came from posh Karachi stock and moved over at the age of eleven, when her father invested in a chain of British discount stores. Her experience of Pakistan was filled with tales of boating clubs and barbeques on private beaches, whereas theirs were of playing cricket in the fields next to their ancestral villages. But Jamila hadn't anticipated this turn in their conversation.

They weren't silent for long when Maryam spoke again, her lips pinched, badly negotiating her noodles with a spoon and fork. 'Sorry, but I don't accept this. Hitting a girl is not right. I can't believe you're going to help him.'

It would have been too easy to steamroll Maryam when Jamila argued for a living, but Jamila didn't want to do that to her friend, not when she was trying to get closer to her. She bit her lip and summoned patience. 'Would you feel the same if he'd hit a guy?'

'Well, no, because—'

'Or a girl hitting another girl?'

'But that's not—'

'Would you feel the same if he was white?'

Maryam's dewy face creased. 'Why do you guys always bring that up? Race has nothing to do with it.'

Jamila didn't want to talk about race, didn't want it to spoil her evening, but race had everything to do with it. Race was what structured the system. It was what decided whose presence was secure in this country and whose was precarious. 'He's British in everything but name, Maryam. He just doesn't have the certificate.'

'All I'm saying is, if you're going to live in this country, you've got to follow its rules and norms. And if he can't do that then maybe he should leave?'

'It's the rules of any country, Maryam. That stuff is universal,' Samir said quietly.

'Well, if it was up to me, I'd deport him.'

'What?'

Maryam repeated herself, with guttural force. 'I'd send him back, I would.'

Jamila couldn't believe what she was hearing. Maryam's politics had always been on the conservative side, but this? She felt the veins in her neck engorge. 'What the hell are you on about? You can't just bin a person off—'

'This is getting too heated now, let's talk about something else,' Samir said quickly. He rotated his lip piercing like worry beads.

But Jamila couldn't forget it and move on. Maryam needed to know. If Khalil had been French, Canadian or Australian, she would never have argued for his deportation. They were not the sorts of 'foreign criminals' that were splashed across the covers of newspapers, linked to rising crime rates and accused of making our streets unsafe. There were no walls built to keep them out.

'Fine, but first let me thank Maryam for her help. I was leaning towards not taking on this case, but you've just made up my mind for me that I will.' Jamila stared defiantly at Maryam, who was drinking from her cup, looking everywhere but at her friend. Maryam was the kind of girl who considered purple an unlucky colour. The kind of girl who could tell the difference between Waitrose and Tesco's chicken. The kind of girl who mused that 'Some things you just can't say anymore'. Jamila assured herself that Maryam's opinion on Khalil didn't matter. Except, with resignation and despair, she knew that it did. Because there were so many Maryams in this country. Maryams with votes and opinions, with convictions, however wrong, that had to be appeased.

'So that was weird?' said Samir, once Maryam had left.

This was why she wasn't allowed to talk about work. Everybody had an opinion. If strangers weren't rebuking her for representing people they disapproved of, then they were patting her shoulder in sympathy at the kinds of stories that she took home. Jamila had invited her friends over to forget about her dilemma, then driven them into a collision with it. How stupid. What a disaster.

Something came over her. She lobbed her laptop at Samir.

'Go on then, work your magic like you promised.'

He eyed her. 'Are you sure?'

She sank into the soft flesh of her armchair. 'I'm allowing it.'

'You do have a lot to offer someone, you know.'

She frowned. 'I know.'

'Maybe you could find a nice Afghan warlord at work?'

'I value my practising certificate, thanks.' She didn't mention that she had caught some clients staring at her strangely, like she was a delicate, charismatic beauty, a jewel they had chanced upon at the bottom of the ocean. She had glowered at them at first, then traced the contours of her jawline, first in disbelief, then affirmation. 'Do you want to do this or not? I'm letting you.'

After university he had always suggested that she try online dating, but she had refused. It was desperate. She wanted to meet someone organically. Then, after a couple of 'organic' experiences, she had withdrawn from dating altogether. There was comfort in being unavailable to men. In filling the void with work and telling yourself that your time would come. Then Zak appeared and she thought that it had.

Now, just a few months from her thirtieth birthday, she was ready to try again.

Samir registered with the dating site, then selected a photograph from her meagre library of selfies. He typed a brief description of her interests (comics, baking, video games), profession (legal wench) and what she was looking for in a man (fun, with a side of commitment). Samir tossed the phone back for Jamila to admire his handiwork. 'Just don't be too picky, okay? I know you. Nothing and no one is ever quite right.'

Seventeen

It was something about the failure of that night in with her friends that had led her down the path of dating again, the desire to make some new decisions and build something that was completely for herself. An online profile made sense. Apps and websites contained wider pools of people, access to like-minded individuals from the comfort of her sofa – but she had forgotten that dating was like trekking through a forest full of goblins and trolls. Online, it was no different, only worse.

From the moment she joined, she was inundated with messages, shirtless torsos wanting one-night stands, faceless profiles that said 'hi' then cursed her when she didn't respond, overconfident young men that asked if she had fallen from a vending machine because she looked tasty. She began to worry she had made a wrong turn.

But, as she hovered over the leaving button, she received a message. Haris had a chipped incisor and a feathered fringe. A thick, muscley body, like her men at the gym. From their brief, but chaste conversation, she learned that he owned three mobile phone shops, had two sisters and collected anime figurines. When he asked her to dinner, she took those sisters as reason to agree.

She met him in Castlefield. He knew good restaurants and suggested a Jamaican on the banks of the ship canal, which had drawn her to the sound of eddying water, its dulsey odour, dining in the cool air. But, upon arriving, they were given a view of the kitchen.

'You look great,' he said, when they were seated.

'Yeah?' She had worn a little make-up and her good kurta, but she couldn't help feeling like one of his old model phones. Not ancient, not rusted, not worth so little as to be discarded. But sitting in a glass case, beneath a layer of dust, slow and missing several key functions. Nerves snaked around her stomach. What if there was nothing redemptive about her after all? She lowered her eyes: Haris filled his suit jacket nicely.

This was a man who worked with handfuls of cash. She saw from the way he had sauntered into the restaurant, his patent shoes squeaking on the polished tiles, fat silver chain clinking on his wrist. The scent of his expensive oud filled the room. Such flamboyant style wasn't to her taste, but with Samir's words in her ears, she tried to remain open.

'So, you're a lawyer?' Haris asked her. 'You must be really smart.'

She smiled. 'I'm a glorified form filler really.'

'Oh, I'm sure that's not true.' His eyes darted around the room.

'It is, I promise.' She found it easy to take this line. Her intelligence mentioned once, twice on those dates in her early twenties – not so much as a compliment but as an observation, and, later, as a reason not to take things further – and she had learnt to share less of herself. 'But taking apart and repairing phones, now that's a real skill.'

He nodded, as if it had never been acknowledged before. 'Hungry?'

'Sure.' She had already chosen the peppered steak.

'You've got to try the jerk chicken burgers, they're amazing.' And without a moment's delay he summoned a waitress and ordered them.

Jamila did a double take. Had he really ordered for her? Was this how men behaved these days? She thought of objecting but didn't trust herself. Perhaps he was genuinely excited to share the burgers with her. She followed the steak heading to another table, steam twining away from the plate, and quashed her unease. Meat was meat. Not at all worth spoiling the date over.

Haris watched her. 'Can I ask if you're practising?'

'Practising?' A practising solicitor, but he knew that.

'Muslim. Do you come from an observant family?'

She hadn't expected religion to come up so quickly. Maybe not even at this date. Between the holiday photos and references to windsurfing, he hadn't mentioned it on his profile. She slipped her hands beneath her thighs. 'What classes as observant to you?'

'You know. Namaz, roza. Is there dhikr in your house?'

Dhikr? Namaz? Her work was her worship. 'I've been on hajj if that counts. You?'

'Alhamdullilah. My shop is next door to a masjid so I can pray with the jamaat.'

'That's good, er . . . Masha'Allah. I wouldn't say I'm there yet.'

He edged forward. 'But do you think you will? Get there, I mean.'

She looked to the ceiling. She was happy with her faith, praying when it felt right, speaking to God in her own way. 'I . . . guess?'

The waitress returned with complimentary fritters. Jamila longed for her to stay – straighten their dishes or polish their cutlery – long enough to launch their conversation into another direction. His questioning felt invasive.

Haris resumed when the waitress left: 'The reason why I'm asking is because I want to raise my kids in the deen and obviously, so much of that rests on the mother.' He tipped his head towards her. 'So, if you knew that you'd get there, that would—'

'Woah, Haris. Slow down. Don't you want to get to know me?' She laughed awkwardly, though inside she was steaming. She didn't need to know much about dating to know that he had committed a cardinal sin. From his choice of religious teacher, for children that didn't even exist yet, she had learnt more than enough about him.

His head wobbled – the first and only indication of doubt. 'I thought I was getting to know you?'

'No, not the Muslim reproductive machine that you think I am. The real me.'

Jamila spent the next few days avoiding Haris's messages. Her instincts had been wrong: his sisters told her nothing about his values as a man. She promised to be more discerning the next time somebody invited her to dinner.

Instead of going out, she spent time at home after work. She baked and listened to music, then brought one of her efforts to the office one Monday in late July. Clients filled the reception, silhouettes pressed against the windows, peeking through cracks.

After Jummah, she portioned out fat slices for her staff. Since they were approaching the end of Nazish's second month working with them, Jamila had chosen the fragrance of clementines and the moistness of almonds because, whenever they went out on their walks, Nazish spoke of little else – everything led back to her grandmother's orange groves, her walnut trees; everything tasted superior when labelled *Produce of Pakistan*.

'How is it?' Jamila asked.

'Delicious,' Sadia said, who had returned from maternity leave that week, much earlier than planned, leaving Maliha with her grandmother. Rather than ending Nazish's employment, Jamila had seen it as an opening for Sadia, to move to the back and assist her with appeals.

'Mmmn,' Nazish said, poker-faced.

Jamila laughed at her. Nazish's letters were strewn with grammatical mistakes and, whenever she succumbed to her own dark thoughts, she forgot to answer the phones, but she presided over the reception like a personal fiefdom. Jamila heard her all day, her voice reaching the corners of the office:

'What I tell you on the phone? We're very busy today.'

'No, I didn't give you appointment. I would remember your voice.'

'Quick, I need water! She is having panic attack.'

Nazish was a strident, stabilising force at the reception. It helped that she wasn't at all concerned with complaints about her behaviour, which only made the clients respect her more. It left Jamila occasionally feeling green and wondering, was it because they recognised her as one of their own?

'How have you found this time with us?' Jamila asked.

'Fine. I'm happy.'

The levity in Nazish's voice lifted Jamila. 'Work is a good distraction, isn't it?' Not that she had ever used work to distract her from her terrible love life. At the end of the evening, she had informed Haris that there wouldn't be second date and walked away almost proud. She wasn't interested in a man with a modern appearance and prehistoric expectations, fixated on the children she wasn't sure she wanted. It felt liberating to have identified those traits early.

Babar and Rubel were late back from the mosque. She handed them their slices.

'Half of that, please,' Rubel said, rejecting his plate.

Babar elbowed Rubel. 'He's dieting, Mrs Shah. Trying to look smarter while he finds himself a wife.'

Babar had been in a sunnier mood of late. His appeal hearing had gone well, and he paraded around the office telling everybody how smart his solicitor was, how functional, how shrewdly she had answered the judge's questions. Gemma never answered her mobile when she was meeting with a client; Gemma never stayed in her office after five. Jamila felt like a dog at the dinner table, desperate for scraps.

'Is that right? You're looking for someone?' She prayed they weren't using the same dating website. If he stumbled across her profile, or worse still, matched, she would die.

Rubel grinned. 'It's God's wish.'

'Really? He communicated that to you directly?'

'He can say the same to you if you want, Mrs Shah.' He laughed.

'Actually, Mrs Shah, I never understand this. When you represented me, I was always wondering, what does she like? Boys or girls? Everything or nothing?' Nazish asked.

Jamila's smile disguised her irritation. It wasn't an especially novel question (everyone from Jahida to Samir had asked it already), nor did it offend her. But there was something about its entitlement, its claim to know who or what exactly powered her desire that didn't feel . . . right. Some rooms in her house were locked. Some rooms not everyone needed access to. Desire was a room that she had, at times in her life, treated as mythical. 'Boys,' she offered reluctantly. 'What made you think I didn't?'

Nazish's face softened. 'Your emotions, Mrs Shah, how you were with me . . . ' Then something shifted, as if she had woken up to realise exactly where she was standing, and that softness slipped away. 'You know, this is good cake. Give to me recipe so I can make at home.' Her voice was synthetic, her expression unrecognisable.

Jamila was confused. She wanted to take Nazish aside, ask what had happened. But then she noticed the slightest movement of Nazish's eyes, gesturing away from Sadia helping herself to more cake, towards the silence that surrounded them. The boys. They were signalling to one other and sharing some unspoken feeling. It was clear that they, too, had thoughts about Jamila's sexuality.

The idea of gossip at her expense stripped and exposed her. Unsure how to respond, Jamila clamped down on her teeth.

Nazish looked towards the waiting area and shrieked. 'No, Mrs Keshavarzi! It is not your turn. Somebody else is before you.'

The woman, who was about to enter Jamila's office, scowled and sat down again.

Nazish smiled smugly. 'See? All you needed was a strong hand.'

Jamila left her staff by the reception and returned to her office. The man who replaced Mrs Keshavarzi looked embarrassed to be standing there. Zulfikar Ali was a sturdy man, with thick sideburns and soiled hands. He had come to her recently on a recommendation. He skidded forward, stretched out his arms and passed her a folder. 'Will you check the documents I've gathered so far? Tell me honestly, are they enough to win?'

So much about this task made her cranky. The collective hours spent unfolding crumpled documents, flattening them, arranging them, reading them, when she had already told her clients what she required. She could have used that time more productively. And perhaps she would have outsourced this task to Rubel or Babar, except for the fact that Zulfikar's was no ordinary case. And his documents weren't the bank statements, bills and pay slips that her clients usually supplied her.

Zulfikar's folder was in perfect order. She went through it quickly, confidently, knowing exactly how to assess it. 'These pictures on Canal Street are fine. Not massively useful, but fine. Most people will tell you to submit them, but I think that anybody can go to a gay club, take a few pictures and grab a wristband. It's superficial. Do you know what I mean?'

'But my friend Kebiru said—'

'And I did his asylum too, remember? He might consider himself an expert now, but I know what you need and I won't steer you wrong. These pictures are fine, but as I said before, I want bigger, more impressive, harder for the Home Office to deny. Letters from your partner, your support group, your volunteering.' Every additional piece of evidence was an insurance against rejection. She pondered Nazish's question. It was true that she became incredibly invested in gay and lesbian asylum claims. Sexuality was a nebulous thing, almost impossible to prove. Her own sexuality felt nebulous too sometimes: constantly questioned; non-existent, for some, without the proof of a partner.

Zulfikar built himself up to say something. 'Kebiru said I should make some kind of—'

'Absolutely not.' She knew what he was going to say. 'We can win this without resorting to smut.'

'No, I don't want to make it. I really don't like the idea of a video, but . . . ' He produced a USB from his pocket. 'I made it already. It's me and my partner.'

She stood. 'What, why didn't you discuss it with me first?' She hadn't pegged him as the type to do such a thing.

'Kebiru says I will get my status quickly.'

'I'm not taking that USB.' She stared at it like it was radioactive.

He locked his fingers together. 'You don't understand, I have to listen to him. I owe him so much.'

She wanted to throttle Kebiru, warn him against meddling in her cases. But Nazish slid back the door and marched in lugging a stack of files. Jamila sat down and gestured to Zulfikar that they had not finished discussing this, and he nodded like he was under no illusions that they had.

'Don't look so angry with me,' he said, smiling.

'I'm not,' she replied through a frown.

How could she be angry? For years, she had submitted the intimate videos and pictures that her queer clients provided as evidence because, really, what good was having moral reservations when the clients with X-rated evidence were granted in two weeks and the ones without were left waiting years? She might have stopped upon learning of the problems with this approach, but she could understand Zulfikar. Authenticity was a luxury that some clients just didn't have.

Once she had placed the files on Jamila's desk, Nazish handed her an envelope and hovered by her ear. 'This one, uh, had no file.'

From the way that Nazish whispered, Jamila knew something was wrong.

'Just give me minute,' she said to Zulfikar. Her fingers trembled as she teased out the papers – just enough to spot the distinctive red and black logo of her regulators, just enough to see the word *COMPLAINT* written in a bold typeface. She shoved the papers back inside and re-sealed the tab.

The letter was a gut punch. Frustrated with the system, clients grumbled all the time, but she had never received a complaint about her service, not in the nineteen months that she had been in charge. What had they accused her of? What would the regulators put her through now? For crying out loud, she was never allowed to get comfortable – never allowed to rest before God returned to test her.

She wrenched her shoulders down from her ears and glanced inside at the pages again. His name was in the subject heading.

Hassan Khemiri.

The bad penny – her bad penny.

Was getting his revenge.

All colour had been leeched from the sky when Jamila left work and drove in the opposite direction to her route home. Beneath it, the city was stagnant. The streets were empty and the trees listless, the air thick and tarry. She wanted to carry on working, batter out a defence, but cancelling her engagement and staying behind was as good as accepting defeat, and she wouldn't let Hassan bring about another breakdown.

In the complaint, Hassan had accused her of faulty advice and of pursuing an appeal when he didn't want to. He alleged that she had overcharged him. She took it all like blows to the body. All those hours she had wasted entertaining his silly delusions; all those nights, how easily they were forgotten now.

Her hands hadn't stopped sweating since she received the news. Even now, in the car, she felt a sick tension in her limbs that wouldn't recede. Her first instinct was to reach for her father, draw upon his calming words. But fearing his shame and hectoring, she called her sister instead. 'Hello. Baj, are you free?'

Jahida's voice filtered through the speakers. 'It's not a great time, what's up?'

Jamila recited what she had memorised of the letter.

There was a delay, the baby babbling. 'And you're concerned with this because?'

'Um . . . I didn't do anything wrong?'

Hassan had been so confident before his appeal hearing. When she tried drilling him in the kinds of questions he would have to answer, he had stopped her and beat his chest. 'Why are you worried, Mrs Shah? This is my life. Mine. As soon as I start talking, the judge will stop everything to give me visa.'

'He fluffed almost every question at his hearing, baj,' Jamila said. 'When asked about his political awakening, he talked about his mother instead of his father, his recruitment into his political party and he mentioned protests on the streets instead of his friend, his role within the organisation, and he wittered on about being a dogsbody. When I summoned him in for an explanation, he sat there scratching his ears.'

'But you must deal with complaints all the time. It happens to everyone—'

'Not me. It doesn't happen to me.' She had taken her career seriously to avoid exactly these kinds of pitfalls. And now that it had happened, she was plagued by the thought that she should have been more careful.

'No, Jam. You might be a lawyer, but you're not that special. Can't you see that this isn't about you? The client is upset about losing and he's lashing out?'

'Yes, but—'

'But Dad was here the other day and he mentioned that you've been sitting on Uncle Saeed's case for months. I thought things were calmer now.'

So they were talking about her again – everybody always talking about her. Never respecting her enough to tell her directly. 'Actually, it's his nephew's case and I'm trying to iron out some problems.'

'What problems?'

'Problems that don't concern you,' Jamila said.

Jahida sighed wearily. 'You're not in court now, you don't have to fight me. But Dad said you threw him out of the office when he tried talking to you.'

Jamila honked at the car ahead. 'Are you serious? You believe that joker?'

'Don't call him a joker, he's our dad.'

Jamila cut the call. Her sister had this way of denying her. Dictating to her as her parents did. She slumped in her seat, flatlining. All she had wanted was a little encouragement, for somebody to reassure her and tell her there was no reason to be afraid.

The café in Didsbury soon came into view. She dawdled towards it and parked on a side street. Sitting in the car, she tried to revert to her old self, the spirited self, the self that didn't know a client hated her. What a moment to be going out on another date. It really would have been better to cancel.

She got out and started walking, revising the profile of the man she had been messaging for the past fortnight.

There were tables outside, on the uneven pavement, decorated with stubby unlit candles. Opposite, a group of Lycra-clad women walked to the church hall, yoga mats tucked under their arms. She noticed him sitting in the large window. She clenched her teeth. They had agreed to meet at the entrance. Now, she faced the additional strain of deciding on an approach. She worked up a smile as she covered the remaining distance.

He lifted his head, sensing her arrival. 'Jamila?' He stood.

'Irfan.' She shook his hand, conscious of the picked skin around her fingernails.

'Nice to meet you. I got out of work early, so I thought I'd come here and wait. Coffee?'

She glanced at his empty cup. 'Tea, but only if you're having another.'

'Of course, I'm in the mood for something herbal.'

She sat down as he strode over to the counter. He looked just as his picture suggested: tall and lean as a street cat, with thick brows and a square jaw. His hair was cropped close, skin visible around the crown. But it was his beautiful eyelashes that had caught her attention: long and spidery, with a natural curl. She breathed deeply as she recalled all the things she knew about him: he was forty years old, a primary school teacher. He liked to bike and play badminton, read and make pottery.

'Thank you,' she said, when he set her drink on the table.

'That's all right. Are you well?' He slotted himself into the chair opposite her.

'Yeah, good.' She spoke quickly, to avoid suggesting otherwise. 'You said you got let out of work early?'

'We've been rehearsing for our end-of-year assembly, so the kids were wiped by the afternoon. I let them watch a movie or nap . . . You're a lawyer, right?'

She nodded apprehensively, wondering where this was going.

'Our jobs are quite similar, you know.'

'Are they? I don't think I treat my clients to TV and naps on the carpet.'

He laughed and touched his throat, as if she had wounded him there. 'My work is very important, I'll have you know.'

'Yeah? How exactly?' She found herself smiling, despite how she had felt before.

'I'm teaching the future of this country. I'm shaping what kind of people they'll grow up to be—'

'So, if they turn out to be monsters, I can hold you responsible?'

'If one of your clients ends up in prison, can I do the same?'

She thought of Khalil then. She scratched her collarbone and searched for one last comeback. This was surprisingly fun. 'Ahhh, you got me,' she said, when the quickness she prized in herself let her down.

He leaned over the table. 'Well, that's good, because you'd feel terrible once you found out that I work with kids who have special educational needs, in one of the most deprived areas of the city. I advocate for people just like you do.'

She took a long look at his open, smiling face then, doing her best to resist the net of embarrassment sweeping over her. Her abrasive approach to the conversation had been partly masochistic, given the day she'd had at work, but also down to her impatience. Behind the genial veneer, she wondered if, like other men, he was brittle and sensitive, or had views that she would disapprove of. She preferred to know now and not waste her time. But, despite her prodding, he had matched and then trounced her. She was impressed.

In a strange way, the embarrassment relaxed her. 'So, what's the assembly about?'

'My kids are putting on a mini musical: *Little Red Riding Hood*. It's a chance to sing a few songs and blow some houses down,' he said.

'Oh, that'll be cute.' She brightened at the thought. 'How's it shaping up?'

'It's still, uh, getting there, shall we say?'

She found his pained laughter endearing. 'We did *The Lion King* when I was in year six.'

'Yeah, that might be a little bit advanced for my kids.'

'I played Nala.'

He smiled. 'Did you always get the lead role in the school play?'

'Never,' she said dramatically, to underscore how mistaken his image of her was. She had never been artistic or popular enough. 'That was an aberration. They usually had me narrating from the side.'

'I played a rat in the Christmas nativity,' he said, his eyes shining.

'A rat?' She laughed again.

'A pretty pivotal role. But then I tripped over my cape and forgot my line and retired from the stage soon after.'

She hadn't expected him to be funny – such things rarely translated in online messaging – but it encouraged her to keep talking.

'It's amazing how tightly we hold onto those moments. Being noticed enough to finally become Nala, I've never forgotten it,' she said, surprised by her own nostalgia.

'Being the main character, for once? The love interest?'

'Can it be both?' Their eyes met long enough for him to convey a flicker of mischief in his, before she looked away. She picked up the book he had left on the table and leafed through. *The Left Hand of Darkness*.

'Any good?' she asked.

'Oh, amazing. Do you know it?'

'I'm not nearly as well read as I wish I was, but I'm trying.'

'I can't believe it took me this long. Did you read the blurb? It's about this diplomat who works for an interstellar United Nations and he's sent to make connections with a previously unknown world. It's got stuff about gender, bodies, war, bureaucracy—'

She rolled her eyes. 'Oh, I know all about bureaucracy.'

'Oh, you might not like it then.'

'No, I'm going to check it out. You sell it so well, how could I not?'

'Now you're just taking the mick,' he said, with a sad shake of the head.

'I'm not!' she protested. 'You got quite passionate. It was nice.'

This time, the smile they exchanged lasted a little longer, encompassing some acknowledgement of the attraction growing between them.

He sipped his tea. 'Immigration. Is it particularly bureaucratic?'

'The worst. Ninety per cent is mindless paperwork – though today maybe not so much. Today was, um . . . ' she rummaged her tired, addled brain for the right word '. . . eventful. We celebrated my receptionist's second month at work. We use any little excuse to have a party – a new car, a driving test, a successful case – it keeps morale up. And, of course, our clients bring us food. We try to refuse, but they insist on doing it because they're happy and, in the process, it makes us feel good too. Appreciated.' Jamila couldn't help smiling to herself – those little parties were some of her happiest moments.

'I should drop in sometime. I only get coffee mugs and cheap boxes of chocolate.'

'Next time, I'll swap you.'

He sat up. 'A mug? Two? Seriously, I've got loads.'

She laughed. This was easy. His confidence unthreatening. It was a good idea to come. 'But yeah, this receptionist of ours – she's great, she's a handful. Got opinions about everything, but learning fast and it's nice to be part of that. But then I— I . . . had a more, uh, difficult situation.'

'Yeah?'

Her mind began to riot, trying to determine what was safe to share, what wouldn't alienate him or misrepresent her. If she was taking this seriously now, she had to be careful. 'My client is gay . . . ' Zulfikar – yes. She latched onto his story, looked better in that one. 'He's claiming asylum and wants to use a video of himself with his boyfriend as evidence.'

Irfan poured a spoonful of sugar into his cup. 'Wait, of them having sex? People do that?'

'They do, and it's annoying because it doesn't prove anything.'

'Only the lengths that people go to for their safety,' he said gravely, stirring his spoon. There was a pause as he contemplated this. 'And I'm guessing you have a problem with his proposal?'

'Well, more and more, the Home Office are asking for this material, so my clients feel like there's no other way to win. But it's degrading and we straights don't have to do it, and it pushes a narrow idea of sexuality and warps the evidentiary standards of the system.' She recalled the NGOs reports and hoped that she had represented them accurately.

'And yet, it's still his decision to make, I presume.'

'But it's my job to guide him. Protect him. He's a grown man, strong and self-sufficient, but I can see his vulnerability. I know what he came from, what it took to accept who he is.' She swayed with emotion.

'He's an adult though. Why can't he decide?'

'Because of all the things I just told you.' She heard the impatience bleed into her voice. Felt an origami of creases appearing in her face. 'Why don't you tell me about your school?'

But Irfan kept rubbing the grey hairs in his chin, like this was an issue she had charged him with solving. 'It seems to me like you're making an example of this person. You're trying to force some sort of communal response to one individual's problem.'

He waved a single digit in her face. The gall of that gesture, the naivety of his diagnosis, was all that it took to rile her. Nobody listened. Once again, she was being told that she was wrong. She leaned back and stared at him.

'How is this an individual problem?' she asked. 'Since when has a cultural or political issue only ever concerned one of us? You know that, you're a teacher. But look, let's talk about—'

'Sure, sure, but listen—'

'But what, Irfan?' she asked, with a jerk of her head. She tried to smile. 'You said yourself you don't know much about my job. Can we change the subject, please?'

Irfan fell dangerously quiet. She tried to recover things, asking him a question about his biking, then pottery. He gave her a couple of short answers and followed up with a query about her hobbies. But, though she did her best to answer him fully, the energy between them had shifted fundamentally. The conversation petered out. She made her excuses and left.

Eighteen

Zulfikar

Each time Zulfikar went to the Gay Village, he felt horses galloping in his chest. On previous visits he'd hidden among his acquaintances, but now he studied the crowd: men making eyes at each other, women holding one another's hips, purple lights streaking their faces and arms. They looked so unencumbered, doing what he had so often imagined for himself. His face grew hot.

Before they'd left home, Kebiru had snatched his baggy T-shirt from him ('Tsk, what's that ugly thing you're holding?'), pressed his favourite tie-dye shirt into Zulfikar's hands and sprayed his neck with CK1 ('The white boys won't know what hit them'). Now, Kebiru pointed to an older man in a light blue denim jacket, standing against the bar. 'That one,' he said.

Zulfikar cast a queasy glance across, then looked pleadingly at Kebiru. 'Do we have to?'

'Sister, if you want to settle in this country, you need someone to help you. A nice British daddy, accommodation included.' Kebiru winked.

'But I am happy alone.'

'Who is happy alone, Zulfi? Nobody's giving you asylum if you don't have a partner.'

They went up and pretended to select drinks from the bottles behind the bar, positioning themselves a table's length away.

Kebiru's eyes were dancing, and he bit his lip to stop giggling. How was Kebiru going to do this? The galloping horses returned.

Kebiru took his hand like they were making an oath. 'Now, remember. Smile. Keep your eyes on the prize.'

Zulfikar latched onto Kebiru's arm, who slipped away, lost in a river of sparkling light, back towards the dancefloor. Zulfikar's heart dropped into his stomach. Staring at the ground, he steadied his breathing. All he had to do was say hello.

The man was already watching. 'Your friend left you?' he asked.

Zulfikar tried to shake off the stench of desperation.

'Fancy some company? I'm Henry.' The man's trainers had split lips; Zulfikar pitied him while calculating that it made him more attainable.

'Zulfikar.'

'All by yourself here, you not much of a dancer?'

'Uh—'

'Can't be that difficult, can it? Swing one arm, then the other?' He mimed a series of exaggerated movements, like an inflatable dancing tube. 'First time?'

How much to share with this man, Zulfikar didn't know. There were no bars like this in Pakistan. He still hadn't found home in the words used to describe them both. Homosexual. Hum jins parast. Gay.

None of that seemed important now.

'Dinosaurs like me don't belong here either. But look at me, I keep coming back.' Henry twisted his face into a smile, but something painful floated beneath. Curiosity drew Zulfikar closer. 'Are you a student?' Henry asked.

'I used to work for a grocery shop.' Zulfikar said the first part quietly. Asylum seekers weren't allowed to work. Most days he drifted through streets, feeling like a bum.

'I'm a tram driver. Have been all my life.'

'Really?' Zulfikar knew of no happiness greater than looking out of a tram or train, travelling to some place he'd picked randomly from a map. The juddering motion passed through him and he smiled, thinking of his trips to the beach, but offered nothing more.

Henry emptied his beer, placed it on the bar. 'Well, that's me done.'

Soapy foam slid down the glass. Zulfikar felt his hopes turn to liquid. They were only just getting started. He hadn't yet asked the questions that Kebiru had coached him in. If he messed this up, Kebiru would be furious. But Henry stood still, watching the game of snooker to their left. A player leaned over the table, lined up a shot.

Henry's hand landed on his shoulder. 'You could come too?'

Zulfikar shuddered from the shock of his touch. A sour, beery smell steamed from his mouth. Henry had a bland face, a shaggy beard and an earring. But Zulfikar stared into his eyes and found something kind, even shy, in the way he was staring back.

He remembered Kebiru's warning. Without a partner, the Home Office wouldn't believe him.

Zulfikar was only eighteen when he left his village and moved to Lahore for university. Three years later, when he received a first-class degree in management science, his father announced that he was selling an eight-kanal plot of land. He wanted Zulfikar to study overseas, work and send money back home.

Zulfikar, who had been performing devotional poetry since he was a child, had listened to his father's plans and began dreaming of becoming a big man. A manager by day, a successful naat khawan at night. He would buy a tractor and field cultivator for his father, a flatscreen television for his mother. Success would come as easily as shaking the trees and collecting the notes gathered by his feet.

And when he arrived, England immediately seduced him. The air smelled of saffron and the tarmacked roads were like an immaculate carpet. Flashy stores sold shoes and perfumes and yellow gold and designer clothes. These things existed in Lahore too, tall shopping malls made of steel and glass, but here everything was cleaner, bigger and brighter.

Within a month, Zulfikar decided to never leave. He refused when his Manchester college lost its license and closed. He refused when no mosque considered him good enough to perform at their religious gatherings. He found a day job shifting pallets for a Pakistani grocer. At night, he delivered pizzas. He saved money and sent it home, nobody caring to ask how these sums had grown.

Lying in the dark at night, unspooling reel after reel of memories, images of his family jammed his throat. But there was one evening he returned to most. The time his friend Junaid had come over to his hostel in Lahore and they had eaten gobi gosht together before lying on Zulfikar's bed playing a video game. It involved a funny little man with a thick moustache, jumping from platform to platform, always falling in between.

When Junaid lost for the fourth time, he dropped the controller and turned to him. 'You know, I like you so much.'

Back then, Zulfikar hadn't heard the thin hope in Junaid's voice. 'I like you too,' he said, reloading the game. Junaid was generous, sharing his college notes and his mother's food. They spent most evenings together, gaming and eating, listening to Abida Parveen and singing along.

Zulfikar felt a hand grip his thigh. When he looked up, his gaze collided with the intense longing in Junaid's eyes. A tremor raced up his legs, charged his groin before dying out in his stomach. He sprung to his feet. 'What the hell are you doing?' he demanded, scrutinising the door, the windows, lowering his voice. 'I'm not . . . not . . . ' He ran into the bathroom and slammed the bolt. For fifteen minutes, he sat on the floor, his thighs convulsing. Junaid had been selfish, stupid, reckless. What if somebody had seen them? Then Zulfikar began to wonder . . . what if he had stayed? But when he came out, Junaid was gone.

Now he imagined that evening ending a hundred different ways.

Zulfikar sat in Henry's kitchen drinking tea. A month had passed since their initial meeting. Every week they met up, and every time

Henry tried to get inside his 'story', like his past was a chocolate bar that needed unwrapping. His story was broken, had no beginning or end. Zulfikar placated him with crumbs:

'Then, last December, after seven years like this, everything changed. The Home Office had a law against hiring illegal people. Fine of £10,000. Now they were raiding more businesses, catching more people. My bosses got scared and asked me to leave.'

'How did you manage?' Henry asked.

'My friends helped me a lot. One was telling me to marry a Pakistani woman for a visa. Eventually, I said, "No, I don't like women," so he told me about asylum.'

'Do your parents know you're gay?'

'They're village people.'

'People can surprise you. When I came out, it divided my lot. But I'd expected them all to reject me.'

Zulfikar pictured telling his family. Staring out into Henry's garden, he noticed the curved outline of a pond, dark and iridescent, like an oil spill. He wondered how deep it went.

No, he couldn't imagine their acceptance. Instead, he told Henry about his Home Office accommodation: 'The heating was broken and there were rats in the kitchen and something black growing on the wall. I was sharing a flat with six guys and they would laugh at me and steal my food, so one day I got angry and hit one of them—'

'Is that how you got the scar on your chin?'

Zulfikar's hand went up to it, rubbing as he frowned. 'Er . . . So then, Kebiru took me to his place—'

'And Kebiru's a friend, or . . . ?'

'He's my sister,' Zulfikar said firmly.

The concern on Henry's face evaporated. 'Well, you know, you could stay here if you want?' Henry lifted his mug and swigged with an air of affected nonchalance, but Zulfikar understood: the proposal had been planned.

'I can't,' he said. The Home Office hadn't asked for it; he barely knew the man.

Henry gripped his arm. 'Sure, you can. No point bothering your mate in his tiny flat when I've got this whole house to myself . . . I could use the company, to be honest. I'm rattling around on my own.' He smiled, but, once more, pain moved beneath the surface. There was nothing hidden in this man.

Outside, a red-breasted bird fought a brown one at the birdfeeder. Zulfikar glanced at Henry and then the house, searching for justification. Both were a little worn. Henry especially – he was gaunt and thin, with an uneven beard and patches of sunburn. A little attention would go a long way, something he could do for Henry in return.

'From my union campaigns, I know how hard it is for LGBT asylum seekers. I could be your partner. It doesn't have to be real – I mean, not unless you want it to be? But living in the same house would definitely help your case.'

This was true; Kebiru had told him so.

The night they first met, Henry had done nothing more than buy him chips and talk. Henry didn't ask for intimacy and Zulfikar didn't offer. Now, once more, Henry was providing something without expecting anything in return. Zulfikar looked up to the ceiling. If God hated people like them, why was He smiling down on him now?

Zulfikar moved in and got busy. While Henry was at work, he fixed the hinges on the kitchen cupboards, filled chips in the hallway plaster, tackled a leak in the bathroom. He bought meat, vegetables and spices, and began cooking meals for Henry.

One evening, a month later, Henry came home late from work. His face was pink; the thumb-shaped birthmark on his cheek uncovered by his new cleanshaven look. But he was quiet and looked tired, skin sagging beneath his eyes. Zulfikar led him into the living room.

'We had another person under the tram today. The driver couldn't stop shaking. I had to stay with him, take him home,' Henry said.

Zulfikar placed a hand on his arm. 'That's awful, Henry. Are you okay?' Riding with him in the driver's cabin, watching the suburbs race by, had impressed Zulfikar, but he had never expected the role to involve dealing with death. He couldn't imagine what that took out of him.

'Yes . . . no . . . I'm fine.' Henry drained his body of air.

Zulfikar guided him to the sofa.

'He was young . . . just a kid, really.'

'Do you know why he jumped?'

Henry shook his head.

Zulfikar shuffled his body closer. 'I'm so sorry. May he rest in peace.'

As Henry described the incident, Zulfikar grabbed a cushion and picked at loose threads. He wondered what had driven the boy to jump, whether he had ever considered the same escape himself. No. Yes. Maybe. The times he was so far from himself it felt easier to disappear. His memory stopped short of the rest.

They sat shoulder to shoulder until Zulfikar became aware of their knees gluing together. They were too close. He was giving Henry the wrong impression. He detached himself. 'You need to eat something. You must be hungry.' Zulfikar knew of no other way to soothe him. He'd never seen Henry so morose.

When Henry didn't respond, his eyes closed, head resting against the back of the sofa, Zulfikar went into the kitchen and started microwaving the salan.

Henry followed when the food had been laid out on the table, getting cold. 'I'm sorry. I shouldn't be bringing this stuff home and loading it onto you.'

Zulfikar smiled across the dining table. 'No, I'm here to listen.'

Henry's eyes were red, as if he had been ripped from sleep. He stretched his lips in appreciation. 'What did you do today?'

'I went jogging in the park.' Whenever he was active, Zulfikar felt a small circle of peace growing inside him. 'Afterwards, I went with Kebiru to see my solicitor. We've almost finished the statement. She booked my screening interview.'

'When will she need the stuff from me?'

'Soon. Next month maybe?'

'No problem, I'm on it.' Henry surveyed the table, his smile growing wider. 'You'll have to stop spoiling me . . . but maybe not yet . . . what's this one called? It smells amazing.'

'Saag gosht.' He'd decided on it because Henry couldn't contemplate a meal without meat.

'Saag.' The word sounded warm on Henry's tongue. Like it belonged there.

Henry's shirt gaped open near the stomach, his white flesh exposed. Zulfikar felt the responsibility surge within him, stronger than any opioid. 'Your button is missing. Give to me after, I'll fix.'

Sitting with the shirt after dinner, he remembered the wives in his mother's Pakistani dramas. They sewed buttons onto their husband's shirts, even as they were wearing them. They cut the thread with their teeth, inches from their lover's necks. He wouldn't do that. Couldn't. He didn't know such intimacy away from a screen.

Beside him, Henry was lost in a *Blue Planet* rerun. In the Russian Arctic Circle, an eagle spread its brown wings and rode the coastal wind. Suddenly, it swooped down a cliff into a colony of seagulls. Henry's love for wildlife reminded Zulfikar of the old women in his village. With nothing to do, they spent whole days staring up at the trees. He preferred to look down, at his sewing.

'I've told you before, you don't need to do this,' Henry said.

'But I do. I mean, I want to.'

Anyway, the button was almost re-attached. Henry placed his head on Zulfikar's shoulder. Zulfikar felt Henry's knuckles brushing against his knees. He imagined those hands moving across his groin, parting his thighs. It took all his resolve not to drag his legs away. The weight of Henry's head was enough.

One morning, Zulfikar made omelettes for breakfast. Outside, a torrent assailed the pond, soaked the grass. The bird feeder was abandoned and dripping. Unlike Pakistan, when the storm clouds gathered in England, he worried they would never part.

But then they did. A miracle. Henry was off from work and insisted on joining him in Platt Fields Park. He sat on a bench with his birding guide as Zulfikar ran three laps of the lake, then they strolled around it together.

Henry pointed to a green-headed bird swimming near them. 'That's a male mallard. A wild duck. You know what ducks are, don't you? And that family of white birds over there, with the long necks, they're swans.'

Of course he knew them, they were common everywhere. He humoured Henry anyway. 'Battakh, in my language, and hanss.'

'There's all sorts around here. Herons and egrets. Woodpeckers and yellowhammers.'

Zulfikar laughed. 'Talk to me about goat, sheep, buffalo, I'll tell you things.'

Walking in rhythm with another person was hard. Henry walked inconsistently, speeding from the lake to the bush and back again. The path was full of puddles. Zulfikar concentrated on the ground, careful not to spatter them. 'Why birds, Henry?'

'Because of my granddad, I guess. We were close and he kept pigeons. When I got older, I joined a club. That's how I met my ex, David, actually.'

'Acha?'

'We were together for ten years. Split last year.'

'What happened?'

Henry contorted his face. 'Oh, I don't know. He claimed we drifted apart. My friends said he was sleeping with someone from the group. I found the usual clues – texts and lies, but he denies it. Of course, they're together now. Traded me in for a younger model.' He paused, a sheen covering his eyes, and Zulfikar understood this to be one source of his hurt, though not the only one. Henry nodded to some small creatures in the water. 'Coots and moorhens.'

Crowded around a traffic cone half-submerged in the water, parents and children, feathers black and dusty, foreheads painted red or white, Zulfikar found their pained squeaking endearing.

'Tell me about your exes,' Henry said.

'I don't have any,' Zulfikar replied, his shoulders tightening.

'You're a man of secrets.'

'Not really.'

'You've told your solicitor. You'll be telling the Home Office soon enough.'

But talking to his solicitor was easier. Her velvet hands patiently searched for an opening hidden inside him. Zulfikar glanced at the island in the middle of the lake, where the trees were bent over, praying at the water's edge. He couldn't. Didn't want to share the few encounters he'd had, both in Pakistan and England, hoping to find himself in other men's bodies. So much had been offered up for the scrutiny of others.

'There's a colony of parakeets living on the island,' Henry said.

'Para— kya?'

'Parakeets. Bright green. They sing and chirp a lot?'

'Tota?'

'All sorts of legends about how they got here, but they're hardy little things. Two hundred in this area alone.'

Zulfikar raised his head to find them. At the same time, Henry reached for his hand. Zulfikar pulled away. 'Sorry, Henry, I can't.' Henry was kind and loving and, more than anything, Zulfikar wanted to please him. But people were rushing into the park. His limbs filled with lead.

Henry held out his hand like it had been burnt. 'Why won't you let me get to know you?'

'Because I can't,' he said with a quiet force. Because he was not Henry's meat and potatoes. It didn't matter how Henry was helping, Zulfikar wasn't obliged to nourish him with his past.

Silence descended. The clouds became one in the sky and the lake turned to steel.

From behind the glass wall, a uniformed officer asked for his name, nationality and date of birth.

'Why have you come to the UK?'

'Why are you claiming asylum?'

'Why can't you return to your home country?'

She had a form in her hand and an impatient look in her eye. Zulfikar turned to the people sitting at booths either side of him and scanned for pricked ears, inquisitive glances.

In the evening, Henry discovered him on the sofa, his head in his hands.

Henry spoke through a clenched jaw. 'What did those bastards do?'

Zulfikar gestured to the phone beside him. 'My family called. There's been flooding in Pakistan. Lots of people have died.'

'Oh, no. Is your family okay?'

'Yes, but all their crops are destroyed.'

'I'm so sorry.' Henry sat beside him, held his knee.

'They need help, but I have nothing.'

'Isn't there anyone else? Any relatives?'

Zulfikar shook his head. 'I have to find a job, send money.'

'But you're not allowed to work?'

'How can I let them starve?'

Zulfikar lay back on the sofa, his wrist taped to his forehead, and saw the land he had grown up on swimming with water. He had spent these years in England thinking of only his family, sending whatever he had to pay off weddings and debts, fund seeds and electronics. Now, when it was his turn to rest and receive, his parents were tugging once more at the rope they had tied around his waist. A part of him wished they would stop contacting him and disappear.

The next morning, he sat nursing a bowl of hot Weetabix. He had spent half the night thinking of jobs he could do, employers willing to hire him off the books. He would lift heavy boxes, wash dishes in a restaurant, even clean nightclub toilets – anything. So long as his family were in jeopardy, his freedom carried no value.

Henry's cold hand covered his. 'If it's money they need, I can help.'

Zulfikar looked up. 'No, no, Henry—'

'You could pay me back. A loan.'

'No, this is too much. I'm going to look for a job today. You're already doing enough.'

Henry pressed down on Zulfikar's hand. 'And what about how much you do for me? It's your family we're talking about. And you're my family now too.'

His family? Zulfikar stared into his eyes and saw Henry's honesty. It was more than he could process, all of it. Emotion coursed through him. He stood up and put his arms around Henry, his head on Henry's shoulder. He brought his mouth to Henry's and kissed him. A thousand doves fluttered across his chest.

That night, they finally made love. Henry grabbed Zulfikar's wrists and pinned them to the bed, pulled his hair as Zulfikar struggled beneath. 'No, Henry. I'm not comfortable.' He hadn't pictured it like this. He wanted to make Henry happy, but couldn't breathe.

'Shit, sorry.' Henry released the pressure on his arms and kissed him slowly. He tasted earthy but sweet, like candied nuts, so Zulfikar tugged his shirt and pulled him closer. Theirs was a friendship, a pact they were altering. If it collapsed afterwards, what would that mean for his case? But Zulfikar found himself lifting his hips so Henry could remove his jeans. Pressing their bodies together to unite Henry's skin with his. Nuzzling his neck so that Henry's scent filled his lungs. Zulfikar found himself living out a hundred nights in one.

Henry had such beautiful eyes. They were rich and brown, reminded Zulfikar of the gravy served with their Sunday lunch. His eyes had the same depth and shine. They flowed through him in the same way.

'How is it?' Henry asked as Zulfikar took his first bite.

Zulfikar reached across the table for Henry's hand. For once, he didn't care who noticed. In this pub, there were only white people.

This was his fourth month living with Henry, but Zulfikar was only seeing him now. Seeing him fully. How his face grew pink with excitement whenever he talked about the rare birds on the Galápagos Islands: the blue-footed booby, swallow-tailed gull and waved albatross. How he cried when watching *Titanic* and laughed, albeit without understanding, when Zulfikar played his Punjabi stage comedies. How he held Zulfikar's hand when crossing the road. How, despite everything, he prayed to God every night.

'What did your mum and Sarah say?' Zulfikar asked.

'About the letters of support? They'll send them over in a few days.'

It had surprised Zulfikar how close he had grown to Henry's loved ones. 'We can ask Mike and Rob when they come for dinner next week, Chris and Iain when you have your bird meeting.' Two months remained until his substantive interview with the Home Office. The grey tower block appeared in his dreams, a blot on every horizon.

Henry squeezed his hand. 'Relax, we'll get everything sorted. Let's focus on going away. What about Blackpool, or the Lakes?'

Despite Zulfikar's attempts to explain, Henry couldn't grasp why a holiday was the furthest thing from his mind. A shard of loneliness jammed into his heart. Sometimes, he felt the weight of Henry's sleeping body beside him and couldn't relax. Never had he imagined himself lying so close to another man. The only solution was to stop thinking. If he didn't picture his family's faces, their judgements. his heart wouldn't race.

Still, if the caseworker asked about Henry, Zulfikar would tell them the truth. He didn't know anything about love; he had spent his life hiding from it. When he went with Henry to the park or the halal grocery store, he could feel the Pakistani people watching and whispering. But he tried not to care, because with Henry he felt safe. Important. He was an asylum seeker, but with Henry he could close his eyes and pretend that his life was stable.

Henry's grip tightened around his hand. 'Were you eyeing him up?'

Zulfikar looked around in confusion.

'The young lad that walked past.' Henry gestured to the toilets.

'I was just thinking.'

'Sure, fine, whatever.' Henry downed his beer. 'Same again,' he called to the waitress.

'But, Henry, too much beer makes you sad.'

A few nights ago, David, the ex, had announced his engagement on social media. Henry came home with a twelve-pack, watched his documentaries and refused to eat, scrunched empties falling around him.

Henry looked ahead, stony-faced, and Zulfikar resigned himself to Henry doom-scrolling on David's profile when they got back, before passing out drunk on the sofa.

But, when they reached home that evening, Henry pushed his beery mouth against Zulfikar's with a renewed urgency. Leaning over him in their bedroom, Zulfikar saw that Henry's eyes were cloudy, as if a heat, a longing deep inside was being released. When he entered Henry, kissing his face and chest, Henry marked his back with his nails. Then, after a while, he brushed his hands across it, and Zulfikar thought of the turtles he had seen on the beach in Karachi, sweeping back sand, coming home to nest again.

For two hours, they waited to see his solicitor. The benches in reception were hard, the upholstery had been pulled apart and the thin foam picked through.

Mrs Shah went through their supporting evidence while peeking at them like they were a puzzle. Zulfikar knew why: he was twenty-nine years old, while Henry was forty-six. Mrs Shah was often brusque in her manner, Pakistani, like the women he hid from in the streets, but he trusted her. She had never asked him for more than she needed.

The big interview was a month away. Zulfikar listened to Mrs Shah's instructions and took notes: 'Make sure you're happy with the interpreter. Ask them to record the interview. The

Home Office will keep asking the same question in different ways. They want to catch you out. Speak clearly and confidently. Take your time.'

'Ji, baji.'

When Zulfikar first started meeting her, his knees had clicked together. Forced to tell his story to a stranger, a story he didn't know himself, felt like dredging something from the bottom of the sea, presenting his guts on the table. He remembered staring at the books and paperweights on the shelves, wishing they could speak on his behalf. She had showered him with time, like he was the only client in her office.

'How's my letter?' Henry asked, interrupting.

Zulfikar sensed that Henry wanted her approval. He had slaved over the letter, describing how they met, how their relationship had developed, what he loved about Zulfikar.

Mrs Shah flattened her lips, nodding. 'Fine. It's just one part of what we're doing here.'

From the slackening of his mouth, he realised that Henry had expected more.

'What are our chances?' Zulfikar asked.

'That's hard to say. You've been together for four months now?'

'Nearly five.'

'You live together, which is good. But given the timing of your relationship, the Home Office might think you're pretending.'

'Pretending?' What they shared now was as real as relationships could be. Kebiru had promised it would help. Zulfikar grew quiet, looked to Henry for guidance.

Henry paused, his forehead dimpled in thought. 'We could get civil partnered?'

Zulfikar's heart stopped.

'Really?' Mrs Shah grimaced, like something cold had hit the back of her teeth. 'The Home Office might accuse you of being cynical. Of doing it for the case. A bit like the tape—'

'But if we're honest and consistent it could also strengthen our case, no? Reinforce it.'

'Yes, but—'

'Yeah, well, I've seen enough cases from my campaigning, and I know that what we have comes from the heart. We're ready to take that step, aren't we?' He kissed Zulfikar's hand.

Zulfikar had never considered marriage – of any kind. There was a time when his parents were always pushing him: 'Come back and get married. You need someone to care for you.' He asked his older sisters to make them stop. Once he had settled in England, he would find a woman here – though he never truly meant it.

'Zulfikar? Is this what you want?' Mrs Shah asked.

They both stared at him, waiting for an answer.

The ceremony was a nervy affair. Zulfikar kept expecting the Home Office to barge in and break it up. Afterwards, they held a reception in the back of Henry's favourite pub, inviting thirty people in total, including Henry's family and Mrs Shah. Wasim came too, the newest member of Zulfikar's support group. He looked handsome in a grey salwar kameez and purple waistcoat, scented with sandalwood.

Zulfikar gazed around the room from his table. People were laughing and eating. He wished his family could have joined them. He tried picturing it, but once again his imagination was too small.

After he and Henry cut the frilly white cake, Kebiru played music from his playlist: Beyoncé and Bruno Mars and that annoying 'Azonto' song he listened to all the time. Some people got up and danced. Zulfikar and Henry visited each table. They asked how the guests were enjoying their night. They thanked them for coming.

Kebiru dragged Zulfikar away. 'I have a song for you.'

It was an old Punjabi song. When Zulfikar was living with Kebiru, Naseebo Lal was all that he played. Kebiru had found her music intoxicating.

The white people who were dancing sat down, but he and Kebiru stayed on their feet. So did Wasim. Wasim knew all the words. He danced confidently in front of Zulfikar with his hands snaking above his head. Everybody watched and clapped. Zulfikar spotted Henry at the bar, drinking, and he waved at him and beckoned him over. Henry shook his head, so Zulfikar continued dancing with Wasim, even as Kebiru drifted away. He raised his hands to the sky, like Wasim did, like the men in his family had done for centuries.

Henry was quiet in the taxi. Though it was only 8pm, it had been a long day, Zulfikar was tired too. At home, Henry filled a glass of water and went upstairs. Zulfikar followed him and sat on the bed, watching Henry change out of his suit. He was rounder, healthier than when they had first met, his complexion brighter. The result of Zulfikar's presence in his life.

'It was a nice day,' Zulfikar said after a while.

'Good. I'm glad it was for you,' Henry said.

'Huh?' Henry's tone was barbed in a way he couldn't follow.

'I was having a great time until the dancing started.'

'Why?'

'You made me look like an idiot in front of my family and friends.'

Zulfikar didn't understand. He'd had such fun dancing. He took off his shoes and rubbed his sore feet.

'That boy you were dancing with. Wasim. Looked like he was going to kiss you.'

'Really? No.'

'Come off it. I saw the way he touched your face.'

The accusation stung. Perhaps for a few seconds Zulfikar had felt the intensity in Wasim's eyes, but no. He and Wasim were from the same part of Pakistan. There was so much that didn't need to be explained. Maybe, in an alternate world, they could have . . . Zulfikar stopped himself. Had it really looked that way? 'I was only dancing, Henry. There is nothing wrong with dancing.'

'You were chasing new dick on our wedding day.'

Such ugly words. Henry had never used them before. Zulfikar tutted and pulled his nightclothes from the back of the door. Regardless of what might have passed between him and Wasim, he would never have acted on it. He was better than that.

'You had your eye on something younger, prettier. Someone of your own kind.'

His own kind? Zulfikar had all but tattooed their vows on his chest. He approached Henry to communicate this, but Henry pushed him away, knocking over a glass on the television stand. Both bent down to pick up the pieces. Their faces close again, he saw Henry's eyes were bloodshot, the corner of his mouth trembling. He saw that old pain, the pain of his ex, never far from the surface. 'I love you, Henry.'

'Lies.' Henry's voice fractured. 'Soon as you get your visa, you'll be gone.'

'No, we're together now. Husbands.' How to convey the seriousness of their relationship?

Zulfikar took the broken glass from his hands and threw it away. He waited to be embraced. They had never disagreed like this before. He didn't think he had done anything wrong. But the longer their silence persisted, the more unjust it all began to feel.

'You know, I've helped you so much—'

'But I never asked you, Henry. You offered all this. And how much did you get in return? How much have I done for you?' He remembered the sick-looking man he had met at the bar. The constant need for gratitude was a tyre around his neck.

Henry looked at him coldly. Zulfikar searched for the man he had trusted his life with.

The sun had almost disappeared that late summer evening when Zulfikar began a lap of the lake. He was out in just a T-shirt and jeans with the cold beginning to bite, but he started jogging as an ache spread across his chest. Geese were gliding along the water, their beaks skimming the surface, sipping and sifting, the sound like the whirring of a machine or the ticking of a clock. Though it was light still, a half-moon had come out already and appeared in three white dots on the water. High up on the island, he heard a trilling. A flash of green that disappeared before he saw it again: a flock of ten, maybe twelve parakeets, sailing from tree to tree and singing.

If only there was someone who could listen and understand. Henry was a sunburned man with a cheap earring and the names of a few birds memorised. But Henry was now his man, and they were bound together legally. Talking to family was out of the question. Kebiru would send him home again. 'Bitch, what are you talking about? All that matters is your visa.'

Zulfikar sat on a bench. Mrs Shah would get him. She would recognise his kinship with Wasim, assure him that Henry was overreacting. Perhaps she would confess that she had never approved of Henry in the first place, and, if he wanted, there were other ways to resolve the question of his immigration status.

Calling now seemed unreasonable – he'd seen her at the reception – but he did it anyway.

She picked up on the first ring. 'Zulfi – I never got to tell you, you both looked so beautiful together, so happy. And the ceremony, I wish I'd never pulled you aside in the office and asked if this was the right decision. What do I know about relationships? But you, you seem to have found exactly where you're meant to be.'

There was a peculiar sadness to Jamila's voice. Despite her words, she sounded so disconnected from him. Zulfikar hung up disappointed and gazed into the water. The air was still and the lake reflected the sky like a mirror. After a while, the wind picked up and the mirror broke, and the pieces surged forward. He got up and started walking, wondering if it was too soon to make his way back, if Henry would be awake waiting when he finally reached home.

Nineteen

The humidity of August had drawn the world's couples out of their houses and onto the streets – at least it seemed that way as Jamila walked back from the bank on Stockport Road. Most of her clients were either homeless or employed in cash-in-hand jobs. They rarely had the documents to open a bank account and paid her in cash. Usually, she entrusted this task to Sadia, but, this Friday, Jamila deposited the takings herself.

The couples were dressed in very little, their fingers interlaced and arms draped over one another, kissing. Meanwhile, the city smelled of rot: hot garbage and overripe bananas. As dandelion seeds continued to drift through the air like summer snow, her thighs chafed in thick cotton trousers. The arrangement of these couples didn't strike her as natural so much as something they performed – something the streets demanded of them – which made her want to knock them loose. The streets demanded nothing of her. She picked a spot on her forehead and ceded none of the pavement.

Her foray into dating had left her feeling plainer than she had for years. Attending Zulfikar and Henry's reception had only made it worse. She had found Henry too pushy, disliked the way he presumed to advise her on how the asylum system worked, but what did she know about love? They had built something together, while she couldn't get past the initial hurdles of a relationship.

Every failure in her life added to her sense of inadequacy: her relationship with her father, the complaint, the breakdown that had led her to try and change things in the first place – whatever it was, she couldn't manage it. Still, work didn't disappoint and judge her; work was certain and had tangible outcomes; work made it easy to forget everything else – so the dating profile had to go.

The news about the 'Go Home' vans had spread. In newspaper articles, on the ten o'clock news, on her staff members' lips. People were shocked, angry. Protests were being organised across the country.

'They're trying to intimidate us into leaving,' Babar said, cheeks spasming with rage. Once again, his status was in limbo. Like Hassan, Babar's appeal hearing had failed: the judge suggested his mother-in-law could move into a care home if she really needed looking after. Gemma was incredulous, appealing certain legal errors, but the decision had left Babar shaky, prone to storming out of the office with Rubel chasing after him to calm him down and bring him back. In private, Sadia told Jamila that he and Habeebah were fighting about trying for another baby.

The vans were part of a pilot that hadn't lasted very long. One month in total – advertisements in Punjabi and Bengali newspapers, flyers in mosques and churches, postcards in Pakistani and Nigerian shops at the total cost of just £10,000 – long enough for eleven people to leave the country, including a twenty-five-year-old Pakistani student, who hadn't been in the UK 'illegally' but had read about the campaign in the newspaper. Jamila searched for more information about him but couldn't find a word.

'It was part of a package that was looked at and agreed,' said the minister, eventually responding to criticism. 'If you are asking me, did I say to them, "It would be a jolly good idea to have vans going round the country," no, I did not. But the package was brought forward and looked at, and there were a variety of elements to it—'

How casually this government defended its language. How smoothly it moved on. Rage tarred Jamila's insides. The vans reminded her mother of the 'P*ki Go Home' graffiti that fascists had once scrawled on the walls. Graffiti that her parents had passed when racing to and from school every day, when skinheads were patrolling the streets, looking for someone to beat up. Her mother's grandparents had been recruited to build the railways in Kenya; she had come to Britain as a citizen, but when thirteen-year-old Ahmed Ullah Iqbal was stabbed to death in 1986, Jamila's mother had stopped believing this country could be faithful to her. How had the government missed this connection?

When Jamila neared the office, she saw the man who lived above the chicken shop lurking outside. He was standing by the front door. Although young, he had aged prematurely. His face was scabby and scarred, his hands wrinkled and blistered. Clutching a bottle in his hands, half filled with straw-yellow wine, he peered in as he staggered about.

She deployed the deepest timbre available to her, the thickest Mancunian accent, which wasn't very thick at all – an accent polished of its glottal stops and slanted vowels over a decade of speaking to those with other languages flourishing on their tongues. 'Y'alright?'

He smelled earthy, like wet tarmac and church incense.

She circled gingerly, with a wide stance, and hopped inside.

He followed her in, like they were both attending the same meeting. Inside the waiting area, he stood and glanced around, making sense of the old toys and magazines. The staff gathered at the window dividing the waiting room from the rest of the office and watched.

He raised his face to them. 'You're all cunts,' he slurred in a heavy but undistinguishable accent. 'Fucking illegal cunts. The lot of you.' He fell against the coffee table, its legs scraping across the floor.

Jamila locked the doors that connected him to her office and the staff room. 'Ignore him. He'll get bored soon enough,' she said, her calves giving way. She steadied herself against the counter, not convinced that he would leave. Some seconds later,

Rubel unlocked the door. He grabbed the man's arm and placed him outside, dusted off his hands. He had done what she couldn't, what she, as their boss, was too afraid to do. She felt ashamed, but life returned to her legs. She dispersed the crowd and headed into her office.

There was an explosion. She ran back to find the front door shattered. Glass confetti scattered across the floor and seats. A broken bottle lay on the welcome mat, liquid pooling between its bristly fibres.

Rubel bolted outside, but the drunkard had vanished.

Jamila picked up the glass with her hands.

Nazish kneeled by her. 'Stop. Let me do it.'

Jamila sighed. 'It's fine.' She felt too morose to say anything more.

'No, you're boss. You call for new glass.'

Nazish fetched a broom, while Babar attended to the calls and Rubel researched security cameras. It came with the territory, Jamila told herself. Whether it was cutting legal aid or appeal rights, making children homeless or into criminals for having the temerity to come here, hiking up application fees or watering down the legal definition of torture – whatever strategy the Home Office adopted in this game she had found herself playing, she and other immigration solicitors were always left to pick up the pieces. She was just lucky that her waiting area had been empty.

Nazish insisted on staying behind and waiting for the glazier with her. Once the glass had been replaced, Jamila went home and sat with Bertha, resorted to playing video games to dull her thoughts. The man had called them 'illegal', as if she and her staff weren't British, weren't closer to Britishness through their work than most people in this country.

Hassan's complaint continued to threaten her. It lived in her mind, and she turned it over constantly, drafting and redrafting her response. Jahida had insisted that nothing would come of it, but she didn't know. They could make an example of her. It was the system's wicked unpredictability rearing its head again – this time, the long arm of the law threatened to wrap itself around her neck and pull her under. She wished that she was stronger. More resilient. More like her sister or her friends. But now, with Bertha flicking her tongue at the cushions, she realised that the scale of the task was too large. She was battling a system that felt as though it had the weight of an entire nation – her nation, like it or not; if any place felt like home, it was Manchester – behind it.

'Every job has pressure,' Nazish tried to reason with her, on one of their walks. 'Go ask a security guard, a waiter, an artist. They will say there's nothing more stressful than what they do.'

Nazish didn't understand. It was the pressure that led Jamila to feel such panic. These other professions weren't tethered to public opinion in the same way, couldn't be derailed in the same way. A firm built over twenty years, her expertise over ten, a family legacy, all destroyed by one false complaint. The prospect of humiliation terrified her.

A fortnight passed. Though she didn't share her fears with her staff – Nazish excepted – they rallied together, nonetheless. Fearing the drunk man's return – or something worse – Rubel and Babar took to staying behind at work and helping her to close the office. Sadia and Nazish visited her at home with food and a safety alarm, or took her for walks and tea in Rusholme, reminding her that she could not back out of the concert they had booked to attend together. The morning of, Sadia called to remind her. Jamila tried to demur – she was writing up her response to the complaint, papers scattered around her – then put on the Syrian singer's CD. She had listened to him before and found him too jangly, too much like wedding music. But in her solitude, something changed. Not the music opening to her, as she might have expected, but her body shifting to the music. The way a Venus flytrap – the image amused her, she indulged it – opened to nourishment: sulky and opportunistic, discovering its appetite as it consumed.

Not until the cool of that Saturday evening did Jamila venture out. A decaying aroma still lingered in the air. Sadia opened her door and led Jamila to the bedroom, where Nazish sat at the dressing table, wearing a pink salwar kameez decorated with tiny mirrors. She was pleased to see Nazish there – Jamila had brought the pair together after work one evening, when they all had dinner in Rusholme. Adrift in a city that alternated between vast and unknowable, closed and provincial, they both needed new anchors.

Nazish held a mascara wand to her eyes and feathered her lashes. 'You should have come to the protest.'

'Crowds aren't my thing,' Jamila said. What would a pro-immigration protest achieve?

'Or you could have come clubbing with me last night,' Nazish said.

Sadia entered the room with a drink for Jamila. 'You went clubbing without me?'

'Paagal, don't spill the juice.'

Sadia sucked her cheeks in a mild rage. 'Did you meet someone?' she asked, handing the glass to Jamila.

Nazish gave her an impish smile.

'Oh ho, you sly fox! Kya hua? Woh kaisi thi?'

'I only have to close my eyes to see her.'

'Lekin uska chehra kaisa tha?'

Nazish opened her eyes slowly. It was an overly theatrical gesture. Watching her in the mirror, Jamila couldn't help but envy how Nazish revelled in the attention.

'How can you describe a rainbow?' Nazish asked Sadia through the mirror.

'A rainbow?'

'Fine, pari. Woh ek pari thi mere liye.'

'Will you see her again?'

Nazish grabbed a brush and powdered her cheeks. 'Don't ask too many questions.'

Jamila admired how elegant they both looked and smelled, Sadia removing the stud from her nose and replacing it with a tiny gold ring. She felt an urge to join in with their beautifying, for herself if no one else. There was nobody she could imagine herself dressing up for.

'I'd love to meet someone,' Sadia said quietly.

'What, no boys, no rishtas?' Jamila asked.

Her divorce was days from being finalised. Sadia uncurled her torso. 'Look at me. Main te buddi mai ho gayi anh. No, my focus is all on me and Maliha now.'

She smiled, but Jamila sensed a reservoir of unspilled tears. Over dinner recently, Sadia had shared how much she missed male companionship, the feel of a male body lying on top of her. A need so great, so existential, it threatened to consume her sometimes. A need that, having spent years squashing her sexuality into an envelope and slipping it into a drawer, Jamila maybe understood. She decided not to share how easy it had been for Akbar to move on, by contrast. She had received an invite to his engagement next month.

Nazish reached over to where Sadia stood and pinched her stomach.

Sadia jolted. 'Ow! Was that really necessary?'

Nazish laughed. 'Yes. No feeling sorry.'

'It's going to bruise now. You're brutal sometimes.'

Nazish nodded, as Sadia rubbed her stomach, mouthing empty threats.

'Well, if it helps, I'm so single people think I'm a lesbian,' Jamila said.

Nazish turned back. 'And what's wrong with being lesbian?'

'Nothing at all. I just—'

'Do you want to meet someone?' Sadia asked.

'Doesn't everyone?' Jamila replied.

'Do *you*? Are you ready?'

These were her friends. They didn't make her feel like a failure, like this was a race she had lost, like some injured animal – she could give them this. 'I am.' She wanted a companion. Someone to share secrets and burdens with. Someone to inhabit her silences.

Sadia squinted at her. 'You know, I've always found it hard to see you with someone.'

Nazish scoffed. 'What?'

'I mean, she's so independent and—'

'Pfft, she's really not—'

Jamila ignored the flaying sensation of yet more people having opinions about her. 'I did go on some dates recently. They weren't great.'

Sadia glanced at her. 'Really?'

Jamila hadn't planned on keeping those dates to herself, but they had all had much bigger things to deal with recently. 'The last guy, he was a divorcee—'

'You're dating divorced men now?'

'You're a divorcee. Don't you deserve a second chance at happiness?'

Sadia pouted. 'Why do you have to expose me like that?'

Jamila laughed. It was tinged with the bitterness of what she was about to remember. 'I'd been so looking forward to meeting him. He wasn't my usual type – very thin – but he had a lovely smile. When we chatted online there was so much zip to our conversation. He was smart, sweet, political. It felt natural to meet up. And it sort of was until we got onto the subject of my work . . . He started arguing with me about how I should handle a case. And tried to analyse my motivations when the complaint had already put me in a terrible mood. It killed the connection between us. He sent me a couple of texts afterwards, but things got so complicated at work . . . and I was too annoyed to reply.'

Sadia dabbed some colour onto her lips. 'That's really sad.'

Jamila pictured Nadeem's legs curled on the sofa, Jahida sitting over them, his warmth becoming hers, a single organism. How much she had wanted that. How much she had allowed herself to believe that it was possible for her. That she wouldn't have to move through the world alone, shoulder its albatrosses alone. If being alone truly was her destiny, she would accept and find happiness within it, but, for now, she felt pathetic, and the cliché of this devastated her too.

Nazish perched on the bed next to her and took her hands. 'Masha'Allah, you are so clever and wise in your work. But, sometimes, I see you don't have experience in life. My Warda used to argue with me all the time. Not bad argument, not bad fighting, but sharing her experience, her opinions, ideas. We need this, Jamila. It's Newton's third law. Honestly, I thought the education was good in this country.'

But, reminded of her sadness again, all Jamila wanted to do was lie down.

The concert was in a cold converted warehouse. Sadia and Jamila ordered drinks at the bar and scanned the crowd for handsome men, studying the imprint of their shirts against their chests, jeans against their behinds. Nazish lapped up the compliments on her 'exotic' outfit. Then Jamila roughed her way to the front and made space for them by the barriers.

When the music started, the three of them turned away from the stage, faced each other and danced. When the dry smoke separated them, they came together again, as one, without touch. The crowd formed an arc around them, and they performed eagerly for their audience. Nazish and Sadia's skin was fluorescent, hips oily, bellies rolling. In a sea of white faces, their ethnicities lent them a flattened, generalised authenticity, but they didn't care. Jamila raised her hands and pogoed and headbanged. All her questions were suspended in the air.

Twenty

Nazish

Nazish stood alone at the bus stop. She was late for work again. Jamila would have questions, but, lately, she was in no mood to answer them. She stared into the distance, spotting a blue-and-yellow bus, grimy as the grey clouds, as the stony skyscrapers, stuck at a faraway traffic light. She squinted to see if it was hers.

It wasn't hers. She fell back against the brick wall behind her. Hard cold spread across her back, the pointed edge slashing her shoulder blades. She rubbed her eyes. She had overslept, having spent another night lost to the woods, dreaming of trees enveloping her as they did when she had visited Dalby Forest at the weekend. Branches wrapping themselves like limbs around her torso. Jamila would surely understand, how they didn't release her until the apartment was bathed in light, the alarm clock subdued on her nightstand.

Every judder of the bus across the crumbling roads sent commuters groaning into their books and electronics. Her knees knocked against the seat in front, but she hardly felt it. She rounded out the bumps, leaned into the turns, planning her escape. Come the weekend, she would head to the forest again. Already, it was calling.

Her phone beeped in her bag.

Her phone. She'd forgotten it. Not even glanced at it since last night, when, spent from the hike, she'd gone to bed without eating. There had been four missed calls. Two voicemails. Nuisance callers, most likely – pension providers and accident helplines – though, recently, the Muslims had found her too – God knows how – and were forever offering Quran classes online.

Now, her heart stopped as she recognised the country code calling. 0092. Pakistan.

The phone shuddered as she brought it to her ear. Nazish hadn't received a call from there in years – not a single call from *them* – and when she moved to Britain, she, too, had broken ties with the past. Not that she'd had any choice.

It took little more than hello to recognise him. He pronounced his own name oddly, as if she was unfamiliar with it, as if they weren't connected by blood, by a single womb – as if that knowledge, those memories could not only be suppressed, but erased completely.

'It's me, Mahsoom,' he said. 'I wanted to tell you that . . . last night . . . our grandmother . . . '

Nazish stopped listening to her younger brother. She already knew.

Their grandmother.

Had passed away.

Now there was no time. Phone, bag, coat, keys. She grabbed them and punched the bell. Shoved past the nurse sitting beside her, backpacks clogging the aisle. When the bus stopped, she hurled herself out onto the kerb and stood there, panting. The city sat on her shoulders. Fine droplets pattered her forehead. She sucked in the cold air. Then the urgency drilled through her again and she set off running down the street, hands over her mouth, tears mixing with rain.

It had happened. She was gone.

And Nazish never got to say goodbye.

In the months after being recognised as a refugee, Nazish had tried so hard to forget the night back in Islamabad that obliterated her world as she knew it. She was returning home after a day's teaching at the university. The watchman opened their squealing black gates. Strangely, everybody was home, their cars neatly parked inside. She drove in and joined them.

The humidity of the house hit her first — that all-conquering summer heat their ceiling fans were powerless against. She noticed them afterwards. All of them. Standing in the hallway space that functioned as their reception room: mor, baba, her two brothers, their wives. What was this? She looked to her grandmother, sat with her back stubbornly facing the front door, a jewelled tasbih moving between her fingers.

Her elder brother spoke first. 'Just tell us if it's true. If you lie, I'll—'

Her father grabbed his arm. 'Ehsaan. She's only just come in. Give her a chance.'

'What's going on?' Nazish asked. From the rooftop her nieces and nephews were yelling. Her hands and underarms moistening.

'Come,' her father beckoned, 'sit.'

Their gloomy faces and the sober atmosphere, the fact that she was usually the first to reach home at the end of the day, unnerved her. She adjusted the bag strap on her shoulder and didn't move.

'What's happened to you? I'm your Baba. Come to me.' He held out his hand.

Nazish caught a strange look in her mother's eyes. A look that made her stare at her grandmother, imploring her to turn and say something. Anything. One word to diffuse all this.

When she approached him, her father placed his hand at her back and spoke calmly. 'I need to ask you something. We've received an accusation, that you have some kind of link with a woman, a colleague. Tell me it's not true. Tell me he made it up and I will destroy that person.'

She feared he could hear her breath shallowing. There was no question about it, she had to do as he asked. 'It's not true.' She squeezed out the words as her throat sealed itself.

'You can't even look at me.' His voice was drenched in disappointment.

Nazish attempted to meet her father's gaze. She rubbed gummy hands against wobbling thighs, staring at the frosted doors behind him, figures creeping on the other side. 'Baba, he's lying.' Her bowels rumbled.

He blinked slowly and didn't respond. She looked to the others for encouragement, was surprised to find Ehsaan marching towards her. Then everything went black. When she came to, a bell clanged in her ears. Voices swam above her. When she opened her eyes, she found herself sprawled back on the grubby tiles. Her right ear wet. A sharp pain ballooned across her face and a dull ache raced over her ribs. She lifted her head and saw Mahsoom holding Ehsaan back, their father go over and slap him.

Nothing much was said after that. Her mother dabbed at her wounds as she would a stranger's. It was fear, Nazish could see now. Fear that had taken residence in the mangled shape of her mother's lips. How could a mother fear her own daughter? Her sisters-in-law appeared with a suitcase. Mahsoom helped their grandmother into the front seat, then threw the case into the boot of his car.

Nazish stared at her family through the rear window, assembled like the posts of a fence.

She didn't know she was seeing them for the last time.

It took four hours to reach her grandparents' house in the valley. Her grandfather was sleeping. The house smelled of cooking gas. Her grandmother wiped the blood congealed around her ear, gave her food and painkillers, sent her to bed without a word. Nazish woke the next day to a cockerel's cry. Her ears gurgled like they were filled with water. She found her grandmother tending to her garden outside, the same garden they had tended together when Nazish was a child. They had sown mustard and spinach, watered potatoes and corn, picked tomatoes and okra. All the while her grandmother would speak of the serenity that came from caring for living things and watching them grow.

The early morning was cold but blinding. Bulbuls and song thrushes sang vigorously. Mahsoom's car was gone.

'Come,' her grandmother said. 'Let's go inside.'

They squatted on low stools in the kitchen and brewed tea. Her grandmother softened a rusk with hot milk, fed it to her. She stroked Nazish's cheek.

'Your father didn't plan for any of this. It's that stupid, hot-headed brother of yours. I could kill him for what he did to you.'

Nazish leaned into her grandmother's touch. She had never expected her family's acceptance so never asked for it. But witnessing herself drop in their estimations – how quickly they bundled her away when the truth unsettled them, the sister that her brothers doted over, whom they consulted before every decision – it gave rise to shame that had never existed before.

In the afternoon, they prayed. Nazish stood on the prayer mat; her grandmother settled on a chair. Afterwards, she handed Nazish another copy of the Quran and the two of them sat together and read. The living room danced with shadows as the sun moved to the back of the house, the rose scent of their fragranced books intensifying. When they finished, Nazish took another painkiller and led them back into the garden. Her grandmother raised her salwar, invited sunlight to her knees.

The valley grew still. Even the song thrushes were mute.

'Before your grandfather comes back from the market, let me tell you that I have decided you should go from here. I don't think you can be happy in this country. I don't think you can find peace.'

Nazish began to weep.

Her grandmother took her hands and kissed them. 'You don't think it hurts me too? To send my own blood away, you don't think my liver cries? But plenty of mothers send their children abroad for a better life, so I'm placing a stone against my chest. I'll talk to your parents when you're gone. I'll make things good again.'

Nazish made arrangements that week. A visit visa for Britain. Flights with a stopover in Dubai. For three hours, a battered taxi descended the misty roads, past wild apricot and walnut trees, and delivered her back to Islamabad. Nazish gazed at the green valleys and tried to memorise everything: the hissing rivers, the feeling of the sky like a roof over her head, the ruddy faces of her people, that unmistakable piney scent. Tears gushed over the dams of her eyelids. She had always wanted to see the world. But she could never have predicted the circumstances of her journey.

It's time to start your adventure.

At least that's what it said on the sign outside. Bright orange adverts hung in the windows. Sandy-haired figures grinned from white beaches. Unburdened and unafraid, they were climbing mountains, scaling cliffs, diving into the sea. Nazish regarded them with disdain as she checked out the destinations and fares.

'I want to book for Pakistan.'

The boy behind the desk was blade-thin and acned. His features, too generous, spilled across his face. Her presence startled him. 'Oh. Right. It's not one of our more popular destinations, but I'll take a look.' He faced the computer, his voice deep and lived in, at odds with his youth and surprise. 'Which city were you thinking?'

'Islamabad.'

'Direct or stopover?'

'I don't care.'

'And your travel dates?'

'As soon as possible. One way.'

The agency smelled of gym socks and photocopying. Fingers clattered against keys. Nazish felt a quiet panic radiating from her. She grabbed a paperback from the boy's desk – *The Art of Saying No* – and fanned herself. She resisted thoughts of the office and their incessant calls. She was going home. Ending the experiment and returning their visa. She couldn't afford to be sentimental now.

The boy stole glances – once, twice – she caught him the third time, but his eyes darted to the safety of the screen. 'Sorry, our system's really slow. Is it business or pleasure you're travelling for?'

She turned away and fanned herself some more.

'Okay, er . . . great, yes, there's a flight going out tomorrow. Four thirty in the afternoon. You'd get into Islamabad at . . . '

Tomorrow? Wouldn't tomorrow be too late? Slim chance, maybe, but what if she could wash the body herself, wrap her in her final garments, apply her last dab of perfume?

The evening flight was sold out.

'What about standby?'

He smiled apologetically. 'I don't know about that. But I can book you on tomorrow's flight and you could try heading to the airport?'

Her phone began throbbing in her pocket. She held it through her jeans and nodded.

'What with it being last minute, the flight's quite expensive . . . '

'How much?' she demanded, though it hardly mattered. She'd pay anything – anything – to see her grandmother's face again.

'Fourteen hundred pounds.'

She sat back and let the figure sink in. It was a huge chunk of her savings. Would wipe out her future fund almost entirely. When she moved into her studio apartment, she had furnished it with second-hand pieces from the Mustard Tree, including a saggy mattress that left her queasy thinking of what had been done on it. And, once she'd started working, she had set aside a part of her monthly salary, aiming to buy furniture without a history one day, items with which she could mark a truly fresh beginning.

She handed the boy her credit card and looked up at the map on the wall. *What's your adventure going to be?* But Nazish's adventure wasn't beginning, no. It was coming to an end. And with it all her pretending.

Nazish stood on Oxford Road and surveyed the city. The dark clouds had cleared, but the wind grumbled on. In the three years that Nazish had spent living in Manchester, she had followed the workmen in hi-vis jackets dismantling the BBC building that once stood opposite. Now, she watched them building something else in its midst. Heavy machinery clawed and grinded. Dust clouds rose like unassailable truths. What was she to do now?

Steadily, a list emerged of things that needed winding up. Bank account and tenancy. Yoga and gym. Jamila and Sadia. Nazish felt another pang; this time she allowed it to spread. They had looked out for her, taken care of her, tried to make her feel at home. In turn she had loved them, guided them and dominated them like little sisters. But here was the thing: though they had been her everything in this country, she had a blood family. A family that she was angry with. A family that she had tried to move on without, but couldn't.

Because there was no use in denying it – her grandmother's death had made this obvious – Nazish didn't understand why she was here. Time hadn't healed her family. Distance hadn't made them reach out. Three years of waiting, praying, forging a new life for herself, no closer to reconciliation. What had been the point?

Her champion, her rock, was gone. And with it all her remaining optimism.

Nazish fell to the ground then. A cry came out of her. A howl that shook the soundscape of this busy city-centre road.

Last Sunday, Nazish had taken Jamila ambling along a country lane. They stuck to one side of the road, cleaving as closely as possible to the limestone wall, avoiding the verges where weeds and wildflowers grew. When the wind picked up, the trees rustled dry and sharp, sounding like the clattering of small bones. Her brother's slap had perforated her ear drum and caused a loss of hearing in one ear – a fact that Nazish kept to herself. But this meant that she couldn't tell if it was the trees playing games with her or an approaching car, tires crackling beneath the asphalt. She kept looking back.

The white sky retreated as they entered Dalby Forest, and the concrete feeling in her bones. She sought out the Deepdale Habitat Trail – the steepest, quietest trail available – and set off walking. Nature's orchestra resounded across her torso: the percussive, swaying branches and leaves, shoes scuffed against crumbling earth, twigs snapped beneath feet. Somewhere the lap of water. Birdsong. Stillness.

Giant oaks, beeches and ashes loomed above them. Moss jacketed the trees. Ferns trousered them and released their spores, spraying a flaxen dust across the forest floor. They climbed the slopes, using the fraying, jutting roots as steps, merciless with their bodies until their calves buckled and burned. To be with Jamila, and yet essentially alone in her thoughts, was a gift.

In the flattened heart of the thicket, they straddled a hollowed-out trunk and slipped off their rucksacks. She pulled out her lunch: a foil-lined package of potato and aubergine pakodas, two apples and a purple flask of tea. They ate, submerged in white arrows of light and swept up in deep gratitude.

Nazish had spent hours as a child tumbling around the hills and valleys of northern Pakistan; as a teenager, she sought solace in it when stumbling over her identity; as an adult, she requested its counsel when deciding to leave. Here, too, the forest answered, providing relief, escape, a reason to keep on living. It was why she returned every weekend. She hoped it would do the same for Jamila.

Nazish shuffled into Sadia's flat. She had been sitting dazed on the ground, beside a multistorey car park and a line of restaurants, when Sadia called. In a moment of weakness, she had answered the phone and told Sadia where she was, then regretted it instantly – because Sadia heard whatever was in her voice and announced that she was coming to get her. Nazish did not contest it. This way she could also say goodbye.

Sadia's apartment was made up like a Moroccan riad. Returning from a holiday to Marrakesh, she had done away with sofas in favour of rugs and scattered cushions. The kitchen was tiled in a geometric print. Chandeliers and table lamps emitted colourful, speckled light. The whole thing was more fantasy Morocco than real, much like the paintings of harems and dancing girls that Nazish had been drawn to in the city gallery, and she didn't like it.

Sadia raced through the apartment, picking up Maliha's toys from the floor and her own clothes, books and magazines. 'I had an appointment with the dentist this morning. Sent Maliha to my mum's, thought I'd have the afternoon to myself,' she said. 'It's nice that we're both off from work. We should make it count.'

Nazish shunned the rugs for a seat at the dining table. 'You were making coffee, you said. Or should I go to a café?'

Sadia kissed her teeth. 'Can't you see I'm trying to make the place presentable for you? Do you want something to eat as well?'

'I'm not hungry.'

'Fine, I'll eat alone. Which errands did you say you were running again?'

'Nothing special. Bank, post office.' Nazish scratched her back, her rain-soaked shirt now stiff and itchy. Sadia tossed the mess into her bedroom and returned with a shiny white packet.

She took out a make-up wipe. 'Your eyeliner is all smeared.'

Nazish snatched the wipe from her hands. 'You know, I can do myself.'

Sadia tutted. 'Try to do someone a favour.' She left the packet on the table and filled the kettle. Nazish rubbed her face. Dissatisfied with the faint grey marks that appeared on the wipe, she got up to head to the bathroom when the doorbell rang.

'I'll get it.' Sadia ran.

Nazish saw the figure in the door and grimaced. 'What's this?'

'An intervention,' Sadia said cheerfully. 'Coffee?'

Jamila nodded gravely as she entered. 'What's going on?' she asked, approaching the table.

Nazish looked away.

'You don't look well.'

'I'm sick,' Nazish said, and when her face spasmed, she believed it.

Jamila touched her forehead. Her hands were cold, rough, impersonal. Nazish noticed her biting away at the corner of her mouth. Which client had Jamila abandoned to attend to her? How did their crisis compare to hers? Jamila would soon let her know.

'You never came to work,' Jamila said.

'I told you, I'm sick.'

'You could've called. Or answered one of mine.'

'I didn't feel like it.'

'You don't think I deserve a call?'

Nazish smoothed the tablecloth. She owed them nothing and everything to herself.

Sadia came over with a packet of digestives and coffee. Jamila sat and took Nazish's hands in a tight, desperate grip. 'Why are you shutting me out? You've never done that before. You know that I've always listened. We're closer than this.'

Nazish gazed into both of their faces and found herself sliding. 'Everything is broken,' she said, trembling all over. 'Sab kuch galat ho chuka hai. I received a message from my brother. Meri nani-ji. Woh Allah ko pyari ho gayi hai.'

Jamila squeezed her forearm. 'Oh, Nazish.'

Sadia smothered her from behind. 'I'm so sorry.'

Nazish collapsed in her arms a little and couldn't stop the tears falling. Then, after some seconds, she took a deep breath and sucked her tears back. 'But I see things properly now. All this was a mistake.'

Sadia pulled back. 'All what?'

Nazish gestured around the room. 'All this. I don't want to do it anymore.'

'What are you on about?'

'Main faisla karchuki houn. I want to go back to Pakistan.'

Nazish tried to gauge their reactions. Sadia moved forwards to catch the expression on Nazish's face but revealed her own bafflement in the process. Jamila, placing a sheet of iron over hers, gave less away.

'You can't go back. You're a refugee. Even I know that much,' Sadia said.

Nazish shrugged. 'They can take away my visa. I don't care.'

'Now you're just being silly.'

'I'm tired, Sadia. I'm not happy. I'm not.'

'Tired of what, though?'

'Tired of this life. This country. This *fucking* place.' Nazish closed her eyes and tried to distance herself from it, then opened them and found – to her devastation – she hadn't moved.

'You sound pretty ungrateful right now,' Jamila said. Her face was pinched and flush.

Sadia clumped her lips together. 'No, love . . . don't . . . '

'No, let me say this. Have you forgotten how hard we worked? What it took for me to get you over the line? People would kill to live your life right now, but you'd rather give it up because you're tired. Sorry, but that sounds ungrateful to me.'

Nazish knew that Jamila felt betrayed. But how could she explain the toll of fighting for recognition? The cost of receiving asylum? It had weakened her to the point of illness, packed cement into her bones, but all they could see was how she had gained. Safety, protection, freedom, but at what price? What did she have to leave behind? If anything, Jamila should have known this and sympathised.

Had Nazish been in a fighting mood, she would have ordered Jamila to itemise everything she had done for her, every penny she had spent, so Nazish could pay her back. She wouldn't be beholden to anyone. But she balled the tissue in her hand and laughed instead. 'Oh, look. Mrs Boss is back. Mrs Boss always telling us what to do, what is best. Always playing God. Aren't you tired?'

Jamila drank her coffee – chastened, hairline damp, throat rusty like a bike chain.

'Look, we get it. You're homesick,' Sadia said.

'This is not about feeling homesick, Sadia. This is about starting over. Even after three years, I couldn't find a place here,' Nazish said.

'But would you be safe in Pakistan?' Jamila asked.

'What is safe, exactly? I'm not safe here. All the time, I'm afraid. Afraid of how this place makes me feel, afraid that I don't wake up tomorrow.'

'But what if you got caught?' Sadia asked.

'What is it you don't understand? Even here, I am not free from violence. But maybe, if I live quietly there, nobody will see me.'

'You know that's impossible. What sort of life can you have there really?' Jamila said.

Her voice rippled at their ignorance. 'You think it's not England, so it must be bad? No, I had good life in my country. I had big car, big house, family, friends and partner. If I had stayed, maybe I would be professor. But here, I have no car, no girlfriend, studio apartment. I work as receptionist. Why?'

She wanted to tell them that England wasn't so special. English people smelled of raw chicken and didn't wash their backsides. They knocked into her wherever she was walking. How many times had they disrespected her? 'N—, Nazi—, Nakeesh – oh, I can't get it. I'll just call you Naz.' In Pakistan, people said good morning, good evening, kaisey hain aap. Her face wasn't a conundrum, and neither was her name.

'How often do you speak to those friends? When's the last time they sent you a text?'

In Pakistan, she hadn't made appointments with her friends the way that she was expected to do here. The evenings were theirs for meals, hookah and coffee. On weekends, they piled into her Suzuki and drove the length of the country, visiting forts, festivals and parks, only stopping to eat, sleep and pee. How she longed for those magic nights in Lahore. When, at the Urs of Data Ganj Bakhsh, his followers descended on his darbar and spent the nights praying and whirling, letting the spirits inhabit them. Nazish would stay up all night with her friends, singing and chanting, green lights flickering above, the air fragrant with hash and incense.

The memory caught in her throat.

'They message me sometimes,' she said, pinching her wrist.

'It sounds like they've moved on,' said Jamila. 'But me and Sadia are still here.'

Jamila passed her a biscuit from the pack. Nazish remembered the first time she had made that gesture and shook her head.

They sat awkwardly. Sadia got up and put something in the microwave. It spun, beeped. She took it out and brought it to the table. Nazish stared at the slop, wondering how long remained until she needed to leave for the airport.

'What about that Gambian girlfriend? Or the girl from the club?' Sadia said.

'It didn't work out,' Nazish replied.

'You know, my dad used to tell me—' Jamila began, her chest expanding.

Nazish smacked her palms on the table. 'Oh God, not her dad again.' She laughed, too loud to convince them.

'—a few months after he moved here, my grandfather passed away. Dad was devastated but couldn't afford to go back. He missed the ghusl, the gatherings, the Quran readings. He'd hoped to lead the funeral prayer himself. I assumed this was an agonising situation for him, but when I asked him recently, he said it wasn't. Of course, he grieved the loss of his dad, but he knew when he left Pakistan that there would be sacrifices. He had no choice but to accept them.'

Wisdom imparted, Jamila shrank down again. No matter how she claimed to have changed, her love of grand speeches was undimmed, but, for once, Nazish was endeared. She reached for Jamila, conveying what she could with touch, heavy eyes and a quiet, pleading voice. 'I need soft life, Jamila. I want to live soft.'

'I understand, believe me I do.' Jamila took her hands. 'But there are no perfect choices in life. Something always has to give. You've got to accept the sacrifice.'

It was so sanctimonious, Nazish erupted from her chair. 'What do *you* know about sacrifice? Rich little Jamila, crying to her parents about her problems. Can you survive without them? Can you wipe yourself without their support?'

Jamila folded her arms. 'I know a fair bit, actually . . . '

Nazish turned to Sadia. 'And you—'

'Wait, why are you bringing me into this?' Sadia asked, hands raised in surrender.

'You run from your problems. From Akbar to your Ammi. From one man to the other. Who are you to advise me? You hide from yourself.'

Sadia scowled at her. 'You have no idea about me, actually. You haven't got an ounce of empathy for anyone else.'

Nazish didn't want to hurt them, didn't want to leave on bad terms, but they were utterly clueless. They had never put continents between themselves and everything they had ever known. They couldn't appreciate the length of her pain. 'Why only I have got to compromise? Why everyone always telling me what to do? All the time, nobody listens, everybody always tries to control.'

'Well, you're deluded if you think running away will solve your problems,' Jamila said.

'Fuck you, Jamila.' Nazish reached for her bag.

Outside she leaned against the building and sucked in the cold air. What if they were right and she hadn't fully thought this through?

When she returned, she immediately wished that she hadn't. They were eating without her. Sadia slipped a plate in her direction and beckoned her in. Soon they were apologising, embracing, reminding her of all that rooted her to Britain: her work colleagues, her friends from yoga, belly dancing and the support group.

'I promise, I won't ever lecture you again,' Jamila said, her neck bent low.

But could these fractured pieces ever form a whole?

Nazish didn't follow her grandmother's decision to leave Pakistan straightaway. It was too drastic. She couldn't imagine abandoning her career, her family, the community she had spent her twenties painstakingly building. She reached out to this community for guidance. Some told her she was stupid for not seizing the chance to leave; others rejected her calls, scared that association with her would endanger them. Nazish took to hiking the tracks she had pursued as a child. The apricot trees were heavy with blossom, ferns thriving in the shade, golden eagles patrolling the skies. She waited for the right path to emerge in front of her.

Even when she gave in, Nazish cushioned the journey with lies. She told herself it was just a holiday. A stopover in Dubai concealed the truth. Wearing a floppy hat and sunglasses, she sniffed spices in the souks, watched the fountains tango and play, paraded the marina where skyscrapers erupted from the ground like giant thorns. But what if her family had followed her? What if they were watching? The whole time her nerves were shredded.

Nobody called. Not one of her friends thought to check how she was doing.

Still, upon arriving in Britain, she kept calling. Their conversations moved with mechanical efficiency: they asked after her before launching into lengthy descriptions of their social engagements and the local gossip. Only once did they call her – all in the week she received her refugee status – each one begging for her formula. What formula? She had bared her truth. But though she agreed to help, she never heard from those friends again.

Occasionally, she called her grandmother. They spoke of their health, the weather, the garden. She didn't dare ask if her grandmother had worked on their family, if they were ready to have her back. Instead, she watered the plants on her windowsill, the apricot seed that wouldn't sprout, and wondered, who was watering her garden at home?

When Nazish finally left Sadia's place, the evening flight had long departed. That plane was perhaps always destined to escape her, but she still had a ticket for tomorrow.

She shoved her hands into her jacket pockets and started walking. It was cold and blood rushed to her face. Under the lights, the quiet streets were the colour of weak tea. She walked and walked, the beat of her footsteps for company, trying to hold in these foreign lands, in numb fingers and hands, the shapeless form of her yearning.

She slowed upon reaching Rusholme. Turning a corner, the neon strip lights of Wilmslow Road came into view. She strolled towards the clothing and jewellery stores, cafés and bakeries, shisha bars and restaurants. She lingered outside each one, gazing through the shopfronts, stepping into their shiny white reflections. Black and Brown faces were smoking out on the pavement. Hookah pipes gurgled. Coal released an amber glow. She smelled apple, grape and cinnamon. Did these people belong to her? The ticket sat in her pocket, digging into her thigh.

Nazish had spent so much time in Rusholme – her, Sadia and Jamila – shopping, eating and smoking. With its comfort and familiarity, with the memories she had made, surely here she belonged? She pictured the Swat Valley, her grandmother's valley, with its flower-filled inclines and pure crystalline lakes, that she had grown up believing were the world's most beautiful. The valley was why she found herself pulled to the parks and woodlands on this island. Because, in the forest, she could be anywhere. In every forest she returned home.

Nazish walked further down the road. She switched sides, circled cars, strolling in time with the bass-heavy music that erupted from them. Stagnant traffic snaked towards the city centre. Drunk-looking drivers honked their horns in frustration. Real life was temporarily paused.

She sat on a slanted yellow seat and rested at a bus stop. A screeching bus soon arrived. Ten, maybe fifteen people lined up to board. On the bus itself, a hijab-clad woman waited to alight with her pushchair. Nazish watched the exchange. The doors opened and some passengers mounted the bus, elbowing past her. Others tutted and waited. But there was a man standing outside the Kurdish barbershop, chatting to his friend and smoking. Slowly, he moved to the front. He lifted one end of the pushchair and eased it down onto the pavement, then fell back to a nearby lamppost.

She glanced at the man and smiled.

The kindness of strangers. In the past, it had been moments like these – inconsequential to some – that had given her the courage to move forward. But the kindness of this foreign land, was it really enough? Could she keep moving forwards with so little?

She got up and crossed the street again, advancing on a red-and-white cart fifty metres away, an old man hunched beneath a large umbrella.

'Aapke paas kaunse flavours hain?'

Nazish began with the pistachio kulfi. A couple of bites and it was gone. She asked for mango next, ignoring the old man's curiosity, devouring it in seconds, rejecting every spectre of shame.

He presented her with the malai.

'For free,' he said. 'For my daughter.'

She unwrapped it slowly.

There it was, from the very first taste, everything at once. The sweet creaminess and tiny hint of spice. Sunlight beaming in from the mountains, over distant crests of ice. She was sprinting beside rivers and waterfalls, brushing past tulips and irises, sheltered by spruces and pines. And, as she plucked their elegant, woody sprigs and traced the ridge between her lips and nose, following behind was her grandmother's voice. Echoing across valleys, she was shouting after her, warning, calling out some loving instruction.

Twenty-one

Over two months after she had instructed him to go to the police, Khalil finally showed up at the office. Jamila waved him inside as he stood at her door. She was ready to resolve his case, decide how they were going to proceed – if they were to proceed at all. In spite of the difficult conversations that had followed, her journey to the woods with Nazish had revived her.

This time, Saeed came with him. They both sat opposite her, red-faced and sweaty in the heat. 'This is all we could get from the police,' Saeed said, passing her some papers.

She couldn't tell whether these pages were his record, or a bunch of documents scraped together by the police. She had never seen a criminal record before. The front page set out Khalil's personal details: name, sex, date of birth, place of birth, address. It had been 'created' on 18 August 2012 – the day after the slap.

The front door creaked open, and her father appeared in the shadowy cavity, wearing a sheepish smile and a shirt that she had gifted him last Eid. A weight plunged through her stomach. Saeed must have told him they were coming.

'Salaam, Dad. You all right?' She gritted her teeth.

'Sorry, I'm late. I was just checking if you need me,' he said, his tone friendly.

'No, we're doing all right.'

He ambled in and stood by her desk.

Jamila took a deep breath. She knew that he couldn't help himself and it was futile to expect otherwise, especially with Saeed here. She returned to the sheets, page after page of empty questionnaires. Then she found something. An indecipherable scribble. She held the page aloft. 'This is the charge sheet, Khalil. You were given a verbal caution, yes, but there's a written record of it. You've even signed it.'

Khalil's throat pulsed, but he said nothing.

'I don't understand. What does this mean?' asked Saeed.

She continued to observe Khalil. His face had grown sallow, his torso crooked like he was nursing a stitch. She felt sorry for him. He may have been an adult in the eyes of the law, he may have spoken to her on occasion with a bluntness she found rude, but he was just a kid.

'If the Home Office sees this, they might refuse your application.'

Saeed leaned in. '"If," does that mean it's not guaranteed?'

'I don't know what they have access to—'

'Why didn't you tell me earlier?' her father interrupted in Punjabi. 'How many times have I said, this case is important to me, my reputation is on the line. You need to deal with it personally—'

She gazed impassively, her voice even and unaffected. 'I did everything myself, Dad.'

'Oh, yeah? So why am I only finding out about this now?' Her father snatched the charge sheet and strained his eyes, switching back to English. 'Okay, this is no big deal. We don't need to tell them. Bringing it to their notice will only cause problems for us.'

'No,' Jamila said. 'It's always better to over-disclose than under.' For all his confidence, he had never dealt with this kind of case before.

'No, Jamila, you don't understand. You need to let the lion sleep.'

'Maybe your father's right.' Saeed looked to him for assurance, and he nodded as if this was beyond doubt, but her father wasn't right at all. What good was letting the lion sleep when they only hunted at night anyway, when the darkness left their victims defenceless? No, there was a time for her to listen and be silent, and a time to trust herself and speak.

She straightened her back. 'It's your choice, but if they find this, you'll have two strikes against you instead of one. One for the slap and one for lying about it in the application. Lying is a big deal for the Home Office. Lying is fraud.' She paused to let that hit them.

'Don't worry, we'll find a solution,' her father intoned.

'No, there isn't one.' She held firm. He couldn't magic up a third way, a hidden route that only he knew the code to. In this instance, there was only the binary choice before them.

Her certainty caused the two men's faces to ripple with concern. That was when Khalil leaned forwards.

'We should tell them. It's my application and I want to be honest,' he said, placing a hand on his uncle's forearm.

'But Khalil—' Saeed began.

'Look, we talked about this at home.'

'But son—'

Khalil tightened his grip around Saeed's arm. 'You promised you wouldn't do this.'

For a moment, neither man gave in.

'Okay, fine . . . ' Saeed's gaze dropped and he played with the zip on his jacket, shrugging Khalil's hand away, which slipped back to his lap naturally. 'You say we don't let you do anything, but we let you walk around looking like a hippy,' Saeed mumbled.

Khalil was undeterred. He swallowed several times before he spoke again, as if he were dislodging something there, but as he did his eyes developed the clarity of spring water and there was colour returning to his lips. He looked at her. 'Does this mean I could be deported? I can't go back to Afghanistan or

Pakistan . . . especially looking the way I do.' He touched his long hair and tattoos.

She slid her chair forward. 'If you'd been to prison on drug offences, maybe. But you're a permanent resident and haven't committed a serious crime.'

'Is there anything you can do to stop them refusing me?'

At last. They had reached the stage that invigorated her: whittling down a strategy. On her fingers, she counted her lines of attack: 'We challenge the seriousness of the incident. We submit evidence of good behaviour. Academic success and progress at university, for example, any volunteering that you might do. We explain that you come from a family of refugees. That you've spent your entire life in this country and all your family is here too. A decision to deny you citizenship because of this small thing is outweighed by the reasons why you deserve it. They'd be leaving you stateless, effectively. This must count for something.'

'And what are our chances? What percentage . . . '

Sometimes, she felt like a merchant of promises. She saw it in their faces, a willingness to trade anything for the tiniest fragment of optimism. Now, she embraced it. 'Look, there are no guarantees in this work, but I feel good about this. We have a chance. It's a balancing exercise for the Home Office.'

Khalil and Saeed forgot their differences, leaned into one another and whispered.

'Okay, well if this is what the boy wants . . . ' her father began.

Nobody responded, Khalil and Saeed stood to leave.

Khalil repeated his desire to disclose the slap to the authorities, and Jamila assured them that they would when Rubel submitted the application in a few days' time. She waited until they had disappeared before closing the door behind her.

She glanced at her father, who smiled and sat down. 'How are things with the complaint?' he asked.

They had barely spoken since their big argument. Jamila had been content with that – no contact meant no interference. But then, last weekend, she visited her parents' house. Her mother, tired of their enmity, had the old photo albums waiting. Jamila knew them well, had spent many afternoons flicking through them as a child, she and Jahida lying on the floor like silverfish, begging their mother for stories to breathe life into them.

Among the photographs were pictures of her father in the knitwear factory he had worked in when he first came to Britain. Jamila remembered the vast metal stairwell that gripped the side of the building, the chattering machines inside. There were pictures of her parents loading the boot of their trusted Datsun with clothes from Pakistan, which they would sell from door to door. 'These ones are embroidered,' she and Jahida had learned to chant, removing the dummies and bottles from their mouths. 'Kadai, kadai.' There was the one photo that Jamila had never forgotten, from the days when her father was practising law from home. It captured the two sisters sitting on opposite sides of his desk, Jamila no more than six years old, curling the telephone cord around her tiny fingers, scribbling on a notepad, seemingly attending to her sister's needs.

'You were your father's shadow. Whatever he did you copied,' her mother said.

Then, a couple of days ago, he had called her to check in about Hassan's complaint, having heard about it from Jahida. His voice, his certainty that there were no grounds for concern, had been a balm to her nerves.

She reminded herself to be gentle with him.

'I sent my response to the regulators yesterday,' she said. She had poured all of her frustration into it, all of the frustration that Hassan had poured into her.

'I could have read it for you. But you'll be fine, I trust you. Everything you know you learnt from me.' He squared his shoulders and grinned.

'Thanks, Dad. Does it mean you'll stop dropping in unannounced too?'

Immediately, his face crinkled in distress. 'Why are you so against me, Jammu?'

She laughed at him. 'Promise me you won't visit for a year.'

He got up. 'What? My own office?'

She went over and wrapped her arms around him. 'Make it my birthday present.'

His neck craned away from her. 'I don't know. I can't promise anything.'

His stash of pistachios rattled in his pockets. Then, gradually, his hands came to rest at the small of her back.

On the last Sunday in August, she finally sent the message her brain had spent days composing. The reply was swift; its content surprised her too. A couple of hours later, she found herself parking up and walking to her favourite café in Levenshulme. Three young boys were playing kerby at the mouth of a cul-de-sac. The air carried a honeysuckled scent. Her palms were sweating and not because of the heat.

Inside, the walls were grey, chalky and water stained. Jars of pickled eggs, cucumbers and kimchi sat on shelves above her. Spider plants hung from macramé baskets, which had given birth to several smaller plants, their umbilical cords uncut. She sat at a corner table and waited with a book.

And waited.

She checked the time. He was late. He wasn't going to come. He had deceived her. She berated herself for pursuing this backwards move. And then he was there, a sinewy figure in the window, coming through the door, approaching her. 'You came,' she said, clambering to her feet, trying and failing to conceal her delight.

'I said I would, didn't I?' Irfan looked wolfish, his silvery stubble glinting in the light.

'Yeah, well, I'm glad. Can I get you a drink? Something to eat?'

'Just a coffee.'

She dashed to the counter, where she forgot what she wanted and ordered two cappuccinos. It was late for caffeine, but it didn't matter, she'd drink it. He had come. She leaned against the bar and stared at the fancy bottles of wine, their syrupy hues, pretending to be interested. She glanced back. He wasn't looking, he was playing with his phone. She steadied her gaze on the counter.

He had come.

Teetering back to their table, she placed one coffee in front him.

'Thanks,' he said.

She sat down. 'So, how have you been?'

'Not bad.'

'Got much planned for the day?'

Irfan looked down at himself. He was dressed in shorts and a sports T-shirt, fabric clinging to the concave of his stomach. 'I've got badminton in an hour. The court was already booked, otherwise—'

'Oh, no, that's fine,' she said quickly. She tried to sound serene, to give the impression that it didn't matter either way, but, honestly, it felt like a setback. 'How's that going?'

'I've got a tournament in Amsterdam next week.'

'Wow, Amsterdam.' She drew the words out, all too aware of how ridiculous she sounded. She wasn't used to currying favour with people, rarely felt like she had wronged them, but it was required of her now. She was the one who had called him here.

'It's only amateur level.'

'I'd love to get away. My sister keeps pestering me to take some time off and go to Lisbon with her. I kept refusing her because work was too hectic, or my employees weren't quite ready to handle my absence, then work got hectic again. But I think I could do it now. I should.'

'You should.' He sipped his coffee and gazed past her.

His dry tone scalded her. It had sounded like she was trying to convince herself. But whenever she got nervous, she gabbled, as if by talking she could pin down her breath, which had become a thing removed from her. She regrouped with a drink from her own cup. 'So, how's the dating life—'

'We not going to talk about it then?'

'About what?' she asked to be funny, but he gave her such an impatient look that she added, 'Of course.' She had come prepared, thinking of her clients – Nazish, Zulfikar, even John – and the strength and dignity that was to be found in sharing the truth as they had experienced it.

And yet, her story was so difficult to share, to an unwelcome stranger at that.

She looked around to check that nobody was listening. The café was half empty. The nearest couple to them, a mother and daughter, were sampling wine and talking about preschools. Jamila lowered her voice. 'A lot happened that day . . . it was a bad one for me.

'Yeah? Like what?'

'It was work stuff. It can get a little intense.'

'You, or the work?' he asked, staring directly at her. If he meant to insult her, she probably deserved it.

'Uh . . . both?' She sought refuge in her cup and a little bit of coffee dribbled through the side of her mouth. Oh, God. She wiped her chin with a hand and prayed he hadn't noticed.

'You got up and left me. You didn't reply to my texts. It wasn't that bad, was it?' He gave her an ironic smile.

'No! I was having a really nice time until then.'

'Until when? A simple explanation, I think you can give me that.' It sounded so reasonable.

But she had behaved so badly, her body wanted to curl away in embarrassment. She pushed through, like a mole digging in the dirt. 'You started deconstructing my job, my advice to a client—'

He leant forward. 'I wasn't criticising you. I thought we were having a discussion.'

'Not one that I wanted to have necessarily—'

'Because you don't like opposing ideas?'

'Because all I get is opposition, especially where my job is concerned. When people constantly try to force me into accepting their judgements of my choices, whether that's in life

241

or at work, it's hard not to react defensively.' Hard to centre her compass, hard to know how a person should be. 'But I'm trying not to be like that anymore.'

He paused, absorbing what she had said. 'But you judged me. You judged me when you don't even know me.'

She found a degree of softness in his eyes. 'I'm sorry. Did I hurt you?' She found his appearance so endearing, she wanted to embrace him. He looked like a sick kitten.

He shrugged. 'Nobody likes being judged unfairly.'

'Does it help that I returned?'

'Is that why you got in touch?'

She pondered this. 'I felt bad. Things were going well.' But in truth it was Nazish who had pushed her towards this. Nazish who had decided to stay in Britain, for now. Who had a way with words and a tendency to pull back the skin and reveal truths as clean and white as bone. 'I didn't want to feel like my work was winning. Why did you respond?'

'Because I had nothing better to do?' He smiled. 'No, you're smart and passionate about your job. I respect that. And I thought we had a connection.'

A compliment. Ground broken. 'Does this mean I get a second chance?'

He raised a brow. 'Are you asking for one?'

She raised hers. 'Are you offering one?' But, as he stared at her without blinking, and the seconds ticked by, she decided it was only appropriate that she concede. 'I guess I am.'

He looked down at the table and said nothing. Then he glanced up and traced his fingers over the glossy title page of her book, smiling and enjoying the suspense. 'Then I am going to need another drink.' He raised his hand towards the waitress.

She sighed with a mixture of elation and relief. 'So now can we talk about something else? What have you been up to?' It overwhelmed her to think about the implications of this.

'Not much, honestly. Pottering about, enjoying the summer, a little bit of prep for the new term. You?'

'I'm good. Work is fine, ticking along as always.'

'What happened with that client of yours?'

'The one with the sex tape? We're still waiting for a decision, actually.' Irfan pushed for details on the case, but she refused to elaborate. 'I saw Omar Souleyman in concert the other day. That changed my world.'

The waitress approached with his coffee. He made space for it on the table. 'Do you like your work?' he asked.

'I guess I'm good at it,' she said, watching the foam on his coffee deflate. 'Do you like yours?'

'Well, yeah. I wouldn't do it otherwise.'

'I like mine too, but I wish there was less of it sometimes. I remember when I first started out, any time we won a case it felt like the world's broken axis had been adjusted a little.'

'And now?'

'Winning always feels good, Irfan,' she said, with an unassailable smile, before taking the question more seriously. 'It can get repetitive, and it tends to take over things if I'm not careful, but I do genuinely enjoy it. My dad built this business for me. It connects me to him.'

He smiled. 'You're such a weird mix of prickly and soft.'

'Yeah, I'm like an egg—'

'If an egg was covered in spikes.'

She shrugged. 'I prefer thorns.'

'Oh, so you have a martyr complex.'

She laughed at the mischief in his face and the certainty with which he seemed to have defined her. 'Maybe. Blame my parents,' she said.

'You talk about your family a lot.'

'Do I?'

'Maybe you don't, maybe I'm just projecting here . . . '

He looked uncertain. She didn't know what to do with it. 'They're a big part of my life. Aren't yours?' she asked.

'Not really.' He tore a sachet of sugar and added it to his drink.

'You don't talk, or had an argument, or . . . ?' She tried to balance his right to privacy with how natural it felt for people to divulge their lives to her – and for her to expect it.

'We're not close. But since my mum died, I get the occasional text from my brother.'

She grimaced a little. 'I'm sorry.'

'Don't be, I'm not. But Eid and Ramadan do end up being very quiet, shall we say.'

He scratched his cheek, and she was flooded with sympathy for him. Hers was a small family, a family that didn't always appreciate one another's choices, but they would lay down their lives for each other and it choked her to think about this.

'Are you close with anybody? Friends, aunts, uncles?'

'Uni friends, yes. And I'm still tight with the boys I grew up with on my estate. Uncles and aunties, they're all busy with their own lives, aren't they?'

'We were all quite close when I was young. But as you get older families expand and priorities change, I guess,' she said.

They talked some more, about books, music and video games – and, more tentatively, the things they could do together.

'We could go to a comedy night,' Irfan offered.

'I'm sorry, I don't do forced laughter,' she said. 'I know it makes me sound weird. But I do have tickets for a bunch of gigs if you fancied coming along?'

'Where we have to shout over the music – and everyone else – to be heard? No thanks!'

'What a grandad.' Jamila rolled her eyes playfully.

He laughed. 'Yeah, I'm old. I like walks and stately homes. So what? Let's go into the countryside.'

Irfan made no mention of his badminton practice, didn't seem to want the afternoon to end, so neither did she. A cool, breathy sensation was rising through her breastbone, a rush of karmic energy that she only felt in a yoga class. She hoped he felt the same.

At some point, they ordered food. An array of small plates: charred hispi cabbage with chilli, mint and broad beans; steamed asparagus topped with roasted almonds and wild garlic pesto; local tomatoes drizzled with olive oil and flaked with sea salt. When the food arrived, they served themselves and waited until the other was done, then took a bite simultaneously. Instantly, their eyes connected, and they smiled in shared pleasure, and confirmation of what they would do when they met again: they would eat.

'So, family is quite important to you then?' he asked.

'There's not much choice, we're a small tribe.'

'It's just that I want to tell you something before we go further. Wow, I'm getting sweaty at the thought.' He shook his hands and rolled his shoulders to loosen up.

His sudden nervousness was attractive – that he cared about her response. When he lay his hands on the table, she ran two daring fingers along the open terrain of his palm. His right hand was soft, save for a leathery callous beneath his middle finger. 'Not sweaty at all,' she said. Her fingers tingled with the feel of him.

'I have two children from my previous marriage. Daughters. They're nine and eleven.'

He had to be joking. No, you wouldn't joke about a thing like that.

'I was going to tell you last time, but you ran away before I could.'

Jamila withdrew her hand and felt her mind go blank.

Part III

Twenty-two

One Friday evening in late October, four Pakistani men of wildly different ages had been camped in her office for over an hour as she tried, in vain, to unburden herself of them. Every time she thought she had exhausted their run of questions, the quaking voice of the oldest man, who kept his body upright with the help of two walking sticks, staggered out of the silence: 'Beti, tell me again. What does it mean? What kinds of grounds are there?'

Rotating her ankles, she threw a desperate glance at the clock. Ejecting a man who nodded as he spoke, whose neck couldn't support the weight of his head, would have betrayed her upbringing.

'Like I said before, uncle, asylum is when you're afraid for your life. Maybe you support the wrong political party. Maybe somebody hates you for your relig—'

'What proof would we need?' asked the middle-aged man stood against the door.

'You might have police reports. If somebody hurt you, there could be medical reports, photographs. It depends—'

'What about earthquakes? Natural disasters?' asked a pock-marked kid with bumfluff.

It was a triumph of no small proportion when they left. She jumped into her car and thundered home, where she donned a sleek leather jacket and jeans and doused herself in too much perfume. Outside the Mongolian restaurant near Canal Street, a man was waiting for her, his face silver and pinked like fresh salmon in the soft autumn light. It lit up when he saw her approaching. She quickened her pace.

'Happy birthday, gorgeous,' he called out.

Irfan kissed her cheek when she drew near. She embraced him and ran her fingers along his spine, their bodies merging. It was indecently warm for October. It smelled of barbeque and bubblegum.

What a blissful end to the summer it had been with him. They had spent it talking and eating in restaurants, hiking and playing video games, watching the long foreign films he favoured, where nothing happened and she fought to stay awake. He showed her how to make pottery. No sooner had they completed one date than he would start planning another, always hungry for more time.

She had forgotten what it was like, answering questions about herself again. She had felt strange initially, like a hoarding squirrel reluctant to part with even a bit of its winter stock. But Irfan's warmth and curiosity made it easier to be open. She felt safe even telling him about Zak: 'We weren't together for that long, but it was quite desi. It got very serious, very quickly, you know? Maybe that's why I found it hard to get over. When he wanted to move to Canada, I ended up refusing.'

By contrast, he presented himself to her like he was completely unspectacular. His childhood with absent parents, friendships closer than blood family, travels that moulded him, his ex-wife – nothing was off limits, and she loved hearing about the lives he had lived before meeting her: 'My ex and I met at university. I'll never forget the day I came home to find her bags packed. She said she was leaving me for another man.'

He often talked up his union work or discussed a piece of immigration news from the paper, to make it clear that he shared her views and concerns about the world. She found this endearing, but it was something else that had solidified their bond. He had also grown up feeling isolated from the world, knowing little beyond the confines of his home and the streets that flanked it, starting Secondary school with no knowledge of singers that were in fashion or the sitcoms that were in vogue on TV. The subsequent years were a scramble to catch up.

'Flirty thirties, eh? How does it feel?' he asked.

'You know, not entirely hateful.' The prospect of getting older had never troubled Jamila; she'd never had the luxury of being young. Instead, she had feared reaching thirty with nothing close to the life expected of her. And yet, having spent the year staring the milestone down, she expected to feel . . . different. Worse.

'You're catching up fast.'

'I don't think it works like that.'

He handed her a giftbag. 'For you.'

'Really?' She grinned into the bag, widening the taped lip with a forefinger and thumb.

He placed his hand over hers. 'Wait until we get inside. We're already late.'

It was not lost on her that she always kept him waiting. He checked his sports watch and tutted whenever she arrived, breathless and apologetic. She couldn't help it – though she carved out more time for herself lately, there were only so many hours in a day and so much to pack into them. She ripped the bag open as soon as they were seated, but the wrapping she peeled back carefully, as though she was unswaddling a newborn.

'Aw, Ghibli?' Her voice rose in surprise. Over the years, Jamila had developed very definitive ideas of what she wanted in a partner. In the absence of one, she had imagined that they would share a common creative language, of which anime would form a strong part. But after a full day of subjecting him to her favourite films, Irfan had scratched his neck and tried to break it to her: they didn't move him the way they did her. The animation was impressive, but he found the stories mundane. She slumped at the news. The movies had accompanied every stage of her life. She had hoped they would accompany their story too.

'I thought it'd go nicely with the one in your bedroom,' he said.

'Which one in my bedroom? What were you doing there?' She angled her face towards him, probing him with her eyes.

He blinked several times. 'Err . . . that one with the troll? In the rain? I saw it when you showed me around.'

'That's a lie, I didn't show you anything.' She aimed to fluster him, exploit the fact that they hadn't yet developed this part of their relationship. Not that she didn't want to. She had regularly indulged the thought of intimacy with Irfan – at the gym, as she showered or dressed, admiring the softness of her belly, tautness of her thighs, wondering what he would make of it. But, unlike Maryam and Samir, she hadn't separated sex from religion and morality, and Irfan hadn't pushed her to either. She was working on it, though, while waiting for a sign, a gesture from Irfan, to suggest it was time to move their relationship along.

As usual, it took more than a pebble to create a ripple effect with Irfan. He laughed at her interrogation and picked up the menu. She glanced again at the framed print he had bought her. The movie's Japanese title was written in hot pink across the top, the young girl's face pale, her bow scarlet against the baked goods behind her. Along the bottom edge, cars from the street outside reflected in the bakery window. It was beautiful. He didn't have to love everything that she did. It was his thoughtfulness that moved her. She placed her foot next to his beneath the table.

After dinner, they walked through the Northern Quarter to the cinema. People were still gathered outside the city's bars and pubs. Their chatter filled the air and gave the streets an alcoholic tang. Jamila's boots tapped along the flagstones. She wouldn't hold Irfan's hand in public, but she kept their upper arms touching, their shoulders connected by an invisible thread.

'How are the girls doing?' she asked while they queued for popcorn, warming her voice in a way that still felt unnatural. His revelation about his two daughters had felt like cruel trickery. She liked Irfan, but was in no position to be a mother – the very suggestion left her cold. She turned to her friends for guidance. Sadia tried convincing her of the joys of motherhood, Nazish told her there was nothing to consider if she didn't like kids, but Samir urged her to trust her gut (though her response was flippant: she had bad gut health) and think one date at a time.

'Why? Are you wanting to meet them?' Irfan asked.

'Um . . . uh . . . um . . . ' She felt her face move through a series of expressions.

He placed his hand on her arm. 'Relax, I'm kidding. They're good, I'm taking them to the Sea Life centre on Sunday.'

'Oh, nice.' No matter how many times he amused himself like this, she faltered. It was frustrating. This was a tender and important subject, and she wanted to be better at it. She recomposed herself. 'I would like to, though. Meet them, I mean.'

'Only when we're ready and the girls are ready. Yes, they've got to want to meet you too,' he said.

She smiled at the reminder that this went far beyond her own well-being. In the end, it was a conversation with Babar that had cemented things for her. On the day he had received news that his second appeal had been refused, he began to hyperventilate. Jamila abandoned her clients and took him outside.

'My baby . . . my baby . . . I can't leave him,' he kept repeating, as Jamila led him through the warren of streets behind them, to a small concrete square with swings, benches and a climbing frame. 'I can't replace him like Habeebah wants to.'

She sat him down and took deep breaths with him.

'Who says that it's a betrayal of your boy, Babar? Who says that it is an exile? Your boy will always be with you. But moving forwards in your life could be a kind of release,' she said.

Babar, ensnared once more in the cycle of grief, couldn't grasp what she was saying. But on the drive home she wondered if it was the same for her. That Irfan didn't represent an exile from herself, but a release from certain expectations around children and motherhood. She had never properly considered wanting a family before. Only an idiot would have outright rejected the opportunity in front of them.

He took her roller skating the next afternoon in Ardwick. He had suggested it a while ago and she hadn't responded, picturing herself red-faced and flat on her back. But he brought it up again when they were planning her birthday celebrations, imploring her to embrace new experiences, pointing out that he had attended Comic Con for her dressed as a Ghostbuster.

The rink smelled of rust and popcorn. Two stripes of teal and maroon raced around the walls. She treaded time on her laces, on the cuff of her jeans, and when Irfan could stand the wait no more, she stomped out on her toe plugs. He stood opposite her, clutching her hands, issuing instructions. She dropped her hips and tightened her diaphragm, shaped her feet into a V and shifted her weight from side to side. She felt a chill on her cheeks. A growing exhilaration as she gathered speed.

Seconds was all it took for her to come undone. One cocky leg, which she raised from the ground, an invisible hand that shoved her from behind. Arms helicoptering forwards, she landed on her chest with a thud. The sound was muffled in her ears, but as children stopped to take pictures and Irfan crouched to see if she was okay, she staggered up and tried again. Gradually, the sting faded from her palms, the ache from her wrist, as a giddiness spread through her stomach and her confidence soared. This is who I am when I'm not burdened by responsibility, she thought. And the next time she lost her balance, she made sure to take him down with her.

Afterwards, they went to a vintage tearoom next to the Mongolian restaurant.

'How are your hands?' Irfan asked, coveting the cakes by the counter.

Jamila rubbed her knees. 'It's not my hands you should be worried about.'

'I'll nurse your bruises if you nurse mine.'

She smiled. 'I thought you knew by now, I'm not the nursing type.'

'Have your parents said what's happening tomorrow?'

'It's a surprise, apparently. I just hope it doesn't involve my extended family and endless questions about when I'm getting married.'

He leaned in, suddenly serious. 'But when are you getting married?'

She shook her head at him, and he laughed. 'I'm nervous about tonight, actually. I offered to pay for the food, help with the arrangements, even to bake my own cake, but Samir won't let me. He says it's all under control and I should just turn up. How can it be under control? He only started planning it a week ago.'

'It takes more than a week to organise a party?'

'It does when your name is Samir.'

'Sounds like he's trying to do a nice thing for you. Maybe try to enjoy it?'

She nodded, but her disquiet remained. Irfan made her feel unreasonable when Samir was sloppy with detail and would surely mess up.

'Or . . . you could sack them off and stay with me. I'll take you to dinner, buy you the biggest slice of birthday cake.'

There was a roguish glint in Irfan's eye – like he had tabled something truly wicked – that she found amusing. She slapped the table. 'Deal.'

He laughed again, then poured himself more tea.

When they left the tearoom, some hours later, the puddled street was dark and gusty. It hummed with the noise of generators. She hugged Irfan and realised that she wasn't ready to leave. 'How about that dinner and cake you promised me?'

'Your friends would never forgive me,' he said.

'Come to the party then.' She took his arm and pulled him towards a taxi.

Standing outside Samir's flat in Crumpsall, she licked her dried lips. What the hell was she doing? She didn't believe in introducing a partner to her friends until past the six-month stage. She was in no way ready to answer the bigger questions about their future. She didn't even think she could deal with her friends disliking him.

But, as she began to panic, wondering if they could abort what she had begun, somebody unclasped the lock. An eye appeared in a tiny slit of space. Glittery and black, the eye watched her for a second, then yanked the door back and ushered her inside.

Samir smothered her in a tight hug. 'Happy birthday, babes.'

'Thanks, love. You look stunning,' Jamila said. He was wearing a loose black shirt and drainpipe jeans, his eyes made up with kohl. Even his lip piercing sparkled.

'I was feeling very gothic today. We could blame it on the pressures of hosting, but I'm not ready to talk about it yet. And you . . . ' He looked her up and down, at the trousers and chiffon top she had changed into at the skating rink, borrowing a little of her sister's aesthetic, the elementary thumbs of blush on her cheeks. ' . . . came. Just kidding, I like it.'

She smiled, taking the comment with good grace.

'And who's this?' Samir asked, moving his attention to the space beside her.

'This is . . . ' She held out her hand as her mind rapidly emptied.

'. . . Irfan,' he confirmed.

Samir smiled broadly. 'Mhmmn. Of course. Come in and make yourself at home.'

In the living room, Maryam and Sadia were laying out snacks on the coffee table. Babar and Rubel were spread across a sofa. Nazish came in from the kitchen carrying a tray of pastries. Jamila greeted each of them. They had all come. A bird sang in her chest.

'You're late,' Maryam said, drawing her into a wiry embrace, as if nothing had happened between them. 'Sorry that nobody else could make it. Wasn't enough notice.'

'It was plenty of notice!' Samir said, his voice leaping over hers. 'What can I do if she's always too busy to celebrate her birthday?'

Her friends stared at the figure she had entered with. 'Oh, sorry. This is Irfan. He's my, uh . . . ' Again, her mind offered nothing. She berated her lack of preparedness. It was so unlike her; she could have brought it up in the taxi over. Not just how to introduce him, but who they were to one another.

'Boyfriend . . . ?' Irfan glanced at Jamila. 'I mean, I think?'

His composure quelled the pull inside her. 'Yes, my boyfriend,' she nodded. And her concern that this label had come too early was quickly displaced by something else. A shuttlecock somersaulting between her throat and stomach. Her limbs and organs drifting like stars in a galaxy. She was happy and lightheaded and needed to sit down.

Sadia took a seat opposite her. 'So, this is the teacher you've been hiding from us.'

'I didn't mean to. It's just, when you don't know where something is going . . . '

'How long has it been?' Rubel asked.

'Two months? I wasn't planning on bringing him, but we were having tea—'

'No, it's good. We can size him up for you.' Sadia raked him with her eyes.

'Look after her. She's very dear to us,' Rubel said, and Babar agreed.

Jamila wasn't like her friends. She didn't enjoy this kind of attention, but she wasn't easily embarrassed either. Still, to meet the occasion, she fashioned a demure sort of look for them, which became somewhat real when Irfan nudged her and said, 'I try, even when she doesn't want me to.'

'If you don't, Samir will have no choice but to hurt you,' Maryam said.

Samir came in from the kitchen with drinks. 'Who am I hurting? I'm not hurting anybody . . . unless they want me to.' He winked and the girls dissolved into laughter.

Samir's boyfriend and Maryam's fiancé arrived with the roast lamb that Samir had ordered from a local restaurant. Its aroma filled the room. Samir and Gustavo had just moved into their flat – the walls were still bare and leeched warmth. But there was a banner with her name on it and glossy, helium-filled balloons floating towards opposite corners of the room. Samir refused to sit, even when asked. He refilled their glasses and snack bowls, brought in condiments and napkins from the kitchen, chewing his piercing in concentration. Jamila's cheeks suffused with shame.

As Samir and Gustavo laid out the food, Irfan talked to Rubel and Babar about the recent Ashes series and Jamila caught up with the girls. At some point she looked over at Irfan, at the bristly moustache he was growing out longer than his stubble, listening to his effortless, animated Urdu, and realised how far she had come. She was doing it. Living. A wave of contentment washed over her.

'So, thirty then. How does it feel?' Sadia asked.

'Like I've let myself go,' Jamila said with a short laugh.

'Shut up, you look great.'

'I mean, I'm trying to let go of things. Don't I seem more chilled out to you?'

'No. Have you got any wisdom that you want to share?'

'Then no,' Jamila retorted, and Maryam snorted with laughter.

Sadia was undeterred. She grabbed a handful of crisps and stuffed them in her mouth. 'Come on, J. You must have learnt something from your twenties?'

'To be honest, I always thought you were older than thirty,' Rubel said.

'I always thought she was younger,' Nazish said.

'I don't feel like I lived my twenties,' Jamila said, shrugging.

Nazish sneered. 'So? You're our big-sister boss. You have a piece of wisdom for every moment. Tell us something.' Nazish seemed happier than she had been for some time, certainly she laughed more and was more cutting in her comments. Although she had stayed in Britain, Jamila knew it was only temporary. She and her older brother were talking again. Returning to Pakistan had become more than a fantasy.

'When I turned thirty, I felt like I was grieving my youth,' Samir said.

'I felt like I was finally an adult,' Maryam added.

'I knew myself better, I felt more in control,' Nazish said, with some power.

Jamila gazed into a bowl of sweets. 'I feel like I know less and not more. I feel like I'm still trying to understand who I am.'

They all looked at her strangely, like they couldn't quite believe it – Jamila passing up an opportunity to lecture them. Either that, or they felt like she was speaking in tongues. Jamila chose not to concern herself with their reactions. She couldn't offer what she didn't have.

Irfan spoke then. 'Why do we fixate on our ages anyway? I'm forty and if I worried about it I'd feel like I was half-dead already.'

'Which you kind of are,' Samir said, then raised one hand in a half-apology. 'Just kidding.'

After dinner, Rubel and Babar brought out a cake with blue frosting. Maryam lit three candles and insisted she blow them out. Jamila closed her eyes and meditated on her wish, then Nazish shared out massive chunks of the cake on paper plates.

Later, a few of them chose to go for a walk, while the others stayed behind to set up the shishas and music. Samir looped his arm through hers as they headed down the street. 'I really like him,' he said, his voice low and conspiratorial.

'Yeah?' Jamila asked.

They strolled without direction, Nazish and Sadia not far behind.

'He's good for you, I think. Takes everything in his stride. I love that he stayed back to help the boys.'

It was a crisp, quiet night. The only noise came from the trees rustling overhead, a tram rumbling low in the distance, and a few leaves scattered on the ground. Jamila smiled into the darkness, and above her to the stars. The air fizzed on her tongue with a sherbet sweetness.

Twenty-three

Khalil's determination had arrived. Within two hours of informing him, he was sitting inside their reception.

Jamila studied the letter at her desk. She had felt like something of a clairvoyant when drafting his submission, trying to step into his body, see the world from his eyes, write using words and emotions plucked from his mind. Afterwards, she had handed those pages to Khalil and he had added his own thoughts to them. All that effort, and the Home Office had given it a superficial glance, then proceeded with its ready-made conclusion: *We have closely considered your application for naturalisation as a British citizen and decided to reject it* . . .

It infuriated her that he was being denied what so many of his peers took for granted – what they would never have to worry about losing. As her consultations wore on, a voice in her head claimed that her father had been right. They shouldn't have disclosed the slap. She was to blame for this refusal. But as she began to punish herself, a smaller voice spoke up. The Home Office would have found out anyway, the voice swore. It had access to any record it wanted. And it could make whatever decision it desired; the system had severed its relationship to truth, competence and integrity a long time ago.

She moved her concern to Khalil. She wondered how he had taken the news, how to comfort him. But when he entered her office, Khalil was tall and dignified, dressed in a long, sleek black coat, his face serene. His shiny black hair, which now went past his shoulders, fell down his back in a single braid, and he had grown a beard.

'I'm so sorry, Khalil . . . '

'Is this it?' he asked. 'I can never be a citizen?'

'No, they're saying you're not good enough to be one yet.'

'So, I'm stateless until then?'

'I don't know if you're entitled to an Afghan or a Pakistani passport.'

He stood between two chairs, looked as though he couldn't decide if he should sit. 'I really thought my CV would save me.'

Maybe it was a question of perspective. 'In the wider scheme of things, how much does this matter? You still have indefinite leave to remain. You could go away and finish your degree, live your life with your girlfriend, and even travel. Then, when the warning comes off your record, I'll be here, and I'll make that application for you again. This need not consume you.'

'How long would that be?'

'Ten years . . . if you stay out of trouble.' She paused and considered what she meant by this. Don't support the wrong causes, don't utter the wrong words, don't gather with the wrong sort of people – where the requirement of 'goodness' began and ended, she didn't know.

Skin tightened around his face. 'How can it not consume me? If they rejected you, if they spent your life telling you that this country was about equality and fairness, then went back on it and betrayed you, could you get over it? I don't know if I can. Don't know if I want to, to be honest. It needs to consume me.'

A cold Monday in early November, the heating had been on for hours and the room was stuffy. Khalil removed his coat and folded it over a chair. Underneath, she was surprised to find he had on a Hawaiian shirt in the gold and red of a Christmas cracker, and between its wide collar she saw something printed on his chest. A tattoo. A marking. Black, with flourishes of red ink.

Staring at the two inches of skin below his throat, she made out a few things: barbed wire and ancient swords, the sharp, pointed ears of a leopard or maybe a lion. She wondered if it bore any relationship to the playing card on the back of his hand. He had dismissed her opinion before, but this time she didn't have a counterargument, nor was she interested in providing one. It was a matter of perspective, she felt more strongly now, and he had already staked his position into the ground.

'What do you want to do then?' she asked.

'I want to fight, I have to.'

'Even if you end up losing?'

He looked at her as if the result hardly mattered.

For a while, she rubbed her hands quietly, pushing her fingertips into every groove, mulling over the virtues of following him down this path. His words had made her think of herself. The privilege of a red passport, British citizenship – though with heritage from another part of the world, hers could be revoked at any moment. The warmth in her chest whenever she got off the plane from Pakistan to be greeted by terminally grey skies and chilly temperatures. This place. My place. Yet, the system had degraded to the point where it was no more than a lottery. He who persisted won.

There was a lot at stake here – for them both – and huge potential reward.

'Okay,' she said slowly. 'I'll support you. I'll write the grounds for an administrative review. I'll even take it to the High Court if you want. But . . . '

'But what?'

'But nothing.'

But she would not let it consume her. Fighting for her clients while holding onto her boundaries. It was the only way that she could win too.

When she left the office that evening, Jamila got into her car and started driving. She slouched in her seat, wound the windows down and turned up her music. When she climbed the ramp onto the Mancunian Way, the sky opened in front of her. She soared over the highway, joining the exodus of cars speeding away from the city. She imagined them filled with dusty Poles and Lithuanians leaving their building sites, sleepy Pakistanis and Bangladeshis departing their taxi bases, harried-looking Jamaicans and Filipinos exiting their hospital shifts – even those that idled all day abandoning their stoops. She left the deserted city in her mirror and looked ahead to her evening.

The bell to Irfan's house was webbed over. When she pressed it, a tiny black spider scuttled into the brickwork. Irfan unlatched the door and she went inside, his footsteps heavy on the floorboards.

'You won't believe the day I've had,' she said, sighing wearily to make up for his failure to greet her. She followed him into the kitchen, where he stood over the sink, his back to her. She caught a strong odour of fish but held off complaining until she had properly gauged his mood. The small, fold-out dining table had been pulled back from the wall. Two places had been set with the fancy stoneware plates he rarely used. Three bowls contained salad, curry and rice. She felt a pang of contrition. 'It really was a lot.'

'You should have texted if you were going to be late. You can't reheat seafood,' he said.

'I did,' she said. 'Check your phone.'

He dried his hands on a tea towel and retrieved his phone from the living room, scrolled through his messages. His pettiness surprised her. Then he quietly put the phone in his pocket and placed the curry in the microwave to reheat. Its briny smell grew in intensity.

Suppressing the urge to gloat, she hugged him and said, in a child-like voice: 'I'm so hungry. It was such a long day.'

'Fine. But you always do this and I'm tired.'

He tried moving away from her, but she turned him around and looked contrite until she forced a grim smile out of him. He instructed her to take the fish out of the microwave. He filled their glasses with cordial. She served them both as they sat down to eat.

'Oh, this isn't bad at all,' she said. 'I was scared. You've outdone yourself.'

'It's my ex-wife's recipe. She was a great cook,' he said.

She raised her brows. 'You're feeding me your ex-wife's food?'

He matched them. 'You're complaining that I cooked for you?'

'Someone's still in a mood.'

'Yeah, well I had a bit of a day too. And you're late to everything.'

She stroked his forearm. She loved the hair there and the surprising heft of his wrists. 'What happened?' she asked, brushing over the second comment, hoping that he would forget it too.

'I had to fill in for a colleague today and teach a full class. Then one of the kids soiled himself and I had to clean him up.'

'Oh, God. Did you shower?'

His arms tensed. 'What kind of person do you think I am?'

'I thought it smelled weird in here.' She sniffed the room and then him, pretended to gag. She would play the clown for as long as he needed.

'Stop, it was horrible,' he said, trying to hold in his laughter.

When they had finished eating, she cleared the table and started washing up. Irfan stood by her, drying the dishes with a tea towel, happiest when they were side-by-side, immersed in this simple domesticity.

'You know, I was actually on time for once, when a client called me up,' she said, passing him a plate.

Just as she was leaving the office that evening, the phones had sparked up. Though Babar had switched on the answering machine, she answered it on a whim.

'Mrs Shah! Help me, its Hassan.'

'Hassan?' She couldn't believe she was hearing that voice again. The voice that only promised trouble. A couple of weeks ago, her regulators had received her response to his complaint, but asked for more information. She gathered her consultation notes, her costs at each juncture, her answers to their questions, and submitted them. As she did, she conceded that she had never known Hassan, never fully understood what he wanted. She had tried constantly to unearth the code that would have unlocked him for her. Instead, he was an obstruction to them both.

'They've detained me and my family. They're putting us on a plane,' he said.

'But I don't represent you anymore. You gave instructions to another solicitor.'

'That solicitor was an idiot. Only you can help me now, Mrs Shah.'

'You complained to my regulators, Hassan. You never said a word to my face.' It seemed cruel to dredge it up now, when he was at his lowest, moments from deportation, but it would have been dishonest to pretend she harboured anything but resentment for him.

'Well . . . well, what if I take that back? Will you help me then?'

'You can't do that now, it's too late—'

'No, but I can. I will. I'll email them now. Tell them that I got angry and made a . . . '

The offer tempted her, but she said nothing. Her pride, she knew it held her back sometimes, but she couldn't trade with this man – she cared about integrity.

'Please, I can't go back to Algeria. I left when there was war and they were killing everybody. I saw them kill my father, then my mother, my sister. I tried to forget, but my mind remembers. My sweet uncle managed to send me out and even he is gone now. What will I do there? I have no house, no job, no family. But I have been living here for fifteen years and I know the streets. My children are in school and I have my people. I'm not asking for something big, Mrs Shah. I just need a place – a small place – where my wife can sleep and my children can play. And when it's my time to return to God, you can bury me anywhere.'

Jamila listened to him then – really, properly listened. He had never told her any of this before. Just how long had he been fighting with the truth?

She advised him to resist deportation at all costs: lie on the floor if he had to, wriggle if they tried lifting him, kick and punch them if they carried him onto the plane. Meanwhile, she locked the front door of the office and retrieved his file from storage, called the removal centre and pled his case, wrote and faxed letters to the Home Office. Without knowing it, Hassan had shown her what to do. She pictured a cellar door swinging open in front of her.

'What do you think will happen to him?' Irfan asked her.

'It's going to take a miracle. But if he somehow avoids that flight tonight, we've got a chance. He's traumatised by the civil war; I need to get him to a psychiatrist. I can't believe it's taken me this long to realise.' She scanned the room for anything else that needed washing. Perhaps she had obstructed herself from helping him all this time.

Irfan pressed his hand against her lower back. 'You can't know what they don't tell you. You've done what you can for now.'

He led her into the living room to watch a medieval fantasy drama. The room, like the rest of Irfan's house, was full of the things he had collected over the years – sci-fi DVDs, gifts from his students, magazine subscriptions – but everything had its place. Jamila pushed her back into a corner of the sofa and stretched her legs across his lap. His fingers dangled over her shins. Every so often, he pushed her toes back and forth in a rhythmic motion.

Ten minutes in, Jamila glanced at her watch. It was 8:30pm; Hassan's flight was due to leave at 8:15. Had the plane taken off? Were he and his family on board? Handcuffed to their seats? Alive? She grabbed her phone from the coffee table.

'What are you doing?' Irfan asked.

'Nothing.'

'You're on your phone.'

She tried to remember Hassan's flight number. 'I'm nearly done.'

The sound of clanging swords stopped abruptly. She looked up and found Irfan clutching the television remote. 'You're not watching.' The series of depressions that had appeared several times on his forehead already that evening had finally conquered his face.

'I am.'

'We're meant to be doing this together.'

'I'm trying to check on his flight.'

He sighed. 'Look, I get it. Your work is hectic. You've been on the go all week. But can we relax and forget about it now? You can't do anything from here.'

She slid the phone into the crook of her armpit, away from his grasp, folding her arms. 'You're teacher-ing me, Irfan. You don't respect my work enough.'

'No, I'm saying that I care about you. You work really hard and I'm proud of what you do. But my work is important too, and I'm exhausted. Don't we both deserve a moment to recuperate? Before the next big thing comes along?'

She inspected the lines around his eyes, the silvery tint of his beard, as if they weren't proof of his age but the week he'd had. He was being reasonable – his voice was suffused in a sincerity she found hard to deny, and yet she felt compelled to do so anyway. He didn't understand; their jobs weren't the same. He could switch off whereas hers was a twenty-four-hour profession.

'You're always so wrapped up in your work, I wish you'd leave more space for us. Sometimes, I feel like you don't really want to be around me.' He had never accused her of this before and it shook her enough to look at him again. His nostrils were flared in that sick, feline way of his, so that she was engulfed with tenderness.

'I always want to be around you,' she said, gripping his calf.

'Well, then.' He gestured to her phone.

She dropped it reluctantly from her hands to the floor.

The clanging and grunting resumed.

Some seconds later, she glanced at him and smiled. She was no good at relaxing. Stubborn and argumentative. Sometimes she needed help. Then, before he caught her looking, she turned back to the television.

Twenty-four

Rubel

They began by fixing the story of how they met.

Rubel didn't understand why. Sadia might have been a married woman once, but her divorce had come through. And while her ex-husband Akbar used to visit the office regularly and was friendly with everyone, he'd not dropped in for almost a year. If it was so important to come up with a story their friends and family would find acceptable, they would have done it already, on those balmy September nights when they'd texted for hours, describing the smell of the air with their heads pushed out of their bedroom windows, exchanging hazy pictures of the moon.

It was a brisk November afternoon as they sat down in the restaurant on the fifth floor of a glass building in Spinningfields. The heat of the open kitchen lay on top of them. Sadia picked up a napkin, slowly tore it into strips. 'But you must have some idea,' she said to him.

It was so obvious he leaned back and smiled. 'We'll say we met online. Simple.'

'Like Single Muslim and all that?'

'Or Hipster Shaadi. Or Pure Matrimony.' He had profiles on them all – had even joined an app recently called Tinder.

Sadia flinched and felt for the dupatta looped across her chest. 'Where I come from, girls don't use apps or go out looking for their own partner. Not on the internet. No.'

'Okay.' Rubel rocked as he thought. 'What about in person? A Muslim singles' event?' Immaculately groomed men and women networking in stately halls, confidence and orange juice flowing freely.

From the bewildered look she threw at him he realised that Sadia hadn't attended one and couldn't imagine doing so.

'You could say our friends introduced us?'

'To my relatives? They'll think my friends are loose and spend all their time with boys. I have a daughter now, I can't.'

Rubel adjusted his chair, heat spotting his forehead. This was getting complicated. 'Fine. Your family then? An auntie?' He pictured marriage bureaus operating from cramped living rooms, the kind he'd visited on more than one occasion, hoping to be matched with a wife. Rubel had time for aunties. They inscribed his details on a cue card and added it to a shoebox behind the sofa, then fed him laddoo as a promise of what was to come. Nobody could object to the community matchmaker.

Sadia sighed. 'How many Bengali families do you see marrying their boys to a Pakistani girl like me?'

'I guess you're right, especially given the whole genocide thing.'

Her face froze and Rubel saw that Sadia had no idea and was too afraid to ask. But how many Pakistanis knew what their country had done during the war? Mrs Shah didn't, and she was the smartest person he knew. A brief mention on the anniversary of liberation had sent her scurrying through Wikipedia for information.

'I'm sorry, I just can't have people finding out. Not until it's clear what this is.'

Rubel considered the remnants of the napkin that Sadia tossed through her fingers like paper spaghetti. *I'm an open book,* she had texted on more than one occasion. *I'm up for whatever.* And Rubel had lain back on his bed and imagined her shapely figure advancing towards him in the rain. That woman, he thought, his breath swelling. That woman he had adored for years. That woman who seemed so cool when she came to work dressed in tight jeans, glass bangles and a designer kurta, gold-sandalled and jasmine-fragrant. That woman who didn't care if she caught him watching her as she worked, who turned back to him as she was leaving and let her eyes . . . linger. Where was she now?

It was funny how initial appearances could deceive. Deflating, really. The sleek restaurant décor had impressed him upon entering, for example, but now, glancing at the bronze elephants and diamantéd gods on the walls, it struck him as hideously old fashioned. From one of the best restaurants in this supposedly forward-looking city, he'd expected better. He considered getting up and going home.

Then Sadia picked up his flower, sniffed it and rolled the stem between her fingers. 'No one's ever bought me a rose before,' she said. Cellophane crackled.

He traced a sweaty hand over his hair, hard against his palm, fat globs of gel holding the wet-look, slicked-back style in place. 'You deserve it.'

Rubel hadn't been in romantic relationships long enough to understand them. Every piece of wisdom he trusted came from Bollywood, such as the fact that heroes only got the girl if they both looked and acted the part. So, here he was, wearing a suit, gunmetal grey, his most expensive. And before meeting Sadia that afternoon, he had combed his local florist for the fattest rose and presented it to her outside.

Sadia twirled the rose again, brought it to her nose and inhaled its perfume. She stared into its dark, velvety folds, as if she'd never seen a flower like this before, and gave him a half-smile. A dart of joy fired through his heart.

Rubel quickly exhausted the conversation topics he had prepared (her daughter, jobs, hobbies). He hadn't expected this – in the office she chatted for hours to anyone who gave her the slightest inroad, but now she said very little. Then the food arrived. She took one look at the silver platters balanced on the waiter's tray – Rubel had ordered enough to feed a family; he was no miser – and sat up in her chair.

'This looks amazing,' she said.

'Eat! Don't be shy.' He urged her with both hands.

She lifted a kebab with her fingers.

He watched her like a boss gifting an underling. 'Any good?'

'Gorgeous.' Her lips glistened with fat.

It was a joy to watch her eating with almost animalistic fervour, staining her fingers and mouth, but then it was a joy to watch her at all. She looked incredible in a mustard salwar kameez, hair braided to one side, nose twinkling with a paisley-shaped pin. When he wore mustard, he looked like the condiment. He noticed new things in her appearance: the marble smoothness of her forearms, the perfect arc of her brows, the fat freckle beneath her left eye. She was beautiful and he longed to hold her.

'There's lots I don't know about you,' he said. 'To be honest, I don't know you at all.'

'Guess,' she said.

'Guess?'

His calf muscles tensed, there was so much that could go wrong – would inevitably go wrong – but she started tapping his shin beneath the chair. 'Anything. I won't be mad.'

So he did.

'You're a Baptist minister and leader of the American civil rights movement?'

'Huh?'

'You're the Prime Minister of a small, powerful country, a war hero and you like cigars?'

She looked at him blankly.

'You're a religious woman from Eastern Europe who has dedicated her life to wearing cheap sandals, blue-and-white saris and serving the poor.'

'Come on, be serious.' Sadia's voice assumed a nasal, whining quality, in a not-too-unpleasant sort of way. He laughed a little too hard.

'You'll regret this,' she said.

'I regret a lot in life.' He cast a superior glance at the table next to them, where an orange-skinned couple were mispronouncing items from the menu. 'Tell me,' he asked Sadia. 'Have you done this much?'

'Done what?'

'This.' He pointed a finger at the table and them both.

'Well, aside from with . . . '

'Akbar. You can say it, you know. Akbar,' Rubel said, as if repeating it would cease his hold over them. They had never made a good match, in Rubel's opinion. He had sensed her impatience with Akbar's eccentricities, noticing how she always dulled herself whenever he visited the office. He was unsurprised when they split, and eager to meet her in ways that Akbar could not.

'Aside from Akbar, no. I did not have good experiences with men before that.'

'What do you mean?'

Her gaze drifted to the ceiling. 'I started getting attention very young. Catcalls in the street. Followed on my way home. Boys at university who wouldn't take no for an answer, like all they had to do was wear me down. It did wear me down. It wore me out.'

A small dimple appeared in her chin. Rubel tried to look thoughtful, hurt, offering what he assumed she wanted, a man who understood what it meant to be a woman. But the more he thought about it, the more he *was* hurt. Hurt as he realised how she had been troubled by men. 'I'm sorry.' He stared quietly at the table.

'Thank you.'

'Is that why you married Akbar?' he asked, once enough time had passed.

Sadia shrugged. 'Akbar was . . . he made me feel . . . '

'Safe?' Rubel offered, trite as it was. As much as he had disapproved of their coupling, a woman financially caring for her husband, Akbar was not a bad man. But, more importantly, neither was he.

Sadia gestured to his plate. 'You're not eating.'

He sprang into action, spearing a piece of fish.

'Have you dated much?' she asked.

'Yes.'

'Oh. Here or in Bangladesh?'

'Both,' he said, trying to sound nonchalant.

'Nice. And nothing worked out?'

He shook his head. There were milkshake dates at college and unrequited love affairs, matches where British-Bengali women rejected him for not having a permanent visa. They didn't get very far and left Sadia far more experienced – but she didn't need to know that.

'When did you move here?'

'Seven years ago, as a law student.'

'And why did you stay?'

'Because I want to be successful.'

She turned a fork in her hand. 'You couldn't be successful over there?'

He straightened his back. 'Not the way I want to be.'

'Define success.'

'I want to be rich. I want to be at the top of my field. People to know my name.' And it was happening, far quicker than ever possible in Bangladesh. Six months from completing his traineeship with Mrs Shah, where the clients adored him, and he was primed to leave her. He'd found a former pet shop for rent in Levenshulme. Started saving copies of the work he did at Mrs Shah's. He fingered his shirt collar. Usually, he kept his ambitions to himself.

His words had impressed her; she gave him a wry smile. 'And what about personal happiness?'

'Of course, I want that too.' Having a perfect family was another kind of success. In this country people fell in love recklessly and, when it faded, they swiftly moved on. But he was looking for something lifelong. No, not lifelong. More than that – a partnership that would continue from this life to the next.

He searched for an intelligent way to articulate these thoughts, but Sadia had moved on. She was filling a fuchka, water trickling along her fingers. She carried it to her lips, one hand rushing the other. The fuchka, a combination of crispy shell filled with chickpeas, potatoes and tamarind, collapsed just as she slotted it into her dainty, puckered mouth. Fuchka water dribbled down her chin.

'Oh, God, I'm such a mess. Can't take me anywhere.' Sadia wiped her chin with the back of her hand, then ran her tongue all the way down her fingers.

Oh, to be one of them.

'Stay this way,' he said, admiring her ability to be nothing but herself.

He handed her a napkin and she wiped her face. Should he have reached over and wiped it for her?

An idea came to him. His pulse quickened. It would be like in those movies – the movies of his childhood – the hero and heroine coming together over a plate of street food. He loaded a fuchka with spicy tamarind water and offered it to her.

She raised a palm to reject it. 'You saw what I just did there. I make a mess of things.'

'No, but you have to.' He moved the fuchka around her fingers.

She leaned back and laughed, not appearing to take him seriously. Why wasn't she taking him seriously? He was trying hard to make this moment a significant one.

He pushed the fuchka closer. 'Look, it's breaking, it's falling. It's going to land in your lap if you don't take it.'

The smile disappeared from her face. She really didn't want it, he realised with horror. But it was already too late to pull back. The fuchka was inches from her lips. Seconds from collapsing. If he retracted, he would look like an idiot.

Sadia opened her mouth and accepted his gift. But every muscle in her face had deadened and so had the light in her eyes.

Before she had even begun to chew, Rubel was searching to rectify his mistake. Then a low moan emerged from Sadia's throat. A strained cough. He looked up and saw her shoulders beginning to judder, her body jerking forwards.

Kuttar fuwa. It had all gone wrong.

'Sadia? Sadia, are you okay?'

She didn't answer. He filled a glass with water and placed it before her. For several minutes, he could do nothing more than watch as she hacked and spluttered, his head so hot it could burst. The whole restaurant was staring, deathly silent. What if he had caused her some lasting damage?

Sadia surfaced and sank the glass. When he caught her gaze again, her eyes were swimming in their sockets. 'You don't do that to a woman, Rubel.' She wagged a weak finger and whimpered.

'I-I'm s-sorry, I don't know what I was thinking . . . I thought you'd like it.' He stared at his hands with contempt.

For the rest of the meal, Rubel picked at his food and exchanged mindless small talk. He felt all stretched out of shape. Next to them, a couple's hands were entwined across the table, a picture of how it could have been. Through the window the city slowed to a thick soup of regret.

The waiter came to clear their plates.

'But you've hardly eaten anything,' Sadia said, sending the waiter away.

'I don't feel like it.' He felt as if he had swallowed a stone.

'Is it because of what happened before?'

'I had a big breakfast not too long ago.' But he couldn't stop replaying the shaky viral videos that circulated the internet – street scenes of irate young women in marketplaces, shopping centres, places of worship, confronting the men who dared to touch them. 'Ladki ko chhedha? Teri maa beti nahin hai kya?' they asked in Hindi, yanking the men by their shirts and pelting them with their slippers. He considered their query. Hadn't the presence of a mother and sister in his life shaped him into a better man?

Sadia reached along the table, some way short of his hands. 'You don't need to feel so bad. Mistakes happen. Forget about it.'

'It was a big mistake.'

'Maybe I'm just glad to meet someone who's direct and knows what he wants . . . but take your cues from me next time, okay?'

He nodded vigorously, grateful for another chance.

She threw a napkin at him. 'You look terrible.'

He wiped the shine from his face.

'Wasn't very halal of you though, was it?' she added, playfully. 'No, straight to jahannam for you.'

And with the rasp in her weakened voice, a current passed between his thighs.

The food in his plate was cold, its flavour dulled, but he was hungrier than he had dared admit and ate ravenously.

'What's your favourite film?' Sadia asked, watching.

'*Dilwale Dul* – no, *Sholay*. I like *Sholay*.' It was important to speak carefully now. 'Action films. *Dhoom*. *Dabbangg*. *Gangs of Wasseypur*.'

'Action, really?' A twinkle of something in her eye. 'But I like *Dilwale*.'

'Shah Rukh is a good actor.' He tried walking into work with an ounce of his confidence.

But what he really meant was this: his life, like cinema, could be split into two – the period that came before *Dilwale* and the period that followed. He had travelled through Europe with friends, gone skiing in the Alps with the object of his affections, made the decision to move to Britain, all like his heroes on screen. *Dilwale* had opened up the world to him, taught him to chase the train that carried his desires.

'I don't like the newer stuff. Bollywood became so superficial. All that money, sex and nudity. It's trying too hard to be Western.'

'Oh?' Rubel was afraid to disagree. 'Which films do you like then?'

'I love *Anmol*, *Maine Pyar Kiya*, *Tezaab*. I'm kind of traditional.'

'Me too,' he said eagerly.

She threw him a look, like she didn't quite believe him.

When the waiter took away their plates, Rubel didn't know what to do with himself. He saw that Sadia didn't either. She moved her hands from the table to her lap and looked out of the window. He counted the cranes in the sky, the streaks of colour among the concrete.

'Isn't the view nice?' Sadia said. 'I've never seen it high up.'

He pointed at the skyline. 'You can see the Peak District over there, and on that side is Saddleworth Moor.'

'I should be telling you these things. I'm the one who's from here.'

'We don't always value the things in front of us. I travel all the time here, but I've seen nothing of Bangladesh.'

'Do you miss it?' she asked.

'Bangladesh? My life is here now.'

'Don't you care about where you came from?'

'No, no, I do. It's just . . . ' Rubel felt the network of veins and arteries in his cheeks surging with heat, an urge to share more, something substantial about himself, about the struggle of life in Bangladesh – how he couldn't even secure an internship because they were reserved for those with connections – but Sadia spoke up first.

'What are your thoughts on religion?' she asked.

'Religion? You mean Islam?'

'Yeah. We didn't talk about what kind of Muslims we are.'

'I guess—'

'Sorry if that's too heavy to talk about. I'm just curious.'

'No, it's fine.' But it was too heavy, wasn't it? He looked around the room. 'I . . . believe in Allah and Prophet Muhammed, Sallallahu Alayhi Wasallam. I fast, I give zakat—'

'Sure, but there's more to Islam than that. More than God and the Prophet. More than no booze and no pork. What do you believe in, Rubel?'

What did he believe? Nothing came to him. The way she held his gaze he felt the terrible possibility of his words exposing him to be somebody not worthy of her time.

'Are you going to answer?' she asked.

'Of course. It's a complicated topic.' Religion wasn't for conversations like this, he wanted to say. Religion was to be lived, embodied, not examined like a rock on a beach. But, from the corner of his eye, he saw something. Someone. His heartbeat leapt. Entering the restaurant was his boss, Mrs Shah – Jamila – and her partner. She wore a bottle-green dress, her hair arranged into glossy curls. Irfan wore a suit. It became obvious that she couldn't see them – a pillar obstructed her view and she wasn't looking – but Rubel could see them both clearly.

Meanwhile, Sadia continued talking: 'Growing up, I never thought about it. I was just Muslim, you know? Born Muslim, surrounded by Muslims, doing what other Muslims do. But when my marriage ended, and people started gossiping, I couldn't stop with the questions . . . '

Rubel had witnessed Jamila's slow transformation but was still surprised. He saw a woman in possession of herself, who kept placing her hands on her hips, like they were the gates to somewhere sacred – like she had discovered them for the first time. Lucky Jamila, to whom everything came easily. The office and business had fallen into her lap. The English language slid off her tongue like water. He was stuck with an impossible question, but she inhabited the room easily, following the waiter to a table far away, chatting to Irfan while a finger traced her collarbone. Jamila, who once shuffled around the office like an old woman, was young again. He felt happy for her.

'. . . I mean, there are people out there who'd have a problem with me not covering my hair or my forearms, who'd condemn me for meeting a man without a guardian. Is that Islam? They seem to think so . . . '

But glancing at Jamila and recalling how she had addressed the challenges in her own life, he realised that this question of Sadia's – that all her questions, in fact – were mere opportunities. He brought his arms down to rest on the table. 'Why do people matter, Sadia? Why do their opinions matter when we have our own? Let them talk. My mother always told me, be good, do good for others, always try your best. The rest is up to Allah.'

Sadia grabbed the air. 'Yes! Yes, exactly. Only God can judge us.'

'Only God, Sadia,' he repeated with conviction. 'Now, don't make it obvious, but Jamila is over there, behind you.'

Sadia snuck a look, groaned. 'What? Why didn't you say so? Oh God, oh God.'

Now Sadia wanted to leave. She used her jacket to slip out unnoticed. Rubel laid his gold money clip on the table and stood up. It didn't matter that Sadia wasn't around to see it, that she was terrified of Jamila spotting them. The afternoon had been salvaged. No, not salvaged, but won.

They came out onto Deansgate and started walking. The city was cold, congested, unfeeling. They followed the direction of the descending sun, past the squat neoclassical library, the gothic Town Hall, the red-brick Edwardian-Baroque of the Midland Hotel. Though he wanted to keep speaking and getting to know her, Rubel feared breaking the spell that enchanted them. Hands in his coat pockets, he took in the sights as if he were viewing them for the first time.

They continued down Oxford Road, Sadia's sandals slapping against the flagstones. It smelled of alcohol and burger grease, fumes from the black cabs and wheezing buses. He felt like a feather had appeared inside of him, the blunt edge scraping against his ribs, digging harder with every step he took. Sadia seemed to feel the same. Outside the Palace Theatre, the doors had opened after a matinee performance of *Sleeping Beauty* and the last of its audience dribbled out onto the pavement. Sadia stopped by the steps. 'What happens now?'

'I don't know,' he said.

'We have to figure this out. Akbar is my ex-husband. My child's father. What if that hadn't been Jamila but someone else? I can't risk people knowing.'

'I understand.'

'Maybe you don't want this. It's too complicated. Too much like hard work.'

'No!' He jumped like he had stepped on a nail. 'I want to.'

'Maybe you think I'm a mess. I don't know where I'm going, I've got a kid . . .'

But in a frenzied moment, he gripped her hand and shifted his body into hers. 'No, Sadia. I want to.' He leaned her against a pillar.

Their eyes met. Her knee pushed against him. Trapped his breath in his lungs.

'We'll find a way. I know we will,' he said, letting go.

By the time they reached Sadia's apartment, the sun was finally beginning to set, the sky ablaze with colour, like a peacock spreading its tail. Rubel stood by the door and examined the dirt on his shoes.

He'd never gotten this far before. On this part, his movies were silent. In the nineties, Bollywood skipped ahead to the happy ending, with the bleeding hero embracing his tired wife and newborn. If only he could do the same. 'I should get going,' he said. But having uttered those words, he stood exactly where he was, hands in his pockets, toes tacked to the ground.

'All day I've been thinking, all through dinner and all through drinks, would I let you in if we got this far?' Sadia said.

'You don't have to,' he said quickly.

'Other people, they know what's right for them and how to go about it. But you and me, we're stumbling around blind.'

'We don't have to do anything, Sadia. We can take our time.'

'Yeah, but what if I want to, Rubel? What if I want to?'

Rubel's pulse hopped around his throat. He kicked the grass towards her. How much he longed for something to happen. If only he didn't have to take the first step.

'Well, I can do what I want. All these years, I did what I thought I was supposed to do, what the system told me was right. Now, I'm doing what's good for me,' she declared.

Rubel stared at the blades of grass, the scattered leaves and, of course, Sadia's feet just metres from his, high-heeled, encased in gold straps and swollen from the walk.

The lampposts would flicker to life soon. A breeze would come and run its fingers through their scalps. But the sky did not possess its healing quality yet – it was still bruising, from blue to orange, pink to purple. The moon had arrived early, company for the dying sun in the last moments of its reverie. They would be standing there like this even when the cold night arrived, with its navy blanket and a silver dusting of stars, no further along in their decision.

Twenty-five

Her father wanted to go shopping – he had actually called her and asked for help.

Lately, he had become obsessed with his health and reversing the toll of time, with undoing whatever damage his sedentary decades at the office had inflicted upon him. He had given up gluten, then meat, then lunch altogether. Jamila would go home to find him juicing bitter gourds and shaping turmeric paste into little pill-shaped balls. 'I want to start jogging,' he said to her on the phone, 'but I don't have trainers.'

Jamila knew a specialist shop in town. She met him there one Sunday in mid-November. At the end of a busy week, there was nowhere Jamila wanted to visit less, but she saw an opportunity to spend time with him alone, as she had when she was a child.

They entered the Arndale Centre through the market. It reeked of dull, murky-eyed fish ageing on ice chips, the iron-rich musk of marbled meat sitting in refrigerated counters, smoked chillies from the Mexican deli. Her father wore a tracksuit and a pious expression; he showed a monastic disinterest in the food stalls preparing for service.

'How's the office?' he asked as they walked.

'Biji biji,' she said, imitating the way he said this.

He didn't laugh. 'And the staff? Your clients?'

'All fine. What are we going to eat?'

'Whatever you want. When have I ever denied you?'

'Ha.' She thought of all the times that he had.

Inside the shop that sold running gear, a young sales assistant had him puffing on a treadmill. Attached to the back of it was a camera, which filmed his heels as he shambled.

'Are you flat-footed?' she asked, switching off the machine.

The belt on the treadmill slowed. Holding his sides, her father caught his breath.

'Yes, he is,' Jamila said. They both were. She couldn't believe how unfit he was – he'd jogged less than a hundred metres. As she considered the costs and benefits of taking him along to the gym, her phone buzzed in her pocket. She clenched it, then her jaw.

'Jamila, kidhar ho tum?'

Her mother was speaking in Urdu. It sounded so formal, so unlike her.

'Mum, you know where I am. I'm with Dad buying shoes.'

She looked up. He had clambered off the treadmill to the seats, where the assistant was helping him try on a pair.

'Come home.'

'Why?'

'You're all over the newspapers.'

Her legs buckled beneath her.

One newspaper. She was all over one, her mother clarified, as Jamila hurried to the bus stop. In Piccadilly Gardens, she dipped into a newsagent's and grabbed a copy. She marched with it folded under her arm. Aboard the bus, she and her father flipped through together.

REVEALED: CROOKED IMMIGRATION ADVISORS
HELPING ILLEGAL IMMIGRANTS AND
SCAMMING THE LAW.

They stared at the headline. There was an image of her – blurry, mid-speech, no bigger than a passport photograph – beneath the snap of another solicitor. Jamila recognised the frosted glass in the background, the teak panelling, her curly hair. They had taken it fraudulently, in her office, perched on the end of her chairs like sycophants, nodding and gobbling her advice. She wanted to scratch the image out of the paper. Hundreds of thousands of copies were already circulating the country.

A solicitor's firm boasted of using European human rights laws to keep illegal immigrants in the UK. During an undercover visit to their offices in Manchester, Shafiq Ahmad, principal solicitor of Ahmad Solicitors, said he would apply the controversial legislation to stop his 'clients' of Pakistani and Nigerian origin who married brides from continental Europe from being deported. He required 'touching' love stories and wedding photographs to ensure the authorities believed the relationships were genuine. In return, grooms would obtain the right to live and work in the UK. 'We will arrange it all,' he said, 'you won't have to worry about a thing.'

She didn't know who Shafiq Ahmad was, but her stomach began to churn.

The article moved to another immigration advisor, a Mr Shirazi who told undercover reporters to file 'gay asylum claims' and promised to assist in fabricating the details. *'Make sure to include details of previous gay relationships and any trips to gay and lesbian nightlife venues,'* he said. The paper had dug into his background and found that he had organised protests against the Iranian government's oppression of gay people. It also transpired that he wasn't a registered advisor.

She also did a lot of gay asylum claims.

Heat piping through her body, she skimmed the subsequent paragraphs to find the bit about her.

Jamila Shah, of Shah & Co. Solicitors in Manchester, advised our undercover reporters to take advantage of lax refugee provisions, pinning their hopes on natural disasters and political crises to stay in the UK. 'Depending on where you are from,' she said, 'you could say that you were affected by the Arab Spring, or that you were caught up in the earthquake in Indonesia.' When our undercover reporters asked about how they would go about proving such a thing, she told them to find 'photographic proof that your house has been destroyed, supporting letters from people who are still living there.'

As soon as they got off the bus, she was sick. Squatting in a corner of her parents' street, minutes from their house, she heaved until nothing remained.

Her father held back her hair. 'Jamila, meri jaan. Why are you worrying so much when your father is here? I would walk through gunfire to protect you. This is nothing.'

The family had assembled at home. Jahida was in the kitchen, boiling ginger, mint and fennel. Her mother sat in the living room with the newspaper spread across the coffee table. Nadeem minded the kids upstairs. Their sombre faces gave the house a funereal atmosphere. All that was missing were the prayers and incense.

Her father sat beside her. 'Do you remember them visiting?'

Jamila shook her head. 'You know how it is.'

'Too many people, every single day.'

The last few months stewed in her mind – Babar, Nazish. . . Hassan, that bad penny – the elements inseparable, indistinguishable, a sloppy mass.

Jahida entered carrying a tray of clinking cups. She placed each cup on the table, balancing them carefully on coasters.

'So, did you say those things then?' she asked, standing back from the coffee table.

Her mother flinched. 'Don't you ever think before you speak, Jahida?'

'They put those lines in there, Mum. Where did they come from?'

Jamila made no attempt to hide her hurt. 'Is that what you think of me, Sis?'

'You know I love you, Jam. I think you're brilliant, smart, generous, empathetic. But I've said this before, you need to stop being so good all the time. So what if you said these things? You're not a robot—'

'I don't know what you're on about.' Jamila ran a hand across the leather sofa. But she did know – in essence, she had battled with that all year – only this wasn't the time to get into it.

Jahida flung a withering glance at their parents. 'They really messed you up, huh?'

Their mother's voice jumped an octave. 'Hain? Assi ki kitha ve?'

'Even if I did say those things, it doesn't mean I said them in that way. I'm not telling people how to lie in their claims. Half of my clients don't even know what asylum means. I've got to explain it to them in the most basic terms. I've got to lay it out with tonnes of examples, otherwise they can't apply it to their own lives and give me the information I need, and all the while I've got a reception full of clients. I haven't got time for them to get it organically. As if that's even a thing.'

Her father nodded and patted her knee.

Nobody said anything. Only the clearing of throats and noses, and the quick, sharp slurps of hot tea, and the ringing of cups returning to their saucers. Jamila looked up to find Jahida pacing the room, scrubbing her heels against the carpet, and was strangely validated by her sister's frustration.

'The thing I don't understand is, why they were so cruel? They could have chosen any other picture of you. And the description, "Scruffy and plump, sporting an egg-stained blouse," what was the need?' her father asked.

'Well, whatever they said, it's done now, finished,' Jahida said.

'It's far from finished. Didn't you catch the bit at the end?' Jamila pointed to the last line of the article. 'They sent a recording to the police.'

'Nothing will happen, Jammu,' her father said. 'You didn't do anything wrong.'

Maybe not wrong, per se, but a feeling jammed her airways, a fear that maybe her advice had crossed a line. As she drank her tea, her imagination ran riot. She foresaw the arrest, the interrogation, the trial. The layers of humiliation, each one mounting, then burying her: the authorities sanctioning her, then closing the office; community gossip forcing her parents' gazes into the ground.

It was a relief when Irfan finally called. She ran into the next room to answer him.

'Are you all right?' he asked. 'I just read the article you sent me.' He sounded spooked.

'I don't know.' She still scarcely believed that it had happened – to her of all people.

'A national newspaper. That's massive, Jam.'

'Of all the immigration solicitors out there, I don't know what drew them to me. They must have come to the office and recorded me, asked a bunch of leading questions and got their quotes.' She had treated those people like they were genuinely in need. She had listened to their fears and shared her honest advice. The more she considered it, the more she felt like she was the one who had been scammed.

'I'm sorry, I wish I could be there for you—'

'It's okay, I'm with family.' Just hearing the bass of his voice was comforting.

'What's going to happen now?' He paused. 'Will the story get any bigger?'

'I don't know.'

'But you've got to have some idea. I mean, I'm about the quiet life, I don't know if I can deal with that.'

Jamila's stomach caved in. 'Right. The quiet life,' she said icily.

'I didn't mean it like that—'

'No, I get it. I'll leave you to it then.' She hung up, his words branding her.

A great loneliness swept over her then. She fell back on the sofa and silently wept.

The television was on mute when she returned. Her father was following the Urdu subtitles scrolling along the bottom of the screen, her mother jabbing out a text message, Jahida studying the article yet again.

Her mother raised her head. 'Kaun si?'

Jamila cleared her throat. 'Just a friend checking on me.'

'Who?'

'What happens now?' she asked, repeating Irfan's question. She couldn't stop herself – his fear had reignited hers, convinced her that the ramifications of this would be terrible.

'You ride it out,' Jahida said. 'Then, when you're ready, take it to them. Put that bitterness and resentment back into the work, show them who's boss. Don't you have an opportunity to do that with Uncle Saeed's nephew?'

Jamila shook her head. 'No, that doesn't work for me. I don't want to feed this – whatever this is.'

Her mother pushed her phone into a pocket in the sofa. 'This is my advice: stop worrying and go to work. Continue as normal. You think you're the first person to be in the newspaper? No, and you won't be the last. Don't let it faze you.'

'Okay. How?'

'Do your namaz, tasbih. When you remember Allah, it will bring you peace.'

For once, Jamila considered this without any scepticism.

Her father turned to her from the television. 'Stop thinking that you committed a sin. When I used to get inspected, the regulators would criticise me all the time. "Why are you dealing with this case, with that case, it has no merits, these people should leave the country." But it's not their job to decide which case has no merit. I'm going to follow what I believe is right, not government policy that is changing all the time. So, trust what you're doing in the office. Clients, media, ministers, somebody somewhere always has an issue.'

'And what if I get inspected?'

Her father swatted the air. 'The jahil's job is to create problems. It's how they keep themselves in business. My friend Zaheer used to say, "Whenever they come to inspect you, agree with whatever they say. If they say yes, say yes. If they say no, say no. And when they leave, kick them on their backsides and get back to your work. Because only you know what you're doing and why and if they had their way, you wouldn't have any clients at all."'

Jamila sat down beside her father. Fighting for everyone without distinction. Looking at every individual life and believing it had value. That had always been her mantra. But resting her head against her father's chest, his advice slid off her. All her progress had been worthless. She could only pretend that none of this had happened.

Twenty-six

She lay in bed semi-conscious, a prisoner to her dreams. In the most disturbing one of all, she found herself slumped back in a wheelbarrow, naked from the waist up. She was paraded around the suburbs, on pavements ruptured by tree roots, with Irfan, then Babar, then Nazish at the helm. Reality provided a welcome escape.

Her head and tongue were fuzzy. She crawled out of bed expecting the world to look different. But approaching her window and peering outside, through the lacy net curtains, she saw that it was an ordinary Monday morning. The tarmac was wet and gleaming. The city sat beneath a familiar white frame. And, in between, a flock of children, hunched beneath the weight of their backpacks, trotted along to school.

Her mother was waiting downstairs. She prepared them breakfast, recited Ayatul Kursi and blew on her, pushed a tasbih into her hands. But when it was time to leave, Jamila couldn't move from her chair.

The office phones were already clamouring for her attention. She went inside and approached the reception desk with some trepidation.

'Shah and Co., how can I help you?' she said, injecting her voice with enthusiasm.

'Good morning, this is Darren Purchase from the Manchester Evening News. We saw the article about your firm in the Sunday paper. Would you care to comment on the story?'

She brought the phone crashing down. Her heart was spinning. Only afterwards did she think, I should have said something, shared my side of what happened. Too late. The phones continued to ring, but now she couldn't touch them. She took to pacing her office, rotating the tasbih in her hand, waiting for the day to begin. Nazish appeared, then Babar, then Rubel and Sadia, each of them waving cautiously through the window and heading straight to their desks.

When she ventured into the staff area, they were arranged in a semi-circle.

Their gazes hooked onto her. She cleared her throat, looked down and saw that her socks were mismatched, different shades of blue. It almost pushed her into collapsing – but she couldn't. There was too much at stake. 'I suppose you've seen, or heard, at least, what happened,' she said, hiding one ankle behind the other. 'I don't know what to say, really. I keep reminding myself that we're here to do our job – a job that hasn't gone away. Our clients still need us, so let's focus on that. If they ask you, tell them we're open and ready to help.'

'What if they have questions?' Rubel asked.

'Uh . . . direct them to me.'

'And what about the police?' Babar added, his worry lines more prominent than ever.

'We don't know that's happening. Let's deal with an investigation or inspection when it happens. *If* it happens.'

None of them spoke. Jamila sensed that she'd tumbled from her pedestal, no longer the big-sister boss of the group, and it made something plummet inside her too. She inhaled deeply. 'I'm . . . I'm sorry if you feel disappointed in me . . . '

A rough hand grabbed hers.

'I know who you are, Mrs Shah. I see you every day in this office and I know your heart. If these people put us in the newspaper, it's because they're jealous, they hate us. But they are the crooked ones, not us, so I don't feel ashamed. No, I am proud to be here and work with you,' Nazish said. She jutted her chin at each of them.

'They are trying to punish us,' Babar said, straightening his shoulders. 'Let the police or the regulators come.' He looked ready to fight once more.

'This is nice, but maybe . . . we should get on with things?' Rubel said, smiling.

Sadia agreed: 'Yeah, guys, it's getting a bit getting cringey.' She pulled a face and broke from the circle, walking towards her desk. 'I don't know about the rest of you, but I've got work to do.'

Jamila gazed at them, hoping for an osmosis of their confidence.

The rest of the day came and went quickly. Clients flurried in and out of her office. Others called in their droves. Most of them weren't aware of the article, concerned only with their specific requests, but too many conversations began the same way: 'I saw you in the newspaper. What does it mean for me? Are you still allowed to represent my case?'

And over successive calls and consultations she crafted the right response: 'Please don't worry, the article is meaningless and doesn't affect you. If you're happy with the work that we're doing for you, please focus on that. I will never stop giving my all.'

Later in the afternoon, the phone rang while Nazish was away from her desk. Jamila picked it up.

'Can I speak to Mrs Shah?' the voice asked.

'Yes, this is Mrs Shah. How can I help?'

'No, I want to speak to a proper solicitor. An honest solicitor, not a dodgy one like you.'

The man's laughter cracked like a whip.

Yesterday's churning sensation ploughed through her. She opened her mouth, but nothing came out. The phone limp in her hand. She passed her mother's tasbih through her fingers, squeezing on each bead.

At the end of the day, she found her staff still clustered in the reception area.

'Maybe we could go somewhere together?' Babar said, by way of explanation.

The gesture made her eyes sting.

Locking up, she checked her phone one last time.

There was still no word from Irfan.

Jamila returned to work the next day, and the day after that. With every successful sleep, she sought to push the event further from her mind, which was difficult when clients constantly barrelled in, having only just heard the news.

Babar took to checking on her every afternoon. 'The clients aren't troubling you too much, are they?'

'Oh, no, no,' she said emphatically. It was a strange role reversal, strange to be vulnerable in front of the people she was used to taking care of. It left her feeling cold and shaky and raw, like an animal that had been hunted for its tusks or horn and then discarded, but it quickly faded. If she couldn't be vulnerable in front of these people, who could she call her own?

'And those strange phone calls?' he asked.

'They've stopped, thank God.' She sensed a chance to move the dial away from herself. 'And you? How's Habeebah?' Their final appeal was still under consideration. What usually took weeks had been keeping them waiting for months now because of a shortage of judges.

'All fine.'

They fell silent, but Babar remained where he was.

Their conversation in the concrete square swirled around her mind, accompanied by the image of Babar bringing his knees to his chest as she urged him to let go of his grief. She had been talking nonsense, as usual; she had no idea what it meant to pursue not exile but release. If she had, she would have known what to do now as she returned to the idea of selling the business and moving on.

'Actually, I've been thinking about what I put you through . . .' Babar slid the door shut behind him.

'Oh, you didn't do anything, Babar.' Her face began to flush.

'All that pressure. Entitlement. I was no better than the clients.'

'You wanted to be held and I couldn't do that for you.'

'Gemma is really good, you know? She's already thinking ahead about applying for Ariba, even though she's soon going to be six. You definitely made the right choice for me.'

Jamila smiled. 'That's sweet. Is it time to start collecting your documents early maybe?'

Babar nodded, as though Gemma had already advised him to. 'Also, Habeebah and I have decided to try for a baby. I woke up one day and thought, why am I waiting? I don't know what is going to happen with my immigration status, but I can't stop living. The time for that is now. And wherever my life takes me, I will go with my children and raise them the best I can.'

He didn't move for a moment. His new maturity confounded her. She took his arm. 'This is really good, Babar, I'm so happy—'

There was a knock on the door. Another client waited in the wings. Without prompting, Babar retreated to the staff area, but, as she attended to the client, Jamila continued to think about what he had shared. The time to live is now. It lingered when Khalil arrived later that afternoon.

'Am I doing the right thing?' he asked, refusing to sit and looking profoundly agitated. 'Is there any point in all of this?'

Though she had sent his documents to the best barrister she could find, they were some way from lodging an appeal in the High Court. She found herself listing answers as they came to her, reminding herself as much as him:

'It's about the principle and accountability.'

'It's about pursuing what others in the system don't have the privilege to do.'

'It's about God.'

When Khalil left, marginally convinced, but much more interested in her advice not to lose himself to the process, Jamila found herself scribbling on a notepad. Drawing lines and spirals and occasional words, she admired how smoothly the ink flowed from her pen, how easy it was to mark the white surface with the smallest stroke, how effortless to join the strokes up and create units of meaning.

Everybody wanted to be held in certainty. They wanted guarantees in a system where all that existed was precarity. Some of that she could remedy, and she made promises to that effect, but the vast majority was out of her control. She, too, wanted to be held and told that there was a logic to her decisions, that every turn she took in life would make some greater sort of sense. With a pen between her fingers, maybe that was possible. The nib touching her notebook sounded like the opening whisper of a prayer.

At the end of the week, she returned to her parents. After dinner, her mother brought out the oldest family album, the one that contained faded portraits of Jamila's grandparents and great-grandparents, dressed in dhotis and chadars, their arms glued to their sides, fingers splayed across their knees. They sat and admired it together, exchanging stories about their past.

'Your father doesn't know who he was – your daddi found him abandoned at her door – but my ancestors were soldiers,' her mother said, turning pages. 'When the raja abandoned them, they went back to their village to fend for themselves. When their crops failed, they moved to the city, where they occupied shrines like gangsters and forced local businesses to pay them for protection. Such pride they had, such stubbornness. You might love your father more, but you're tough like me.'

Later, she called Irfan.

'How are you holding up?' he asked, his concern still palpable.

'I thought you didn't care, I thought you were about the quiet life,' she replied sulkily.

'I was joking when I said that. You overreac—'

'You weren't joking, Irfan.' Her voice was a blade.

'But . . . a national newspaper, it blew my mind a little bit.'

'You weren't there for me.'

He paused. 'I got scared.'

'But I was scared too.'

'But you could have had a little more trust in me. I'm not used to being with somebody in the spotlight. You cut the call before I could explain.'

Jamila mulled over his words and found them hard to deny; she had been rash. Her voice grew small. 'I guess I'm just used to people not thinking about me. Zak . . . he never asked what I wanted. He never thought that it mattered. Instead, he wanted me to choose: me or work, my family or him. Don't make me feel like I need to do that—'

'I would never expect you—'

'Help me to believe it's not one or the other.'

'I thought I had shown you these past months, I'm not like that. I care about you.'

'Really?' she asked quietly, scarcely believing it.

'Of course.' He sighed. 'You really are my little egg, aren't you? Silly, spiky, difficult to crack—'

'Call me a century egg, if you have to. I'm softer, more tender than I've ever been.'

Twenty-seven

The Lake District was cold, the trail steep, wet and slippery. Despite the thick, rubbery soles of her shoes, shards of slate and stone dug into her feet. But Jamila kept her head down and climbed, working her thighs. She paused occasionally and took in the scene around her. Moss cushioned limestone walls, ferns jutted from tiny gaps like arrows and spears – pleasure drawn from the noticing and naming of things. The rusted beds of heather that gave the landscape a bronzed antique appearance, sub-zero temperatures that had stopped the flow of the streams, iced and cracked their surfaces. Nothing but the wind for company. It was a whole life, this.

She pushed on.

At the top of the hill, Irfan had stopped and turned, his bald head shielded from the elements by a cap, a fleece and waterproof padding out his frame. He grimaced against a gust so strong it threatened to topple him.

She took a picture of the trail she had climbed, then of him clutching the straps of his backpack, nothing but the open sky behind him. He gritted his teeth and counted the seconds until she was done. Even pale and hollowed out by the cold, discomfited by the camera's glare, she found him so attractive.

'We need to talk about where we're going, Jam,' he said, when she had joined him.

'It's not that hard. Across and up again. You've got the map,' she said.

'No, I'm talking about us.'

'Oh, right.' Jamila looked away, towards the shaggy, grey-coated sheep grazing on the other side of the valley. The tendons in her feet had begun to tighten and warp. 'You want to do this here?'

He looked at her like, where else?

'Okay.' Another gust blew through them and she wrenched her eyes shut, trying not to look as though she was considering her options. Whenever she had sensed him looking for an opening to this conversation, she had pre-empted it and asked him for more time.

When the wind died, she pulled down on the toggles of her hood and took off. Irfan was the more experienced hiker, he was leaner, more compact and built for endurance, but she had the power. She used this to spring up the path now, her feet moving fast, her lungs working like little factories. She put twenty, then thirty metres between them, then glanced back to take in Irfan's surprise.

In the weeks since the newspaper article, Irfan had sent her flowers. He had paid for countless meals. He explained repeatedly, for Jamila's benefit, the smallness of his life and how he feared a media circus could affect his girls. And though Jamila wondered if she had overreacted, or simply expected too much from someone she hadn't known for very long at all, she reminded him again that this was who she was. That the job, with all its attendant joys and miseries, was the baggage she came with. The job, whether she liked it or not, was key to how she understood herself. But Irfan refused the binary she presented before him. There was nothing to accept or reject. 'It's an adjustment, is all.'

'And you're all adjusted now?' she asked.

'I'm all adjusted,' he said.

And, having opened herself up to the kinds of connections she had deprived herself of, having accepted her limitations and learned to maintain boundaries, Jamila reminded herself of all the ways she had adjusted too.

He caught up some minutes later. 'What the hell was that?' He caught his breath, blinking rapidly, his heavy eyelids flapping like Tibetan prayer flags in the wind.

'It's a big question. I don't know where I'm going.'

He glowered at a tree. 'I told you, I won't let you down. Let me show you I mean it.'

'I don't know if I can rely on someone like that again.' She swallowed the emotion this sprung in her and stepped back, standing on one foot, then the other. Something stubborn like a boulder refused to shift inside her. She had been waiting for it to, believed that it would with time, but it had stayed there all these months, blocking her. She couldn't bring herself to look at the tormented and almost feeble reaction it produced in him.

The path ahead grew narrow. Both sides were backed by tall stands of thorny bushes with a few withered berries still attached, that plucked and clawed at them as they passed. She followed him in silence, glad to see nothing more than his back, concentrating on the climb and the sound of their rustling jackets and rocks clicking together beneath their feet like marbles. When they turned a corner, a mountain came out of hiding, like a rare and ancient animal. Here I am, it seemed to say, announcing itself. Here I am too, she replied, suddenly exhilarated. This was the most alive she had felt in years.

On their slow descent, fat clumps of snow fell from the sky. A small tarn below was dark, still and glistening. When Irfan took her hand, she let him. Her legs were spent from the climb.

The snow fell quickly, as if it was eager to obscure a parcel of land that was sparser now, more open and more workmanlike. Many of the trees here had been felled and there was less vegetation. Cows grazed here too, she saw from the patches of dung – their hooves had rucked and knuckled and overturned the earth. But even as a thin white sheet settled over it, all Jamila saw was abundance.

Irfan guided her over a spring. 'I just want to make you happy.'

He said it so quietly, so ordinarily, an utterance so impossibly profound, a shiver went through her that made her want to cry out. She had never heard such a sentence directed at her before.

'I want you to meet my family,' she said, discovering her rational self. 'I don't like keeping you from them.'

He nodded and squeezed her hand. 'I want you to meet my girls. Do you think you're ready?'

'Yes, but I don't want to marry you.' She had known this for some time, talked it through with her sister, then Sadia and Nazish, growing firmer in her beliefs. She could give him the keys to her house, live with him – they could enjoy a good life together. But she refused to become his wife, a mother to their children. She wouldn't pick up the second shift. And yet, this was not a rejection of motherhood, care and nourishment. She provided that to her clients all the time. To her niece and nephew. To Maliha. One day, she could extend that to his girls too.

'This small bit of time ahead, it feels important. I feel like it has to be mine,' she said.

'And you're sure I fit into it?' he asked.

She stood on the other side of the stream and rested her whole body against his. 'I don't know. But if you help me, I think we can make it.'

Twenty-eight

A scream rang through the office. She dropped everything and dashed to the reception. There, on the other side of the glass, a familiar face with sunken eyes, red ears and a new waxed combover had pressed his hands against the reception window. He was laughing and chatting with the staff, his eyes gleaming like gold teeth, with the sound of children yelping around him. When his gaze fell on Jamila, he yanked back the door and threw himself into her arms, before apologising.

'I can't, I just can't believe it. I am here, finally. When I lost all hope, Mrs Shah made me keep on fighting. Even after everything I did to her, keep on fighting . . . ' He choked on the last of these words, coughing to force them through. 'Mrs Shah, you told me, don't hide, don't be ashamed of your story, time is running out, tell them everything you have been through. And only then I realised, sometimes you have to hold your nose and climb into the dirty water.'

Hassan. Hassan, who had buried his past and refused to share it with the system, just so that his children would have a chance of living a life unaffected by it. Nazish had called this morning to inform him of the good news: the Home Office were planning to grant him a visa. All they needed was four passport-sized photographs.

Hassan was loose-limbed and excited. He hopped back into the reception area and presented them with a fruit basket bigger than his children. 'I brought something – it isn't much at all, it's what I can do right now – but I wanted to thank you for everything you have done for me, all of you.' He handed the fruit to Babar and fell against him. Babar's awkward arms, his trepidation and surprise, amused them all, but he returned Hassan's embrace. 'When I get back on my feet, I will bring something better for you all, I promise you.'

'No, please,' Babar said. 'This is already too much. We're just happy for you.'

Hassan glanced back at Jamila. 'Thank you for everything, Mrs Shah. Finally, I can do all the things I want. I can work. I can make a garden. I can rest my head in peace. I am so tired.' And she witnessed his muscles completely slacken then, including those in his face, which had carried him for so long.

Babar held him. Jamila touched Hassan's shoulder and smiled.

Afterwards, the staff stood around dissecting what had happened.

'I've never heard a scream like that,' Sadia said.

'Honestly, my ears are still hurting,' Nazish said.

Rubel elbowed Babar curiously. 'He gave you the biggest hug of all.'

Babar shrugged. 'The rest of you found him too difficult to deal with.'

Jamila left them to bathe in the afterglow. In her office, she read over the appeal grounds that her new barrister had prepared for Khalil's run to the High Court. Maybe this was where she belonged. An uncertain space, but one that she could grow into. She took out a letter from her drawer and peered at it again: *We are writing to inform you that the complaint against you has been withdrawn . . .* She scrolled through a series of headlines on her phone:

French food critic attacks Michelin guide.

Afghanistan troop cuts will likely lead to Taliban surge.

Migrant shipwreck in Italy kills 59.

But there was no chance to click on the stories and read them, no time to absorb the headlines or descriptions because, as she was accustomed to by now, there was a knock on the door and two new clients walked straight in, bowing as the door swung shut behind them.

'Good afternoon, Mrs Shah,' one of them said.

'Good afternoon,' she replied, and she motioned for them to sit down.

Author's Note

Since 2012, the term 'hostile environment' has evolved to describe a raft of policies introduced by the British government, and the broader culture of disbelief and disdain that informs Home Office decision making. It is known as such because, in the words of then Home Secretary Theresa May, her aim was 'to create, here in Britain, a really hostile environment for illegal immigrants' and deter potential migrants from choosing to settle in the country. Perhaps, given the huge rise in decisions to strip Britons of their citizenship (and deny those who had the right to apply for it), the aim was also to remind people with non-British heritage that their right to live in Britain was unfixed and conditional.

The 'Go Home' vans remain the clearest encapsulation of the hostile environment. As part of 'Operation Vaken', the billboards were driven around six London boroughs and followed by the placement of adverts in six community newspapers and 300 local shops. For this novel, I have exercised some artistic licence in bringing the vans to Manchester rather than London, in April 2013 instead of August. Theresa May did not make her comments defending the vans until October 2013. Everything else I have written about this policy, however, has its basis in fact.

Acknowledgements

I spent the best part of eight years working on this novel. It took a village to get me there – a whole town, maybe. A huge thank you to:

Mum, Dad and Haseeb, for your love and support. This book is dedicated to you, to the kind of life we've lived, the kind of values you've instilled in me.

Tom White, for encouraging my writing and steering me through endless drafts.

New Writing North, particularly Will Mackie. Thank you for all the ways you've aided my development as a writer.

The Arts Council, for supporting this novel with a DYCP grant.

Kerry Young, for reading an early synopsis and recognising that this was Mrs Shah's story.

Leone Ross, for just about everything – your honesty, generosity, care and mentorship. Anytime you liked a sentence or passage of mine, it felt like the most gorgeous validation.

The tutors at UEA: Andrew Cowan, Giles Foden, Julianne Pachico, Philip Langeskov, Tom Benn and Trezza Azzopardi, and all your valuable lessons about craft. Also, my workshop group there: Alistair, Ariane, Derek, Hannah, Max, Michele, Ope, Polly, Rose and Trisha, for your feedback on early chapters. Thank you to everyone who read full or partial drafts of this manuscript, including Helen, Jonathan and Twishaa.

My agent, Matthew Turner, for understanding what I was trying to achieve and helping me to get there without compromising on the values that underpin this book.

My editor, Rose Green, for getting *Determination* immediately and for your gentle, intelligent edit. Thank you to everyone at Footnote, especially Fritha Saunders and Vidisha Biswas. Thank you to Vicki Heath-Silk for your meticulous copy-editing.

Tom Benn, Jyoti Patel, Rebecca Watson and Guy Gunaratne, for the early endorsements.

My non-fiction editor, James Pulford, for always championing me – Rebecca too.

Karen Powell, Laura Bui and Sophie Parkes-Nield, look how far we've all come! Writing and publishing is such a gruelling process at times. I'm so glad that we have each other to rely on as we muddle through.

Leyla Jagiella, Amna Siddiqi, Niven Govinden, Shahid Iqbal Khan, Chris Nield and Jessica Johnson.

Finally, my young cousin, Sufiyaan. Sorry to have missed you from the acknowledgements of the last book. I hope that this one inspires you to write your own one day.